Copyright 2021 Cal Clement
All Rights Reserved

The characters and events portrayed within are fictitious.
Any similarities to real persons, alive or dead is coincidental and not intended by the author.

No part of this book may be reproduced or stored in a retrieval system or transmitted in any form or by any means, electronic, mechanical, photocopying, recording or otherwise without express written permission of the author.

ISBN-9798599464976

Cover Artist: Juan Padron
Printed in the United States of America

H.M.S Valor
Treachery and Triumph

by Cal Clement

This book is dedicated to the brave souls of the 2nd Battalion of the 7th Marine Regiment I had the distinct honor of serving beside.
And to the heroes who never returned home.

"A Ship is safe in harbor, but that's not what ships are for"
- William Shedd

PART ONE
A Storm Gathers

'Whereas the Two Houses of Parliament did, by their Resolutions of the Tenth and Twenty-fourth days of June One Thousand eight hundred and six, severally resolve, upon certain Grounds therein mentioned, that they would, with all practicable Expedition, take effectual Measures for the Abolition of the African Slave Trade in such Manner, and at such Period as might be deemed advisable, And whereas it is fit upon all and each of the Grounds mentioned in the said Resolutions, that the same should be forthwith abolished and prohibited, and declared to be unlawful'

- *British Parliament*
  June 24th 1806

Chapter 1

Aug 4, 1808
Office of the Admiralty, London

Lieutenant William Pike stood in a massive hallway outside of the naval boardroom, stifling, in his dress uniform he awaited his fate. Outside, the dreary London morning had given way to a hot August sunshine and with it pouring into the large windows, the hallway had become uncomfortably warm. William could feel perspiration gather around his collar and beading on his head as he looked across the great passage adjoining the boardroom with the offices of the commanding Admirals of the Royal Navy. Great portraits of Admirals past and present lined the hallway, unsmiling and grave, they all seemed to be looking directly through William's soul as he anxiously awaited to be summoned into the boardroom. William closed his eyes momentarily, longing for a gust of wind and the spray of the sea to cool him. The sea. She had been both his loving savior from the orphan homes and the cruel mistress who deprived him the joys of typical adolescence relished by so many. It was more to William than a trade, the sea was a living thing as much as any creature with a heartbeat. She was freedom and joy to the skilled sailor and sure death to all who underestimated her.

He pictured the bow of a ship, sliding over breaking waves and rolling with wind at beam reach and a spray spackling his cheeks with every slap of water against the hull. That relieving thought was both joy and torture as the minutes dragged on for what felt like forever. Exacerbated by the ticking of a large ornate clock flanking the door on the far end of the hall, William fought his wandering mind, willing himself to maintain his discipline and reserve.

    Inside the boardroom three Admirals of the fleet had deliberated away the morning, reviewing evaluations from commanding Captains and Lieutenants, assessing combat and inspection performance for scores of line officers. Their determinations could make a career or condemn one, in the competitive field of the naval officer corps progression was inextricably tied to the findings of the Admiralty Board. Few officers petitioned in person, fewer still were permitted an audience. Admiral Torren had received petition on behalf of Lieutenant Pike from the young man's most recent commanding Captain, a man Admiral Torren knew very well and had mentored as a Lieutenant over a decade before. Lieutenant William Pike's service record was in fact, spotted, several mentions of unorthodox tactical decisions had caused a previous commander to pause before recommending promotion for the lad.   But his most recent commander had specifically petitioned for promotion, citing his bravery and leadership ability, noting several instances of such when engaged with both American and French privateers. Still, the board was very hesitant to promote and assign command to anything but an exemplary record. This made battlefield advancement the surest way in a young officer's mind to advance in rank, thus any assignment likely to engage in combat was a more competitive endeavor.

After what seemed like an eternity, William was finally beckoned in by a Royal Marine Sergeant who rigidly opened the door and formally called William by his full name and rank. With a deep breath, William mustering the most formal military bearing he could, proceeded into the room and reported to the board. His first step in was like going from the pan into the fire, the room was remarkably hotter than the hallway. Will eyed a fireplace across the room to his right with a robust blaze crackling away. He made a note to himself of how advanced in age the Admirals were and decided perhaps they were warding off the chills of death.

"Mr. Pike, good afternoon." Admiral Torren started, appearing oblivious to the oppressively sweltering boardroom as did the other Admirals, "We have reviewed your records, recommendations from several of your previous commanders and your most recent." The Admiral gave a slight pause, looking to the officers flanking him momentarily before resuming the board findings to the young lieutenant.

"It is the final opinion of this board, that despite your most recent commander's insistence, you are not yet ready for a command of your own. However, you are to be assigned to the next open first Lieutenant billet aboard a frigate command. This will afford you a sufficient opportunity to develop further, perhaps command is yet in your future, but not today."

The Admiral's monotonous tone and the board's collective unchanging demeanor coupled with their dress uniforms and formal wigs conveyed the gravity and finality of their decision. Lieutenant William Pike had been passed over for command. He could feel his face flushing, the perspiration, which was now increasing, utterly failed to cool him. William fought the urge to argue his case, challenging these findings could jeopardize his future opportunities to command. He couldn't believe it and at the same time had dreadfully expected this outcome. A frigate assignment, however, was far from a dead end, his chances to advance were better on a frigate than just about any other assignment he could have gotten. He thanked the gentlemen admirals of the review board and made his exit from the board room. Retrieving his new orders from the clerk in the front atrium, he barely disguised his haste to leave. William made his way out of the massive building housing the Admiralty offices and began walking. He made his way up the narrow London streets toward an ordinance depot he knew that would certainly have a wagon or cart headed toward the shipyards he could hitch a ride on.

Reaching the depot, William searched through the dirty window of the front office for any sign of life within.

"I suppose you want a ride to the navy yards johnny sailor bold?" a voice from behind Will grumbled. Will turned to see a one-legged man driving a cart loaded with heavy shot. A scraggly, unkempt beard did little to disguise the man smiling at his own jest. Though it was far from a comfortable carriage with the company of a beautiful girl, it would be better than walking all night to get to the shipyard.

"I am. Would you be so kind?" Will asked, hoping the man didn't demand some form of payment as he had little money after several weeks in London.

"Climb on up then sailor, er, Sir! My apologies Lieutenant! It's been too long, I forget myself sometimes." the driver cackled. William could not quite tell if he was the butt of another joke or if the man was genuine.

As the cart wound its way through London's streets toward the naval yard, the sun started edging into the western sky.

Evening would soon set in and a breeze from the east was carrying the salty air of the sea mixed with various smells of cooking food and wood smoke. Finished with the formalities of the board, William was grateful to relax, taking off his dress coat and hat, the breeze brought welcome relief from the stifling constriction he had endured most of the day. He eyed the cargo in the back of the cart and asked the driver he had managed to convince a ride from,

"Those look like eighteen-pound shot. Are you hauling to a man o' war?"

"Aye, I am, though it may not be on the same end of the yard as the inn, not sure, you may want to part ways with me before I head onto the pier," the cart driver explained, simultaneously navigating the street while repacking his pipe.

"Not to worry, I do appreciate the ride. Which ship?" William pressed, watching apprehensively as the driver fumbled over his pipe, barely paying attention to much else.

"Ah, Pier twelve I believe, I forget her bloody name, here take these," the driver said, handing the reins to William. The driver began digging into a shirt pocket that had several pieces of paper, then handed William his pipe and sorted through them one by one. "Here it is," he exclaimed, "the last foundry order for the H.M.S Valor."

William dug into his jacket pocket,

fumbling for the envelope containing his orders. He opened the envelope, hearing the name H.M.S Valor brought a skip to his heartbeat. He hadn't even seen for himself which frigate he had been assigned to yet, the chance he was assigned to the Valor was exhilarating. She had been the talk of town, having just returned from the Americas and recently taking a French privateer sloop as a prize. Her Captain was reputed to be one of the finest commanders a sailor could serve with. Opening the seal, he unfolded the parchment and scanned through the formalities for her name. *"I do hereby on this day the fourth of August in the year of our Lord eighteen hundred and eight assign Lieutenant William A. Pike to service aboard the H.M.S Valor..."* William's disappointment in being passed over faded in the crescendo of his excitement. This was an assignment any Lieutenant hopeful for promotion would kill for! This new revelation fresh on his mind inflated the young officer's spirit, he could barely contain it. He slapped the cart driver on the shoulder, almost causing him to lose his grip of the pipe.

"Well, good man, it happens that you have rated escort from the ship's new first lieutenant for this load of ammunition! Where is a pub along the way? I feel like having a drink and I'm sure you wouldn't mind indulging me, if not joining me for one?" William asked overflowing with this new joyful discovery.

"I don't suppose we have the time lad; I spoke with the Captain yesterday when I delivered, he is preparing to set off, this is the last load from the foundry for shot. There were barrels of food and water being loaded yesterday when I left and powder the day before. It looked to me like she will be making way soon, perhaps as soon as this last load is aboard." The cart driver eyed William, kind of leaning away as he spoke.

"Well, whatever the case, I shall certainly want to celebrate, this is a tremendous assignment!" William exclaimed; his giddiness was apparent though he could see his companion did not share in it. The cobbled streets eventually gave way to dirt and graveled roads as the taller buildings of London faded into the countryside replaced by farmhouses and softly rolling hills. William noted heavy storm clouds lumbering in from the north as the sun dipped below the horizon, painting the sky a beautiful sight. Oranges and violets floated high in the heavens and eventually twilight began to appear. For the last part of his ride, William mostly kept in his own head, questions about the new assignment had him spinning.

What was the Captain like? Was he a hard man? Was the crew a tough group? William knew they had seen quite a few engagements lately, though he was no stranger to combat himself, there was a nagging sense in his mind that the crew would doubt his capabilities. As William pondered to himself, along the horizon in the fading light he saw masts from the shipyard. Very faintly he could hear bells chiming out the hour and as they drew closer voices giving command and whistles piping. As they pulled in nearer to the shipyard the road became busy, sailors walked about to the shops and inns that lined the road. The briny smell of the tide was hanging low in the dense air and it only served to stoke William's excitement. Turning at the large naval depot complex, the cart driver clicked his mouth a few times and gave the reigns a slap on the team pulling their cart. The ride was jarring, as it had been much of the way, until they finally pulled onto the wooden pier. Passing several smaller sloops and a brigantine, they finally pulled to the very end of the pier where H.M.S Valor stood, awash in light from lanterns and buzzing with activity. Men were scurrying through rigging, loading supplies up the gangplank, painting, cleaning brass and all manner of preparations. As William dismounted the cart, a sharp looking Midshipman was standing by the bottom of the gangplank. Flanked by two imposing Marines, the young Midshipman looked barely sixteen years old as he was meticulously writing in a logbook while sailors loaded wares onto the ship.

"Mr. Shelton what have you there?" the

Midshipman called.

Shelton, another Midshipman who looked to be about the same age, was leading a group of sailors carrying goods aboard. "A crate of pistols, three large sacks of flour and three more small barrels of fresh water." He replied.

The Midshipman at the gangplank turned and took notice of William.

"You must be our new First Lieutenant, I am Midshipman Ordman. The Captain is expecting you, Sir." The Midshipman rendered the customary salute and introduced himself, "He is up in his quarters now, reviewing the new charts for our cruise. Lieutenant Cobb is the watch officer, he will show you to your berthing. He's up there on the quarterdeck." William looked aft to see a portly gentleman in a high-collared officer coat, his face was beet red and his tone seemed more than a little irate as he snarled at a petty officer. Will looked back at Mr. Ordman and raised an eyebrow.

"You'll have to forgive Mr. Cobb, Sir. He is at his wits end with the fresh crop from the press gang. We were told most would be from the fishing fleet or merchant men. They brought landsmen, twenty-six men and none with experience at sea. Although, Mr. Cobb's normal disposition is not so different," said the Midshipman shrugging his shoulders. At that, he turned and went back to inventorying the incoming goods. William donned his jacket and hat before following the sailors up the gang plank. A sense of anxiousness and excitement was in the air and not just for the young officer. They were setting off soon.

Aug 4, 1808
Guinea, Africa

Omibwe hushed his little sister. The pair had been out gathering wood for a cooking fire when they first heard the shots. For hours now, they had hidden in tall grass a few hundred yards from the edge of their small coastal village. Darkness had set in and his sister, Anaya, was restless and scared. Through the trees Omibwe could hear foreign voices and occasionally saw the light from lanterns held by the European men. He knew this was not good. Traders frequented the coast and Omibwe had met European men before, he had even learned some of their words. But the men he had met had come for ivory or hardwood logs, spices and skins. They would carry muskets and sometimes swords but never fired them, these men had. The white men Omibwe had met before sailed into the bay and would come ashore in daylight. No sail had announced the presence of these hostile men. Another shot cut through night air and Omibwe heard a woman's cry. Anaya squirmed a little and he quickly hushed his little sister, doing his best to hide his own fear. They had to stay silent, he knew, if the men heard her or suspected their presence they would surely come looking and find them.

Omibwe had been warned about men like the ones now in his village. His father had told him about groups of white men who came in the night to steal people. They didn't care about trade goods and anyone who resisted these men was killed. When he was younger, Omibwe thought it was just a story to scare him into minding his parents. That was until a neighboring village had been visited by men like these. A battle had taken place costing many of the villagers their lives, the white men left defeated that night, but returned several weeks later. They burned the village to the ground and left none alive, not even livestock escaped their wrath.

Crawling several feet through high grass, Omibwe strained his ears for any indication of what was occurring in his village. He heard voices from the whites and from his people, every few minutes another shot would pierce the darkness and send Anaya into another fit. Omibwe's arms and back were soaked in sweat and burning from the tension he felt. He could see the edge of the village and through the darkness and intermittent lantern light, his eyes strained for any sign of his parents. Hours went by, the voices quieted but all sounded foreign. Eventually the lanterns started moving around, some came out of the village. At one point a man with a musket and lantern had come close to Omibwe and Anaya, close enough for them to make out features on his face. He was a large man, with a big bulbous nose jutting out from a bushy mustache and his face had scars on it. Most white men wore hats, this one had no hat but Omibwe could make out scars in his hairline, dividing his scalp in several places. He was wearing a sword and several pistols on his belt. The man wandered out, drawing nearer and nearer to Omibwe and Anaya's hiding place, at one point he was so close they could hear him relieve himself. But he carried on, eventually disappearing into the tree line behind them.

In the hot African night, Omibwe's eyelids eventually grew heavy. Anaya had drifted into sleep, still latched onto his leg tightly. Even in sleep her grip on him had not slacked. His ears still straining for any sign of activity, Omibwe finally relented and let his eyes close. He was exhausted from the tense night spent hyper vigilant to any noise, any movement. The dark of night was fading as dawn began drawing a faint glow to the eastern skies. The village had been silent for hours and the smoke from several smoldering huts mixed with a low-lying early fog gathered through the coastal region where the village sat.

A party of men gathered at the edge of the village, holding lanterns and torches, they were all armed. The men fanned out in a line and began walking away from the village. In the pre-dawn light, their lanterns cast formidable shadows that danced back towards the village. Their gait was slow, each man near enough to the man next to him to hear without yelling. They walked in line for several hundred yards in silence, passing right by the sleeping siblings and then into the tree line.

Omibwe awoke to an awkwardly silent morning, no birds singing, no voices from the village. He instinctively reached down to check his little sister. She was still there, clung to his leg and still fast asleep. He woke her gently, gesturing for her to remain silent. The pair crawled as far as they could through the tall grasses beside the village, pausing every few seconds so Omibwe could listen for anything amiss. Finally, reaching as far as they could go in the tall grass, Omibwe stretched his head up out of the grass as far as he dared. Looking around he couldn't see anyone. He took Anaya by the hand and together they crept low to the ground into the village. The now breaking dawn revealed carnage in the village. Many men and women lay dead in the open, huts had been burned. Omibwe couldn't believe what he saw, why would anyone do this to his village? Tears welled up into his eyes, he struggled to cover Anaya's view, not wanting her to see her home and the elders who lay dead. He did not see his parents or any sign of survival of the others in the village. His hands shook as he looked around unsure of what to do. He didn't know if the men had left for a ship or headed overland to somewhere else. Or maybe they would return. As he struggled over these thoughts and looked around the village, tears now streaming down his face uncontrollably, he did not notice that the masts of several ships now protruded from behind the thatched roofs of the village. Omibwe's wander took him south through the village towards his own family's home. Hoping against all hope, his entire being longed to see his family unharmed. His father would know what to do and that thought brought him both an uneasy comfort and foreboding sadness.

Approaching their family home, Omibwe noted it had not been set fire, the thatched door was intact, the few hand tools they owned were in place. It seemed as if he could walk in and find his mother and father inside, perhaps eating breakfast. After instructing Anaya to stay out front, Omibwe entered their family's hut. Their belongings were scattered, what food they had been preparing to eat was all over the floor, and there was a small spatter of blood across the back wall, but no one inside. It was small relief not to find anyone, but he still did not know their fate, and this troubled him almost into a panic. Coming out of the hut, Omibwe thought to check on the beach. It is possible his family went that way to make it to another village up the coast. Starting up the path Omibwe cleared his eyes and looked up, seeing the masts. His eyes followed a mast that led down to a ship only a few hundred yards off the shore.

Omibwe quickly realized he needed to get out of the village, he needed to protect Anaya and get her somewhere safe in case the white men returned. He took Anaya's hand and they began to hurry back toward the grass that had hidden them through the night. The pair came around from behind a hut to the sight of the search party returning. The large man with the big nose and scarred face in front, the party spotted the two right away. Omibwe heard some shouting, a shot rang out and the men started running. More shouting, Omibwe could hear clearly but didn't understand the words. They didn't sound like the men he had met before; their words were different. He held his sister's hand tightly and ran away as quickly as he could, Anaya fell, unable to keep pace with her brother. Omibwe dragged her back up to her feet and they continued running through the village. The pair turned down a path that would lead to the shoreline, frantically racing away from the group of men now in pursuit.

Racing to the shoreline, Omibwe quickly outpaced Anaya who stumbled again. He slowed momentarily to scoop up his little sister to carry her and took off again, this time with everything he had. Omibwe was a powerful runner and strong enough to carry his sister for miles, if he could get far enough away that the guns couldn't hit him, he knew he could lose the following men. As he sprinted to the shore, he could already tell he was opening a gap from his followers. Cresting over a small ridge, Omibwe came within sight of the sea and the ships. What he hadn't seen before was the inhabitants of his village, all sitting, surrounded by several men with guns. There were small boats laden with people from the village being ferried off to the large ships. Omibwe was shocked, he almost froze at the sight, but he turned and kept his sprint up the shore hoping none of the men down on the beach had seen him. His legs burning from the pace, shoulders already aching from carrying Anaya, Omibwe searched desperately in his mind for a plan. He could hear yelling behind him, a piercing shot rang out and snapped in the air over his head. A shrill voice screamed out his name, then Anaya's! Omibwe turned his head to see the source of the screams. His mother was crying out for them from the group of villagers, upon seeing her fleeing children she panicked, inconsolably crying and trying to leave the group to protect her children.

Omibwe heard the shot, he stumbled down to the sand, instantly coating his sweat soaked body, the sand cushioned his fall. Anaya scrambled to her feet, Omibwe could hear her gasp and start to cry and then her cries turned to screams. He rolled to his back, trying to command his feet to lift them both and carry them away, but they would not obey. He felt a strange, sudden rush of cold, a chill he had never experienced, and a nausea swept over him. He struggled to sit up, his head felt like a boulder. He had heard the shot, he saw three of the pursuing men now just moments from getting to him, his head swooned, and his vision was failing. In the distance Omibwe could see his mother, struggling against their captors, fighting to get to her children, a man raised up a musket and struck her with it. Omibwe, filled with rage, attempted to muster strength that seemed to be slipping through his fingers again trying to stand. His right leg would not obey, it lay crooked and as he looked at it Omibwe saw the wound. Just below the knee, a massive hole with blood running out soaking into the white sand. His head swam, feeling heavier by the second. The men approached, now walking, looking over him with disdain. Anaya's screams and cries faded from hearing and he could no longer sit up. His torso crashing back into the sand, he watched helplessly as one of the men grabbed Anaya's arm and drug her back away towards the rest of the captive villagers. Then Omibwe's vision finally succumbed and unconsciousness swept over him.

4 August 1808
Haiti, Near Port-Au-Prince

In the past few months, Lilith Gereau had suffered trauma upon tragedy. She was the illegitimate daughter of a French slave owner in Port-Au-Prince, Haiti. The result of his salacious and depraved acts against her mother. Lilith had grown up never knowing that the man whom she feared more than anyone, the man whose volatile temper caused so much pain and torment to her mother, was actually her father. Learning this truth was difficult, but when Lilith's mother told her that she would soon likely have to endure the same type of abuse, she could not stand the thought. Her mother had, up until then, attempted to shield her daughter from the wicked realities of life on the plantation. But having just reached sixteen years of age and due to her beautiful features and lighter complexion, Lilith was told she would be given "inside work". Her mother could not stand to see her daughter go into the estate home unknowing of some very hard truths. Lilith's mother came to her the evening before she was to begin working in the kitchen of the estate owner.

"I don't wish this for you my darling, but in some ways, it will be better than working cane in the fields." Lilith's mother lamented. She was braiding Lilith's long hair as they sat by the only lantern in the long bunkhouse. The building that housed all the slaves of the French estate sat situated near cane fields, at the bottom of the hill the estate house was on. It was a low, long building with dirt floors, no windows, poor ventilation and a slant roof that did little to keep out water in the rainy seasons.

"Mama, I don't want to be near him." Lilith said, struggling to see through the tears welling in her eyes.

"Baby, we have no choices here. It will be okay, but you need to keep busy and try not to be caught alone by him," her mother said through a deep sigh, knowing how impossible that endeavor would be.

"No, mama. I don't want this. I don't want the kitchen or cleaning or the cane fields. I want to leave. We need to leave." Lilith said, a spark kindled in her eyes with the thought of even the possibility of a future away from here.

"Lilith, we have spoken about this. There is only one way that path ends. Baby, I cannot watch you hang…" her mother's voice trailed off. Lilith could see tears running down her mother's cheeks when she looked back at her and felt a wave of sadness over their situation. It seemed hopeless, but Lilith was desperate to avoid the same fate her mother had suffered for years. The night found her in restless fits, sleep elusive until the wee morning hours when exhaustion finally set her off into a sleep laden with strange dreams.

The following morning, Lilith reported to the head servant in the estate home. She was given a set of clothes, strictly for while she was in the home. The dress she was expected to wear was constricting and stifling in the hot Haitian morning. In addition, she was told to wear an apron and head dress which only added to her discomfort. As soon as she dressed, she was ushered into a washroom adjacent to the kitchen in the large estate home, loads of pots and pans and plates and flatware waiting for her to begin.

Lilith worked diligently at cleaning the dishes and meticulously placing them away in their designated spots. As she was nearing completion of her first task, Francis, the estate owner entered the washroom. He was an older man, in his late fifties, rotund and with a receding hairline typically hidden by his wig. He stood in the doorway between the washroom and the kitchen, watching Lilith for a moment. An awkward tension filled the kitchen and washroom, the other slave women shared glances amongst each other. Soon Lilith noticed the other workers making themselves scarce, leaving the kitchen for some task either instructed or implied. A heavy feeling came over her, she had been warned about this exact situation by her mother, her hands began to shake, and she felt as though she could not catch her breath. Francis entered the washroom and closed the door behind him, he walked over to the window near the large wash basin Lilith stood at and reached up to pull the curtains shut. Momentarily over his shoulder, Francis ran his eyes up and down Lilith's figure, bringing a sick feeling to her stomach. Lilith averted her eyes from the Frenchman's and searched the room. On a counter behind her, Lilith's eye caught one of the large kitchen knives she had yet to clean. She reached her hands behind her onto the counter as Francis finished drawing the curtains. He turned towards her, looking her up and down with an unmistakable intent in his eyes.

"Let me introduce you to your new surroundings girl, there are a few things I'd like to teach you about serving a man such as myself." Francis said, the words oozing from his mouth. He reached out a hand and placed it on Lilith's shoulder. Then with a sudden force that took Lilith by surprise, Francis spun her around and shoved her into the counter. Francis pushed against her hard and her hip bones could feel the biting edge of the counter through her dress as Francis pushed harder and harder, lifting her feet from the floor. Lilith looked over, seeing the large kitchen knife laying on the counter, just out of reach. Francis began pulling at her dress and she squirmed involuntarily, he stopped moving momentarily and before Lilith could process what was happening, she felt his hand hit her square on the back of her head. The impact was hard enough that it forced her forehead into the cabinet above the counter.

"Don't you try and pull away from me, I'll take what I want girl." Francis hissed through clenched teeth and resumed pulling up her dress. Lilith filled with rage, realizing this was the heinous treatment her mother had received for years and it was about to repeat with her. She stretched herself and could get a fingertip onto the handle of the knife. Then she felt Francis exposed her buttocks and push her dress hard against the back of her neck. The sound of him unbuckling his belt with his free hand sent a chill through her nerves, cutting so deep goosebumps rose all across her skin. She felt an urgent rush of panic and knew she had to stop him, or she would fall victim to Francis the same way her mother and surely many others had. Lilith kicked her right foot back hard, finding Francis' knee with her heel. His leg buckled from the impact and his hand left Lilith's shoulder and dress to hold his balance from falling. Lilith, using the leverage from her contact with Francis' knee, lunged for the kitchen knife. With a solid grasp on the handle, Lilith pushed with everything she had off the counter with her other arm and turned toward Francis, slashing the knife hard. The edge of the knife found Francis' brow and cut him across his nose and deep across his cheek. Francis reached his hands up, instinctively trying to grab Lilith's arms to stop a second swing, but Lilith's next attack was not a swing or slash. She plunged her arm in, stabbing Francis directly in his throat. The man's eyes bulged, blood gushed and frothed from his neck as he tried to breathe. Lilith withdrew the knife and pushed Francis over onto the floor. Then, standing over him, Lilith stabbed again, this time into her attacker's groin. She withdrew the blade, wiping the blood off with a dishrag from the wash basin. Breathless and shaking, Lilith dropped the rag onto Francis' chest as he writhed on the ground attempting to hold both his groin and his throat while blood pooled around him on the washroom floor.

    Lilith stood over Francis, watching him squirm, she felt no guilt, no pity, only a fiery rage. Then fear closed in around her. She could hear voices out beyond the kitchen and her anger was replaced by an icy chill that cut her to her core. Once Francis' body was discovered she would be sought after and killed for his murder, it did not matter how the act had come about. She scooted a large wooden case of pots in front of the door, it took every ounce of strength she had in her slight frame and the better part of ten minutes. Once she was satisfied that the case would impede anyone easy access to the washroom, Lilith pulled the window open as far as she could. She tucked the knife into the waist of her dress, crawled through the open window and walked away at as brisk a pace as she dared. So far, no alarm had been raised and she feared running would do just that. As she approached the bunkhouse, Lilith looked around for her mother, but she was still laboring in the cane fields. That was a good thing though, Lilith thought, none of the other white men would be around the estate home for some hours. She would have some time to effect an escape.

Lilith shed the apron and head dress and kept to a path away from the road that allowed her to stay out of sight from the cane fields. She walked in the scorching heat and humidity of the Haitian sun, only pausing to look back momentarily when the thought of her mother crossed her mind. Hours drug by and the sun dipping ever lower over the western horizon did little to lower the temperature. It seemed even the breeze off the sea brought little relief and in the constricting dress, with no water, Lilith was soon exhausted of the walk. Port-Au-Prince was only a couple miles away and she could see the masts in the harbor, little beacons of freedom and escape to Lilith. She stopped to rest near a squat tree a way off the road. She finally found respite from the sun in the shade of the tree, looking over the beautiful Caribbean coast. Carefully watching the road, Lilith knew that by now Francis' body had to have been discovered and his people would be looking for her. If they got to the port before she did, they would be watching for her there as well. With nothing but a kitchen knife to defend herself, she suddenly began to feel like her escape plans were hopeless. Francis was a fat old man and she had surprised him during his attack on her. It would be much harder, if not impossible, to defend herself against someone trying to apprehend her. These thoughts ran through her mind, gripping her with a carnal fear of being caught and killed or worse, returned to the estate.

Noises down on the road caught Lilith's attention and snapped her thoughts to her immediate situation. Riders on the road, carrying lanterns and armed with muskets were on their way towards Port-Au-Prince. Lilith could see they were not soldiers and studying them harder she recognized one of the faces. They were from the estate, no doubt searching for the murderer of their collective employer. Lilith waited for them to pass completely from sight before she roused herself from her hiding spot. With any good fortune at all, she could skirt the edge of town and make it to the dockyards. From there, she hoped to stow away aboard a vessel heading somewhere and leave Haiti forever.

Moving in the moonlight, Lilith felt exposed and kept to the shadows as much as she could. In the pale glow, she could still see decently well enough to make slow progress across the rough terrain towards the harbor. Trying to work out in her mind how to get aboard a ship, Lilith was careful to avoid roads and paused often to listen for signs of pursuit. After hours of methodical progress and with the moonlight about to fade away Lilith came to a halt a short distance across the bay from the harbor. There were several silhouettes of ships in the harbor and some smaller vessels moored up by the pier. From her vantage across the bay, Lilith watched sailors returning to their vessels under the brilliant tapestry of stars in the dark night sky. The water of the bay was placid calm, the tide ebbing slowly out exposed a broadened beach that would allow Lilith to walk within a couple hundred feet of the pier. She carefully edged her way out onto the exposed rocky shores and made her way as far as she could towards the pier.

Reaching the water's edge, Lilith eased into the water up to her waist and took a deep breath trying to adjust to the chill water. Then she plunged in the rest of the way. She could swim, not well, but well enough to cross this small stretch she thought to herself. As she approached the boats docked at the pier her legs began to fatigue, her arms burned, and she struggled to keep her face above the water. Her dress felt heavier and heavier by the second and soon she was gasping for panicked breaths while fighting to buoy her face out of the water. All forward progress stopped as she was consumed with a struggle only for air. The chill of the water overcame Lilith, her strength to fight her head above the water failed. Clawing at the surface felt impossible, her feet felt like lead weights, her chest felt as if it would explode, her vision faded. Sinking slowly to the floor of the bay she succumbed to unconsciousness.

H.M.S Valor
6 Aug 1808
50 Degrees 40'N, 1 Degree 38'W

William stood on the quarterdeck of the valor, observing the hands as they milled about their work. Captain Grimes, currently below in his cabin, would be on deck soon. William was already in awe of his new commander, a sailors' Captain, as far as William could tell he was a supremely disciplined man but also very fair with the crew. He had spoken with Mr. Ordman, the Midshipman whom he had met on the pier accounting loading supplies, about their commander.   William learned of an instance where Captain Grimes had derated a Midshipman, causing him to become an ordinary seaman for a time because the young man was not proficient enough in basic seamanship and gunnery tasks. This sort of thing happened regularly throughout the King's Navy, but it was a horrid sentence for a young hopeful officer. This sort of handling though, would often teach the young man the most basic of fundamentals and give him enough perspective from a viewpoint he was previously unaccustomed to make him all the better an officer in the end. William had also discovered, in his conversation with Mr. Ordman, that Captain Grimes had stayed the hand of the Master at Arms very recently when a landsman pressed into the service had been caught stealing from the officer's mess. This was a very unorthodox treatment of crew; William had never heard of restraint like that amongst the fleet.

Their departure from port had been a hurried affair, William scarcely had time to retrieve his belongings from the inn in between preparations. His introduction with Captain Grimes had been similarly rushed and informal although William suspected now that the ship was underway, he would very soon get to know him better. Even as William was in awe of his commander, he had heard Captain Grimes' reputation far before setting foot on the H.M.S Valor. Jonathan Grimes was known for his extraordinary skill at seamanship and combat, but in some circles, he drew ire and criticism as being a bit of a rogue. Bucking tradition and protocol were often career ending mistakes, but the Lords of the Admiralty overlooked Grimes' occasional departure choosing to relish in his almost exclusively successful exploits. This caused a resentment among competing officers of the fleet, especially those who did not personally know Grimes. Usually, once a man met Captain Johnathan Grimes he would be endeared by his charm and eventually made a friend by his relentless loyalty. Captain Grimes would give a man the shirt off his back if in need and as several sailors could personally attest, his boat cloak on a cold watch at night.

Captain Grimes materialized from his cabin and made his way up the stairs to the quarterdeck. His uniform coat and hat missing caused no confusion among the crew, passing sailors all touched brow and spoke their greeting. Grimes was a man of formidable stature and composure, his blouse did little to disguise his powerful broad shoulders and chest and his sleeves, though designed to be loose fitting, barely contained the man's arms. William instantly began to understand some of the unflattering things he had heard about Captain Grimes. For a commanding Captain to present himself this way before the crew was unheard of, although the crew responded to him all the same. Discipline aboard seemed to be of the highest order, in fact the ship was the cleanest and most kept William had ever seen. It seemed odd to William but at the same time, strangely endearing. He had never worked for a Captain who was as approachable or informal as this man.

"Lieutenant Pike," Grimes said beckoning

him, "Follow me forward man, we have a few things to discuss if you will humor me."

"Aye Sir," William responded, instantly following his leader and simultaneously struggling to keep pace with him.

"A brisk walk in the wind should help the mind digest." Grimes said, almost as much to himself as to William, then turning toward the quartermaster at the wheel, "Make your course south west by south, we should be into channel rollers in two hours' time, if the wind holds we will make our way west." Grimes looked over to the officer on watch, "Young man, top gallants and royals if you please and see to it that the sheets are addressed on the main, they look slack to my eye." Midshipman Shellam turned and began issuing orders to the crew, causing a cascade of officers and petty officers to give in kind directions to accomplish the Captain's orders.

"William," Grimes continued to his new First Lieutenant, "It may not seem as such, but our crew is out of sorts. The press brought in mostly landsmen and we are still fourteen men shy of full compliment. Our tasking from the Admiralty will take us across the Atlantic to the Caribbean, such is not for an un-seaworthy crew." Grimes stepped over a line and seeing it laying about on the deck, uncoiled and a mess, began to set it right himself. A passing bosun's mate, recognizing the situation, rendered his respects and interrupted the Captain mid-task.

"My apologies Sir, I should have caught this long before you, Sir. Here Sir, I will finish it and double check the rest." The bosun's mate said.

"No apologies, get a seaman to do it and ensure the crew understands the conditions for line on a King's Ship." Grimes responded, again setting off to walk the deck with William.

"I will see to it at once Sir." William said, "Also, I meant to ask you when you would permit me to gun drill the crews?"

"You may start as you see fit Will, the sooner the better, old bony still has men o' war prowling about and I won't be caught with my pants down. See to it that the men understand quarters though first, they need to be in the right place when contact is made. Anyone dithering about in the face of the enemy won't fare well through a fight." Grimes continued as they approached the bowsprit in the very front of the Valor. Grimes took a step up, bracing himself on a line and stepped onto the rail. William, sensing he was expected to follow suit, also stepped up and looked out over their intended course. He could see the gently rolling waves ahead gleaming in the midmorning sun. The southern horizon was foreboding and showed large, dark cloud formations hovering over the English Channel almost warning the Valor's crew of the ever-present threat from the seas compounded by the current state of war with France.

"As First Lieutenant, I want you to understand the extent of our orders," the Captain continued, still looking out over their course. "We are to cross the Atlantic to report to the fleet in Nassau. From there we will be making patrols through the Caribbean, hunting for Bonaparte's privateers. They have been causing all manner of havoc for the East India Company, especially in those waters. There is however special instruction for all manner of King's ships currently. These are secret instructions, so I expect you to keep these to yourself as You and I are the only officers aboard who know and it must remain that way unless one of us perishes at sea." Grimes paused momentarily and then continued in a lower voice, "No ship of His Majesty's Navy is to board any ship of The Company, we can approach to four cables, but under no circumstances any closer no matter the distress, not even if they hail us to. Do you understand William?" His tone had turned very grave and he made no eye contact with William.

"I understand, Sir. But if I may ask, why? Why would we be prevented from assisting a Company ship in distress?" William asked, genuinely perplexed by the intent and broad nature of the order.

"I do not know, nor do I understand fully the benefit to allowing a ship sharing our colors to perish. However, those are the special orders for all ships operating in the Caribbean. We will follow them." Grimes stated, finally stepping off the rail and heading aft along the larboard side. The pair continued their walk along the deck toward the rear of the ship, stopping several times for Lieutenant Pike to address crew and have something corrected. Each time Captain Grimes would make comment or conversation with members of the crew, encouraging good handling or redirecting poor. Finally reaching the quarterdeck and completing their tour topside, Grimes turned to Lieutenant Pike, "I'll leave you to it then, I'm going aloft, see to it we maintain our course out. Westward once we get into the channel rollers."

"Aye Sir." William replied, noting a disturbing change in the Captain's demeanor. Something seemed to be troubling the man, though Lieutenant Pike could not determine quite what it was. William thought it could have something to do with the state of affairs with France, maybe the number of inexperienced men through the crew or possibly the odd special order to the fleet. Whatever it was, it certainly did not slow the man's vigor up the ratlines and high aloft, William noted, watching the Captain through the rigging faster than any man he had ever seen.

High aloft and away from the crew, Captain

Grimes mulled over his current state of affairs. Tasked with a Trans-Atlantic voyage, while the channel fleet has recently reported several French men o' war slipping the blockade. He was short manned and many of the hands he had were quite inexperienced. The Valor could hold her own against just about anything and had in recent memory. But Captain Grimes had reservations about this cruise, with special orders from the Admiralty. For the life of him he could not work out in his mind why, why would they be ordered to keep clear of the Company? How was he, a Captain ordered to stop privateer interference in their trade, supposed to accomplish this if he had to stay at maximum cannon range at the very closest? Johnathan Grimes toiled over it in his mind, making some silent resolutions to himself and cursing the circumstances forcing him to make decisions such as these. The channel rollers were starting to pick up with England far astern and he could feel the Valor beginning to change course, just as he had ordered. "We have work to do, so let us quit this pathetic sulking and heave to, for God's sake we are the pride of the fleet!" Grimes spoke aloud, to the ship and to himself. With that, he scurried down the ratlines as the ship's movements became more and more pronounced by the big rolling waves in the channel.

    The deck of the Valor was a swarm of activity when Captain Grimes rejoined the crew. Uninitiated sailors were not hard to spot and were typically pausing between tasks to be sick over the rail. The landsmen tripped over their own feet on the moving deck in the heaving swells, winds from the west and northwest blew hard and propelled them along at a rapid pace. But with seas this large, too much speed could be a disaster. Captain Grimes turned toward the quarterdeck, but as he was about to call out command, Lieutenant Pike summoned the officer of the watch over and spoke something to him. Then in a flash, the watch officer scurried off the quarterdeck issuing command, "Hands, make ready to reef royals! Quartermaster make your heading west by southwest. Below watch check all cargo and cannon are well secured, look lively men, come on!" Cobb the Second Lieutenant called out. This caused a flurry of secondary direction and commands from midshipmen, petty officers and the crew were instantly in action to set the ship condition to Lieutenant Pike's orders.

"This bastard is going to blade himself off to the wind to avoid damaging masts and square rig as he reefs sail, then slug it out with the rollers with main, topsail and jib. Not what I would do, but, effective, I suppose." Grimes said to himself. Rain was now pouring, soaking all on deck, then Pike beckoned Cobb back over and another condition change was ordered.

"Hands, reef royals and top gallants, come

about westerly once that is done, double line those aft braces." Cobb crowed out in his usual manner. It was a slight change, but Grimes was irritated by the half step. Crews must have confidence that the orders they are receiving are correct, the first time they receive them. Anything less than this erodes a crew's confidence in their command and can lead to nightmarish problems. Grimes made a mental note to correct this with Pike. Even if he must delay the change of sail momentarily to be sure of his decision, he cannot appear to be second guessing himself. Despite his irritation, Grimes took notice of how well the Valor got along running before the wind under main and topsail. He was endeared to Pike, watching him command the ship, even though he had made the half step, his final command was exactly what Grimes himself would have ordered. Other Captains would be threatened by proficiency such as this in a first lieutenant billet, Grimes loved it. He smiled as he looked out into the gathering swells and weather in the course ahead.

"Mr. Pike, about those gun drills..." Grimes yelled over to the Lieutenant through the foul weather.

"Aye Sir." Lieutenant Pike responded, both bewildered and intrigued by the Captain's choice of timing. Then he turned to the crew of the Valor and cried out, "BEAT TO QUARTERS!"

Chapter 2

"Gazelle"
12 Aug 1808
N 2 Degree 4' E 8 Degrees 13'

Omibwe awoke in a feverish sweat, his head spinning and his eyes unable to focus. He was in a dimly lit room and seemed to either be sick or everything was moving, or both. Omibwe rolled on his side, as he did his eyes started to focus. He was startled by a tall, thin man sitting close to him. Omibwe started to vomit and the man held a pail for him. While he wretched, Omibwe became aware of a terrible pain in his right leg, like it was burning. He rolled back and tried to sit up, but his strength failed him. The thin man leaned forward, pail still in one hand and spoke some words, nothing Omibwe could understand, then he tried again putting a hand out onto Omibwe's shoulder.

"Your wound was bad. I had to take your leg." The man said to him, this time in a language he knew. He then wet a cloth from a wash basin and put it on Omibwe's forehead. In the candlelight Omibwe looked around, where was his sister? His parents? Where was he? He felt awful and weak, hot and cold at the same time, his head awash with questions and waves of nausea beating him down onto the hard-wooden slab he lay on.

"Your sister and parents are here. They are on the ship with us." The man said, opening up a bottle and pouring some of its contents into a small cup. The mention of a ship snapped at Omibwe, the men chasing him, who had shot him, they had taken his family on their ships.

"Drink this," The man said holding out the small cup," you need to rest, or you won't make it my friend."

Omibwe drank the contents of the small cup. It was horrid, he coughed and gagged a little but held the liquid down. His spinning head felt heavier. After a few minutes, his pain subsided and soon Omibwe drifted off unable to remain conscious.

The tall man stood next to Omibwe as he fell back asleep. His shoulders and back ached, his mind was exhausted. He took the pail Omibwe had been sick into and left the small room, in a passageway on his way topside he looked and saw the little girl he knew to be Omibwe's sister. He tried to make eye contact with her, but she buried her face into her mother's arms. He then continued to the ladder well and went topside to the deck of the ship.

"Hey Frenchman, did you save that little shit, or do we need to dump him over?" the large man with a scarred face asked him.

"I would say he will be fine. But all I can say

is he will recover." He replied, "And my name is LeMeux."

"I don't give a damn Frenchman, if it were up to me you would be hangin' by yer neck with the rest of your crew and we would've left that running welp to bleed out on the beach!" the man sneered, drawing nearer to LeMeux as if to strike.

"Enough!" The Captain of the ship approached the two, "Go about your business doctor and be thankful you are still breathing." Turning toward the scarred man, "I'm not sure how many times I have to tell you, dead men collect no price. Now, you have filled the holds yet again and you will collect fair wages, but do not antagonize my prisoners or you will be in irons among them Mr. Sprague. Do I make myself clear?"

"Aye, Sir," Sprague replied, his countenance toward the Captain just as ragged.

LeMeux emptied his pail over the side and immediately headed back down for his patient. He paused momentarily near the cell where the young man's sister and parents were. He considered trying to get their attention but the sentry roaming the passageway was too close. He continued on to see to the young man instead.

This was the second voyage to Africa LeMeux had made since being pressed into the service of this slaver ship. A year ago, he had been sailing to Martinique aboard a French merchantman. LeMeux's medical education had saved him from the grim fate of the rest of the crew and passengers aboard the small French trade vessel, but he was nonetheless a prisoner on the ship. The doctor obtained a rudimentary grasp on the native language of the region the slavers were targeting on his first voyage to Africa and it was useful on that trip as he was kept quite busy treating the abducted. Omibwe had been brought to him in what would have likely been the young man's final hours. Unconscious and bleeding profusely, with a shattered tibia the strong young African's condition improved somewhat after LeMeux stopped his blood loss. But infection had set in rapidly and LeMeux made the perilous gamble of amputating Omibwe's lower right leg. It had worked and the young man was recovering. To what end the doctor was unsure of. This crew of brigand men were delivering Africans to market, to be sold off as slaves in the Americas. LeMeux spent the first few days just keeping Omibwe off of death's doorstep, over the course of the next few days he would tend to the young man as best he could. It was difficult enough were he caring for a patient under normal circumstances, this situation was extreme. Not only was his patient a prisoner and subject to a diet almost too meager to survive on, he was also. Additionally, the pitching and rolling of the ship made almost all of the prisoner occupants ill. This coupled with the smell of dozens of prisoners in cramped quarters, in severe heat and with poor ventilation below deck made a putrid concoction which amplified every misery experienced aboard. Their captors were merciless animals who often tormented and abused their prisoners as entertainment. Though Lemeux noticed, this was never done within sight of the captain.

    Their days were long and miserable and nights just as horrid. After a few days the occupants of the ship grew more accustomed to the perpetual motion and the sea sickness lessened slightly. Any prisoner who resisted anything from the crew was beaten savagely, any prisoner who died was unceremoniously dumped overboard. LeMeux, after days of caring for Omibwe and bringing him into relative good health had formed a bond with the young man. The two had spent many hours talking in LeMeux's cramped quarters, broadening one another's perspectives and knowledge both to pass time and out of genuine interest. LeMeux's elementary grasp on Omibwe's native language deepened to the point he could communicate conversationally with him after the first week. Omibwe's leg was healing well and LeMeux was beginning to fear that the ship's captain would demand he be placed into the cells with the rest of the

African prisoners.

Omibwe's strength returned to him, day by day, aided in great part that Dr. Lemeux was giving him the majority of his own rationed food in addition to the sparse rations he was allowed by their captors. Lemeux fashioned him an improvised crutch with a board he managed to barter away from one of the ship's carpenters and some ragged clothes he had been instructed to use as bandage. It took several attempts and with much assistance from the doctor, Omibwe could manage to move about the very small cabin. Omibwe and his French doctor grew ever closer through the experience. LeMeux promised the young man that he would take him up the passageway to see his family at the first opportunity and despite Omibwe's general distrust of everything due to his recent trauma, he believed his doctor.

LeMeaux awoke on the first particularly rough night at sea with his new patient. They had been sailing for ten days and were getting into larger rolling waves. Omibwe was awake, visibly scared out of his wits, pouring sweat and weeping. He had been sick onto the floor and was sitting up, bracing himself on the wall and the edge of the slab he lay on. LeMeaux tried to calm him but Omibwe began to call out for his mother. Fearing the crew would hear and knowing they would react horribly, LeMeux tried a different approach.

"Have I told you about mermaids?" LeMeux asked, desperate to draw the young man's attention to anything but the heaving ship and rolling seas.

"No." Omibwe replied, "What is a mermaid?"

"Oh, you have never heard of mermaids. You are in luck man; I know all about them. I can tell you about them if you'd like."

"Tell me." Omibwe answered, still visibly tense but now interested, LeMeux could see.

"The mermaids are an ancient people. Mermaids and mermen, keepers of the sea. The Mermaids, from the waist up are the most beautiful women you could ever imagine. Their bottom halves are like sea creatures, a tail like a dolphin." said Lemeux keeping eye contact with Omibwe. He could see he had piqued the young man's interest. Of course, he thought to himself, all young men like hearing about beautiful women.

"Have you seen one?" Omibwe asked the doctor, unsure of what he was being told.

"I have my friend and I will tell you. They certainly are beautiful creatures. Kind and beautiful. They love sailing men, in fact, they often trail behind ships like this." LeMeux continued, now with the young African's full attention, "Mermaids have been known to rescue sailors that have fallen overboard in foul weather. They will pull them to shore and sing them sweet songs. Many sailors have stories of rescue from mermaids."

"I know how to swim, my father and I dive in the sea from our village, but Anaya, she doesn't know how yet." Omibwe said, visibly becoming upset again mentioning his sister. Quickly, LeMeux sought to redirect his attention.

"Oh, she will be fine Omi," LeMeux said, using the shorthand name he had taken to calling his patients, "This ship is big and sturdy and built for far fouler weather than this." At this mention, Omibwe seemed to ease and the conversation slowed until LeMeux looked over when Omibwe had paused and saw his companion had fallen back to sleep.

LeMeux felt pangs of guilt for spinning this yarn to the naive young man. He felt many things about this situation. Powerless to stop what was happening and guilty for being a part of the society that was allowing and enabling it. He felt dread for Omibwe and his family, he dreaded their future and what it held. He was developing a kinship with the young African and felt a fondness for his family in the cell just up the passageway. Sorting through these thoughts and feelings, LeMeux tried to think of a way he could help. To interfere with the journey meant a swift and certain death at the hands of the crew, Mr. Sprague in particular would take joy in killing him. Escape for the Africans aboard was a futile endeavor, they were too far from shore for even the strongest swimmer to survive, plus the African coast was notorious for its population of sharks. Escape near their destination would be similarly impossible, they would all be in no shape to swim anywhere by that point of the voyage. These thoughts drifted LeMeux into a restless and fitful sleep and even unconscious, the gears of his mind ground away towards a plan to reinstate freedom to them all.

H.M.S. Valor
11 Aug 1808
48 Degrees 36'N, 7 Degrees 27'W

The routine of sailing in a Royal Navy frigate had settled in, the sailors were familiar with their battle quarters and becoming more and more proficient in the drill of clearing for action. Lieutenant Pike had exhibited leadership ability and technical prowess in training many of the new hands. He had led the gun batteries in drill twice daily since departing, dry runs early in the day and live fire in the evening. The ship's combat abilities had improved dramatically in the short time since their departure. Captain Grimes demanded a very high standard and while they were not quite there, even he would admit, the crew was well on their way and on the right heading. A week of drill and discipline had laid a foundation for the newest of the crew and the experienced hands let none slack, knowing the captain would accept nothing other than excellence.

Lieutenant Pike had just come off his watch, he stood midnight to four bells as a matter of principle, after seeing the oncoming watch settled in, he made his way below to get some rest. It felt as if he had just laid himself into his hammock, almost before the slack was out of the lines suspending it from the timbers of the ship when a midshipman appeared in the berthing.

"Lieutenant Cobb's compliments Sir. He has requested your presence on the quarterdeck."

"Alright Mr. Shelton, I'll be along." William responded, biting down a flare of temper and wondering what could possibly be worth preventing his sleep in the pitch dark of night. He slipped his pants and shoes back on, grabbed his coat and headed back topside. Once on the quarterdeck, William immediately noted the wind had remained steady, sea conditions had not changed enough to note, perhaps the swells were even a bit smaller.

"Mr. Cobb, what seems to be the issue?" he asked, mindfully keeping an even tone with the junior lieutenant.

"I heard a bell that wasn't ours Sir, out of place like, and when I went forward to look, I swear I saw a light for a moment." Cobb replied in a hurried, hushed tone. The implication that they could be in that close of a proximity to another ship sent a chill up and down both men. William immediately turned to the petty officer on watch.

"No bells or whistles, no calls, pass the word." William instructed, "Quietly now, no shouts, no calls and douse all lanterns."

"Aye Sir," the petty officer responded and immediately began passing word to each individual man on deck, before climbing ratlines himself to pass the command to hands above in the rigging.

"Mr. Cobb, station lookouts and men to pass the word on larboard and starboard bow," William ordered, then turning to another petty officer, "wake the gun crews and stand by smartly, no calls and no shouts. Then give the Captain my compliments and request his presence on the quarterdeck. Lively now man. Go!"

"Aye Sir!" the sailor replied in a hushed tone, hurrying below to complete his tasks. Watch had changed not more than ten minutes ago. "If we can hear their bells, they could have heard ours." William mumbled to himself.

"Hold steady course quartermaster, I'm going forward to have a look." William commanded, departing the quarterdeck and walking up the starboard rail for the bow. There was dead silence aboard the Valor, just her hull sliding through small rolling waves was the only sound to reach his ears. Satisfied that his orders were being heeded, William had just begun to question in his mind Cobb's senses when he smelled something. It was just a passing sensation but through the salty sea air, William could almost detect the smell of something cooking. His mind was trying to process how this could be, Cobb specifically pointed ahead of the bow, the sound, the light he thought he saw was ahead of them and most importantly and problematically for William's logic, downwind. This was important if the ship that was out there was hostile, but if William was smelling cooking there could possibly be another ship and they would have the weather gauge on the Valor!

Captain Grimes came to the quarterdeck and got a report from Cobb, then proceeded up to where William was scouring the dark for any sign of a ship out ahead. The winds held steady out of the east and the Valor was moving along at a slight 6 knots with her top gallants and royals reefed. Grimes reached William just as a faint sound floated in over the gentle swells.

"What was that?" the Captain asked.

"Not sure Sir, I heard it also, Mr. Cobb was alerted by what he thought were bells. But I think our situation could be more complex than that." William said, bracing himself, unsure of what Captain Grimes' reaction would be to his suspicion.

"What is it Will?" Grimes pressed, looking out over the bow.

"Sir, I smelled cooking food as I approached the bow. It was only for a passing moment, but it could not be from us and it could not possibly have come from a ship downwind." William stated, flatly presenting the dilemma he had been working through.

"Very well, Mr. Pike. Good observation. We need to come to some kind of conclusion then. If we approach the ship ahead and she is hostile, which is quite likely given our relative position to France, we will be forced to pursue and engage. However, if there is another ship out there, this one with the weather gauge on us, engaging a ship and giving away our position would be folly. But if there is no other ship, we risk losing contact with this bugger." Grimes was now looking at the deck, deep in thought, talking to William but also himself. Before William had a chance to respond Grimes straightened his neck, looked out over the bow and seemed to come to an internal conclusion.

"What hour is it Lieutenant? I have misplaced my pocket watch." Grimes asked.

"Half past four I believe Sir, um, approximately." William said. The two were now walking at a quick pace to the quarterdeck.

"Dawn will be nearing and before the sun breaks, we have to gain weather gauge on whatever ship was behind us." Grimes stated with confidence and conviction, then turning toward the quartermaster, "Come about, hard a-larboard bring us close hauled to the wind and adjust sail and remember, silence man."

"Aye Sir," the quartermaster replied, immediately passing word to begin setting the conditions the Captain specified.

The bow of the H.M.S Valor nosed southward, swiftly at first and then more slowly as she came up into the wind close hauled as the Captain commanded. There were a few snaps at the canvas as sail filled and sheet tightened, each causing crew on deck to grimace and look toward their Captain. Johnathan Grimes stood on the quarterdeck, seemingly immune to the tensions running through every other man aboard ship. Above the deck, high in the rigging crewmen were making sail adjustments, coaxing every bit of speed they could while the quartermaster held course. Minutes dragged on and the faintest glow could be detected in the eastern sky. Grimes calculated in his mind, if the two ships were cohorts, they would keep relatively close proximity to provide each other mutual support and aid if necessary. Perhaps they would increase that distance slightly to avoid mishap at night, especially under the sliver of moon and overcast skies. But they could be only a few miles apart, it was difficult to determine how far away the ship had been off their bow but the ship that was upwind of them had to be within a few nautical miles. Smells travel with the wind, but William smelling cooking food caused Grimes to believe they were close, perhaps within a mile. The challenge would be slipping by them undetected into an advantage before dawn unveiled their position. The eastern sky was glowing more and more intensely by the minute it seemed, and Grimes silently thanked the overcast conditions for giving him an extra few minutes of precious darkness to cover his maneuver.

As the eastern skyline grew lighter and lighter, the seas immediately surrounding the Valor began to come into view. Captain Grimes had the Valor tack over larboard and bring the wind in close haul on her starboard side. As the ship settled into her new heading and all adjustments completed, Lieutenant Pike had stationed himself on the larboard edge of the quarterdeck, scouring the waning darkness for any sign of a ship. Through his glass William scanned, from in front of the bow to far astern pausing intermittently to look with his naked eye and listening intently all the while. His tiredness had faded away in the tension and excitement and he was set on finding both ships. William could hear voices in the shadowy stretches of the pre-dawn glow. Muffled and distant but definitely present, he slowed his breathing to try and hear better, desperately trying to hear something definite a word, a phrase, some kind of indicator of their nation of origin. The voices floated in again over the gently rolling sea, but no words were distinguishable. William alerted the Captain by tapping him slightly on the arm and cupping his left ear at the rail. Johnathan nodded in agreement, he heard voices as well. Steadily the pair monitored the sporadic incoming sounds from the ship they had yet to see. They tracked as near as they could reckon the source of the sounds until both were confident it was astern of them.

The increasing light of dawn finally began to illuminate enough horizon that a sail would not hide for long and neither would the Valor. Now it would be a question of speed of action for the crews and the skill of decision for officers. Word was passed that a sail sighting would end the order of silence as the officers on deck would need to react immediately. Tense moments dragged as every available hand searched the gathering light for sign of another ship. Sunlight finally emerged enough over the horizon that even through the dense cloud cover the seas were growing visible. As William and Johnathan could now see more farther than pistol range from the Valor, things began to unfold in a mad rush.

"Sail off the larboard stern, she's about a mile out Sir!" called down one of the marines stationed up on the mizzen top.

"Colors?" The Captain shouted up in reply.

"She's French!" the marine exclaimed.

"Quartermaster, hard a-larboard, make your heading west by northwest," the Captain ordered, then immediately turning to Cobb, "Sheet the top gallants as we come about, and beat to quarters." Captain Grimes then turned to his steward, "If you will, fetch my hat and sword. Lieutenant Pike's as well, hurry man." As soon as the Captain had finished speaking the same marine who had spotted the first sail called out again,

"Another sail Sir! She's about three miles farther out than the first! No colors yet." The marine's voice was followed abruptly by the drums signaling the Valor to clear for action. Every man aboard who had not already been stationed by Lieutenant Pike earlier scrambled to their designated post. Both batteries opened their gun ports and ran out loaded guns, all while the Valor made a tight turn towards the stern of the nearest French Ship, her name still not distinguishable through the dim dawn and distance.

"Sail! Two points off the starboard bow Sir! Ship of the line, looks to be a third rate!" the sailor on watch up on the main topsail called down. This sent a chill through every hand, including Lieutenant Pike. They had expected the sighting of two ships and even though they still had weather gauge on all three, a three on one engagement could be disastrous for all but the most skilled of crews. Captain Grimes wasted no time, immediately grabbing William's sight glass and furiously pacing up the ship to the bowsprit. He opened the telescoping glass and scrutinized the third sighted ship. As he looked on her stern the large ship with two decks of gun batteries was unfurling her colors, she was French as well.

"Damn the luck William, that bastard will prevent us from taking any prize this day." Grimes uttered to his second in command. William, completely taken aback, couldn't believe what he was hearing. Any commander William had ever worked with would be trying to find a way to survive their current predicament. Captain Grimes was still working out his plan of attack!

"The closest Frenchy is a sloop; she can match our maneuvering and possibly our speed. We must disable her first, run out the long nines on the bow and aim for those masts. Fire at will, Will." the Captain said, pausing slightly to emphasize his pun.

"Aye Sir." William responded, completely bewildered. The Valor was about to be in a serious engagement and her commander was cracking jokes. He instructed the gun crew to load the bow chasers and run them out, the first shot would give them range to set up a possible hit on their second.

"Larboard gun fire when ready." William

instructed. With a thunderous roar, the cannon fired and recoiled violently. The crew set about immediately, swabbing the bore with a sponge then a powder bag and wad with another nine-pound ball immediately after. William looked for the impact of the first shot, it sent a plume of water into the air just behind their target.

"Starboard gun increase elevation four turns, fire when ready!" William shouted.

5 Aug 1808
Governor's Mansion -Kingston, Jamaica

Admiral Elliot Sharpe exited a large, comfortable carriage in front of Lord Governor Alton's mansion. Governor Alton expecting his arrival, greeted him on the front steps leading up to the grand mansion. Colonial soldiers guarding the premises and it's occupants snapped to attention when the two men came into sight.

"Admiral Sharpe! How good to see you, please, I am expecting additional company, a dinner party. Would you join us?" Alton said. The Governor spoke everything with an air of contempt and elitism that the Admiral could barely suffer. His ample build and the walk down the stairs caused the last words to come across a little hurried as he ran out of breath.

"It would be my pleasure Lord Governor." Elliot replied. A stark contrast to the obscenely overweight governor, Admiral Sharpe was a tall, slender man. He spoke in measured, careful tones and always maintained his officer's reserve. Years of command in the Royal Navy had embedded discipline and bearing into Elliot, his tone was the same whether he was accepting a dinner invitation or ordering a shore battery to open fire. His opinion of the governor couldn't be lower, the things Elliot had sacrificed and worked for his entire life, Governor Alton was born into. It was a symptom of a class system that defined life in Britain and all of its colonies and protectorates. Governor Alton wielded commander in chief powers of the Caribbean fleet and so Elliot must suffer his presence and pander to his oddities and incompetence.

The two entered the mansion and proceeded through a large, ornate atrium and into a study. The room was filled with bookcases, a large desk sat at the rear of the room facing inward from picture windows displaying a gorgeous backdrop behind the mansion. The Jamaican evening was setting in, casting orange and pink hues over the hills and cliffs overlooking calm, almost serene seas. The evening glow served to illuminate the study and Admiral Sharpe took note of charts scattered across the Governor's desk. A large map of the Caribbean painted on the north wall and flanked by more bookcases loaded with volumes. Governor Alton stood behind the desk and settled into the high back plush chair behind it. He removed his wig and dabbed at his forehead with a kerchief, barely abating the onslaught of perspiration.

"There is to be a few additions to your fleet Admiral. I have received correspondence from London, and you should be expecting an additional frigate this month and next. As well as two ships of the line the following month and two more the month after." Alton said in between recovering his breath.

"I didn't realize we were in need of additional ships, with the pirate problem nearly abated…" the admiral began to reply.

"I know you didn't realize, but I have foreseen the need and have requested the additional sea power." Governor Alton snapped, interrupting the admiral, "I want the frigates assigned to covering the East India Company shipments between Barbados and Kingston. The larger ships, third rates I believe, are to be deployed as a squadron to defend Kingston harbor."

"Yes, Lord Governor. I will see to it. But, if I may Sir, might I inquire into the need for additional escorts for the East India ships, we haven't lost any to pirates in quite some…" Admiral Sharpe began to respond, but was again interrupted.

"I am aware of threats to the East India fleet of which you are not Admiral. Those are your orders; I see no need for further discussion." Alton huffed out, growing visibly irritated with Admiral Sharpe.

"Yes, Sir. Might I also inquire as to the standoff orders we are currently issuing to the fleet. It would aid in their defense if the fleet could rely on the East India ships for mutual support as well as approach to render aid if the East India ships are in distress." Sharpe said, hurrying his cadence slightly to avoid being cut off again and internally irritated at the Governor's rude habit. Through it Elliot maintained his military bearing, insulted as he was that the silver spoon Governor kept insinuating his subservience while also implying a sense that Admiral Sharpe was somehow ignorant of his duties.

"The standoff orders are to remain Admiral. The East India fleet are aware of these orders and have been so directed as well. Approach at your own peril, it will be charged as treason to disregard these orders. We cannot afford to quarantine any of your ships and that is exactly what the result of close contact will be." Alton continued, his arrogance dripping from his words. The conversation turned to other matters, the current state of the fleet, ships refitting and those in need of refit. There were several troop movements that needed attention from the fleet, both carrying troops and escorting those movements as well as ship battery supporting a ground assault on a rebel encampment eastward up the coast from Kingston. The Governor's indifference grew in each new matter discussed until he caught Admiral Sharpe's eye gazing upon a particular map of the Jamaican interior. Alton quickly overturned the map and gave a self-satisfactory smile. Replacing his wig onto his head and giving Sharpe a blank stare awaiting conclusion to what was obviously information he believed beneath his station.

"Yes, Lord Governor. I will ensure those orders are carried out exactly." Sharpe replied evenly, disguising his simmering distaste for the Governor and his continually declining situation.

"Very well, now that we have that unpleasantness concluded. I'm sure you have kept me from greeting some of my dinner guests. But we will carry on nonetheless." The Governor stated flatly, almost to himself, pulling his large frame up from his chair. The Governor started toward the door and opened it to reveal a crowd of guests awaiting his arrival in the large atrium. Immediately the Governor's countenance changed as he was pleasant to each guest he greeted and to Admiral Sharpe as well while all the introductions were made. With each introduction Elliot's discomfort grew, he would much rather be in an officer's mess amongst line captains and lieutenants aboard a ship with marginal food.

Dinner was a grand and formal event, obscene in both portion and number of courses. Elliot found himself quite satiated early on and longing for an excuse to exit. He felt out of place being a bachelor among a company of married couples. He did note several lasting stares from a couple of the society type wives and Elliot Sharpe desired no confrontation from a jealous husband. The only other bachelor at the dinner party was a man whom the Governor introduced as Mr. Timothy Sladen, a tobacco farmer and merchant from the former colonies, now United States. The presence and demeanor of Mr. Sladen did not sit well with Elliot. He was obviously American; his accent was distinct when he spoke and his conduct consistent with that of other Americans Elliot had encountered. But a scarred brow and neck in addition to scarred hands belied something other than the gentleman plantation owner the Governor had introduced him as.

At the conclusion of the meal, the men gathered on a large balcony to partake in cigars while the ladies continued their conversation in the dining hall. Elliot chose this as his opportunity to exit, exchanging parting pleasantries with each gentleman in turn and the Governor last. He entered a waiting carriage which would deliver him to a shore boat which would in turn eventually deliver him aboard his flagship. Riding in the carriage Elliot replayed his conversation with the Governor in his mind, the new ships arriving to the fleet and the peculiar orders the Governor seemed so touchy about. In addition, the supposed gentleman tobacco baron from the Carolinas did not sit well with him, his demeanor and unveiled interest in Admiral Sharpe seemed out of place. This, before considering, that tensions between the Crown and the former colonies were again on the rise, Elliot could not quite place why the American would be a welcomed guest at the Lord Governor's home. Elliot mulled these questions until his escort arrived at the pier, he then gathered himself and proceeded to the longboat waiting to take him out to his flagship the H.M.S Endurance. His mind eased by the improvement, in his opinion, of company and the familiar demands of naval service.

On the balcony, the gentlemen had congregated into several groups each enjoying cigars and rum provided by the Governor's servants. Nearest the door Mr. Sladen stood solitary, puffing at his cigar and looking intently at the Lord Governor. Alton, noticing Sladen's focus, excused himself from a discussion with several of his guests regarding a slave revolt currently in progress inland. He made his way over to Sladen, acknowledging several compliments on dinner from his guests along the way and the duo walked to the rail on the side of the balcony.

"I'm not impressed by your Admiral. Is he going to become a problem?" Sladen asked in a very hushed tone.

"No no, I've got things completely under control. I assure you, any issues we come against from the Royal Navy will be handled according to the articles of war. No Sir, there will be no problems." the Governor insisted quietly.

"I could hear you in the study Governor, the Admiral is already questioning his orders. If this turns into an issue now it will make for an inconvenient reception when they return." Sladen said.

"The Admiral will do his duty. He will follow his orders exactly; you have nothing to worry about." Alton replied.

"Well, I should hope not. For your sake as well as his, my partners and I have already invested quite an advance to you. It won't turn out well for anyone if there are any unnecessary..." Sladen paused, "Problems."

"No, no no. I am certain. Things will progress just as we have agreed. I am expecting minimal problems and nothing we cannot easily overcome. I assure you Sir, your investment is in good hands and will reap you exactly what you are seeking." the Governor said even more hushed so his guests would not hear him in this position with someone.

"That's good. You let me know if there's anything else you need. This endeavor cannot fail." Sladen said, putting out his cigar on the rail and walking away without observing any departing gestures.

5 August 1808
Port-Au-Prince Harbor, Haiti

Lilith awoke on the hard-wooden deck of a ship, a group of men looked on as she coughed and sputtered up water and retched on the deck where she lay. A sick feeling engulfed her and even though the night was warm, she shivered violently. A large, imposing man with a bald head and graying beard brought Lilith a blanket and wrapping her in it, lifted her from the deck of the ship. He had a kind manner about him, though his scarred hands and face belied a propensity for violence that Lilith noticed as he took her up.

"You gave us a scare young lady; another few minutes and you'd be beyond saving. You must feel like shit." The large man spoke, soft in manner or at least he was trying. A gentle look in his eyes reassured her, this man meant her no harm.

"Thank you." Lilith sputtered out in between coughs. Her shiver continued even now wrapped in the blanket and held tightly in the strong sailor's big arms. With a slight motion of the deck Lilith quickly looked about, instantly anxious about her new surroundings and the strange men who had rescued her.

Seeing this, the sailor tried to ease her discomfort,

"Relax miss, not an evil will befall you whilst you are among this crew." the man spoke reassuring Lilith. He carried her below decks to the galley and gently placed her in a seat near the wood stove. Lilith could feel her chill easing and the sailor poured some coffee into a cup and handed it to her with a smile.

"My name is Charles; this lot all calls me Chibs or worse sometimes I'm afraid. But you can call me what you like miss." He said sitting in a seat across from her. He opened a wooden crate near the stove and produced a small loaf of dark bread which he tore in half. He handed half of the bread to Lilith, who immediately began to eat. She was famished, the bread and coffee were devoured with no observed formality, which brought a huge grin to Chibs' face. He had taken a bite of his half of the loaf but surrendered the rest to the girl who gladly took it and wolfed it down.

"I'll have our cook, fix you something proper after you've had some rest. But, that wench of a screw is god awful if awoken and she is sleeping now. Speaking of which, you must be about done in. There's a hammock you can use here in the galley, I wouldn't want your shiver to keep, so you sleep here. I'll go fetch a hammock."

"Sir, where are we sailing to?" Lilith asked sheepishly.

"You've nothing to fear lady. The authorities have no idea we scooped you up and we have no further business in a French port on this trip. Not any French port that would be looking for you anyhow." Chibs answered but without really giving a specific destination. Lilith was confounded. How did he know she was avoiding French authorities? Where were they headed and what French port would not be looking out for a runaway slave who had murdered her former captor? Chibs could see confusion and concern crossing Lilith's beautiful face.

"Sir. Where do you sail to?" Lilith asked again, a stern, determined note entering her voice.

"Well, ah, little lady. We haven't a particular destination as of yet. A few options have been discussed but having taken in a fugitive in Port-Au-Prince, I think Haiti be good only astern of us for now. The Cuba trade routes have made us a good profit before, or perhaps the Louisiana coast. The crew will hold a vote when we've put out a little farther from Haiti." Chibs replied, hoping his answer would placate the girl. It didn't.

"How do you know I am pursued? And why would you help me?" Lilith pressed.

"Your former master did not survive his, ah, encounter. His employees spread word all over town and the docks. We found you as we were returning to the ship in the longboat. There are only so many reasons for a young lady to be attempting to swim the harbor that late at night. We assumed you to be the wanted woman. My apologies if we were incorrect. But you were in obvious peril, so we did the only rightful thing. As far as your escape from Haiti, I think you will find this crew is a bit patchwork like. You wouldn't be the first escaped slave we've taken on, nor fugitive." answered Chibs. "In fact, our Captain himself is an escaped slave. But that is a conversation for another time."

"What sort of crew votes on their destination? Don't toy with me mister." Lilith asked pressing further.

"Well miss, ah, we vote on destination and duties. The captain still commands as he will, but at least this way he knows the desire of the crew. We deal in all different manner of cargo, but never human cargo." Chibs answered. He could see some of the girl's fears eased and other suspicions arose. He would have to leave it at that for now, he could see Lilith struggling to remain awake despite her investigative questions. "You need to rest lady. Fear not, you're safe, but I'm afraid you may catch a fever if you don't beat those shivers and get some sleep. Now, let me fetch you a hammock," said Chibs. He disappeared out of the galley and Lilith was already nodding off when he returned. Lilith opened her eyes momentarily as Chibs lifted her into the freshly slung hammock, she smiled slightly and drifted off into sleep with the gentle pitch and roll of the ship.

"BOOM!" Lilith awoke to the thundering of a single cannon shot. Startled awake and in a panic, she scrambled out of the hammock, hitting her head and knee in the cramped galley quarters, she raced to find out what was unfolding. Finding her way out to the passageway she ran, barefoot and clothed only in the torn remains of her dress, to the stairs leading up onto the main deck. On her way Lilith passed a gun deck with crew members all manning cannons. She scanned the crews looking for Chibs but found only unfamiliar faces intently staring out open gun ports. Not a single one even looked her way. Lilith continued on up the stairs, finally she emerged from below onto the main deck. Lilith squinted as the bright sun hit her eyes which had been accustomed to the dim light below deck. The loud thunderclap of another cannon sounded, and smoke rose from the side of the ship she was on. Men were hustling about on deck and Lilith was frantically searching for Chibs. Then she spotted him, he was standing near the wheel of the ship, but focused out over their larboard rail. Lilith made her way over, weaving in between men and women alike moving about on deck. She approached Chibs, who was so focused over the larboard rail he hadn't noticed the beautiful girl approaching him.

"Chibs?" Lilith raised her voice trying to get his attention. It failed. Another man was standing about two feet behind Chibs and stepped forward slightly to speak to the large sailor.

"Hoist the black Chibs, let's see what this lot is made of," the man said.

"Aye Captain." Chibs replied, then he turned toward the rest of the deck and repeated the command. "Run up the black flag boys! Fire another round across her bow!" Then looking out over the deck of the ship Chibs finally noticed Lilith, who had been standing there trying to get his attention.

"Ah, Good morning there, my dear, you may want to be getting below decks, maybe even the hold girl. If these dogs return fire it could turn into a bloody mess up here!" said Chibs, pausing slightly and then raising his voice mid-sentence after another outgoing shot from a cannon.

"What is going on? Who is on that ship?" Lilith demanded, pointing over at the ship off the larboard rail.

"Some American merchantmen dear." Chibs replied, giving up on persuading the girl to return to relative safety below as she walked up to him, "We are going to relieve them of some excess cargo as it were."

As Lilith walked over to the larboard rail

with Chibs next to her, the ship's captain approached the duo from where he stood. The crew aboard were running up a large black flag, Lilith could see the likeness of a skull with horns coming from out atop its head. Behind the skull was an angled trident with a broken chain crossing the bottom of the black field. Lilith watched as the large black flag filled with the morning breeze. Almost as soon as it was run up to it's highest point the American ship began to lower their stars and stripes.

"Striking their colors Cap'n," Chibs sounded out excitedly.

"Ready a boarding party Chibs. Lay us up alongside pistol shot and grapple them in. Not a soul harmed unless they provoke it." the Captain rattled off his orders. Lilith looked him over, he was dressed in the same manner as the rest of the crew, raggedy, he stood a full head shorter than Chibs and quite narrower at the shoulders. He appeared young, Lilith put him no older than perhaps thirty and his clean-shaven face was almost the only one she had seen on board except for the women. Lilith understood now why Chibs had been so elusive about revealing details last night. She was aboard a pirate vessel. Her head spun, a mixture of excitement and fear washed over her. These men obviously meant her no harm, not yet anyhow. She couldn't help but be caught up in her thoughts and hadn't noticed the ship pulling closer and closer into the surrendering American vessel.

A woman approached Lilith, eyeing her over with an inquisitive look. Her mulatto complexion was only slightly darker than Lilith's and her hair was wrapped up in a bandanna. She wore ragged pants over boots that looked a size too big and a torn-up sailcloth shirt that revealed several scars on her torso.

"You're new. Pretty thing, but that won't do a damn bit of good for you here. Take these, you're coming over with us." The woman said, handing Lilith a pistol and a thin rapier sword. "When the planks go across you follow me, don't use those unless you see me using mine. Try not to get killed if a fight breaks out, losing your pretty face would break my heart."

"Trina, we just fished her out of the drink a few hours…" Chibs began to object, seeing Lilith being armed up.

"She's on the ship so she'll earn her way Chibs. We've no time for a vote but the crew won't have able bodies freeloading. Unless the Captain objects. She goes." Trina snapped back at Chibs, who looked over his shoulder at the Captain. He had been watching as the young lady's situation developed.

"She goes, but Trina, you've insisted so you will watch over her. If she does not return, then neither should you." the Captain replied.

"Alright then, you girly, get your first taste today. Have you ever killed a man?" Trina asked.

"Just one." Lilith replied as casually as she could. She could feel Trina's inquisitive stare as she walked to the larboard rail. The cross planks were about to go down and the raiding crew all gathered on deck to flood across to the American ship.

"Well, hopefully you won't have to today." Trina said, "Keep close to me and if a fight breaks out, I'll try to keep us both alive." The planks clattered home onto the American ship's rail and the pirates started climbing their way over.

Chibs was the first man across. A pistol in each hand, he expertly balanced the cross plank and dropped down onto the deck of the American ship. There were sailors with raised, empty hands scattered across the deck. Some of the sailors kneeled, some remained standing, all showed empty hands. There were no weapons laying on deck, something Chibs immediately took cautious mental note of. With a number of the pirate crew now aboard the American ship, Chibs walked up the quarterdeck and pointed his pistol directly into a sailor's face.

"Where be your Captain? Cowering into his cabin?" Chibs asked, cocking the hammer of the pistol.

"Aye, he is." the sailor stammered responding.

"Go and fetch him. If he comes out armed, we'll kill everyone on deck before we burn this tub and leave you to swim boy." Chibs hissed, shoving the young sailor to the gangway. "My name is Chibs, I'm the Quartermaster aboard the 'Drowned Maiden,' none of you cowards will be harmed if you keep your mouths shut and do as you're told. Lift a finger against my crew and I will see every one of you dead." Chibs shouted over the remaining crew, who were now being forced down to kneel on the deck of their ship by the boarding pirates. Lilith had crossed the gang plank and was now standing by Trina, aiming her pistol at a kneeling sailor who looked to be her own age. The young man still had a fair complexion and no beard, as he knelt, Lilith noticed his hands were shaking and tears ran down his face. A puddle of urine gathered around the deck where his knees touched.

Lilith, trying to remain focused in her own right, felt an edge of pity over the young sailor. She quickly snapped out of it when the sailor Trina had her pistol trained on tried to stand. Trina, in one swift motion raised her foot and kicked the sailor square in the throat. She then swept her pistol down, hitting the man over the head with the edge of her hand and handle of the gun. The remaining sailors on deck kept still, this show of instant force snuffed out any ideas of heroism among them.

The American Captain appeared from his

cabin ready to accept his defeat, his shoulders slumped, head hanging. He approached Chibs to offer a formal surrender of the ship. Lilith watched as the events toward the quarterdeck of the American vessel unfolded, but she caught a smell, an awful retching smell that caused her to recoil slightly. She paused, wondering what the source of the offending odor was. It smelled like death and passed almost as soon as she had detected it. Again, it wafted into her senses and almost caused her to gag.

"What in the bloody? That'd gag a shit eating maggot!" Trina shouted, confirming Lilith was not the only one who smelled the foulness. Lilith stepped over to the netting covering the hold and peered downward, the smell was wafting from below and as she leaned over the hold there was no passing smell, it permeated her nose engulfing her senses. Lilith started to recoil and step away when something caught her eye, in the shadows below deck under the grate covering the hold Lilith saw a set of eyes. Her eyes adjusted to the shadow under the deck and Lilith started to make out faces. Just below the grate covering, Lilith observed them momentarily, people.

"Trina!" Lilith called over gesturing for her new mentor.

"What? What is it?" Trina snapped, stepping over and looking into the hold Lilith motioned toward. Trina gasped, both from what she witnessed and the overpowering smell. At once she called out to Chibs who had heard the commotion but was intent on dealing with the surrendering American skipper.

"Chibs!" Trina called, "You'd better come and look at this!"

"Hold on there," Chibs began to respond. At that moment, an American sailor came from the hold, a tomahawk in one hand and sword in the other. The tomahawk raised to strike Chibs from behind. Lilith raised her pistol, squeezing the trigger prematurely sending a ball careening in front of Chibs' would be assailant and meeting the wooden wall behind Chibs. This gave the attacker just a second of hesitation, which when Chibs spun to see who fired a shot was enough for him to level his pistol at the attacker and send the round into his chest at point blank range. This precipitated a reaction from a few more of the Americans, who were dealt with in the same manner and speed.

Chibs made his way over to the hold and looked down through the grate.

"Mother of god, what have these... what in the bloody name of Mary..." Chibs stammered but could not finish a sentence, his face flushed red offsetting his white beard. He raised his unfired pistol in one hand and grabbing the surrendering captain with the other placed the muzzle of the weapon directly under the man's chin.

"Where did you take them on?" Chibs demanded through gritted teeth.

"Jamaica, please don't shoot..." the captain stammered back in reply.

"Where in Jamaica you bloody fool? It's a big enough island!" Chibs hissed through his teeth louder, his patience for the man gone.

"It's, it's a secret port. We take on goods in Kingston and then we are paid to shuttle the slaves as well," the driveling captain barely had time to finish his sentence. Chibs discharged the pistol under his chin, sending the shot through the man's mouth and head, throwing him backward to the deck in a rain of his own blood and brain matter.

"Trina, empty everyone from the hold. Get them across to the Maiden." Chibs instructed, still staring down at the man he had just killed, "Then you may gather these prisoners of ours up. See to it they are placed down into their own hold, shoot any who resist. Bring three of the bastards across with you when you're done, the Captain will want to ask some questions."

Chapter 3

H.M.S Valor
11 Aug 1808
48 Degrees 12' N, 9 Degrees 4' W

The starboard bow chaser on the H.M.S Valor roared, sending its nine-pound iron projectile hurling towards the French sloop's stern. Lieutenant William Pike looked on intently at the sloop for sign of impact, after a brief moment of flight the ball struck her target sending deadly shards of wood and glass from the aft castle flying.

"Larboard gun, four turns of elevation! Fire when ready!" William ordered as the starboard gun set about reloading. The starboard gun thundered sending another ball into their target, this one hit slightly higher than the last sending more shards of wood across her quarterdeck. A brace line snapped, and screams could be heard across the quarter mile gap of sea between them. The sloop had begun a hard turn to bring her larboard guns to bear on the Valor when the second ball had impacted, her turn stalled and her bow drifted back down wind.

"Her quartermaster must have been hit by debris! Both guns, Fire at will!" William shouted at the bow gun crews as they hurriedly made their guns ready.

The bow cannons were firing as fast as the

crews could make ready, pausing momentarily only to adjust their aim. Their fourth and fifth rounds again found their target high on the stern of the French sloop causing chaos and destruction aboard the ship. Through the calamity aboard the sloop, she doggedly began her hard turn again.

"Captain!" William called out, "She's coming about to fire! Larboard side!"

"Quartermaster bring her about four points to starboard, larboard battery prepare for raking fire as she passes," Captain Grimes called out, each recipient enthusiastically repeated their order and carried about completing their task. Below deck, both batteries of guns were ready and run out, each crew awaiting their orders anxiously. William turned momentarily from the sloop to see how the larger warship was reacting to the cannon fire. The third rate had come about close haul with the wind off her larboard side aiming her bowsprit at an angle toward the Valor.

"Bow guns, make ready and hold fire, let me know when we have that one close enough to range her." William instructed, "I'm headed for the quarterdeck, starboard gun leader take charge."

"Aye Sir," the gunners mate replied.

On the quarterdeck Captain Grimes took careful stock of the position of the sloop, his own course and the course of the much larger warship now beating towards the Valor.

He calculated a course in his mind and quickly inventoried the Valor's capabilities. With a plan put together, he walked up to the quarterdeck rail and looked over the crew quickly. All were ready, hands aloft awaited sail change, gun crews below had all reported ready. William came onto the quarterdeck.

"Mr. Pike, raking fire as we pass the sloop. Then have larboard battery make ready with chain shot and run out, once they are run out, I want max elevation and I want them to unship their rear wheels. See to it that starboard battery's guns are all at the ready for full broadside fire on that ship of the line as soon as we have fired on the sloop. We won't have any room for error. Tell Lieutenant Davitts his Marines are to hold fire on the sloop, we're going to fan in front of that line ship within musket range, they can open fire on her." Captain Grimes rattled off his instructions with dashing confidence. William's broad smile went unnoticed by the Captain, no one else but he could see the commander's plan beginning to take shape.

The sloop came in line with the forward guns on the Valor's larboard battery while she was still at an angle leaving her broadside ineffective. The first two guns fired, followed by the next two and the next two after that. Each pair of guns sent eighteen-pound projectiles directly into the sloop's stern and aft larboard quarter, until all twelve guns of the battery had dealt their blow without the sloop being able to return fire once. The French ship was a flurry of snapping line and cable, shattering wood meeting flesh and sail. Smoke was pouring from the gun ports in the rear before Valor's battery had completed firing. Moments after the last shot, an explosion from in the sloop's hold blew away a massive part of her larboard side sending debris and bodies flying outward, the flames spread quickly and she listed down on her side, thoroughly and decisively beaten.

"Quartermaster ready for hard a larboard, marksmen at ready, starboard gun crews full broadside on my mark!" Captain Grimes bellowed out, preparing the crew for their next fight. The third rate had acted just as Captain Grimes had anticipated they would, in an attempt to aid their countrymen they had made a course to intercept Valor and cut her off from the sloop, setting up a devastating broadside. But the Valor's speed and maneuverability foiled their course. Grimes was able to fire all twelve-larboard cannon at the sloop and now was running before the wind setting up to launch a full broadside at the bow of the French ship beating directly towards them. The entire crew of the Valor was awaiting the Captains orders and as the large French warship drew closer, tense moments drug by and finally expired with Grimes' shouted orders,

"Quartermaster make your turn now! Starboard battery, as she comes about, fire!" Captain Grimes directed.

The Valor cut her turn directly in front of the approaching warship, William guessed the range was less than two hundred meters. The starboard battery opened fire with impressive unity as the French ship came into their aim. Several rounds from the volley found their target, one smashing a large hole in the enemy hull just above the water line. The crew aboard the Valor all cheered loudly, cut short only by the shouts of officers redirecting their efforts back to their tasks. The Valor turned slightly again southward, and she was beam reach to the wind.

"Mr. Cobb keep your heading south by southwest, she will no doubt start firing bow chasers at us and we need to open a gap before our next move against her." Grimes instructed, the opening salvo of the French bow guns confirming his predictions as he spoke. Their first shots fell slightly short and Grimes knew they would now have their range. Before Cobb could even respond, Grimes reissued his orders, "Run up every auxiliary sail, top gallants and royals on main and fore and get every bit of slack from the sheets, we must make every knot we possibly can."

Cobb went about setting his Captain's conditions while Grimes looked back over the fantail of the Valor. He could see the French gun crews readying their bow guns. The other French ship, the one Cobb had originally heard in the dark, had come about also and joined the pursuit of the Valor. With all her sails flying, the Valor rapidly created a gap between herself and her pursuers. The only hit she took was to the aft castle, wounding one sailor and killing another from the wooden debris caused by the ball. It took only forty minutes for Grimes and the Valor to create enough of a gap for the Captain's planned maneuver. Grimes ordered the quartermaster to come about hard, turning with the wind until it was close reach off her starboard bow. This put the large Frenchman on her larboard side and just as Valor hit her heading, within range. The Marines fired swivel guns and muskets as they came about, causing the French sailors to scramble for cover. Valor's larboard battery fired their guns, loaded with sail and line destroying chain shot. Without rear wheels though, the guns only recoiled a fraction of what they normally would, making reloading painstakingly slow.

The Valor's salvo of chain shot ripped through much of the French line ship's sails, shredding her main and topsail on the mainmast, severing many of her brace lines and breaking the larboard side yard for her mainsail. French sailors scrambled away from falling debris, several jumping overboard to escape the hail of fire from the Valor's marines.

Captain Grimes immediately ordered a hard-larboard turn again bringing them dangerously close to the massive French ship who was now severely disabled and in chaos on deck. The Valor's quick turn was not as tight as her Captain had hoped she could make though, and she momentarily came into the field of fire of the French warship's larboard battery. Grimes recognized the danger they were in immediately and began ordering crew to take cover. The French broadside sounded with a thunderous, deafening roar. Impacts along the starboard rail of the Valor sent jagged wooden debris flying and several brace lines flailing. Below deck, the forward most gun on the starboard battery took a direct hit next to their gun port, the impacting round destroyed the cannon, killed the gun crew and wounded several men from the adjacent gun crews. William himself was struck by a shard of wood, the jagged piece lodging high into his cheek by his left eye.

The Valor, wounded but still maneuvering smartly, passed out of the line of fire and crossed the bow of the line ship. Captain Grimes went below himself and ordered the remaining starboard battery to open fire. The volley of fire impacted on the bow and larboard side of the French line ship to deadly effect. Several holes were smashed into the French hull making the conditions for the already disabled ship desperate. She started listing heavily onto her larboard beam and smoke was pouring from all of her gun ports.

Captain Grimes ordered the quartermaster to maintain course westward and went about seeing to his wounded while assessing the damage Valor had taken. There was still another French warship approaching, this one considerably faster and more maneuverable than the line ship that was now fighting to stay afloat and extinguish a fire. Grimes arrived on the gun deck to William holding a wound on his face while he worked to restore order from chaos. He had already ordered all guns reloaded and run out, so Grimes began reorganizing gun crews to compensate for the dead and wounded. Once the gun smoke and confusion had settled, Grimes and Pike assessed damages to their ship and crew. Several sections of the starboard rail were shot away and the large hole by the forward gun port on the starboard side was the worst of it. The severed brace lines were already being replaced and the damage to the aft castle could wait for repair until a more convenient time and condition.

When the Captain and his first Lieutenant returned to the quarterdeck, the remaining French sloop had overtaken her countrymen on the line ship and were pursuing the Valor about half a mile off her stern. Far in the background William noted the line ship was struggling to battle their fire as thick black smoke bellowed up through her rigging and plumed high into the sky.

"They are unlikely to recover her." Grimes stated, he paused momentarily staring at the struggling enemy vessel, "I intend to run us west and south. Mr. Pike get the crew organized. When that sloop comes close enough, we are going to come about on her and take her as a prize. We can take her to Nassau and let Admiral Sharpe do with her as he pleases. Perhaps she will be your first command." The mention of command surprised William, who was not sure how to respond. His mind still reeled from the first part of their engagement and he was baffled how they had come out of it as well as they had. Captain Grimes had led his ship against two enemy vessels one of far superior firepower and size and one of near equal speed and maneuverability, leaving both in their wake, soundly beaten. Having witnessed Johnathan Grimes' decisiveness and conviction in combat, William now understood more of the reputation the daring Captain held.

"Oh and Mr. Pike." Grimes started again.

"Yes Captain?" William said.

"Have that wound attended to, you can't carry about all afternoon holding your face like that." Grimes said with a grin.
"Aye Sir." William responded. He hadn't forgotten the wound, it was too painful for that, but he was taken aback a bit that the

Captain showed as much concern as he did. His other commanders retired to their quarters after battle, Grimes was making rounds with the crew, checking wounded, lamenting over the dead, giving instruction to the sailors where it was needed. This man was completely present, in tune with his ship and his crew. William's chest swelled with pride, both in his Captain and in their crew and what they had collectively just accomplished. With a French warship still in chase, there was an air of tension about, but the victorious crew was high on adrenaline and stiff following winds.

"Three cheers for Captain Grimes! Master of the seas! Master of the Valor!" a sailor cried out.

"Hip hip huzzah!" the crew responded in turn.

A song broke out up in the rigging as they pulled further away from the sloop, at one-point Captain Grimes could be heard lending his voice to the chorus. It was a glorious hour to be on the deck of the Valor and the entire crew's confidence was with their Captain and his First Lieutenant.

16 Aug 1808
Governor's Mansion - Kingston, Jamaica

Governor Alton sat at the desk of his study. He was nervously awaiting a visit from Timothy Sladen. Disturbing news had arrived from a mutual associate of theirs in the United

States. Their most recently expected ship, containing thousands of pounds of raw sugar had not arrived when expected. There were no reports of storms yet, though the season was approaching. The chances of the ship being taken by a pirate vessel still lingered, or perhaps the captain had gone rogue and taken the cargo for his own profit. There was also the chance, however small, the vessel had been taken as contraband by an American Navy vessel. These matters weighed on the Governor in his stuffy study as the sun beat into the west facing windows behind him. He shifted and fidgeted uncomfortably while examining charts of the route the missing vessel likely took. Likely, they had been very specifically instructed to adhere to a designated route. Both for their own protection and that of the mutual proprietors organizing the endeavor. Alton knew he was out of his depth looking over navigational charts and trying to decipher anywhere trouble would have arisen. He needed a man skilled in naval matters such as Admiral Sharpe, but that was a risk he could not afford to take. Attention from Elliot Sharpe in this matter would undoubtedly result in difficult questions arising, questions Governor Alton could not afford to have answered, questions he had sworn to ensure remain unasked and unanswered.

Timothy erupted into the study door, letting it swing and abruptly hit the adjacent bookshelves. It impacted with enough force that several books tipped and rolled charts sitting high atop the uppermost shelf fell off dropping to the floor. Mr. Sladen's face was flushed red, his scarred neck all the more pronounced through the added circulation of his temper.

"You guaranteed Alton. You guaranteed us safe passage and we have now lost a ship. There are parties who will be expecting compensation and some god damned answers. I am here to see to that," said Sladen. His tone failing utterly to disguise his contempt toward the fat governor.

"You may be irritated with me Timothy, but you will remember. I am a Lord and the Governor of the colony in which you are conducting your enterprise. You would do well to remember that and address me according to my social rank and title," said Alton, his tone growing more indignant with each syllable. The tension in the room simmered and Sladen walked back to the door, gently and deliberately closing it as Alton spoke. He slid the bolt closed between the double doors leading out into the grand atrium and turned back to the governor as he finished his arrogant drivel.

"I warned you, Lord Governor," Tim began, sarcasm dripping from the title as it left his mouth, "There is far too much invested into this enterprise for it to fail. I assure you, Lord

Governor, you are amongst the lowest order involved, whether you care to accept that matters not. You will see to it that this situation does not repeat itself. There are other Lord Governors and there are other islands." Tim had walked back in front of the Governor's desk and now stood looking down at him. Timothy's countenance toward Alton had never been to the Governor's liking. Governor Alton preferred sycophants, unquestioning and unchallenging, typically of lower ambition and intelligence.

"I can arrange a search for the missing vessel. It will take some time, but I believe we will be able to recover it and at least some portion of her profits." Alton replied, hoping to placate the American.

"Very well, Lord Governor," said Sladen, his tone softening slightly. "But the cost of that lost vessel goes far beyond a ship, a few bags of goods and a lost crew." As Tim spoke, he slowly turned sitting in one of the plush ornate chairs in front of the Governor's desk. He very deliberately drew out a thin dagger which had been concealed in his waistband as he sat. Tim placed the tip of the dagger on the arm of the chair and spun it in his hand, drilling a small divot in the wood of the chair arm. The blade flashed off of the sunlight pouring in behind the Governor and menacingly glared into his eyes with each turn. Sladen continued, "Perhaps, we have the appropriate island. I'm just unconvinced we have the ideal Governor for such a sensitive and profitable operation. Arrangements could possibly be made to rectify this." He spoke almost to himself. "But I believe you can salvage this situation, Lord Governor. Please make search arrangements with all haste. That vessel is to be located only. Under no circumstance should any Royal Navy vessel approach beyond maximum range. Locate her and report her whereabouts back to me immediately upon discovery. I will handle the recovery of her cargo myself."

"I will dispatch instruction to Elliot immediately then," Alton began to reply.

"Absolutely not, that man already has far too many questions. If it were up to me, he would be assigned elsewhere and replaced with someone more amiable," Sladen interrupted.

"Ok. Admiral Sharpe is the commander of the fleet assigned to the Caribbean. I could, however, issue special orders to the frigate I am expecting late this month. I will dispatch orders to the Governor in Nassau, sealed for the Captain of the frigate. His first task will be to patrol the north Caribbean for our lost merchant ship, locate and follow her, sending word of her whereabouts at the first opportunity. Will that suffice?" Alton replied almost pleadingly, his concentration broken by several glances at the dagger under Tim's index finger.

"Very good, Lord Governor. I suppose we won't be needing this after all." Tim said, replacing the dagger into his waistband. "You would do well to keep me informed Alton. These matters need to be handled with every manner of urgency and care." He stood and in his usual manner, without observing any departing gestures, left as abruptly as he had entered. Governor Alton sat, thoroughly unnerved as he penned the discussed orders to the incoming frigate. He called for one of his servants as he sealed the orders into the envelope.

"Yes, Lord Governor?" The servant said as he entered the study.

"Have this sent at once on the next ship destined for Nassau. If you cannot find one, inform me at once and I will commission a clipper myself." Alton said, handing over the sealed envelope and immediately mopping sweat off his brow with a kerchief.

"Yes, my Lord." The servant replied. Exiting at once to accomplish his task, he examined the envelope as he placed it into his pocket. On the front it read, "For the eyes of the Captain, H.M.S Valor by order of Lord Governor Alton."

"Drowned Maiden"
5 Aug 1808
18 Degrees 46' N, 74 Degrees 44' W

Aboard the main deck of the "Drowned Maiden" a debate was ongoing amongst the senior crew. The Captain looked on as the conversation covered everything from what to do with the captured ship and its crew to the fate of the freed slaves. Chibs had remained uncharacteristically silent through most of the arguments back and forth, remaining at the Captain's side. The two had quietly held a discussion amongst themselves and Chibs waited until a lull in the debate to present their plan to the crew.

"I say we load all the goods aboard. The slavers are all locked up! Let the Africans make their own way!" said one of the crew with small reaction from the onlookers.

"They won't make it half a day on the sea without any experienced crew among them. We should elect another Captain for her and refit the slave hauler as another for us!" another sailor shouted. This drew a much warmer response and several cheers of approval. Chibs shared a satisfied look over his shoulder with the Captain, who nodded his approval.

"Very well then." Chibs announced, walking to the middle of the crew on deck, "We will hold an election for a Captain of the prize ship.

She will sail in concert with us and we will assist in her refit. Do I have any opposed?" The crew remained silent, mostly looking at each other in a sense of solidarity.

"What of the slaver ship's crew?" Trina shouted over as she assisted one of the newly freed women up to the cross plank.

"What to do with the slaver crew?" the Captain stepped onto the rail shouting out above the crowd of crew and refugees. "What would we do with a man who would sell another into bondage for profit?" He looked out over the crew and freed slaves who had all fallen silent, their collective gaze locked upon him. "This matter won't be left for a vote. Chibs robbed me the pleasure of cutting down their Captain. We keep three, to identify their port in Jamaica, the rest are to be bound and tossed overboard. Any hand who disagrees, meet me on the quarterdeck with steel in hand!" Silence followed until the Captain stepped off the rail back onto the deck of the Maiden, when a cheer erupted from the crew. Every hand set to work, bringing the slaver crew up to the starboard rail of their ship, binding their hands with hemp rope and promptly shoving them overboard.

Lilith had avoided much of the commotion involved with the slaver crew, not that she objected to the Captain's orders, she had occupied herself with helping several of the freed slaves across to the Maiden. Once she had them settled in on the deck a group of four of the Maiden's crew met her on the cross plank, escorting the chosen prisoners to their Captain for his approval.

"Separate that first man there, girl. He was the slaver's first mate. The Captain will be wanting a word with him first," rattled one of the men. Lilith, unsure of how to proceed with taking the large man to the Captain, hesitated momentarily.

"Here beauty," Trina interjected, "Place that sword to his back and grab the back of his waistband." She demonstrated while instructing the Maiden's new recruit. "If he struggles or resists you girl, you hit here, on the back of his knee and then drive your blade through his neck and out his throat." Lilith was thankful for the quick instruction and she promptly marched the man over to the Captain who was very eager to glean information from the man.

"Fetch me a chair and some line, girl. We'll exchange our introductions when you return, it occurs to me we haven't properly met." Said the Captain as he lit a brazier on the larboard rail.

"Aye Captain." Lilith replied, imitating Chibs' manner as best she could. She went below and sought the items the Captain requested. Finding both requested items quickly with help from Trina, whom Lilith felt a slight kinship with after the morning's events, she returned to the quarterdeck. Lilith found the Captain holding his sword in the flames of the lit brazier.

"She returns!" He said, "You two," he gestured to Chibs and another sailor standing nearby, "Tie this man to the chair and lean him back onto the rail. We will see what each of these are made of." Lilith's blood ran cold. Could he be referring to her also? What had she done that would cause him to say this? The Captain approached her, his unbuttoned shirt revealing a deeply scarred chest and handed her the sword which was red hot near the point.

"My name is James. What's yours girl?" He asked making deliberate eye contact with Lilith.

"It's Lilith Sir," she answered, her heart still pounding from the thought he had held some ill intention a moment ago.

"Ok, Lilith. Well, we are going to get some answers out of this shit stain of a slaver. When I signal for it, you pull that blade from the brazier and you put it flat on his damned chest. When I tell you to remove it you put it straight back into the flame. Do you understand?" Captain James said holding eye contact so intense Lilith could feel a sense of broiling rage just under the surface of his demeanor.

"Yes Sir." She answered. Captain James walked over to the man, now tied to the chair and held in a lean against the rail by Chibs and the other sailor. He stood over the panicking prisoner for a moment and removed his shirt, exposing his scarred chest and back glistening with perspiration in the tropic heat. The sailor's protests escalated from murmurs to shouts and then seeing the Captain's scars, he fell silent.

"I'm going to ask you a few questions sailor. We'll get some answers out of you, or we won't. It really makes no difference to me. I already have my scars, they've all healed. How many you get depends on the speed and quality of your answers. Understand?" Captain James asked.

"Y y yes," he stammered.

"Where do you take on the slaves?" James began the interrogation staring down at the quivering man.

"We've picked up slaves from an anchorage off the nor'east corner of the island. Always after we make port and take on goods in Kingston," the sailor stuttered and stumbled over his words, rushing to get them out.

"Very good, and where are they destined?" James asked pressing further. An instant look of panic crossed the man's face.

"I don't know where this lot was headed. We've unloaded them in several different..." he began answering. The sailor's answer was not to Captain James' liking, James motioned over to Lilith. There was no hesitation from the girl, she hefted the large cutlass and placed the glowing blade flat across the captured sailor's chest. The man writhed against his restraints and screamed in agony; the smell of seared flesh permeated the air. Lilith looked to Captain James for his sign to remove the hot blade, but it did not come. Instead, he leaned close to the sailor he was questioning.

"I got these scars on my chest in this very manner. From a man like you, on a ship like that. I watched him throw my family overboard. He stole my mother from me, he stole my father and my siblings. Then he delivered me to market where I was sold to the man who gave me the scars on my back," said Captain James. His voice was low, full of simmering anger. He stood, waving Lilith off back to the brazier with the cutlass. James turned, looking out over the fantail. "I'll ask you again. Where was your destination?" He asked in a menacing voice.

"I know we were destined for the Carolinas, which port I don't know exactly, God's truth Sir, I'm never told exactly which port the slaves are to be delivered in until we are almost there. It was the Captain's way," the man rattled out. He struggled to fit words in between his panting breaths and Lilith could see he was struggling to stay coherent.

"Your anchorage in Jamaica. How many slavers does it harbor? And how far inland are the slaves held?" James asked. His voice returned to a somewhat even tone, though Lilith noted he was glancing over at the cutlass as he spoke.

"At least five ships. The most I ever counted was four anchored plus ours. The slaver camp is only a few miles inland," the sailor choked out. James smiled, apparently pleased with the now forthcoming information.

"How many in the camp?" asked James, the smile almost immediately gone from his face. The sailor squirmed again, panic returned to his face and he looked at James with pleading eyes. Before he could offer any reasoning or plea for James' mercy, the captain motioned for Lilith and the cutlass which was once again glowing with heat. Lilith drew the sword and moved to place the blade flat on the man's chest again. James leaned over and with one hand rotated the blade slightly to bear the edge against the sailor's flesh. Lilith let the cutlass rest on the man's chest just below the last burn.

"Please, no, no. I never went ashore there! Please girl, no!" the sailor pleaded, screaming through smoke from his own flesh and blood sizzling and crackling off the hot blade. Lilith looked over to James who slowly shook his head, she leaned more pressure down on the hilt of the cutlass. The sharp blade had worked it's way deep into the man's chest and his screams were fading with exhaustion and a state of delirious shock from the pain. Captain James grew tired of the line of questioning, he walked over and broke Lilith's grip of the cutlass with his own. Then, taking the sword in two hands and with a sweeping blow James relieved the sailor of his agony along with his head.

Lilith stood in a slight state of shock, she could feel her limbs trembling. James walked away as Chibs and the other crewman dumped the body overboard. Blood lay in small puddles at the foot of the chair, the wind had shifted slightly and was now in Lilith's face. Despite the breeze she could feel her face flushing and her chest felt hollow as if she could not get enough air into her lungs to satiate the urge to breathe. The rolling of the deck exaggerated and suddenly the world around her started to spin. Lilith made her way to the rail and heaved the contents of her stomach overboard. There were shouts and cheers from the crew. Almost instantly feeling better Lilith turned, embarrassed by her lapse of constitution she looked for direction from Chibs. He gave the young girl a warm, knowing smile and escorted her up to the bow of the Maiden.

"You wouldn't be the first among us to lose their breakfast over the rail girl. In fact, Trina spent her first month aboard looking green and spilling out everything we fed her." Chibs said consoling her. The combination of the smell from the slaver ship, the motion of the seas and the sight of Captain James' ending the former first mate of the slavers had accumulated and hit Lilith overwhelmingly. As they walked, crew from the maiden were already preparing the slave ship to sail.

"Who will stay aboard the Maiden Chibs? Where will the other crew sail to? What's going to happen to me?" Lilith had so many questions she almost couldn't get them out quick enough. Chibs could sense a nervous apprehension in her, more so than most newcomers and even most freed slaves that had come onto the crew.

"Well, I suppose we will find out soon enough. The Captain intends to hold a vote, he'll ask for a dozen or so able sailors to go with our prize ship and most likely train the freed slaves themselves to crew it. I will stay aboard the Maiden; you are free to go wherever you decide. You could even leave the ship next time we make port if you so desire." Chibs answered. He had pulled and packed a pipe with tobacco while he was talking, then pulling out a wick he stole some flame from an oil lamp as he finished answering Lilith he began puffing away.

"How long have you been on the Maiden?" Lilith asked.

"Since before she was the 'Drowned Maiden' girl. She started as the 'Lord's Maiden' a ship of the East India Trading Company. I was her first mate. My last voyage under the authority of the company was a load of spice and tea from the far east to Kingston. We took on human cargo, much like that bugger we just captured, one of those we took on was our Captain James. He had been captured and bought and sold, whipped and beaten, hid as stowaway and betrayed, tortured and shot. He is probably the toughest person in the world, but I've never met a truer soul in all my days, I'd follow him to the ends of the earth," explained Chibs.

"How did she come to be a pirate ship if you worked for the East India Company?" Lilith asked.

"Ah. We mutinied on her former Captain, dear. There were a few members of the crew who took issue with the leadership of our Captain and the decision to take on slave cargo was the last straw. We killed the bastard and took the ship." Chibs recalled.

"How did James come to be Captain then?" Lilith asked, still intrigued that a freed slave like herself could become a Captain on a pirate vessel.

"We voted on it, though he wasn't our first elected Captain after the mutiny. The Maiden was pursued by the company and naturally, the British fleet. We wound up in an engagement with a pair of large line ships. James came up with an idea to sail in a circle around an island, we set a couple longboats ashore with cannons. James and a few of the crew set them up right on the beach and when those Brits come around the bend those boys lit into both of them. The warships turned all their attention to the shore guns, they really had no choice in the matter, James had them dialed in after the first shot. Those big ships were at a disadvantage close into shore, they draw more depth under their keel, and we hove the Maiden farther out, pinning the bastards between our guns and James' on shore. Between accurate fire from the beach and the volleys from the Maiden, those big warships didn't stand a chance. James is a smart lad, he took two twelve foot lengths of chain with him, they heated those up red hot in a fire and loaded them into the cannons. They set those ships ablaze and the crews couldn't reload and fight their fire quick enough to withstand the volleys we laid on em." Chibs looked aloft into the evening as he spoke, pipe smoke rolling out of his nostrils. "The first Captain we'd elected was killed in that fight. One of the only shots they landed on us that day, hit our rail and cut the poor sod clean in half. Once we'd sunk the pair of warships and everyone realized James' plan had made it all possible, it was unanimous."

Lilith's head had settled, and her stomach seemed more at ease. The whirlwind of events leading her here had seemed to escalate towards this very moment and she was thankful for the calm skies and steady breeze. Almost as if he were reading her mind, Chibs spoke again.

"It'll likely be fair seas tonight and tomorrow. The red and pink hues up there don't often lie. But we'll need every bit of good fortune we can get. There's a fight brewing in the Captain's heart and that means for every soul on these ships as well." Chibs exclaimed, smoke rolling down from his mouth as he spoke. It was a sweet smell that Lilith only recalled smelling in the estate home, it wasn't connected with fond memories but for some reason the smell comforted her, and she felt very close to Chibs. He had a fatherly quality in his voice when they talked, and Lilith felt safe just being near him. He was the oldest man on the Maiden, but he projected a strength and calm Lilith had never seen before. From her experiences, white men all seemed so angry all the time but Chibs' kind manner endeared her to him.

H.M.S Valor
14 Aug 1808
46 Degrees 23' N, 14 Degrees 12' W

Will stood high above the deck of the Valor aloft of the main and top sails. The view was spectacular, the wind at his back and the smell of early dawn lifted his spirits as high as the thin wispy clouds stretching across the sky. The sun peaking above the eastern horizon brought the promise of another day at sea and yet another day of pursuit from the French sloop. Will had climbed high atop the rigging to be the first to spot her sails off behind the Valor. Several times in the last two days of steady pursuit, Captain Grimes had turned the Valor to and unleashed cannon fire to stave off the French ship. Still, the dogged pursuit continued. Will had spoken with the Captain at length of their tactical options. They could surely outgun the smaller French warship and if they boarded her would easily outnumber the crew, even after the casualties they took engaging the others. But Captain Grimes insisted on toying her along, lengthening the engagement. The fight had wounded the Valor and she was handicapped in battle without her lead starboard gun, but still very capable in combat.

"Just hope we don't have to trade broadsides with any frigates our class," said Will to himself as he searched the horizons for the French sails. In the pre-dawn light, he hadn't been able to locate the sloop and with the sun baring all to his eye he scoured the horizon, revealing no sails. It was a small relief, even with a heavy advantage against the smaller ship and crew, every engagement carried the chance of losing their ship and crew to the depths of the sea. William scanned across the horizons again searching for any sign of the enemy warship to no avail. They had lost her, no doubt she was still out there, but probably had turned away from their pursuit. Captain Grimes had intended to draw her out from their first engagement weighing whether there was another squadron of ships in cohort with the first three. Just thinking of it again made Will's chest swell, they had engaged three ships, one of which was far out of the Valor's class and succeeded. It would surely be a high note in the Admiralty's report to the crown when word traveled home about their engagement.

Climbing down from the rigging, William met Captain Grimes on deck.

"No sign of the French sloop Sir. It appears she has broken pursuit." William reported.

"Perhaps Will, but we must remain alert. Let's keep an extra lookout for the next few days." Grimes answered quickly. He was obviously distracted by something; Will could tell his thoughts lie elsewhere.

"Is something amiss Sir?" Will asked. Captain Grimes made fast eye contact with his first lieutenant and motioned for him to follow. The two walked aft to the quarter deck and when the Captain was certain they would be out of hearing from the rest of the crew, he leaned in slightly to William.

"Lieutenant Cobb has raised questions of Mr. Shelton's conduct in our engagement with the French. Apparently, he ordered the young man to assist with the recovery of the starboard battery when gun one was struck by the French shot. Cobb has informed me he saw Mr. Shelton coming up from the hold after the engagement was over." Said Grimes. He was visibly disturbed by this revelation and William could see the matter was consuming to the Captain.

"If he was in fact in the hold during the engagement Sir, that would constitute cowardice in the face of the enemy." William replied. It was an obvious statement and he knew the Captain had already come to that conclusion; the gravity of the charge however gave them both pause. If in fact Midshipman Shelton had been hiding in the ship's hold below the waterline, he was in fact guilty of cowardice in the face of the enemy. The only prescribed punishment for which would be death. William knew Captain Grimes had a fondness of the young Midshipman, often giving the youth extra instruction in matters of navigation and seamanship. It was no secret that Shelton's father was a friend to Captain Grimes, both serving together as midshipmen early in their careers. This made the matter even more difficult for the Captain, his duty would require him to see the young man put to death on the high sea.

"Would you see to it that Mr. Shelton is put into irons. We will have an inquiry today and standard will be at dawn tomorrow. There must be no favoritism in this matter Will, the service demands absolute action where cowardice is concerned. His father will understand," said Grimes, his tone low in both volume and spirit.

"I certainly will Sir. But if you would permit me. I know there is no lost love between Cobb and Shelton, perhaps before putting the young man in irons I should examine his claim further?" Will asked. Captain Grimes hesitated slightly. It was no secret that Cobb did not care for the young midshipman, often displaying a tendency to be harder on him for it. But even the suspicion of favoritism among the crew could have terrible consequences on the good order and discipline aboard. But, then also, the false accusation of such would also create its own set of problems. A moment of silence fell between them as each pondered the predicament they were faced with. They shared a look and William could see the gravity of the decision on the Captain.

"Very well William, see to your investigation into the matter. But come sundown, Mr. Shelton goes into irons and barring any new revelations, he will be hung at dawn according to the articles." Grimes replied, his voice devoid of emotion.

"Aye Sir. I will see to it personally." William stated, turning sharply and heading off about his task.

William's plan was to first question Cobb and see where he could either validate or refute his claim of seeing Mr. Shelton emerging from the hold at the conclusion of the battle. William also thought it would be prudent to see if others among the crew recalled seeing him at his station during the fight. William was suspicious himself; he did not recall seeing Shelton amongst the starboard battery when he had gone down to the gun deck. William asked the watch officer to summon Cobb to meet him in the Captain's quarters. Waiting in the cabin he reviewed what he could remember of the battle. Cobb was present on deck for the initial encounter, he was the watch officer who had summoned William. He knew Cobb was present for the beginning volley with the French sloop, but after that when the Valor engaged the third rate, he did not recall seeing Cobb on deck. Cobb entered the cabin interrupting William's thoughts, he appeared flustered before William even had the chance to begin the conversation.

"I was inspecting the repairs underway to the starboard gun port damage Sir. What could not wait?" Guffawed the irritated lieutenant.

"Well, Lieutenant Cobb." William said, ignoring his insubordinate tone. "I have some questions about crew conduct during our engagement with the French. Mr. Shelton was seen exiting the hold after the engagement. Can you tell me more about that?"

"Why, yes Sir. I can." Cobb replied, his tone melting as his temperament changed rapidly. "After the hit on lead starboard gun, I did see

Mr. Shelton coming out of the hold. He could not have been at his assigned place of duty during the engagement."

"I see and where were you when this took place Mr. Cobb?" William asked, his tone and facial expression unyielding.

"Well Sir, I went below to the gun deck as we were coming about to lay our broadside on them. I knew if we took any impact every available hand would be needed." Said Cobb earnestly.

"Very well Lieutenant, you may go and see to repairs. Please do send Mr. Shelton along and also the gun three leader if you will," said Will. "Do remember Mr. Cobb, I am second in command aboard this ship. If you are summoned, it matters not how inconvenienced you are, I am not disrespectful to you. I expect the same." William turned to look out the row of windows across the fantail as he spoke, hoping to conceal his awkward manner of dressing down a subordinate.

"Aye Sir." Cobb replied, a glimmer of anger flashing across his eyes.

This matter of accusation among the crew completely unsettled William, especially now as the French sloop had suddenly broken off contact. She could be anywhere and with good handling and favorable winds, could run out of sight around the Valor and be laying in wait somewhere. France has their spies in London and elsewhere as does the British

Crown, anything was possible. This was certainly not a time to be dealing with discipline issues. But there really is no good or convenient time for matters like this. The steady pitch and roll of the ship altered slightly, no doubt a change in course ordered by Captain Grimes. William noted the bright sun was racing toward noon just as the bells tolled out confirming his observation. "This matter needs to be resolved before sunset. Damn it if I'm going to have to slap that shod in irons on Cobb's word alone," he spoke to himself. The hatch swung open and Shelton reported in along with the gun leader on starboard gun three.

"Good afternoon men." William began, bypassing any pleasantries. "Mr. Shelton, I have been made aware that you were seen coming out of the hold immediately after the engagement with the French. More specifically, that you were not at your assigned place of duty when we took the hit to starboard one's gun port. Explain yourself man."

"Well, Sir, I was. I was behind the gun line for the whole ordeal. When we took the hit, I myself tipped starboard three's water over the powder charges laying about the wreckage from the cannon." Shelton stammered. His face flushed and he looked angry and nervous at the same time.

"Why did Cobb see you coming out of the hold then?" William pressed.

"It was Lieutenant Cobb who ordered me to go there in the first place Sir. He told me to fetch the surgeon and a litter for the wounded." Shelton answered, his voice steadying.

"I can attest Sir. I heard the order. Mr. Shelton shoved me down when the shot hit Sir, saved me life. Then he grabbed our swab bucket and soaked the powder charges that were exposed, might've saved the ship Sir." offered the petty officer.

"Very well you two. Thank you. You are dismissed." William replied.

Lieutenant Pike found the Captain on deck and briefly covered his conversations with the three men bringing Grimes apprised of the missing details Cobb had omitted. The two officers shared a concerned look, each knowing what was required to maintain order and discipline on the ship. The Captain was silent, William could see he was deep in thought. Both men knew the accusation Cobb had made, if supported by a witness or some form of evidence was enough to put the young man to death. But falsely accusing an officer was also a grievous infraction and Shelton had a witness supporting his claim. Grimes and William agreed that Cobb's accusation was largely self-serving. It was no secret aboard the Valor, Cobb held disdain for Shelton.

"Very well William, I have changed my mind. Default will be tomorrow at noon. Have the crew assembled and have Lieutenant Davitts arrange for the Marines to stand lookout while we conduct our affairs. I won't be caught off guard by the damned bloody Frenchman while we sort this lot out." Grimes instructed.

"Sir, do you want him placed in irons in the meantime?" William asked.

"No Lieutenant Pike, I think what I have in mind will send a clear message to the crew. I will not tolerate a coward, nor a liar. These two will be dealt with accordingly. See to the crew Will, we will handle this. Have the master at arms there and ready with the cat and a hangman's noose. That will be all Lieutenant," said Grimes. The Captain then abruptly turned and left the deck, retiring to his cabin. Will was left on the quarterdeck to organize for the default. The crew would all need to be assembled and in proper uniform and prepared for whatever Captain Grimes had in mind.

William's mind was abuzz while setting the crew to task, unsure of what the Captain planned to do exactly. He believed the account from Shelton, but did the Captain? What was he planning with the noose? Lieutenant Pike tried to remain focused on the crew, but the questions kept nagging him. If the Captain intended to punish both Lieutenant Cobb and Midshipman Shelton it would not be the first injustice he had witnessed in the King's Navy.

Chapter 4

"Drowned Maiden"
18 Aug 1808
19 Degree 36' N, 72 Degrees 59' W

The Maiden and her recently captured prize ship sailed in concert approaching a narrow inlet near the north finger of the island of Haiti. Captain James had timed their sail precisely, doubling back several times over the last few days to ensure the pair of ships was not being followed. The inlet he was navigating towards was not on most charts carried by European navies and the sandbar guarding its entrance was only known to a handful of the most experienced sailors in the Caribbean. As the sunset blazed its way below the western horizon throwing magnificent violet and orange hues high into the sky the pair of ships slipped their way into the inlet, carefully navigating past the sandbar. A compliment of experienced sailors had gone aboard the prize ship, undertaking the process of teaching the freed slaves aboard seamanship and sailing. The disposal of the slaver crew bought a quick but uneasy trust from the former captives and it took days before they let their guard down enough to participate whole heartedly. But with careful and skilled instruction from the members of the Maiden's crew, the recently freed slaves began handling the prize ship aptly.

The Maiden led the way into the mouth of the inlet, Lilith sitting on the larboard rail facing the shore her feet dangling precariously over the water. She gazed up at the high cliffs overlooking the entrance to the inlet as they approached, the brilliance of the painted dusk starkly broken by the shadows of the bluffs. Lilith traced her eyes along the shore, scanning the coastline and high cliffs that descended farther inland. The inlet widened as they crept inland and Lilith could see in the failing light the cliffs descended to meet the water at a white sand beach overshadowed at its upper edge by the dense canopy of rain forest. Behind them only a narrow channel of open sea remained visible and the high bluffs concealed their ships and masts from view. Anyone pursuing them would only have a slight field of view inward to spot the hiding vessels.

The hues of dusk finally faded away as the ships found their destination deep in the inlet, giving way to a tapestry of stars bold and beautiful like Lilith had never witnessed before. The crews made quick work of reefing sail and stowing line, dropping anchor with the Maiden facing her starboard broadside at the mouth of the inlet and the prize ship anchored just inland. They were close enough to swim ashore, but Lilith had no mind for that, yet she was taking in the cooling night air and marveling the heavens. The crew was finally able to unwind in the relative safety of the cove, drinking and conversations carried softly in the air from both vessels and soon the smell of cooking meat and spices filled the night. Lilith looked about the deck of the Maiden for Chibs, she had grown close to the fatherly sailor and often enjoyed conversing with him in the evenings. As she scanned the crew on deck a slight tap on her shoulder caught her attention. Lilith turned to see Captain James, a warm smile on his face and a mug in each hand.

"Our introductions the other day were not under favorable circumstances. I was hoping you would allow me another chance. I swear this time I won't ask you to burn anyone." James said holding up a mug for Lilith to take.

"Of course Captain." Lilith replied taking the mug and drank deeply. It was a strong ale and Lilith coughed slightly after drawing a chuckle from James.

"Star gazing for miss Lilith tonight? Have you eaten yet?" James asked.

"No Sir, I'm afraid I don't have much appetite." Lilith answered, sitting back on the quarterdeck and looking skyward again. "I've never really seen stars like this before. I can't believe I've gone my whole life never noticing, never taking even a moment…" her voice trailed off.

"Living as a slave, it's survival, you cannot

fault yourself for that lady," said James as he sat on the rail by where Lilith leaned back. He could see in the faint light from lanterns on deck her eyes welled with tears. "I was stolen from my village with my family by Dutch slavers. They sailed us to Curacao and we were all sold at market like goats. We were all bought by cane and coffee farms in Jamaica. Unfortunately, I was destined for a different farm than my parents. It took me several years and I had to kill a man, but I made my escape to search for them."

"Did you find them?" Lilith asked as James paused slightly, drinking his ale.

"I'm afraid not. I was caught days after my escape, beaten and sold to another slaver who arranged for my transport to America aboard this very ship. It was Chibs' mutiny that saved me from that fate, I owe him everything. He taught me seamanship and sailing. He taught me how to handle a sword and gunnery, navigating by day or night but the most precious thing Chibs ever taught me is that there are good men in this world. No matter how hard it is to come by them at times, there are good people." James replied. He looked skyward with Lilith and drained the last of his mug. The night had cooled to a pleasant, comfortable temperature and the skies were clear and brilliant. Songs from both ships echoed in the cove and James could see Lilith's eyes had cleared as she still gazed up at the heavens. After a long moment of silence, he began pointing out stars for navigating, constellations large and small. He told Lilith the stories and myths behind the major constellations as the glow of the moon rose over the cliffs on the eastern edge of the cove. It was a waxing moon past quarter full and her pale light shone down illuminating everything in sight. In between the tales inspired by the constellations James looked to see if Lilith was still engaged, pausing momentarily once, he was caught off guard by her beauty. The moonlight reflected off her features and shined in her almond eyes, giving her an angelic glow. Catching his thoughts, James resumed the story he had been telling only to find it more and more difficult to focus.

After a couple of hours, the songs from the crew had died away, sailors made their way to their hammocks, retiring for the night. Eventually, all that remained on deck was the sailors on watch, Lilith and James. James was fighting a yawn and telling the eternal hunt of Orion for Taurus when he looked down to Lilith and saw she was fast asleep, her mug of ale tipped over and a small dribble spilled onto the deck. James fetched a blanket from below deck and draped it over her as she slept, he gave one last look at her face and figure in the glow of the moon and disappeared below to his cabin.

The first glow of dawn brought a flurry of activity to the Drowned Maiden and her prize ship. Crew set about refitting the slave ship from her old profession. The iron bars creating cells below deck were stripped out, shackle mounts were removed and gathered into a barrel so the iron could be re-purposed elsewhere. Cleaning below deck was arduous and gut-wrenching work. Piles of feces had to be shoveled out and deck boards all washed, bulkheads and hatches all needed to be washed and the galley was all but gutted. Above deck, line lockers were in disarray, several blocks in the rigging needed to be replaced and even the rudder line that ran through the ship's wheel was in questionable condition. Long into the hot Haitian afternoon crews went about cleaning and repair, shuttling back and forth to the Maiden for supplies and tools on longboats, bringing fresh hands for work with every trip.

On the quarterdeck of the Maiden, Captain James and Chibs discussed the information they had learned from the slaver crew. Neither man seemed to notice Trina and Lilith at the foot of the stairs that lead down to the main deck, the pair were splicing line while Trina educated Lilith on sailing maneuvers. James had brought a chart out from his cabin and he looked over it with Chibs while they discussed plans to present to the crew.

"We just took one of their ships. The

Caribbean fleet is going to be out in force looking for her. The prudent thing would be to wait it out for a while." Chibs said.

"I disagree Chib. I think if we strike now, we need to hit the slaver fleet before they realize we have taken one of their ships. Right now we have good information on their anchorage and the camp they are using. We could burn their whole fleet at anchor, we could raid their camp and set scores of captives free. But we lose our surprise advantage the longer we wait." James countered. Chibs could only shake his head. James was a stubborn man and a bold tactician of Chibs' own making. James' plan had its merits and when presented to the crew would likely carry the vote. Other matters were discussed, candidates for Captaincy on the prize ship and the name of the vessel were foremost.

With the refitting of the prize ship underway well into the evening, Captain James halted their work to call the entire crew of the Maiden and the freed slaves together onto the deck of the Drowned Maiden. Lilith stood amongst the crowd of sailors, freedmen and women taking in the chatter around her. The warm evening air was thick with tension and excitement. Captain James climbed up onto the rail of the quarterdeck, wearing the same cutlass Lilith had used to torment the captured slaver. He unsheathed the sword and held it out over the crowd.

"Quiet down you lot of brigands!" James yelled out over the ship. His shouts were met with raucous laughter, cheers and shouts in reply. James laughed and turned to Chibs, who was taking a deep drink from a rum bottle pilfered off their prize. Chibs handed the bottle to James and climbed up beside him onto the rail. James took a drink for himself and Chibs held his hands up in the air. The crowd of sailors cheered and shouted all the louder. When James had finished his pull from the rum bottle he handed it back to Chibs and drew a long pistol out of his waistband, he cocked the piece and held it up firing into the air over the side of the ship. After a moment of the shot echoing through the cove and the smoke clearing away in the gentle breeze, the crew finally began to settle, quieting enough for their Captain to be heard.

"We have a vote to call tonight! But first, we have a ship to name!" James shouted out with a show of fanfare. The crew cheered again in a frenzy of shouts, but this time as the Captain started to resume speaking, they quieted in turn. "The slave ship was named 'Carolina Shepherd', which is too fine a name for the lot of us!" The sailors went wild shouting and cheering, clanking together mugs and slapping shoulders. Several shots rang out into the air from pistols in the crowd. Chibs stood and raised his voice to meet the chaos, "The Captain has seen fit to name the prize himself!

She will be the 'Unholy Shepherd'!" This sent the whole crowd into another fit of cheers and shouts which lasted several minutes until Captain James raised his voice again.

"Now we will hold our vote for the Shepherd's Captain. Whoever hopes him or herself a Captain of the Unholy Shepherd, to command and sail her from the hour you set foot on deck until your death, step forward and be considered." James commanded. The reaction for the crew was much quieter, a murmur of chatter among them and two sailors stepped up toward the quarterdeck. Trina, the woman who had taken to teaching Lilith the ways of seamanship stepped forward. Immediately after her was a very large African man known as Big Bob who had been on the crew of the Maiden as long as Captain James, his stature was massive as he was broad of shoulder and stood a full head and a half taller than everyone on board. Big Bob was a name given to the large man by Chibs himself when they found his native name quite unpronounceable. James and Chibs looked over the two who had approached for the crew's consideration, a silent nod of approval was shared between Captain and Quartermaster.

"Both these sailors would prove good commanders; they carry the approval of the Captain and myself. All in favor of Trina as Captain raise a hand and hold it high." Chibs said, hands arose all through the crew. It was an obvious majority though Chibs went through the measure of counting each hand in the interest of thoroughness. "And all in favor of Big Bob." Chibs continued, counting through the show of hands, though every man and woman aboard already knew the outcome. Chibs, leaned over to Captain James and muttered something. With a big smile James stepped back up towards the rail and announced, "Cheers for Captain Trina! Step up here Captain and name your First Mate."

"Big Bob will be First Mate on the Shepherd. It's only fair to keep him on the quarterdeck, there's no way the giant will fit below deck!" Trina announced, jesting at Big Bob with a broad smile. The crew cheered and laughed, Chibs smacked Big Bob on his massive shoulder in congratulation. Drinking and song carried on throughout the remaining evening and well into the night while the Captains and both First Mates withdrew to Captain James' cabin to begin making plans to present their respective crews in the morning.

H.M.S Valor
15 Aug 1808
44 Degrees 10' N, 18 Degrees 9' W

All crew were assembled on the main deck of the Valor as the last bell signaling the hour of noon was struck. A watch crew of marines and sailors ensured the ship remained on course and kept a sharp watch for sails on the horizon. Captain Grimes walked onto the quarterdeck with Lieutenant Pike at his side, both looking magnificent in their full formal uniforms. William called the crew to attention and Captain Grimes read aloud the articles of war. William could feel his legs tighten and feet ache as the process drug on, the articles were exhaustive but regulation and tradition demand they be read aloud once per month and before all disciplinary proceedings aboard ship. It took the better part of half the hour, but each article was read aloud outlining disciplinary infractions and their subsequent required punishments. When Johnathan began reading the article dealing with cowardice, misbehavior before the enemy or refusing to engage an enemy when ordered, a chill shot up William's spine. Captain Grimes gave no emphasis or significance to the article as he read it and continued to the next when he finished. A surprising number of the articles were punishable by death, but William's mind was stuck on misbehavior before the enemy. His mind raced, wondering if Grimes was about to hang Midshipman Shelton, if not, why had he asked for a noose to be hung? Why had he asked for the cat of nine to be on hand? Would he flog a man and then hang him?

At the conclusion of reading the articles

Captain Grimes paused momentarily, looking out over the assembled crew.

"Master at Arms bring forward Lieutenant Cobb." Grimes commanded. His tone belied no emotion, no hint of pride or sadness or grief under the protocol of military bearing. Lieutenant Cobb was escorted in up in front of the crew, facing the Captain, a petty officer at each shoulder. "Lieutenant Alexander Cobb, you are hereby brought forth under my command as Captain of the H.M.S Valor under the charge of falsifying testimony against a member of this crew. The officer in question was accused by you of cowardice in the face of the enemy, when in fact witnesses to the event have stated that you did order the man to complete a task which would remove said officer from the line of fire. I am further charging you with conduct unworthy an officer of the naval service for the malicious nature of your conduct, which if left unchecked by a witness would have resulted in an innocent and dutiful member of this crew being hanged this day. How do you respond to these charges?" said Grimes.

"I have nothing to say Sir." Cobb responded, his voice ragged, rage broiling under the surface.

"Very well then. Master at Arms, remove Cobb's jacket. Alexander Cobb, you are hereby relieved of the rank of Lieutenant. You will receive twelve lashings and serve aboard as an able seaman from this day forth. You shall be paid as an able seaman and receive no promotion for one year." Grimes rattled out. The Master at Arms and his petty officers removed Cobb's jacket and began binding his hands to a wooden lattice to receive the corporal portion of his discipline. He was given a doubled over leather strap to bite into. Every man aboard not on duty was required to watch as Cobb received exactly twelve reminders of the hierarchy aboard ship and forever embedding the consequence of lying to his commanding officer. The first two lashes of the cat of nine tails were met with a nothing more than a silent grimace from Cobb. He looked through the lattice he was bound to, hanging aloft just feet away and overhead was a hangman's noose. Captain Grimes' not so subtle indicator of the grave consequences when discipline broke down. The third lash broke the skin and Cobb let a gasp and writhed from the pain, a fourth followed shortly scattering blood on the petty officer wielding the whip. Cobb cried out and a fifth stoke hit him as his voice rose into the rigging. William could feel the skin on his back crawl and his stomach was in knots. On the sixth hit Cobb lost his footing, he received the rest of his punishment dangling by his wrists bound to the wooden lattice. By the twelfth and final lash Cobb was in a state of shock, barely conscious with his back dripping blood, inflamed and his limbs trembling beyond control. He was cut down and assisted by two sailors to the ship's doctor to be bandaged up.

"Mr. Shelton, approach." Captain Grimes commanded. Will's hair stood up on the backs of his arms, his neck felt a sudden swelter and legs a tremble. Midshipman Shelton presented himself before the quarterdeck, slightly pale and visibly nervous himself. "Mr. Shelton, I have been informed of your behavior before the enemy on the gun line. It seems that if it weren't for your quick thinking this ship would have suffered grave consequence, both to the ship and her crew. Remove your coat lad, you've new rank to go on it. I won't have a man show such mettle and remain a mid a day longer on my watch. It just so happens there is a vacant billet aboard this vessel." Will could not help but smile, if not for the young man whose face was also beaming with pride, but also for his ridiculous inclination that Grimes was about to punish him. Though William had seen injustices aboard ship, hanging the accused midshipman would have been the gravest. Mutinies occurred over less.

Will entered the Captain's cabin to find Johnathan Grimes brooding. The day had turned hot as the afternoon wore on and a shift of the wind, while favorable for the course they were sailing, gave rise to the worries of foul weather. The captain had a chart and the ship's log spread out on the table he was seated at. Johnathan had entrenched himself into the charts on the table and scarcely looked up at William as he approached.

"The key to this Will, is going to be finding a route into Nassau that won't leave us exposed or at a disadvantage should that French sloop reappear." Johnathan muttered. "We can't afford to be caught off guard, but we most certainly must take on fresh water in Nassau. I tinkered with the idea of bypassing her and making sail straight for Kingston, but if we wind up engaged, we could find ourselves in bad footing, half ration of fresh water in the Caribbean in late summer. That won't do."

"Nassau seems our best option Sir." Will offered, looking at the chart. "The Frenchman likely came to his senses, they did witness us defeat two ships in one encounter, one considerably out of our class. Perhaps we crossed out of their limits of engagement even. I doubt we should see that particular warship again Sir."

"I agree with your assessment Lieutenant, but we must consider all possibilities. Something else has been troubling me though and I want to discuss it with you. See to it there is no lurker listening outside the door." Johnathan said. William silently got up and checked the gangway outside the door to find no one, he shut the door and returned into the cabin wondering at his Captain's odd behavior.

"No one Sir. Is everything quite alright?" Will asked.

"I'm unsure Will and growing more so every day. We discussed our ship's orders the day we left port and I fear that I didn't level with you entirely on my concern about the standoff orders for East India Company ships. It's just odd. Our tasking involves escorting them, stopping French interference in trade, but we cannot approach. Why? Why in the bloody imagining would we be restricted from aiding them if they are in distress?" Johnathan pondered aloud. William realized it was not a rhetorical question as he looked up from the charts and saw Johnathan was looking directly at him, awaiting a reply.

"I couldn't say for sure Sir. I thought the order odd when you mentioned it as we left port. But then again, I haven't made it habit to question orders, Sir. I've done it aloud once and I honestly believe I would have my own command right now if not for that." William replied. "Perhaps their port of origin has an outbreak of some sort. Plague or such. The Royal Navy wouldn't get along well with half its sailors dying and the other half quarantined. Or maybe their cargo is of a dangerous nature."

"Astute Will. Good man, good form. Both reasonable solutions to the dilemma. That answers why there is a general standoff order, but the orders specifically list remaining four cables at a minimum even if there is distress at sea. I'm just vexed by the matter." Johnathan said, furrowing his brow and continuing, "But, I am honestly supposed to watch a countryman in distress at sea and not approach closer than four cables? If she's afire? Or engaged by the enemy? What in God's name?"

"Yes, Sir. But, if the Crown is overly concerned about an outbreak in a port of origin, wouldn't that still ring true. We can't have half the navy dying and the other half quarantined or heaven forbid we bring some awful malady back to jolly old England. I mean, the channel fleet is engaged blockading Brest, all through the Atlantic ships stand to engage the French. On top of that Sir, there's trade enforcement and dealing with smugglers and the like. I shared a pint with an officer I'd known since boyhood in London, Sir. He was on the H.M.S Dawn Fire, they had just returned from a cruise enforcing and interdicting Parliament's ban on the slave trade. Some of the stories he had, Sir, they'll turn a stomach." William said, his voice trailing off as he felt he was starting to carry on too long. Johnathan stared blankly at the charts, lost in his own thoughts on the matter when Will concluded. Johnathan looked up at Will.

"I won't let a ship of my countrymen

flounder in distress, Will. I have my honor, I have my decency. Whatever the inspiration is for these absurd orders, if circumstances call for such, I will not stand off a ship in distress and watch sailors perish. So. Young man, we never had this conversation. We never had our conversation off port and you know nothing of these orders. Do you understand?" Johnathan said. His voice carried grave implications, an edge that hadn't been there before. Not even when he was calling down discipline to Cobb from the quarterdeck had Captain Grimes held a tone like he was with William.

"Yes, Captain." William replied.

"That will be all in that regard Lieutenant. Be sure that you keep a close watch on Cobb, de-rating an officer and flogging him like that surely wounded the man's pride. But I won't carry on with an officer who has dishonored himself in such a manner, not on my ship, not on my watch."

"Aye Sir," said William. He promptly exited the cabin and went about making his rounds before turning in for the night.

Alone in his cabin, Captain Grimes had turned from his charts and logs, consumed in his mind over the matter of the standoff orders. William had touched on his deep suspicion, just not in direct terms. It was common knowledge through the fleet that parliament had abolished the slave trade, levying fines against any ship flying the union jack caught for every slave aboard. Is it too far a stretch that the company would take advantage of the near monopoly this would create? How high would they have to collaborate with the admiralty to favor the standoff order? If that was the case, did the admiralty even know? Or was it disguised under likely cover of an outbreak somewhere in Africa? Turning back to the charts laid out across the table, Captain Grimes put his mind back onto his current situation. Temporary repairs to the damage Valor had sustained engaging the squadron of French ships would hold them until Nassau, but the disabled cannon would need to be replaced and permanent repair would be necessary before beginning their tour in the Caribbean. He poured over the charts, analyzing the approaches, shoals, small islands and reefs. The Bahamas and the Caribbean overall were notorious for making ruin of seasoned Captains who had become complacent or overconfident. The oil lamp and charts were the Captain's companions long into the night as he balanced studying charts and making strategic plans with his turmoil over secret orders he still could not make sense of.

18 August 1808

Jamaica, east of Kingston

The evening sun painted the western sky into a breathtaking spectrum of oranges and violets as a column of red coated infantrymen marched from the edge of Kingston into the surrounding hillsides. At the head of the fifty-man double column rode a squadron of twenty dragoons led by Tim Sladen. By his side were two more Americans, both rough looking bearded men who were heavily armed. The column had wound its way from the barracks in Kingston to its outskirts and began ascending into the hills as the sun dipped low. Passing farm and field on its way east from Kingston the column continued their slow steady march upward along the road that wound its way between sugar cane fields. Torches were lit to illuminate the way as the blaze of sunset gave way to dusk and eventually faded into twilight. Despite the absence of the sun, the air hung heavy in the night, hot and muggy with little breeze to relieve the marching soldiers.

The road snaked between hill and field, climbing and falling with the land skirting the shores of the Caribbean. The pace they kept, while leisurely for those mounted, was grueling for the infantry. Every ascent uphill became a challenge to the soldiers' weary legs and soon their uniform coats were soaked in sweat and caked in dust from the road.

Darkness only added to their frustrations and fears as ambush from bands of rebels were a common occurrence after nightfall. But the column drove on, goaded by the three Americans up front. Several of the foot soldiers could be heard cursing and complaining, but none within earshot of Mr. Sladen. The American's position was a mystery to the British soldiers. Their commanding officer had been summoned before Lord Governor Alton the day prior and issued specific instruction to accompany Mr. Sladen on a sortie against a band of escaped slaves. Tim Sladen seemed to have a manner of intelligence about the escapees, but the lieutenant in command of the soldiers was perplexed why the Governor would grant him any more authority than a common informant.

Tim halted his mount and after a short exchange with his two countrymen riding next to him, he turned his mount and approached the Lieutenant.

"They are camped on the hill just east of the one in front of us Lieutenant. Now would be a good time to get your men formed up and make ready. Come dawn, we will move in to take them captive." Sladen instructed.

"What makes you so sure they will throw down arms and surrender to captivity again Mr. Sladen? Most of these slaves turned rebels we have dealt with have fought dearly. They are more likely to flee, Sir," the Lieutenant challenged. His demeanor was stern, and he was quite doubtful of this American.

"You'll do best to do as your told Lieutenant. I'm taking your mounted men around the rebel position; we will cover the north and east. You hold your line below the crest of the hill in front of you. At dawn you will see that there are Royal Navy sails just off the coast. Do you have the signal flag I gave you?" Sladen cut back, his words dripping with disdain.

"I do," the lieutenant answered, suddenly losing any inclination to carry the conversation further.

"When dawn breaks, make sure that signal flag is visible. We will be flying one at our position to the east and the ships will begin battery of the hillside in between. If you see the escapees surrendering, drop your flag immediately." Sladen ordered, his accommodating tone of requests and suggestions from earlier in the evening as they departed Kingston disappeared. Now he seemed to be about his business and the Lieutenant could gather that he had serious personal interest in the escaped slaves, far beyond that of a simple informant.

Sladen departed with all the mounted troops with the exception of the Lieutenant, who remained with his foot soldiers. The infantry dispersed out and formed a skirmish line just behind the crest of the hill as instructed. At first, forming a skirmish line and awaiting dawn was a welcome change for the line of infantry. They could sit and rest their weary legs and sore feet, some even removing their shoes. After the first half hour the stillness of the night set in, only slightly cooled the humid air hung over them and each man had to fight to stay awake. The hours drug by slowly as each weary soldier watched the hillside and fought his eyelids. Sounds floated in on the night air, voices from the opposing hillside. A bell could be heard off the coast in the long hours before sunrise cast its first glows on the horizon. About a half hour before daylight the lieutenant walked his line, steadying his men and making sure everyone was ready. The muggy warmth had given away and the morning air felt crisp as a steadily increasing glow to the east threatened dawn break.

Finally, with the first fingers of sunlight stretching out from the horizon word was passed through the line to fix bayonets. Each soldier swallowed a lump in his throat, no matter how experienced in battle as he mounted the ghastly appendage to his gun. Sails appeared off the coast; the signal flag was raised. Each man readied himself for a fight to begin as the first ship passed by the signal flag. The first boom of a cannon thundered across the water and echoed up off the hill. It was followed by a second and then a third, forth and fifth. Musket fire intermixed with the echoing reports of the cannons and a group of two men and one woman came bounding over the hill in a sprint for life. As the trio ran down the hill, the lieutenant started to call out for shackles to bind them when they ran up to the skirmish line. A shot sounded out, one of the fleeing men fell to the ground. No weapon was visible to anyone in the skirmish line. The lieutenant began to shout down the battle formation, demanding to know who fired on the unarmed group. "Sir, I believe it was them," one soldier said, pointing up at the crest of the hill. The three Americans sat mounted on their horses, one still shouldering a musket. A very different fear began to take hold of each man on the infantry line.

H.M.S Endurance
19 Aug 1808
17 Degrees 51' N, 76 Degrees 34' W

Dawn broke over the Jamaican coast revealing a low hanging fog clinging to the shore. Lookouts had been posted throughout the squadron of ships that sailed in concert with the Endurance. There was the H.M.S Endurance in lead with Admiral Sharpe on board, then the H.M.S Hunter commanded by Captain Nestor and the H.M.S Bayonet commanded by Captain Brant brought up the rear of the formation. Admiral Sharpe's instruction had been issued very clearly. The

Endurance heave to slightly farther offshore and west of the target area while the Hunter and Bayonet sailed through in a circuit delivering battery on target for as long as was necessary.

Standing on the bow of the Endurance, Admiral Sharpe looked ashore for the signal flags, locating them easily just above the misty line of fog hugging the beaches. Tide was slacking and time was certainly of the essence for maneuvers this close to shore.

"Commence fire," Admiral Sharpe said in a low tone.

"Aye Sir," replied a petty officer who had been at the Admiral's side. He immediately turned to the signalman and shouted, "Commence fire!" The signal flags went aloft into the rigging of the Endurance and the two frigates in cohort started their assault by fire. Admiral Sharpe watched on closely through looking glass, observing both ship and shore. The Hunter ducked in close to shore, raking fire one gun at a time on target, Captain Nestor was a seasoned commander and had a reputation for commanding fine gunnery. The Hunter's fire was landing seaside on the hill, just below earthen mounds where rebels had dug in, each ball sent up a showering plume of dirt as it struck into the target hill.

The Hunter's last larboard gun fired, and she peeled away from shore in a steep starboard turn, her crews already making their guns ready for another round of fire. The Bayonet came in just a few minutes after, slightly farther out from the shoreline than Hunter had been. A grimace of concern flashed across Admiral Sharpe's face, Captain Brant was his newest Captain and the Admiral was bracing for the young new commander to make folly of his first run at the target. At first shot, the ball landed very high on the hill, sending a shower of dirt high into the morning air as the shot hit earth and then skipped up sailing over the hill. The second shot from the Bayonet was adjusted to deadly effect, landing directly on one of the dug in positions the rebels were occupying. Sharpe scoured the impact area through his looking glass, he could see smoke from musket fire and dead men on the field. He immediately checked the signal flags ashore again, both were still flying, no surrender yet. Three more blasts of cannon fire came from the gun line aboard the Bayonet, each impacting with deadly effect. Sharpe watched as the line of rebels broke from their dug in positions. There were men and women among them, even from a distance Elliot Sharpe's heart sank as he could distinguish female forms. They were caught in a deadly crossfire between naval gunnery and the mounted soldiers closing on their position.

The signal flag on the eastern edge of the engagement disappeared, Elliot in turn ordered for a change of signal aboard his flagship. All fire from the ships ceased, the Bayonet and Hunter turned out from shore heading for deeper waters. Admiral Sharpe lingered momentarily with his flagship close to shore, he had a deep suspicion he wished to disprove before departing. Through the large looking glass Sharpe watched the events on shore unfold, he scanned back and forth between the advancing mounted troops and the line of infantrymen. A cluster of surrendering men and women had thrown down their weapons, though a small group of three fled. Elliot followed the path of the fleeing trio down the western slope of the hill. One man fell with the sound of a shot rippling through the air.

"You won the day lads, no need to shoot down a man running for his life. In the back no less." Sharpe mumbled to himself. Elliot scanned back up the hill, searching through his growing anger for the source of the shot. Near the crest of the hill were three riders not in Royal Army uniform. He was far too distant to make out faces, but the tall slender man with musket still in his hands Elliot suspected was the American he had met at the Governor's mansion. He watched as the riders separated, two continued down the hill in pursuit of the fleeing, the third man lingered atop the hill on his mount.

Elliot watched the lone man for a long moment, internally he could feel an urge to run his battery out and rain cannon fire on the man. The urge passed; his temper cooled. His eyes sunk down to the deck of his flagship. He asked himself silently what grievous thing he had done this morning. Was he serving king and country? The leadsman along his larboard rail called out a reading, reminding the Admiral of the slacking tide. There were dangerous shoals in the area with the tide running outward beneath him he ordered his flagship to depart from the coast. Admiral Sharpe passed word for his signalman, pacing the rail as he awaited the petty officer's arrival.

"You summoned me, Sir?" said the sailor as he approached.

"Yes, signal orders for the squadron to make sail with us," the Admiral replied. Turning towards the quarterdeck Elliot increased his volume slightly. "Officer of the watch."

"Yes Sir," a young fat faced lieutenant answered as he hurried over to the admiral.

"Pass the word, I want lookouts fore and aft, double the watch. Set a sailing pattern as close to the coast as we dare. Scour every inlet, every beach, every cove and bay. Set our course eastward and follow the shore around to the north side of Jamaica. I want an immediate report of any irregularity." Elliot said as he walked toward his cabin. His tone was distracted, his mind already occupied by questions that wouldn't easily be answered. He would set about to find out more information, as much as he could anyways. His next visit with Governor Alton would not go the same as his last and he desired to know as much as possible before he walked in.

Chapter 5

"Drowned Maiden"
19 Aug 1808
19 Degree 36' N, 72 Degrees 59' W

The morning sun shone brightly through the cove, warming Lilith's shoulders as she stood high up in the rigging of the Unholy Shepherd. Her task since waking had been assisting Trina and Big Bob in replacing lines and blocks through the intricate workings of the upper rigging. Their purpose was twofold, replacing line and block was surely part of their effort, but getting the freed slaves off the deck and up into the rigging was another essential task. There would be some from the Maiden who crossed deck to remain on the Unholy Shepherd, but for the ship to sail efficiently at least two dozen of the freed slaves had to become competent sailors. Learning the rigging was a critical skill aboard any ship, but especially so with a small crew. The plans discussed amongst the two Captains would demand skilled ship handling and superb seamanship from the entire crew. Unlike a Navy ship or even a merchant vessel, a ship that intended to fly black colors demanded a broad range of mastery from her crew. They must trim sail and register gunnery with the same proficiency, ready to wield hand tool and weapon alike. Lilith was being indoctrinated in skills alongside the new crew and was beginning to get a sense of bearings up in the rigging. All the different lines, each with their own purpose, all the commands, preparatory and executing, sail positioning, course change and so much more. It was enough to make her head spin.

Lilith felt there was so much more she should know even having only been aboard for a couple of weeks. Trina was a good teacher, as patient as Chibs would have been though not as much of an expert. Lilith paused for a moment to take in the spectacular beauty of the cove. Under the brightly shining Caribbean sun the waters shimmered in bright greens and deep blues, the air smelled sweet from the native fruits ashore and the white of the beach sands contrasted the deep greens of the forest canopy. Lilith imagined a life lived in the cove, swimming and fishing in the brilliant emerald waters, lounging on the white sandy beach in the sun and exploring through the mysteries of the forest beyond.

"Girl! Are you paying attention?" Trina spoke, snapping Lilith from her daydream.

"Yes, Captain." Lilith replied.

"I was saying, you need to keep your feet about you up here. Always, always mind your feet girly. When you must move a foot, you must keep two hands. It may seem simple here in the cove sweet thing, but out there in the pitch and roll you can lose yourself in a snap.

It's a long way down, love, just prey if it ever happens you land on water and not on wood," said Trina. Her eyes locked on Lilith's, conveying gravity and a sense of responsibility for the young addition to the crew.

The two descended from the upper riggings, climbing ratlines down to the deck of the Shepherd. Lilith's heart was torn, she could not decide which vessel she would stay on. Though that morning the Captains had presented their plan of attacking the slaver camp in Jamaica and both crews would play a role in the plan, Lilith did not want to separate from Captain Trina. Nor was she fond of the idea of leaving the experience of Chibs and Captain James. Ultimately, she knew, she would have to make a choice and soon. The pair would be sailing from the cove, the Captains' plan began with a sneak attack on any ship at anchor near the Jamaican camp.

James insisted they would have to sink or burn whatever vessels the slavers commanded before they could storm the camp. A direct assault would run the risk of sinking a vessel that was already loaded with slaves, which was pointed out repeatedly by the crew, especially the new crew of the Unholy Shepherd, being captives themselves not long ago. James fought through many interruptions and was finally successful in laying out their rough plans. After much back and forth, suggestions came in from across the crew.

Finally, a vote was called. After a few dissenting voices were heard, the crew elected to follow their Captains' plan.

"Slaves are not sold for free, there is a man somewhere profiting from this and I mean for us to take that gold." James shared at the conclusion of their gathering, to an uproar of approval from the crew. Unholy Shepherd would not be long until she was ready to sail and along with the Drowned Maiden, would be a terrifying sight to behold on the horizon for any crew.

H.M.S Valor
12 Sep 1808
Nassau, Bahamas

The port in Nassau was a welcome sight for the crew of the Valor after their Atlantic crossing. Strong Caribbean breezes blew the fragrance of the tropics mixes with the old familiar smell of the sea. Those who were new to the ship by way of press gangs in London marveled at the beauty of the pale blue seas and white sands. These islands were a stark contrast to their home and a sense of adventure renewed the spirit of many of the sailors, old and young alike. The market ashore was teeming with activity, spices from the far reaches of the British empire, coffee, exotic fruit, spiced rum and beautiful women. Merchant ships came and went from the port daily, some arriving and leaving on the same day. Captain Grimes granted every man a day ashore on their arrival, offering another day ashore once refit was finished before setting to sea again. The repairs and loading of fresh provisions went about like clockwork, each man setting to his task heartily for the chance to go ashore again.

In three days' time, the battle wounds Valor had endured had all been repaired. Her destroyed cannon had been discarded and a new twelve-pound gun sat in its place. Food and water reserves were loaded and one last evening ashore was granted to the crew, except for Cobb and another man who were confined while at port.

Grimes received his envelope with orders from the governor of Jamaica. He was to patrol the north coast of Haiti and the southern coast of Cuba for a missing American ship. A frigate named the Carolina Shepherd had not made rendezvous with her escorts and she was feared lost to the sea. Grimes also received a report that the French had commissioned more privateers in the effort of disrupting trade between Britain, it's colonies and the United States. Small wonder Grimes thought to himself, the Carolina Shepherd was probably at the bottom of the Caribbean and her goods in the hold of a French privateer. Trade between the colonial island and the United States was a fledgling endeavor anyway, tariffs being what they were and the probability of another war on the horizon.

With many of her hands in port for their last night of freedom and debauchery before setting sail again, the Valor seemed almost a ghost ship. A skeleton crew of sailors and marines remained to stand the watch, Captain Grimes himself had remained aboard, deferring the opportunity to enjoy an evening ashore to his subordinate officers. Johnathan watched as the sun had set, seeing several merchant ships set off into the dying light. Lamplight created an eerie effect on deck, raising shadows that danced with the movement of the oil flame. Johnathan paced the deck, inspecting line and checking on the watch. As the moon arose, longboats ferrying crews back out to ships could be seen littered across the port. Songs and shouts floated through the night air; Johnathan smiled. In his experience, morale makes a crew all the better. A few dust ups in port and some hungover sailors at daybreak was a small price to pay.

The light of daybreak revealed bruised faces, aching hangovers and to Captain Grimes delight, not a single desertion. Johnathan passed orders to William to take the Valor out of port and the hands responded smartly. Sails trimmed and snapped crisply in the morning breeze and Will made short work of their maneuvers out to sea. In the matter of hours, Valor was plowing ahead full sail and tilt toward the southern edge of Cuba to begin her search pattern for any sign of the missing merchant ship.

Days passed without sighting of another ship. Captain Grimes ordered a sailing pattern by all coves and bays where a ship would likely take refuge from weather. They searched and scanned the southern coast of Cuba, doubling back to search along the north coast of Haiti to no avail. The crew quickly grew weary of the search and Captain Grimes wholly doubted the ship was still afloat. No wreckage or flotsam was found along the coast, no sign or sighting anywhere along the most likely course. A week had been spent searching for any sign of the missing ship when Captain Grimes decided to call off their search. He summoned Lieutenant Pike to his cabin to inform him of his intent and elicit his input on their next course of action, something he made a point to involve his subordinates in. The officer of the watch passed word for William, who was aloft in the rigging with his telescope, scanning shoreline. Will made his way down through the ratlines and hurried to report to the Captain, still in his linen shirt. The rigidity and formal manner he carried when he first assumed his post aboard the Valor had slowly but surely relaxed, he conducted himself with far more latitude and even a bit of swagger. Much of the crew had taken notice and approved, the petty officers and seamen found it endearing, their First Lieutenant was becoming more a part of the Valor every day.

"Captain Grimes Sir, you passed word for me?" William said, stepping into the cabin.

"I did Will, here, have a seat son. We've some matters to discuss." Grimes said, ushering the young officer to the table where he had charts spread out. "I've decided to call off this wild goose hunt. We haven't seen any sign of the Carolina Shepherd, I'm beginning to believe her Captain may have had other plans for his cargo, whatever the case. The Admiralty tasked us with protecting the India Company shipping from privateers and I think that a bit more pressing than spending our days chasing down some missing American tub. By the sounds of things in Nassau, we'll likely be trading shot with the bloody yankees at sea again anyways," said Grimes.

"Yes Captain, what shall I make our next heading then?" William asked.

"Kingston, Will. Let's sail for Kingston and hope Admiral Sharpe can set us on a more sensible course of action." Grimes answered his tone low.

"Perhaps he will have some answers for you about the standoff orders Sir." Will offered.

"I would certainly hope so Lieutenant. On a different note, Lieutenant Shelton will be officer of the watch tonight and Cobb will be on lookout. See to it there are no problems Will, however you see fit."

"Aya aye Sir," Will responded. Immediately his thoughts were occupied by this, Will feared Cobb would try to undermine the newly promoted Lieutenant. "Perhaps he should be shifted to another watch Sir?"

"Not a chance Will. I refuse to accommodate that dishonorable wretch and I won't see the young officer babied along. He will take command of the ship for his watch and nothing less. Any action by Cobb to undermine or otherwise interfere with Shelton fulfilling his duties is punishable by death. I'll tie the damn noose myself if need be. Keep an eye on it and have a strong master at arms on the quarterdeck for his watch, that is all."

'Gazelle'
14 Sept 1808
17 Degrees 27' N, 74 Degrees 43' W

Flashes of lightning broke the darkness over the Gazelle as she pitched and rolled through heaving seas. The storm had come upon her after sunset and escalated fiercely until it was everything the crew could do to keep her upright. Below deck, the captives in their cells were tortured by the constant violent movement of the ship. Many became ill and all were fearful. In his small cabin LeMeaux was utterly failing to console Omibwe. The young man was panicked almost to hysteria. Omibwe worried for his parents and his sister, he heard screams from the other prisoners outside the cabin. Each time a wave broke over the bow of the ship the walls and floors trembled; seawater seeped from the ceiling while the deck above was in a constant wash of wave upon wave. Lanterns swung precariously, threatening to spill their flames out and engulf the storm-tossed ship.

A slamming knock came on the door, Dr. LeMeux got up to answer it stumbling slightly with a heavy pitch of the ship. Lemeux opened the door to find one of the sailors, soaked from head to foot and holding a lantern,

"You better come wit' me doc. It's the Captain, he fell in his cabin," the sailor said.

"Ok, let me grab my bag." Lemeux replied, he turned to Omibwe, "I need you to stay here, young man." Omibwe struggled to get up, fear plagued across his face.

"No friend, no don't go, don't leave me," said Omibwe, grabbing at Lemeux's arm.

"I must go Omi, you will be fine here, I won't be long. Stay here." LeMeux answered, pulling the boy's hand from his arm. He grabbed his medical bag and followed the sailor out into the passageway, stealing one last glance at Omibwe as he shut the door. He could see the pain of fear wracking across the young man's eyes. Lemeux whispered a silent prayer to himself, hoping his companion would stay put.

He followed the sailor up the passageway, both men unsteadily making their way as the ship continued its violent roll side to side. On their way the two passed numerous cells including the one containing Omibwe's family. LeMeux nearly gasped looking through the cells, the numbers had dwindled severely. Where once each cell barely afforded its captives room to sit with legs pulled to chest, the imprisoned Africans numbered far fewer. He knew this would happen from the last trip he had to endure, but this time was far worse. If they kept losing captives, they would arrive with only a very few still alive at their destination. LeMeux cared not for the profit of their endeavor, only in the toll of human life lost.

They climbed the stair up the companionway to the main deck, where the sailor heaved up a weather hatch creating a rush of seawater that slammed into both men nearly washing them back down the stairs. Step by step, they worked their way through the hatch and above to the deck steadying themselves wherever they could. Although LeMeux had been at sea on the Gazelle for months now he was far from experienced on ship during storms and his legs were unaccustomed to the challenging conditions. They reached the door to the Captain's Cabin in the aft castle as a wave broke hard over the rail of the ship, washing sideways it took LeMeux's legs out from under him and pushed him helplessly across the deck. He reached out for something to grab onto, thrashing against the water sweeping him towards the blackness overboard. Lightning flashed and illuminated the ship for a fleeting moment, LeMeux looked frantically for something to grab ahold of, clawing in vain at the deck to stop his perilous slide. From what seemed out of nowhere, the sailor who had retrieved him from below grabbed the back of the French Doctor's collar and wrenched him up onto his feet.

"Thank you!" LeMeux said, gasping for air.

"Don't mention it Frenchman, really, if Sprague finds out I didn't let you wash overboard, he and I'll be for crossing blades. Now quit flopping about the deck like a fish out of water, the Captain needs your attention," the sailor grumbled, pushing LeMeux back toward the door to the aft castle. LeMeux opened it and flung himself into the cabin, closing the door just as another wave crashed over the deck. It took a few moments for his eyes to adjust to the dimly lit interior, but when they did, he could see the ship's Captain sprawled into a hammock. Mr. Sprague stood next to the hammock, watching intently while the hammock swayed, stopping only as it came to rest against Sprague's steady stance. Sprague, an unquestionably experienced sailor was steady as a rock against the motion of the ship, not even the impact of the hammock seemed to sway his stance.

"Come have a look at him Frenchman. I'd be surprised if there's anything you can do for the old man, but you'd better see to it." Sprague grumbled.

"Yes, by all means. Can you tell me what happened? Did anyone witness it?" LeMeux asked.

"What do you mean did anyone witness it? Why would you be asking me what I know? Can you help the man or not?" Sprague snapped, his questions too rapid for LeMeux to process, much less answer.

"Let me see him and I'll have a better idea." LeMeux responded, his tone becoming as icy as he dared let it. Sprague had left no question about how much he disliked the doctor and now that he was laying unconscious in his hammock LeMeux knew he'd best tread carefully. He examined the Captain's head, a split in his scalp was deep enough to reveal a band of skull near as wide as LeMeux's thumb. He was still bleeding profusely and completely unresponsive. LeMeux carefully bandaged the man's head, stemming the blood flowing from his scalp. He sat on the edge of the Captain's desk, looking at the injured man intensely.

"His skull was cracked in the impact. It's difficult to say if he will survive, even if he does there's no telling the condition he will be in after such a blow to the head," said LeMeux, his eyes unmoving.

"What do you mean, condition?" Sprague asked, his tone a bit softer. Softer than LeMeux had ever heard.

"A head injury like that can, well, it can change a man. He may survive, he may be completely normal, although, he may not. Sometimes men are shades different, sometimes they can't even remember who they are and sometimes they survive but never truly function again. It's hard to say, we will need to watch him closely." LeMeux said solemnly.

"Who's this we, doctor? You are the doctor. You nursemaid the old man." Sprague said, his softened tone had disappeared. "I'll have him moved below to the crew quarters, so you can look in on him. You may need to get rid of your pet African, the Captain comes first." LeMeux could feel his face flushing with anger, he fought the urge to air his opinions to this belligerent blowhard. Biting his tongue, quite literally, so hard it drew a taste of blood into his mouth. "Back below decks with you doctor, fetch that slave boy and put him into a cell. Go on." Sprague hissed, contempt in his words and hatred seething from his eyes.

"Mr. Sprague, the boy, well, an amputation is a serio…" LeMeux stammered to respond, trying to illicit some leniency.

"Enough! The boy goes into a cell! Or so help me, I will make you throw his entire family overboard while he watches! Do you understand me Frenchman? Is the King's English plain enough for you or should I draw you an illustration? Put that one-legged slave boy into a god damned cell like the rest of those animals!" Sprague shouted. LeMeux took his leave back out into the storm, fighting against wind and wave to make his way back below deck. As he walked the passageway, he couldn't help but steal a somber glimpse into the cell with Omibwe's family. They looked hollowed and weak from their time at sea. Horrid conditions, sea sickness and stomach-turning rations barely able to sustain children had taken their toll. LeMeux was beside himself, unable to process. He knew Omibwe's condition would deteriorate rapidly, his father had been the picture of strength for the first few days at sea. Without the benefit of LeMeux giving the boy part of his rations, he would lose strength. Strength he needed to cope with his life's new reality and the conditions his future would hold.

Reaching his cabin's door, LeMeux paused momentarily, bracing himself for the unpleasant task ahead. LeMeux opened the door to find Omibwe struggling to stand with the help of his makeshift crutch. He stepped into the little cabin and began to shut the door when a hand wrapped around the door's edge holding it in place. LeMeux turned to see the rough face of the sailor who had come to get him earlier and who had also saved him from a grim and watery fate.

"Mr. Sprague says I'm to see to it you move gimpy out to a cell, he says the boy can't be within sight of his family," the sailor said. Lemeux could see he was less than enthusiastic about his orders.

"Sir. Suppose we just allow the boy a night here and move him after the storm?" LeMeux asked.

"What are you saying? Sprague told you Frenchy, he will 'ave you shovin' the boy's family over and make 'im watch! You want that? I'm no saint, but I won't be a party to it. Give him over," the sailor snapped at LeMeux and then grabbed Omibwe's arm. Omibwe, unaware of what was going on resisted the sailor pulling away from his grip. The sailor struggled to keep the boy's arm, but Omibwe wriggled his arm free.

"Come here, you shit!" the sailor shouted, stumbling with a pitch of the deck and Omibwe's pull he fell forward onto his face. Without thinking, LeMeux reared back his right arm and hit the sailor square in the jaw as he turned to get up, crumpling him into an unconscious pile. LeMeux shook his hand after the hit, it hurt worse than he'd thought. The Gazelle heaved as if she knew what was occurring within her bowels, throwing LeMeux and Omibwe against the door. LeMeux started to realize the perilous folly he'd made.

"I've struck a crewman! Jesus, God, what in heavens name was I thinking? I mean, I'd planned to do something, but now? In a storm? Even if we take the ship, we're doomed in this storm without someone who knows how to sail her!" LeMeux said aloud, to Omibwe and to himself.

"We will be ok doctor. Open the cells. We will fight the crew, they can't beat all of us." Omibwe said, a stubborn bravery in his eyes.

"Oh, my dear friend. You have no idea. There are so many fewer and all so weak, everyone out there is too weak! No, it won't work." LeMeux rebutted. He saw a leather strap hanging from the sailor's waistband with several keys attached. "We are committed now, I suppose, for better or worse. Damn it." LeMeux said, leaning down and retrieving the keys from the unconscious sailor. He helped Omibwe to stand.

"Omi, we are going out to the passageway. You and I will figure out which of these keys will open the cells. Then I will take the rest to see if I can find arms, they must have a weapons locker somewhere in the hold. We must work quickly Omi. Come now." LeMeux said, steeling himself for their perilous task. He opened the door to the passageway slightly and peered out, seeing nothing but shadows dancing across the wooden bulkheads of the ship from the swaying lanterns. LeMeux opened the door farther and he and Omibwe edged out into the passageway, steadying themselves against the bulkhead as the ship heaved. They came to the first cell, mostly occupied by grown men, though they were all in about the same shape, gaunt and tired looking. LeMeux fumbled through the keys, checking over his shoulder with each try to open the cell lock. There were three keys on the leather strap, LeMeux tried the first two keys, swearing each time they did not fit. On the third key, the thought crossed LeMeux's mind that the key for the cells might not be on this set. The click of the lock dispelled his fears and he swung the iron bars of the cell door open. The faces of the men inside were riddled with confusion and fear, until Omibwe crossed behind LeMeux and appeared into the cell. His familiar face calming their fears, but not their confusion.

"Come with us. This man is going to help us!" exclaimed Omibwe in his native tongue. The men in the cell shuffled to their feet with a burst of energy heralded by the prospect of escape. LeMeux separated the cell key from the strap and handed it to Omibwe.

"Open the rest my friend, I will go look for weapons. Hurry, I'll be back as quick as I can," said LeMeux. He disappeared up the passageway toward the stairs leading deeper into the hold of the ship. Omibwe handed the key to one of the men from the cell they had just opened and asked him to help with opening the rest. They moved to the next cell and had it open in a moment, Omibwe explained what they needed as the door was opened and man and woman alike came forth from the second cell into the passageway. On the third cell, the man helping Omibwe with the key struggled, the key bound within the lock and he had to wrench on it hard to break it free. Finally, after a few attempts the key turned in the lock and with a click the cell door swung open. Omibwe's fear was rising, there was fourteen prisoners crowded in the passageway and LeMeux was nowhere to be seen. With the fourth cell opened the number in the passageway grew to nineteen and they moved to the next cell. Omibwe's heart soared when he saw Anaya's bright eyes appear inside the cell.

"Anaya! Mother! Father!" Omibwe exclaimed, "We have to hurry, my friend is going to help us, we're going to escape!"

"What do you mean escape? We are on a ship on the ocean boy!" his father replied, a concerned and doubtful look across his gaunt features.

"We have to fight the crew father, if we can take over this ship, then maybe we can go home." Omibwe answered his challenge. Together they all crowded into the passageway and moved up to the next cell. "Where is the doctor?" Omibwe muttered as he struggled to make his way farther up the passageway. His arm was already chafed from leaning on the makeshift crutch and his good leg was feeling the strain of exertion from carrying his weight compounded by the constant movement of the deck. In the crowded passageway now had two dozen people, but LeMeux had still not returned. Omibwe started to wonder if he should have unlocked all the doors and then awaited his return, that way if a sailor happened his way into view all would appear normal until the doctor returned with weapons.

Immediately confirming Omibwe's fear, they heard as the weather hatch was lifted and a flush of seawater spilled down the stairs announcing the entrance of one of the ship's crew below deck. The sailor came into view starting with his soaking shoes, a flash of lightning danced through the open hatch as he stepped carefully down the stairs into view. Omibwe studied the man's waistline, he did not appear to have any weapons on him. The sailor stepped onto the bottom two steps of the stair flight, letting the weather hatch slam down above him shutting out the wind and rain. The sailor turned and looked up the passageway, at first not registering what he saw. A desperate look crossed the sailor's face and he turned to race back up to the main deck. The two nearest the sailor were Omibwe and a woman a few years older than him.

Omibwe scrambled to hop toward the fleeing sailor and the woman followed passing him in two swift steps. She grabbed at the sailor's feet and clung her arms around his legs. The sailor had one hand on the weather hatch and was trying to lift it as the African woman pulled at his legs with everything she had. The weather hatch cracked open only a sliver, spilling some seawater into the hold for a split second. "Help!" the sailor shouted before losing his footing and being drug down to the bottom of the stairs. He landed in a pile on top of the woman who had pulled him. "You damn wench, get your filthy hands off of me!" the sailor spit out in a venomous rage. Omibwe hobbled right next to the two and lifted his makeshift board crutch, slamming it into the sailor's forehead. The man appeared dazed and a laceration was opened across his forehead, but he reached out toward Omibwe, so the young man struck again, this time with all the strength and weight he could muster behind the blow. The sailor went limp at the impact of the second strike and Omibwe fell over as the ship pitched in a wave.

Dr. LeMeux returned from the hold below, running up the stairwell with a brace of pistols in one arm and three scabbarded swords under the other. He immediately began handing out arms to men and women around him, when he reached the side of the deck where Omibwe was struggling to get back upright, the doctor reached down and assisted the young man. Then he saw the sailor with the gash across his forehead laying on the deck and assisted the young African woman to her feet as well.

"I see you've been busy in my absence Omi. I've only found a few weapons, these will have to do for now." LeMeux said.

"What now? What do we do now?" Omibwe asked, fear and panic taking hold in his eyes.

"The Captain is seriously injured, so I think Mr. Sprague has taken command of the ship. If we can get to the cabin in the aft castle, I think we could take Sprague by surprise. But Omi, I think it would be smart to bide our time and wait out this storm. If any of the sailors come down from the deck, we can overpower them here at the stairs. Once the weather calms, it would be foolish to attempt anything in this storm." LeMeux said, improvising a plan as he spoke. "We need to get this man into a cell and the one in my cabin, before they come to." Omibwe explained to the other prisoners, much quicker in his native language than the doctor could've. They set about, dragging the two sailors into a cell and binding their hands and locking them in. Omibwe instructed those with weapons to position by the stairs, guarding for crew coming below deck. They all settled in, waiting out the storm and bracing themselves for the fight to come.

H.M.S Endurance
14 Sept 1808
18 Degrees 2' N, 76 Degrees 15' W

"Weather on the eastern horizon Sir, could be severe by the look of it." Lieutenant Cormer said, informing Admiral Sharpe who had just come onto the quarter deck a moment before.

"Very well Lieutenant. Signal the squadron, we will weather the storm in the bay to our west. High tide still, is it?" the Admiral replied knowing full well the exact conditions of the seas. He made a habit of testing whatever officer was on watch whenever he came on deck, his not so subtle way of reinforcing seamanship.

"Yes Sir, rising tide for the next two hours. According to our charts we'll have enough depth inside the bay to weather slack tide, Sir," the Lieutenant responded. Elliot was pleased, the young officer not only answered his question but also sufficed the question he planned to ask next. The admiral allowed a slight smile to break his stone bearing for just a moment.

"Alright Lieutenant bring her about," said Elliot.

The course change was quick and orderly, the signalman hoisted his flags and within moments his orders had been acknowledged by the two ships sailing in concert with him.

Within minutes the ships were all edging their way toward the mouth of a large inlet bay on the eastern Jamaican shore. The steady wind out of the northeast had shifted, giving way to a much cooler and stronger wind from the southeast heralding a storm on its way. The foreboding cloud formation seemed to be expanding by the minute and flashes of lightning could be seen within the dark skies beyond the cloud front.

Admiral Sharpe had spent the last few weeks sailing around Jamaica, investigating every nook and cranny of coastline finding nothing to substantiate his suspicions. This had only served to vex the admiral as he was wholly convinced something was afoul and he was being used as a pawn in someone's misdeeds. Years of officer conduct and reserve prevented him from sharing his true concerns with anyone, it would be dangerously inappropriate in his mind to give any of his subordinates reason to doubt his judgment. He continued, passed his orders when necessary and contemplated each situation that had led him to these scandalous conclusions all the while. His interactions with Governor Alton lately had become awkward and tense, even adversarial. The presence of the American he had met at the Governor's mansion baffled logic and he strongly suspected that American was indeed on the field where his ships had recently provided their firepower to quell a supposed rebellion. He questioned himself most of all, whether he was interpreting events and behaviors accurately, even asking himself if he had become paranoid. He shook off the notion, years of service grounded him and honed his instincts, something was afoot. He just needed some confirmation of his suspicions.

As his flagship approached the mouth of the bay Elliot walked up to the bow, he observed the conditions of the seas and scanned the inlet for any ships taking anchorage. The gentle waves breaking along the shores outside the bay were beginning to intensify as the wind picked up gradually, but within the bay the sea was calm and the only indication of incoming weather was the trees ashore beginning to dance with stronger and stronger gusts of wind. After sailing just a few minutes through the opening, Elliot could see that the inlet split off in two directions, the largest part branched north in a broad bay sheltered from the open sea by a thin rocky finger. But towards the southwest he could see another opening, a branch of the bay he was unaware of. Elliot's face flared red with embarrassment, though no one except him could have ever known what from. The Admiral prided himself on his seamanship and navigation savvy, to have sailed these waters as long as he had without knowing the true nature of this particular bay was to him, appalling. He turned to a midshipman passing behind him.

"You there, fetch me the chart we have for this shoreline. Lively now." Admiral Sharpe said snappily.

"Aye Sir!" the midshipman replied, he took off toward the chartroom at a quick pace.

Elliot pulled his looking glass and extended it, scanning the shores to his southwest. As he examined, he could see where the inlet snaked around farther west, occluded by another finger of land with a formidable tree line. From the open sea the inner inlet would be obscured from view, camouflaged by a tree line that seemed to blend together with that of the shore just beyond.

"The chart you requested Sir," said the midshipman, interrupting Elliot's thoughts. "Compliments from the officer of the watch. He asks if there is a specific part of the bay you wish to anchor the squadron?"

Elliot took hold of the chart and found the bay they were sailing into, studying the shape he could see plainly that the chart did not include the hidden inner cove.

"South by west, drop anchor where we can weather this storm and slack tide. Signal the Hunter to lay her guns covering the mouth of the bay and signal the Bayonet to lay her guns covering the mouth of that inlet." Elliot rattled his orders.

"Begging your pardon Sir. But what inlet?" the midshipman replied sheepishly. Elliot smiled broadly realizing he was the first aboard to discover the inner inlet. He put a hand on the shoulder of the young officer and gave over his looking glass.

"That inlet, young man. See to it, and have longboats made ready. I want a compliment of marines ready to go ashore within the hour from all three ships," said the Admiral. With that he left the midshipman standing on the bow, as he headed to his cabin Elliot tried to think of the last time he had personally led a party ashore.

PART TWO
Take The Helm

Chapter 6

'Drowned Maiden'
14 Sept 1808
18 Degrees 2' N, 76 Degrees 11' W

The brunt effects of the storm had enveloped both the Drowned Maiden and the Unholy Shepherd. Howling winds combined with large rolling waves, battering both ships as they made their way toward the eastern coast of Jamaica. Waves broke on the bow of the Maiden, washing seawater across the deck and making walking near impossible for all but the most seasoned of the crew. Lilith fought through waves of nausea on the constantly rolling deck, tending lines according to the orders Chibs barked through howling wind. Several times, the Maiden rolled so hard Lilith thought she was going over the rest of the way. It was by far the worst storm she had ever experienced. Chibs seemed unmoved by the severe conditions, calm even as the ship was tossed about through wind and wave.

"Land ho! Land off the bow!" the lookout aloft called. His voice barely audible over the wind.

"Aye, land!" Chibs called back. The lookout yelled something else down, his words lost to a wave breaking over the bow. "What?" Chibs called back up at him. Again, the lookout called something down, but the words he shouted were drowned out in the storm. Chibs, shaking his head turned to Lilith.

"Girl, go and fetch the Captain. Let him know we've sighted land." Chibs said, wiping seawater off his brow and wringing out his beard.

"Aye." Lilith responded. She scurried across the deck, stopping to grab onto the rail as a large wave broke over the bow sending a wash of seawater across the ship. When she reached the door to James' cabin she knocked loudly,

"Enter," came James' voice from within. Opening the door, she found the Captain leaning against a table with a chart spread out atop.

"Such a loud knock from such a small and beautiful creature. You intrigue me Lilith." James said with a warm smile.

"Aye Captain, I wanted to be certain you would hear me." Lilith replied slightly embarrassed by his flattery.

"I can think of worse interruptions. What brings you miss?" James asked.

"Lookouts have spotted land. Chibs told me to inform you."

"Very good. I suppose it's time I came out and got wet with the rest of you. It will certainly be an improvement of company, if not condition." James said, giving her a sideways look and smiling all the more.

Above deck Captain James lurched and

staggered his way through the motion of the ship up to the bow. He extended his looking glass and did his best to peer through the weather. Meanwhile the lookout and Chibs were still shouting back and forth trying to communicate through the blustering wind and breaking waves. The lookout reluctantly pointed to the foot of the ratlines, signaling Chibs to meet him there so he could pass his message without competing with the weather. When the two met, Chibs spoke with the man only for a fleeting moment before he took off across the ship towards the Captain. Oblivious to the movement of the deck the rain and waves Chibs seemed to be in a panic.

"Captain!" Chibs shouted over the weather, "Captain there are masts sighted in the bay!" He stumbled up right next to Captain James, who instantly turned back outboard and peered back through his looking glass.

"So there are Chibs. Let's make our course west by north. We'll have to skirt the coast north until the weather settles." James replied, shouting over the wind.

Chibs scrambled back to help adjust course, Lilith trying her best to keep up behind him. As the two made their way back, a rogue wave slammed against the side of the Maiden throwing both to the deck. Lilith looked up to see Chibs awash in a flood of seawater struggling to his feet, just beyond him the ship's wheel spun freely the helmsman lying unconscious at its base.

"Lilith!" Chibs cried out slipping from his feet in the rush of water, "Lilith! Take the helm! Take the helm or we're doomed girl!" Lilith stumbled and slid, falling to her knees. She pulled herself back to her feet and made it to the wheel. Lilith grabbed onto the wheel and was nearly lifted off the deck by the force of it. She put all her weight into trying to right the wheel.

"Chibs! I need help, I can't turn it back!" Lilith screamed. In an instant and seemingly appearing from nowhere Captain James grabbed hold on the other side of the ships massive wheel.

"Ready girl? Hard a starboard," James shouted. The wheel moved grudgingly but with James and Lilith both laboring at it the ship started to correct course. As the bow swung back to where it was and then edged north James looked over to Lilith.

"Can you hold her steady?" he asked.

"I believe so." Lilith answered, a little unsure.

"Well, we'll find out in a hurry if you can't," James quipped as he let go and stepped away to see to the fallen helmsman. The man had taken quite a hit to the head when the wave threw him into the wheel, and he was out cold. Captain James tried to wake him with little result when Chibs approached.

"We strayed closer to the shoreline than I

thought James. We aren't going to hit the rocks, but those ships in the bay will surely see us." Chibs rasped. He looked like a man drowned in the sea and returned from the abyss.

"Not much we can do about it now I guess; they've probably spotted us already. No matter Chibs, we'll ride out this weather and be waiting for them when it clears. This must be the anchorage the slaver told us about, wouldn't you say?" James asked.

"Aye, Captain, I'd say it is." Chibs concurred.

"It won't be the sneak attack we'd hoped for. But when those slaver ships leave the bay, I mean to lay them on the bottom," said James. A flash of lightning danced across the sky as he spoke illuminating has face and emphasizing his deadly intentions.

"Captain, we risk killing all aboard. If they have slaves in their holds…" Chibs voice trailed off as the Captain met his gaze.

"I know Chib. The best we could hope for are empty holds I suppose. How could we know with any certainty?" James asked. Lilith, still at the wheel had overheard the dilemma.

"Captain, the Shepherd was taking slaves from this anchorage to America. If those slavers turn north once they exit the bay, that would mean they are holding slaves, yes?" Lilith said, both men looked at each other and then at the girl manning the wheel. The solution had been staring at them, they both had just failed to see it.

"Aye, Lilith. If they turn north, they will surely have to be hauling slaves." Chibs answered.

"What would you do then girl? If the ships leave the bay and turn north?" James probed. Lilith squinted a little thinking through the scenario thoroughly.

"I suppose if they turn north, we could follow them at a distance perhaps? Maybe lure one of them off and force her to strike colors the way the other Americans did?" Lilith said. It seemed almost too simple a solution, but it was all she could come up with. Chibs laughed, drawing a sideways look from Lilith.

"I suppose that's the best plan any of us could hope for. Lilith, you may make a fine Captain someday. I'd sail under your banner," he said warmly. Lilith smiled at the compliment and stowed her reservations at Chibs' humor, irritated with herself for thinking he was laughing at her expense.

"Once the storm breaks, we will do just that. But I hope those bastards turn southward, I have a mind to put them all on the bottom. Chibs, hold this course for now. We'll circle back around and hopefully catch them as they leave," said James. The tone of his voice betrayed his blood lust, an almost tangible excitement at the prospect of engaging the slavers ship to ship. "Then we will storm their camp with every available hand." Lightning emphasized his point again, flashing through the sky and silhouetting the rigging against the decks.

After just a couple hours the winds began to slack to a stiff but manageable level. The rains waned as well as the seas until there was just a steady drizzling over short choppy waves. The Maiden had turned east after running up the coast for about an hour and with the storm dying down, Chibs had her come around back toward the coast. Sunrise crested over the eastern horizon, filling a thin band of open sky between the horizon and a cloud line of overcast grey with brilliant sunshine. The sun burned through its path not quite two hours before it was occluded by the thick layer of rainclouds stretching across the sky. The storm from the previous night seemed to be summoning an encore, the southern skies were lined with thick, dark cloud formations that hung very low in the air above the sea surface. Captain James had remained on deck, allowing Chibs' to get some needed rest after manning the watch during much of the storm. Lilith came back up on deck after short rest. Her clothes were still soaked through and with the seas calming she relished the breeze, the smell of the sea seemed even stronger after the storm.

"Lilith!" Captain James called over to her as he looked over the bow through his glass. The eastern coast of Jamaica peeking back into view on the horizon. "Fly the black, girl."

"Aye Captain!" Lilith answered a chill of excitement running down her spine.

"Someone fetch Chibs from his hammock and see to it the guns are all made ready!" James clamored out, sending deckhands scrambling.

Lilith raised the ship's black flag, with its horned skull, trident and broken chain. Lilith felt a sense of pride sweep over her as the breeze filled the flag. She looked at the white broken chain running across the bottom of the black field and a knot rose into her throat. She thought of her mother, wondering what had become of her. She thought of Captain James and Chibs and all the changed fates of the slaves aboard the Shepherd. She remembered the washroom from the estate in Haiti and the ill intent of Francis, she vividly pictured his eyes, how they glazed over with fear when she plunged the knife into his throat. The sound of gun ports opening interrupted her thoughts and a woman on the crew approached handing her a sword and a set of pistols.

"Miss Lilith, the Captain's ordered us all to prepare for battle. You'll be needing these."

"Thank you." Lilith replied, she buckled a thick leather belt around her middle tucking sword and pistols into place. Looking back up at the black flag her eyes met the empty black eyes of the horned skull. She then turned her gaze out over the larboard rail where the Unholy Shepherd matched pace abreast of the Drowned Maiden. They unfurled their black flag; the horned skull and trident were identical but the broken chain across the bottom was blood red. It was Captain Trina's subtle nod to James, a confirmation of sorts that the Maiden remained the flag ship of their small fleet. Aboard the Shepherd the crew was in a flurry, arming up and readying their guns. Captain James walked up onto the quarterdeck and nodded over to Lilith.

"Beautiful, but fearsome." He said.

"She is, well both ships really Captain." Lilith replied looking back up at the black flag raised high over the stern.

"I agree. But to be honest. It wasn't the ships I was speaking of." James looked over, meeting her gaze.

"Captain I…" Lilith started to reply but her words cut short by a lookout up in the crow's nest.

"Sail HO! Captain, a ship outside the bay!"

H.M.S Valor
14 Sept 1808
18 Degrees 2' N, 76 Degrees 6' W

"Man overboard! You there, a lifeline and be quick about it!" shouted a petty officer at the rail. A sailor from aloft had lost his footing when the Valor was rocked by a wave and had fallen. Luckily, the man did not fall onto the deck of the ship missing by only a few feet. Sailors scrambled to get a line out to save their shipmate. The fallen sailor's head bobbed up the crest of a wave, he was only a few feet off the side of the Valor and just out of arms reach below the rail. When the line was thrown, it hit the water trailing just in front of him. Will had run to the side of the ship along with the rest of the crew on deck. The movement of the Valor drug the line away from grasp just before the man could reach it.

"Another line! Hurry men! Get a line out on the stern!" William shouted. In a flash of lightning Will could see a large swell approaching the side of the Valor. In an instant it hit, before Will could warn anyone, the wave smashed into the side of the frigate battering everyone on board and causing another man climbing down from the rigging to fall. He was not so lucky as the first, hitting the deck of the storm-tossed ship with a sickening thud. Blood spattered the men standing near as he hit the deck and mixed with the seawater still frothing across the ship. Midshipman Ordman stood over the man's body, mouth agape, face twisted by fear and shock. Around him, a flurry of activity continued, but Ordman was frozen. He was the officer of the watch and had ordered the crew aloft to reef and tie the top gallants, now one man was swimming for his life and another likely dead. Will watched as the man overboard swam furiously for a grasp at the second lifeline, he missed the end of the line by mere inches. Another line at the stern drug by him, but the force of the waves was pulling him farther away from the ship. Each lunge the man attempted seemed to just barely miss. Sailor aboard the Valor screamed out encouragements to him, they started at the rail on the side of the ship and each time he missed a grab they yelled for him to keep trying. Eventually, the men were shouting over the fantail of the ship back at the man. His swim pace had gone from frantically racing at first, slowing as he tired and as the Valor slipped further and further away until he surrendered to just fighting to keep his head above the water.

Ordman's distraught look betrayed his thoughts, Will knew exactly what the young officer was about to say. One man was likely dead, he would order the ship around and attempt to save the other. Will stepped over to say something to Ordman, trying to prevent him from making an order he shouldn't. But before he could Ordman shouted out,

"Bring her about, helmsman hard a larboard. We have to rescue him!" Ordman yelled.

"Belay that order! Hold your course man!" Will interrupted, grabbing Ordman's coat by the shoulder he turned the Midshipman towards him. "Don't make a bad situation worse by panicking. He is lost to the sea lad, that's the truth of it. We can't endanger the entire ship by attempting to turn her around in this weather." Ordman looked at Will with sullen and defeated eyes, he was out of his depth in the storm and losing two of the crew was only compounding his missteps. The ship lurched forward again, lightening split the sky revealing both fearful and somber looks across the deck. Kingston was their destined port, but until the storm died all William could ask was to hold course and try to keep the Valor upright. It was by far the most severe weather he had ever sailed in. Wind and wave battered the ship and tested the crew. Interspersed by flashes of lightning, the darkness of night with no moon or stars quickly became disorienting. Lanterns that went out had to be taken below deck to be relit on account of the wind. The night drug on slowly, watch change brought no rest for the sailors being relieved. Below decks smelled of sickness as stomachs spilled into buckets or onto deck boards. Even the saltiest sea hands were fighting motion sickness and panic below decks.

Captain Grimes made a tour through the ship shortly after midnight. On deck he visited with the officer on watch, shouted words over the brunt gusts of wind under hats dripping from rain and seawater. They were keeping the Valor perpendicular to the swells and maintaining a westerly course as best they could, the officer assured him. Grimes calculated their land sighting would come just after dawn, but he made the climb up to the lookout anyway, just to ensure they remained alert through the difficult conditions. Climbing back down to the deck proved treacherous and difficult even for an experienced man like Johnathan Grimes, the motion of the ship was greatly exaggerated at height above the deck and the ratlines were all soaked through from the driving rain. Grimes made his way below and checked through the officer berthing, seeing to it the officers fresh off watch were taking rest as best they could. Then he made his way down into the hold, checking on the men working the bilge baffles and seeing to the carpenter's mate as he took measurement of the standing water in the hold.

"What are we at?" Grimes asked as the man in near waist deep water took a measurement.

"Two feet eight inches Sir, we were holding around two feet for a while, but we took on quite a bit of water through the last hour. I'm afraid the bilges won't be able to keep up if this storm keeps tossing us about the way it is Sir. We could be in real trouble," the sailor admonished, a cautious look on his weary face.

"They'll have to. This storm isn't likely to just vanish, and we won't be near enough land to make a run for calmer water until dawn at least. Keep the bilges running, relieve them with men from the resting watch if you must." The Captain replied curtly. He gave the sailor a knowing look, it was a difficult task but crucial to the survival of the entire ship and crew.

"Aye Sir. We'll see to it." The man said turning back to his pump crew.

The ship's surgeon, Doctor Crowsner, was seeing to the sailor who'd fallen onto the deck when Grimes opened the door to the doctor's cabin.

"How is he Doctor? Will the lad survive?" Grimes asked.

"Not sure yet, though time will tell. It's not likely I'm afraid and even if he does a blow to the head like that can leave a man a fool for the rest of his days. If he survives, but like I said," his voice trailed off.

"Right. Ok, as always Doctor. Thank you for your services. Please, if the young man expires, do come inform me immediately." Grimes said, his tone betraying the heaviness he felt at losing another sailor. It was not the first man the Captain had lost under his command and there would undoubtedly be more. Grimes carried in his mind the face of each perished sailor, men he'd come to know well. Serving in cramped space and austere conditions had a way of bringing men together closer than brothers. Each one surrendered to the sea or lost to the enemy was a family member gone, yet the journey continued in their absence. Relics were often left behind, a set of initials carved out in an obscure spot aboard ship or a possession taken up by a particularly close friend. These brought some comfort to the remaining crew, as if their shipmate carried on as part of them while their relic was still aboard. A stocking cap or a looking glass, a sailor's favored mug, a song or a tale of a girl in some port somewhere. Each man left his mark on the crew as a whole and even after their deaths, their impact remained.

Retiring to his cabin Johnathan crossed paths with Will on his way down from the quarterdeck.

"Any show of relief from the storm Will?"

"No, Sir. Unfortunately, not. I've never seen seas this fierce before." Will said, wiping his face with his sleeve.

"The seas will calm; the storm will subside. We must keep the crew about their wits, first and foremost. When everything is hell out there, your best place to focus is right on deck lad," the Captain encouraged.

"Yes Sir." Will replied.

"We should have a sighting of land shortly after five bells, so long as we haven't drifted off course too far. I'm going to get some rest Will, wake me before dawn and see to it extra lookouts are posted around four bells," said Johnathan.

"Aye Sir," Will answered, "Does the Doctor have any news of the sailor who fell to the deck Sir? He was alive when he hit, the crew on deck have been inquiring."

"Nothing good. The doctor is seeing after him now, though he may be waking me before you get the chance to, I'm afraid. We'll see to arrangements for him when we know more lad."

"Sir. There's something bothering me about the circumstance. It was Timmons who validated what Mr. Shelton claimed happened during the engagement last month." Will extolled hurriedly.

"Aye, what of it?" Grimes replied with a confused note playing across his look.

"Sir. Timmons validated Mr. Shelton's story, Cobb was derated and flogged and then Timmons falls from the rigging? Cobb was aloft with him, though I don't know how close the two men were working. Timmons was, er, is an experienced hand. I wouldn't have thought twice about it, even with the coincidence of other circumstances involving Cobb. But it wasn't a landsman who fell from the rigging and that makes me suspicious." Will rattled, barely able to get the words out fast enough. Grimes could see his second in command was severely troubled by his suspicions. But too many questions remained for anything to be done about it at the moment. Had Cobb done something aloft to cause him to fall? Would Timmons survive his condition? Would he be right in the head if he did survive? An ache filled Johnathan's temples.

"We must watch the man. See to it that Cobb

is not left alone, least of all with Shelton. There isn't proof enough to place the man in irons, let alone hang him, though I'm beginning to suspect, Will, it won't end until we do just that," said Grimes. His look was weary, even more so after Will bore out his suspicions. The Lieutenant regretted sharing his suspicions. The Captain went into his cabin, as Will returned to the quarterdeck to find the winds subsiding slightly. The ship still heaved and rolled with the swells, but gradually over the next two hours wind and wave both lessened. Rain still drizzled, keeping the soaking sea hands aboard from dryness or comfort.

As the eastern horizon began to show the early glow of coming dawn, William called for a sailor from the watch.

"Pass my compliments to Captain Grimes and inform him it is half past four bells, dawn is neigh." Will instructed.

"Aye Sir." The sailor replied, snapping to his task. Will turned to the quartermaster's mate at the helm and began to reckon their heading. They had been holding steady on a westerly course for the last couple hours, if the Captain had judged their course correctly, they should be sighting land soon. Tired from night and battered by the storm, the crew relished rest but the morning would be need to be spent pumping out the hold, drying out what supplies could be salvaged and sorting through any damage sustained in the foul weather. To Will's knowledge, a stay on the foremast would need to be replaced and the blocks for the top gallants on the mainmast were fouled. Along with a tack sail that had split in several places, the tasks ahead promised it would be hours before he took rest.

Will had placed extra lookouts aloft and on the bow as the Captain had asked, he was on his way forward to take a look toward the western horizon when Grimes came up onto the deck. The massive rolling swells had reduced into a sea of short, choppy waves under a strong but steady west blowing wind.

"Well done Will. Let's get the crew set to it. Any damage from the storm?" Johnathan asked. Will began to go through the list of tasks he had just been thinking through when the lookout above relayed down,

"Land on the horizon. Two point off starboard bow." The sailor drolled.

"Good. Let's get about it then. I'll get a fix on our exact position." Grimes continued.

"Sail! Sail off the starboard stern rail Sir! Two Ships!" the lookout cried down, this time a streak of adrenaline fueled his voice. Grimes grabbed his looking glass extending it as he ran across deck to the stern. Reaching the rear of the ship Grimes and Pike looked out over the fantail into the growing light of the rising sun. Two ships sailing abreast bore down on their position, weather gauge in their favor.

Lieutenant Pike's stomach turned into knots as he found the silhouette of two warships to the east. Scouring their view of the ships the two officers stood together trying to discern the warships' colors. In their view behind the Valor, the ship to the right in the duo changed her course slightly. The flag flying over her stern revealed a fearsome looking horned skull over a black field, a tilting trident behind the skull and a length of broken chain beneath.

"Captain." Will said, "Do you see those colors?"

"I do lad. Beat to quarters." Grimes replied sharply. Looking over both ships, the sting of a chill ran up Captain Grimes' spine. They were in his class, both appeared to be frigates but there were two and unlike his bold confrontation with the French in the Atlantic he was at a disadvantage with his opponent upwind. That was before he took into account his damaged sails and rigging. The drum aboard the Valor sounded briskly while the crew erupted into a frenzy of activity to make ready for action. "Well, let's bloody get to it then." Captain Grimes muttered to himself. He looked over to Lieutenant Pike, "Run her towards the coast and make a hard-larboard turn facing us south. I want a volley as soon as we come about Will. Have the bosun and his mates get those damaged sails replaced as we make the run up. We're going to need them." Will smiled devilishly as he went about issuing his orders, Captain Grimes was in his element again.

H.M.S Endurance
14 Sept 1808
18 Degrees 2' N, 76 Degrees 16' W

The rains intensified after sunset and combined with a wind from the east that battered the ships anchored within the safety of the bay. Elliot had donned his oilskin cloak and large hat, but it only took a few minutes on deck until he was soaked through down to his skin. The longboats from his other two ships arrived at the stern of the Endurance, Elliot climbed down into one of the two longboats from his flagship. His longboat led the way toward the shore of the bay, Elliot instructed the marines to make landfall away from the mouth of the inner cove. The intensifying weather made conditions in the longboats miserable, even within the cove short choppy waves slopped over the surface of the water. With the sun down and the heavy wind and rain, visibility was limited as well; which brought a wry smile to Elliot's face. He liked miserable conditions especially if he wanted to do something aggressive. Pouring rain and howling winds would discourage even the most ardent watchman.

After making landfall Elliot waited until he had his entire compliment of marines before heading inland. They formed a column trudging into the tree line on the finger of land separating the inner cove from the larger part of the bay. After only a few minutes of weaving through the dense forest Elliot could see the opening of the cove ahead.

"Douse those lanterns men, four of you come with me. Everyone else form up and stay put, we won't be long." Elliot said to the marine closest to him. The order was quickly passed in hushed tones through the column of soaking wet men. Elliot moved cautiously toward the opening, peering through the trees to the inlet ahead. The visibility had only deteriorated but as Elliot approached the edge of the tree line, he could see a light on the cove. He sent one of his four-man detail back to retrieve the marines who had stayed farther back. When the main body of the landing party all came up to Elliot's location, he looked them over momentarily and addressed them quietly.

"Alright lads. You're probably all scratching your heads and wondering why the old man is dragging you inland in the pouring rain and wind, marching you through this damn mud eh?" Elliot said stone faced. A few grins and chuckles ran through the formation, a marine toward the rear grumbled. "Something has been going on in Jamaica, in the Caribbean. I mean to get to the bottom of it men. If we come across anything up here, it's going to be a close engagement so fix your bayonets and keep your powder dry. Fan out and sweep the tree line, we need to cover this entire inner cove. Keep a weather eye on the water as we move, there's a light out there which means a ship. Best not be taken by surprise. His Majesty expects excellence from his marines as do I. I've always said my marines are superior soldiers to any landsmen the Crown's army has to offer, don't make a liar of me."

 The landing party formed a skirmish line and moved through the trees along the shore of the cove. Progress came slowly and with great difficulty through the wind and mud. Elliot remained just a few paces behind his skirmish line, weaving his way between trees and watching the cove every few steps. After a couple hours of pushing through the dense forest, the line inexplicably halted. Elliot looked out to the cove; he could still faintly see the dim light he had spotted earlier. A marine approached him, leaning in close to inform him why the formation halted.

"Sir, we've come across a path leading uphill away from the cove. What are your orders? Shall we continue our sweep?" he whispered.

"No. Send three to the beach and see if there are longboats. Then I want you to take three men and follow this trail up the hill. Be wary man, don't be spotted and for God's sake don't fire a shot if you don't absolutely have to." Elliot ordered. He looked for a dry spot to sit and rest his legs, finally giving up and sitting on a soaked slick fallen log. He no more than took his weight off his feet when the marines returned from the beach,

"We count four longboats on the shore Sir. But there's something more you should know Admiral." The marine paused, almost hesitant to continue.

"What? What did you find son?" Elliot encouraged.

"There's fortification Sir, earthen bunkers flanking both sides of the trail head. They're plain as day from behind Sir, but a ship out in the cove would never see. They both have twelve-pound guns fixed on the cove." The marine informed him in a hushed, hurried voice. A chill rocked Elliot, his mind raced but he dared not give even a hint of panic to these men.

"Very well. These cannons, were they bronze breech guns?" he asked.

"Didn't look Sir, I can surely go back and see." The marine replied.

"Do that. If they are, unscrew the brass fitting from the touch holes and bring them to me." Elliot ordered.

"Aye, Sir. Something else you ought to know Admiral. The trail, well Sir, ah. They've got men hanging next to the trail." The marine informed.

"What?"

"Aye Sir, I wasn't sure of what I saw at first. But there's two down by the longboats, two more by the bunkers, and two not even twenty feet up the trail from those. All blacks Sir. I thought you should know."

"You might've led with that son. I think I've found more than I wanted to find out here. Get me two men, I need runners lad, get me quick goddamn men." Elliot said. As he finished speaking the sound of a shot cut through the wind followed by two more. Then a rapid succession of gunfire erupted, lasting several seconds. The remaining marines quickly started moving toward the sound of the gunfire up the trail with Admiral Sharpe following close behind. Slipping and stumbling through the mud and rock the marines followed the path up hill. As they progressed, the trail crested the top of the rise and led into a large open area. The formation stopped at the edge of the clearing where they came across the dead bodies of two of their comrades.

"I sent three, where is the third?" said Elliot.

"Sir, we should return to the ship and come back with more men," one of the marines suggested.

"No lad, we'll press on. There's a missing man and I want to know who they exchanged fire with." Elliot replied.

A chill set into the men as they continued into the clearing, in the dark with the rain and wind without the cover of the forest canopy, it wasn't long until many of them were shivering. Elliot formed the marines back into a skirmish line and they pressed on through the clearing. As they proceeded the winds finally began to relent and the rain slowed to a steady drizzle. A light came into view ahead of them, as they drew nearer a second appeared. Slowly they moved toward the lights, seeing in greater detail as they approached a camp of sorts. Elliot again halted the formation. He called the senior man from the detachment to him.

"Choose two men to go in and search the camp. The rest we'll hold on the edge here and cover their retreat if necessary." Elliot whispered. "I want a good search and anything they find brought back to me at once."

"Aye Sir," the marine replied and set off at once. The waiting was an awful business, the men fought against shivers and tried to remain alert. The skies above started to grow lighter as dawn approached and soon there was enough ambient light for the men to clearly see the camp. Elliot's heart sank as he began to make out the silhouette of the crude construction within the camp. The two-man search party returned and reported to the Admiral.

"No sign of our missing man Sir, the camp seems abandoned and quite in a hurry by the look of it. There's lanterns still lit."

"Right. Our detail must have met some of them on the trail, the gunfire raised the alarm and they've fled. Cowards." Elliot replied.

"The camp Sir. It's like a prison of sorts. There are log cages all through, empty, but they have certainly been occupied before." Said the other marine.

"Yes. I expected we would encounter a smugglers camp here. Though it seems I was correct just in a manner I didn't calculate something of this magnitude. Nor did I figure on human smugglers." Elliot replied. "It explains the hanging bodies down the path. Alright men, we need to be headed back for the ships. Hope to god these slavers don't return with reinforcements."

The pace up the hill had been quick, the march back was relentless. Leading the way, Elliot lost himself in his thoughts and took long hurried strides. The evidence clearly indicated someone was trafficking slaves, whether it had anything to do with the Governor and his curious association with the American man was another matter. When they reached the bottom of the hill by the shoreline of the inner cove, Elliot paused their progress only long enough for his men to disable the cannons. They were newer, American made guns, so there was no bronze breech to unscrew. Instead they had to settle for temporarily disabling the pieces by snapping off their flint firing mechanisms.

Back aboard the Endurance, Admiral Sharpe went below into his cabin in a fury. He drafted written orders for both the Bayonet and the Hunter. He then sealed each set of orders along with a letter, immediately returning on deck to a single waiting marine from the detachment of each ship.

"You are to proceed back aboard your ships and hand these orders directly to your Captains. Not the officer on watch and not his steward, directly to each Captain do you understand?" Elliot said, each word in a cutting tone that left nothing to misinterpret.

"Aye Sir," came their response, almost in unison.

"Very well then. Off with you, snap to it men." Elliot said clapping his hands. He turned to his officer of the watch, "Fly sails young man, bring us out of the bay and make course for Kingston at once."

"Sir, there's something…" the midshipman began, before being interrupted by the Admiral.

"Honestly man, make sail. We need to be making way for Kingston with all haste."

"Sir! Two ships arrived outside the bay with the dawn. They both fly black flags Admiral." The midshipman said with a tremor in his voice. He snatched a looking glass from out of the young officer's grasp and stepped over to the rail. Extending the glass, he could see two ships beyond the rocky finger sheltering the bay.

"Officer of the watch see to it the ship's log

is updated, 'encountered and engaged two pirate vessels immediately outside anchorage used as port for slave smugglers', that is a direct quote, write it word for word." Elliot snapped. Through his scope he could see that both vessels were frigates, their gun ports were open, and they appeared ready for action. Elliot looked at the banner flying from the stern of each ship. Pirates flew their own colors, sometimes when they sailed in concert, they would match the lead ships banner. No pirate on the Caribbean currently had that sort of notoriety, it was nearly a century ago when Edward Teach sailed under his skeleton and goblet banner. He'd had a squadron of ships trailing behind the Queen Ann's Revenge all matching his banner. It was a curious and bone chilling sight to behold, two ships bearing down their guns on the mouth of the bay both sailing in concert with one another. They were beholden to no nation, bound by no law and Elliot assumed, would give no quarter.

"That's fine you bloody buggers. I won't be asking for any today." He said to himself. Then he turned back to his officer of the watch, "Well. Make sail and beat to quarters, look lively man. If we wait much longer, they'll think us cowards."

"Admiral, a third!" the Midshipman pointed across the mouth of the bay to the southeast. Elliot snapped his looking glass back open and examined the third ship carefully. Union Jack was flying crisply above her stern as she made a tight larboard turn to face southward. The Admiral focused closely on the fantail as it came into view and smiled broadly when he read the ship name. "Captain Grimes and the 'Valor', Johnathan, it will be good to see you old friend," Elliot said aloud to himself. As he collapsed his looking glass, the exchange of cannon fire began.

Gazelle
15 Sept 1808
17 Degrees 53' N, 76 Degrees 01' W

Dawn approached, unknown to the captive slaves holding guard against the weather hatch. The seas had calmed over the last several hours, but no sailors had made their way below deck yet. Tension hung in the thick air of the hold and Dr. LeMeux tried to reassure everyone, including himself, that their fight would not be in vain. He reasoned that there could be no more than twenty above deck. The party they had gathered numbered no more than two dozen and of that only half would have the strength to fight. LeMeux tried to reason with himself that this entire endeavor wasn't folly, that he hadn't signed the death warrant for everyone aboard by inciting this rebellion. Then a thought occurred to him, with the weather calming, now could be their best chance. Now with the crew weary from the night and the storm, if they stormed the deck and took the Captain's quarters, perhaps they could kill Mr. Sprague perhaps then they stood a chance. He turned to Omibwe, who was being fretted over by his mother and sister, both lamenting over the young man's loss of his leg.

"Omi, we have to get everyone up. If we are going to be successful, I think the time is now." LeMeux said over the young African's shoulder. "We have to take them by surprise." Omibwe translated to the gathered captives, his father the first to move to the weather hatch. The doctor's throat tightened when he saw this, unsure if the Africans realized some of them would not survive this fight and most likely the first on deck would be the first to die.

Omibwe's father lifted the heavy weather hatch slightly, sword in hand. Daylight poured into the opening as he lifted. Voices from the sailors could be heard, but no alarm had been raised yet. Omibwe's father looked down into the faces surrounding him, ensuring they were ready. Then as if he were taking a plunge off a tall cliff, the African took a deep breath and pushed hard, forcing the weather hatch open. With a massive thud, the hatch swung over and landed on the deck. In a headlong rush the crowd of African captives moved up the stairs and onto the deck of the ship. LeMeux, for his part, made his way up the stairs amid the main party. When he stepped out of the hatch onto the deck, he heard the first sound of alarm,

"The slaves have escaped! Down to the deck everyone, the slaves are out and some of them are armed!" a shout from overhead came. The crew of the Gazelle all raced to storm the Africans and their French leader. Pistol shots sounded in rapid succession, several of the Africans fell from the first exchange along with a pair of the closest approaching sailors. LeMeux scanned the deck for Mr. Sprague, not finding him.

"Sprague must be in the Captain's cabin!" the Doctor shouted over the fracas of the fighting. Omibwe's father looked over to him and followed, the two making their way to the door of the cabin in the aft castle.

LeMeux shoved open the door to the cabin to find Sprague pulling on his trousers. Panic and rage plagued the man's face when he saw the French doctor in his doorway, sword in hand.

"I should've killed you, you damn shit eating dog," Sprague shouted angrily, reaching for his sword.

"Indeed. You should have." LeMeux said, running into the cabin all his strength and momentum behind a right sideways swing with the cutlass. Steel rang on steel as Sprague brought his sword up to parry. Another desperate slash from LeMeaux met Sprague's sword from the opposite direction, loosening the startled sailors grip on his weapon slightly.

LeMeux saw a flash of fear cross his opponents face and he swung his sword in rapid succession, each blow growing in strength and fury meeting against Sprague's rebuttals. The sound of the steel swords connecting filled the cabin until LeMeux felt his sword impact soft flesh and bite into bone against Sprague's wrist. The sailor dropped his weapon under the flurry of blows from the raging doctor. LeMeaux freed his blade from the man's arm and plunged with a great thrust, diving his point into Sprague's chest. A guttural gasping noise escaped from Sprague, deep in his throat. Blood poured out of his wound, dark red and quickly soaking through his clothing. Sprague's strength slipped away, and he crumbled onto the deck. LeMeux pulled hard, removing the blade from its target.

A shout from behind snapped LeMeux out from slipping into a trance of shock as his eyes locked onto the face of the man he had just killed. Outside the cabin on the main deck, swords collided as the African's battled the crew of the Gazelle. Each party to the fight seemed to lose their taste for the battle quickly as bodies scattered the deck of the ship. LeMeux scanned over the onslaught as the Africans drew into a semi-circle enveloping him and the cabin entrance by the weather hatch. A standoff developed as the crew of Gazelle faced the circle of Africans. It seemed as though neither side would initiate a second offensive for a moment and there were only shouted threats and taunts from the crew. Doctor LeMeux looked up into the rigging to see four sailors still aloft. They had either refused to join in their crew's battle or were being held in reserve, he could not decide which. From the weather hatch, Omibwe struggled up the last couple steps into LeMeux's vision. The doctor dropped his sword to step forward and assist his young friend coming up on deck, keys still in his hand.

"I'll not be having anything of this sort on my ship!" a voice shouted out from behind LeMeux as he pulled Omibwe up the last step onto the deck. He turned to see the Captain; head still bandaged with a trail of dried blood striping the side of his bearded face. He held Omibwe's father in front of him, a pistol in hand pointed at the African man's head. "You all drop your weapons. Doctor. Don't even breathe a word to them. I know you speak their savage tongues, when I get them all back in their cells, you're a dead man. This is your doing, I should have listened to Mr. Sprague, he wanted to open your throat in the first place."

Omibwe struggled against his board crutch leaning onto it for support in between the doctor and where is father was held by the Captain. A moment elapsed, Omibwe looked down at the blood streaked cutlass LeMeux had dropped onto the deck just moments ago. None aboard dared move, until the Captain's rage boiled over.

"So be it! Kill the lot of them!" he shouted, firing his pistol. Omibwe saw his father's head jerk sideways from the impact of the ball. A shower of blood splattered the deck and his lifeless body crumpled, thudding onto the planks. The Captain turned his pistol in hand and swung it like a club at LeMeux, taking no notice of Omibwe as he dove for the cutlass on deck. The Captain's pistol butt connected with LeMeux's jaw causing him to stumble backwards, falling down the ladder well leading into the belly of the ship.

The fall jarred LeMeux and he fought to grab the steps on his way down, failing he collided with the deck below. His vision doubled over, and his head spun, the doctor placed his hand on the crown of his scalp and felt warm, sticky blood oozing from a gash. Gathering his strength, he fought his way back up the steps, crawling hand over hand trying to gain traction with feet that wouldn't fully obey his command. His ears rang with a deafening tone that all but drowned out the noise of the battle above. When his eyes crested back over the edge of the deck, LeMeux caught a glimpse of Omibwe. Sitting atop the bloodied body of the Captain, Omibwe hacked with the cutlass relentlessly. The Captain raised his arms to shield himself and a downward blow from Omibwe quickly separated his right arm from the elbow down. Then with a following slash into the man's face and throat, and another followed by another. The Captain went limp, blood pouring out onto the deck of the Gazelle. LeMeux pulled himself up the last step and onto the deck, turning he could see the other side of the battle unfolding. The four sailors from the rigging had stubbornly remained perched high above the deck. Meanwhile only a scant few of the Gazelle men remained, outnumbered by the uprising twice over.

On the horizon to the west, unnoticed by any soul on the deck of the Gazelle, sails appeared on the horizon with the eastern coast of Jamaica stretching out behind them. The sailors aloft in the rigging took notice and began to split their attention between the battle unfolding on deck and the sails moving against the backdrop of the island. When the two ships closest unfurled their black banners, the four men up in the rigging sounded down to the deck with alarm, "Pirates! Two of those ships out there are flying the black!"

The three remaining sailors on deck took to the rail, cautiously watching for an attack from the Africans. LeMeux passed friend and foe alike to run to the bow of the ship, looking out over the expanse of sea separating them from the spotted ships. One look confirmed, the two ships closest to them were flying black banners. Though they were miles from the nearest one, the sound of echoing cannon fire floated in against the breeze at their backs. For a moment everyone on the Gazelle looked out of the water, seeing more sails appear from a cove in the island shore.

"Whoever wins that fight, it won't matter for us. If we get caught up by either side, we are doomed!" one of the sailors in the rigging shouted down. "We need to get this tub sailing somewhere else!"

"If those are the Royal Navy..." LeMeux began to reply.

"You'll be hanged as a mutineer, use your head man!" the sailor cut him off. "Take the helm and get us turned, hard a larboard. We can sort out what to do with the ship away from here, with our heads still attached to our bodies and our necks not in a noose."

The doctor made his way to the helm and began making a hard turn. The Gazelle lurched with the turning of the wheel. Off in the distance the reports of cannon fire continued while a front of dark clouds crept slowly across the southern skies. For the moment an uneasy truce seemed to settle in on the Gazelle, each of the African captives weary to let down their guard and the sailors cautiously returned to the business of handling the ship.

Chapter 7

H.M.S Valor
15 Sept 1808
18 Degrees 2' N, 76 Degrees 16' W

The H.M.S Valor had turned hard southward just off the baby opening, her guns run out, men all at their battle quarters awaiting further orders. Below deck Lieutenant Shelton's voice could be heard, "Steady now men, hold fire, no wasted shots." Grimes took a small moment of joy, his father would have been proud of the lad, he thought to himself. Looking out over the larboard rail, Captain Grimes could see the approaching ships, their black flags billowing in the wind. Off the stern of the Valor, Admiral Sharpe's fleet lay at anchor within the bay. At first sighting, Johnathan had been relieved to see friendly ships who could aid him in an engagement. After reconciling charts and the size of the bay opening, with the direction the wind was blowing, he soon realized there was no way for the ships to exit the bay. At low tide they could only traverse the center of the bay opening without risking running even one of the frigates aground. With the wind coming stiff from the east an attempt to do so would put the ship 'In Irons', headlong into the wind with no way to propel themselves forward. The tide was on its way in, but by the time there was enough depth to traverse the mouth of the bay at angle the engagement would likely be over, for better or worse. They could offer fire support from their cannons, but with no maneuver capability they weren't much better than helpless bystanders, especially if the enemy vessels kept out of their fields of fire. To complicate matter further, the damage the Valor had sustained in the previous nights' storm rendered her at a significant disadvantage in maneuverability. Something Johnathan would sorely need trying to engage two ships who had the advantage of the wind. Their options were limited and narrowing with every passing moment. Glancing over at Lieutenant Pike by his side, Grimes steeled himself for the coming engagement.

"William, the rest of the fleet is wind locked in that bay at least until high tide. Even then they will present a nice target until they have full wind out in open water. I suspect Admiral Sharpe will attempt to provide us some aiding cannon fire, but we should presume nothing. If they bear southward, as I believe they will, we will need the fastest broadsides our gun crews have ever put out." Grimes rattled his orders.

"Aye Sir. We are in sight of the Endurance, shall I have any signal flags run up?" Lieutenant Pike asked.

"Yes, signal the flagship to inquire after tea lad." Grimes said flatly.

"I'm sorry Sir. Did you say tea?" Will asked,

twisting his face in confusion.

"Yes lad. Tea, and let me know the response. That will be all Lieutenant." Grimes answered. His tone belied no further illumination on the issue, nor did it leave the impression he would elaborate any further if pressed. But Johnathan Grimes had served at length with Admiral Elliot Sharpe, aboard the same vessels and within the same fleet. The two men were of like mind and though every single sailor may question the meaning of the signals being passed, Johnathan knew Elliot would understand exactly what he meant. It was not tea he was asking about; tea had not been on his mind since he left port in England and tea was not the burning question he desired to ask.

As the two frigates approached Admiral Sharpe let off a single cannon shot sending a massive twenty-two-pound projectile hurling through the air. The cannon shot struck the sea ahead of the northern ship sending a plume of water skyward. Nimbly, the pirates in the ship closest to the impact adjusted their course. Bow chasers of both approaching vessels answered his fire, but their shots were concentrated toward the Valor and accurately fired as Johnathan observed.

"Long nines on their bows. William, we will be in their range before they are in ours." Grimes said flatly, then silently to himself he wondered if he should sheet his sails and run south to try and gain advantage through maneuver. The Captain shared a tense and grave look with his second in command.

"Sir. We could run up max elevation and range them on their way in. Perhaps even score hits before they can bring a full broadside to bear." William offered.

"Aye, do that and check if we have a response from the flagship." Grimes replied.

"We do Sir. The Admiral signals back in the affirmative." William answered his voice betraying his confusion.

"Very well, don't concern yourself with it lad. I'll explain it all later," said Grimes, "Focus on our situation for now. We may take a few here, but once they're in range we need to get repeating fire out and quickly. They'll lose their taste for it. These buggers don't often have a stomach for a real fight."

"Yes Sir, I'll be below then, assisting Mr. Shelton with the gun crews." William replied as he turned to head below deck.

Elliot has answers, Johnathan thought after hearing the reply to his signal flags. At the conclusion of this engagement he would surely get some answers to the questions that had been nagging him for weeks.

The impact of a cannon shot sent the crew of the Drowned Maiden reeling, Captain James was on the bow and looked in toward the shore through his looking glass. "Bear us off away from those guns," he called to the helm. The ship they were approaching had turned southward and looked to be making a stand against the coast, guns run out and ready for action. No smoke reported a shot from any of its guns though. James scanned north toward the mouth of the cove they had run by the night before. There were three ships inside the bay. Two frigates and a massive line ship,

"Look at this Chib, likely some lofty Admiral type is sitting on that, powdered wig and all that." James mused, handing his glass over to his first mate.

"Aye, she's a big one. Likely fourth rate, maybe a third. Two gun decks. She's the one who fired, she'll have big guns. Twenty pounders, maybe even twenty fours. Captain, we'd best steer long clear of that beast and give her wide berth if she makes her way out of the mouth of that bay there. We get caught by one of those broadsides and we are all dead." Chibs said over James' shoulder as he was looking through the glass.

"They're wind locked in that bay Chib, you ought to have figured that before me." James replied quizzically.

"Yes Captain. But if we get into it with that frigate and they manage to slip out, we're fit to be tied, by the neck." Chibs answered, a hint of frustration creeping into his voice. He knew his captain and James was not likely to shy away from an engagement. Unless it was spelled out very plainly and even then, it would be difficult to dissuade him.

"We'll make a pass at the frigate then, Chib. Lay what fire we can on her and see if we can draw her out." James offered.

"Aye Captain. We'll make a pass then." Chibs stroked his white whiskers as if it somehow would soothe his anxieties.

"Chib. Let's open up with the bow guns on our way in." James added.

"Aye Captain. That'll be a good start for it," Chibs replied. Chibs had the bow gun crews on the Maiden begin firing and soon after the Unholy Shepherd began firing her bow guns as well. Through sporadic smoke clouds from the forward cannons, the frigate ahead grew larger and larger as the distance closed. Each round from the approaching pirates honed in on their target and it wasn't long before splintering wood signaled their accuracy.

James stood onto the larboard rail and shouted over to the Unholy, "Bear off south and give them a broadside! We'll follow you up with another!" His shouts were met with acknowledgment and cheers aboard both vessels, cut short by an impact on the Maiden from one of the defending frigate's guns. Wood splinters flew from the impact on the bow, narrowly missing Chibs but wounding several who were standing near him. The next shot impacted on the Shepherd's larboard rail and screams from the wounded could be heard floating between both ships. Captain James was bloodied by a large splinter lodged in his right upper arm and another low on the side of his left hip.

The musket fire came next, it started with a volley that swept the decks of both ships but was largely inaccurate. Then a trickle of individual shots followed, intermittent and accurate. On the decks of the Maiden and Shepherd sailors all took cover wherever they could and returned the musket fire with their own. Then the Shepherd made her turn south. In a series of successive cannon shots, she dealt a deadly hand of accurate fire. The returning fire blew away the deck rail in two spots and then ceased as calamity broke out aboard the navy ship. The impacts of the Shepherd's shot tore into their target, blasting into their gun deck, maiming crew aboard and severely damaging their larboard rail. A single cannon shot found its mark on the foresail mast, boring out a gaping wound and splintering shards all across her bow. Moments passed, the sweeping turn of the Maiden brought her battery to bear on the Navy frigate and she unleashed her broadside almost in unison. Shot tore into the gun ports, blasting wood and metal, maiming sailors all across the gun deck. What was left of the larboard side of the vessel was shattered in the volley. As the Maiden slipped away moans and cries of the wounded on the battered ship were drowned in furious shouts and cheers and taunts from the victorious pirate crews.

William opened his eyes, sunlight filtered through clouds and rigging lines shone into his eyes and he winced. He was laying flat on his back and all around him sailors cried out. Wailing cries of the wounded floated over shouted commands and responses from sailors trying to recover from the attack. His head spun and pounded, he tried to get to his feet but found his strength failed him. He rolled to his side, coughing and retching he pressed himself up onto his hands and knees. A sailor seeing his Lieutenant on the deck stopped and abruptly pulled William to his feet,

"Sir! We all thought you dead."

"Where is the Captain?" William asked.

"He was on his way forward when they let fly with their broadside. I haven't seen him since," the sailor replied, "Do you have orders for us Sir?"

"A damage report and have any Officers you see meet me forward. I'm going up to see to the Captain." William said, still gasping through his speech.

"Aye, Sir," the sailor answered as William stumbled his way forward to the bow. Much of the larboard rail was blown away and the deck was in tatters in several places. After a few moments of stumbling, William found his steps coming easier. A warm oozing alerted

Will to a wound on his side. His jacket was torn and reaching his hand into the tear to check his wound brought a wave of pain that almost dropped him back to the deck of the ship. He pressed on toward the bow of the ship, searching through sailors dead and wounded scattered across the deck.

"Will!" cried out a man hunched over the starboard rail. His shirt was covered in blood and his hair undone and obscuring much of his face, but William could see it was his Captain.

"Captain Grimes! Are you alright Sir? Let me see to your wounds." Will said, reaching in to help Johnathan stand.

"I'll be fine. A few cuts and a chunk of the Valor in my shoulder. Most of this blood belongs to the lad who was next to me. Where are they Will? Are they coming about?" Grimes asked in a growl. The ships, Will hadn't even given thought of the possibility of them coming around for a second exchange. He stood, looking out over the bow he could see the sterns of both pirates. Their black banners billowing through the westerly winds. Both were full rigged and making sail south, no sign of turning to finish the engagement. Off in the distance, a third ship was making her way south as well, though no banner flew from her stern lines.

"No Captain. They're full tilt southward. There's another ship out there also." Lieutenant Pike answered, pointing out over the water as Grimes looked.

"Damn them Will. I erred and they did not let it slip. We shall not give them the same chance again. What of our dead and wounded?" Grimes grumbled as he looked out at the ships beating hastily away.

"I've asked for a damage report, I'll go see to it Sir and be back to you." Will said stepping off to begin getting the ship back in sorts.

"Lieutenant Pike." Grimes called after him.

"Yes Sir?" Will said turning back quickly. Grimes collapsed onto the deck before he could get out his next command. Will rushed over to the Captain whose wound had been bleeding far more severely than he had let on, he was unconscious, pale as death. Will could barely contain his distress, screaming for the ship's doctor. Several sailors came and assisted carrying the Captain to his cabin with Doctor Crowsner following behind them. On their way to the cabin Lieutenant Shelton came alongside Will and pulled him away.

"The foremast has been damaged Sir; we can't make sail until it has been repaired or replaced. Larboard rail is all but destroyed and there are several holes through the side on the gun deck level. Nineteen souls lost right now, another twelve wounded not including the Captain," the young man looked at Will's side oozing blood, "Or you Sir."

"It's nothing. I'll be fine. Are we taking on water?" William said, covering the wound just above his hip.

"No Sir," the young officer replied, "All battle damage was taken above the waterline."

"Very well Shelton, let's get to it. Repairs must start immediately, rudder and mast first."

"Aye Sir." Shelton replied. William awed for a second at the resilient spirit of the crew. After the beating they had taken and already men were making order of the chaos. No, Will thought to himself, we're not beaten just yet. Before descending into the Captain's cabin to see to his commander's condition, Will turned and surveyed the deck of the Valor. Sailors were already at work righting fouled lines and tossing debris overboard, the repairs would take days maybe even weeks. The sight of the ships that had engaged them escaping south while the Valor sat in tatters brought a visceral rage boiling through Will's mind. "So help me," Will said aloud to no one in particular while he pointed at the escaping pirates, "I will kill their skipper and lay those ships on the bottom."

16 Sept 1808
Kingston, Jamaica - Governor's Mansion

Governor Alton awoke to the sound of his chamber door slamming open. Peering out of bed curtains with bleary eyes he could not distinguish who approached. Sitting up, he tried to rub sleep from his eyes. "What is the meaning of this?" he demanded.

"You have disappointed me for the last time you bumbling fool. I'm here to rectify your incompetent errors," came the voice of Tim Sladen. In a flash the bed curtains were torn away, and Governor Alton could clearly see Mr. Sladen standing at his bedside with a pair of fearsome looking men standing beside him. One held a lantern which cast an eerie glow onto their faces and drew towering shadows onto the wall of the chamber. The sound of furniture being overturned in another room alerted Alton that these men were not alone. Fear clamped the Governor's breath in his throat, an icy chill ran up his spine.

"I wouldn't worry too much about your belongings Governor or your servants, you should be a bit more concerned with your neck. I warned you." Tim said through clenched teeth, then turning to the men with him, "Bring the swine, we need him to write a letter for us." Governor Alton was dragged from his bed in his nightgown and forcefully marched from his bedchamber. In the light of the hall Alton could see the flurry of destruction Sladen's men were inflicting. Paintings and tapestries ripped from their rightful place along the hallways. Throughout his home bookshelves, tables, cabinets and cases were being emptied and overturned. Every item of value was being stripped away.

Vases, busts, sculptures and all manner of finery were being sacked and carried away indiscriminately by Sladen's band. The men all had a rough look to them, they carried themselves like men eager to engage a fight.

"What have you done? What are you doing?" Governor Alton stammered, unbelieving of what his eyes saw.

"You've cost me, again. I'm here to collect on that debt on behalf of The Order. Your only value to me is now making good on that debt, the second I think you have outlived that ability will be your last." Sladen hissed into the Governor's ear as they surveyed the atrium of the mansion from atop the stairs.

"What do you mean debt damn you? I don't owe you, that was never part of the arrangement!" Alton began. Tim interrupted him with a savage push sending Alton tumbling down the curved staircase, crashing abruptly onto the tiled floor.

"It was never part of the arrangement that you would send the fleet to our anchorage. It was never agreed upon that under any circumstance would my camp be invaded by your god damned admiral. There were no such concessions Alton. However, you and I agreed that any such losses would be made right by you. Did we not? Just a few weeks ago in fact?" Sladen shouted down as he slowly walked down the stairs. The governor was a pathetic sight, bleeding from a cut on his scalp and from his nose, in his linen nightgown. He tried to lift himself from the floor to address his assailant with some form of dignity only to be shoved back down by Tim's polished black boot.

"I made no such agreement; you just make demands. You seem to think you can order me around, like I'm some piss bottom commoner. I am a Lord and a Governor! You will stop this, this treachery! It is treason!" Alton shouted back between winded breaths.

"Spare me your sanctimonious drivel. Treason would require me to be a subject of your monarch. I am in fact an American, as for treachery, well, you may have me there not that it matters much to us." Sladen said, smiling to his companions. "Take the Lord Governor into his study, let's get a quill and paper into his hands so he can be of some use to us." The two men following Tim stepped around him, grabbed the governor by his ankles and drug him unceremoniously across the atrium to his office. Once inside the larger of the two men prodded the Governor with a large knife, prompting him to climb up into his chair. Tim followed the trio into the study as men were carrying arm loads of valuables out. One man passing by carried a sword with an intricate and ornately designed hilt and hand guard, its scabbard bore gold inlays that caught Tim's attention. He prompted the man to hand over the weapon and unsheathed it, examining the blade.

"Such a fine weapon, Governor. Tell me, what does a fat sack like you do with a blade like this?" Tim said smiling as he looked at the governor from the corner of his eye. "My guess is you consider it a novelty decoration, don't you? You couldn't wield a weapon like this if your life depended on it." Tim arced the blade in a spin by his side, admiring the balance and edge. "Take your quill, you are going to pen orders for that bag of bones admiral."

"What happened Tim? What is going on?" Alton stammered. Tim swung the blade in a high arching blow, landing the edge across the governor's desk and biting his forearm with a glancing slash that immediately produced a crimson drip of blood.

"You know full well what has occurred. That pet Admiral of yours sent a detachment of marines into our prisoner camp, killed four of my men and as of last report, is still blockading access to my bay!" Tim shouted, rage seething and building with every word.

"I didn't, I didn't know Tim, I swear it," the Governor replied, cowering away from another anticipated swing of the sword.

"Then you are incompetent. The result is the same either way. Now Governor, head your letter." Tim said, lowering his voice and narrowing his glaring eyes. "You will write Admiral Sharpe and demand he return the fleet to anchor in Kingston harbor. He is to withdraw all landing parties and ships anchored within the bay. Any prisoners he has are to be released immediately, if he fails to comply with these orders he can expect to be removed from his command and hung under the charge of treason against the Crown." Tim rattled, noting he did not see words forming on the paper yet. "Governor start writing. I could cut you into ribbons before you are unable to pen orders, if that's what it requires." The Governor inked his quill with shaking hands and hurriedly began scrawling Tim's orders.

"What do you intend to do once they anchor in Kingston?" Alton asked, wincing slightly as though afraid to hear the answer.

"That is of no concern to you Lord Governor. Now pull yourself out another paper, you have a letter to write to the garrison commander here in Kingston." Tim said easing himself into a chair.

"Who should I have deliver these orders?" Alton asked timidly.

"We'll say it won't be you and leave it at that, now get to it Governor. You wouldn't want to agitate me further, would you?"

Drowned Maiden
18 Sept 1808
17 Degrees 48' N, 76 Degrees 7' W

The wind filled the Maiden's sails under a sky of roiling dark clouds threatening to open into a storm at any moment. Lilith dutifully stood at the helm, a new duty to her since the last storm but one she found greatly to her liking. She felt powerful at the wheel of the ship, in control of her destiny in a way she had never felt before. Minding the course she was given while adjusting for wind and wave kept her mind focused. In addition to the feeling of control and power, Lilith enjoyed being near Chibs and James as they were never too far from the helm for very long. The feeling of wind on her face and the smell of the sea spray lifted her spirits higher than the masts reaching far above the deck. Occasionally songs would break out on deck and Lilith loved that most, she only knew certain parts, but hearing the crew pitch together in unison meant their spirits were good and it endeared them all to her fondly. Rough and haggard by appearance, Lilith had learned that most of the sailors on the Drowned Maiden were good, kind people who had made tough choices in extreme circumstances. Even Captain James, who at times displayed a fierce propensity for violence that made her blood chill, Lilith had seen James' tenderness. Lost in her thoughts, she did not see Chibs as he approached her.

"You're doing a fine job Miss Lilith but tend her a bit closer to the wind and we'll coax another knot or two of speed. There's a sail off yonder and I think Captain James is of mind to catch her." Chibs said in his familiar brogue.

"Do you think they're more slavers Chib?" Lilith asked as she made the correction he suggested.

"No telling Miss. There are a hundred reasons they could have been headed for the bay. They may not have even intended the bay at all, that weather may have forced them off their destined course. But. There's a chance they're hauling slaves and James isn't going to pass at least having a look." Chibs replied. He'd lit his pipe and smoke billowed through his nose and mouth as he spoke. Lilith thought for a moment.

"Chibs. Are slaver ships they only ones the Maiden has taken?" She asked lowering her voice just a little, she almost feared the answer.

"Well. No dear. No, we've plundered several ships strictly carrying cargo. But James has never let a slave ship cross our path without challenge. Even one who had us outgunned. An old refitted ship of the line, she had us dead to rights if she would've gotten the wind on us. I had James shift two of the guns to the windward side of the ship, we had her doing fourteen knots! We darted away from them in quite a hurry." Chib said emphatically. "But my dear, we are a pirate crew. Freeing slaves doesn't put coin in pockets. To the contrary actually, we've captured two slaver ships including the Shepherd and both times the size of the crew grows with very little income for it. It is a problem James is going to have to confront and soon I fear."

"Do the slaver ships carry no gold Chib?" Lilith asked a puzzled look on her face.

"Well, yes dearie. They do. Though most often it amounts to very little. James has a fancy that one of the slavers ought to be carrying a massive haul of profit back to Europe." Chibs replied puffing away at his pipe and looking out toward the sail they pursued.

"I see. What do you think Chibs? Do you believe there is some ship with a hold full of riches destined for port in Europe?" Lilith asked.

"Well. It's hard to say dear. James keeps saying someone has to profit and that's true enough. The ships belong to someone, none that we've taken so far have been owned by their captains. But if the slavers are taking profits back to Europe, they'd be sailing in a convoy, heavily armed no doubt." Chibs answered. Neither he nor Lilith had seen James approach, though he had only heard Chibs' last reply.

"They will be guarding her. Heavily, I'm

sure. But I will have her, I will take everything from them. Just as they did to me," said James, drawing a look from both Lilith and Chibs. "But even if I'm wrong, suppose we sail for another year we could capture two, maybe even three more. Freedom for those souls is enough reward in my heart."

"Aye Captain, but the crew can't follow the reward of your heart forever." Chibs replied not unkindly. "With two ships James, we could take any single vessel on the Caribbean."

"You aren't wrong Chib. Perhaps. But time will tell Chib. Don't give up on me yet." James said jarring Chibs' shoulder with a smile. He motioned to the sail on the horizon drawing slowly nearer, "How long until we overtake her?"

"Nightfall, if the wind holds. They're sloppy on the lines Captain, like no crew I've ever seen. She is a mess, if they had to tack over the wind, they'd stall her." Chibs remarked.

"That's odd Chib. The slavers have all had experienced crews, even the Americans on the Shepherd handled her well." James said frowning and watching the ship closely. Chibs was right, even from a great distance, James could see sheets running slack, course corrections were frequent and anything but smooth. "Chib, it's almost like they're sailing with half a crew."

"Aye Captain. It's a wonder they weathered that storm." Chibs exclaimed.

"That may be the very reason they are struggling. It's possible they sustained enough damage and loss to cause such haphazard handling. In any case, run her down. We will flank her between us and the Shepherd, if the crew is in any degree of peril already, they'll strike colors quickly." James said with a broad smile.

"Will you take her as a prize as well James?" Lilith asked adjusting the wheel slightly under Chibs' gentle guidance.

"That depends heavily on the manner of her crew and their surrender," replied James.

"Three ships would make a formidable force Captain. Likely we could extend our reach out of the Caribbean with such a fleet," added Chibs hoping to encourage the outcome.

"Likely. But all the more sailors we would need and all the more split for anything we capture." James said, his voice losing some of his usual luster.

As the day wore on toward evening, Lilith watched in anticipation as the sails they pursued on the horizon grew larger and larger. The Shepherd had moved in abreast of the Maiden about a half mile off her larboard rail and they prepared to close in on the vessel ahead. The wind had held steady through the afternoon but as evening approached it shifted from the east to the southeast and the struggling vessel took far too long to adjust. Their dogged sail changes were slow and sloppy, ill-timed with the helm revealing a crew that either wasn't seasoned to working together or was far too inexperienced to be handling a ship. James came and took a grasp of the helm next to Lilith.

"Miss Lilith are you ready dear?" James asked.

"Aye Captain." Lilith replied.

"Fly the black, we are close enough for them to see and too close for them to evade us if they were capable." James said, then turning to Chibs standing along the larboard rail, "Chibs, give them a shot off their bow. Let's see what they do."

"Aye Captain." Chibs replied excited scurrying towards the bow.

Lilith carefully attached the black banner to the hoist line and ran it up hand over hand. Again, as she watched it unfurl into the wind, she felt her skin ripple with goosebumps. It was bold and terrifying, the black eyes of the horned skull seemed to bore a hole right through everything they laid their gaze on. The broken chain underneath made her eyes well up with tears until the flag was a black and white blur. Again, thoughts of her mother crept into Lilith's mind and she wondered what she would think of her daughter's adventures. The roaring boom of Chibs firing off a cannon shot snapped Lilith back to reality. Smoke from the shot drifted back and she could taste the acrid powder mixed with the sea spray. She stepped over to the larboard rail to get a look. The stern of the vessel was not clearly visible.

"Lilith, what name do you see on her stern?" James called over to her.

"I can't make it out Captain, but Chibs is looking through his glass now. He may be able to see it." Lilith called back. As soon as she had replied, Chibs made his way back to the helm.

"James, she's the Gazelle." Chibs informed him with a sober look of caution.

"A little slow for a Gazelle wouldn't you say?" James said jesting.

"No Captain, that's not my point. She is a company ship, I know it for a certainty." Chibs said.

"Ready the crew then Chibs. Their shoddy sailing may be some ruse to lure us into a trap. Keep a keen eye out for any other vessels nearby," said James, his tone turning grave in an instant.

"Exactly what I was thinking Captain," said Chibs as he turned to prepare the Maiden for a fight.

H.M.S Endurance
18 Sept 1808
18 Degrees 2' N, 76 Degrees 16' W

In the days since the Valor's engagement with the pirates, Admiral Sharpe had maintained a respectful distance. At first, he had sent over a deck officer to offer the assistance from the rest of the fleet. Of course, Johnathan Grimes proudly turned them away, sending the officer back with another inquiry about tea. On the third day however, Elliot was concerned that Captain Grimes had not come over to the Endurance to see him. So, he loaded into a longboat with a detachment of sailors to assist in repair and left the bay to where the Valor was anchored. The sea was fair and distance short enough the trip took only twenty minutes, the threat of rain loomed over them in a gray overcast sky. Their manner of reception was lackluster, Elliot noted and seemed haphazard like an afterthought. Elliot's concern escalated as he climbed up from the longboat and looked through the welcoming party to find Grimes missing.

"Where is your Captain?" Elliot asked the officer greeting them.

"He is below in his cabin Sir. I'm afraid he was wounded in the exchange of fire with those pirates, quite seriously Sir," Lieutenant Pike answered while rendering his salute.

"You look a sight yourself lad. I can see you took a wound also, are you well?"

"I am Sir. Well enough, mine was grazing really, no debris remains lodged in my wound Sir, I should recover in a day or two according to our ship's doctor." Pike answered. Elliot noticed his bearing was there, he was a navy man to make the King himself proud.

"Very well son, show me to your Captain." Sharpe commanded, following Will below deck, "Who is your ship's surgeon?"

"Doctor Crowsner Sir," Will replied.

"Ah. I feared as much." Elliot replied with a scowl, he turned to a lieutenant that had come across with him from the endurance. "Run back to the Hunter, have them send over a compliment of carpenters and their surgeon, straight away lad."

"Aye Sir," the lieutenant said snappily turning to execute the directive.

"Apologies Sir, the Captain is out of sorts. He isn't in condition to receive a flag officer properly," William warned as he opened the cabin door.

Elliot could see immediately the dire condition Johnathan was in. The light settled into the cabin softly from the aft windows and he saw Captain Grimes laying shirtless in his hammock. Pale as a ghost, drenched through in sweat. As soon as he stepped in Elliot's senses were assaulted by the smell of the Captain's wound, corrupted flesh has putridity matched by few other odors. Johnathan turned his head; aware someone had entered his cabin.

"Admiral?" Grimes spoke a growl almost too faint to hear.

"Yes lad. Keep where you are. Let me see that wound." Elliot instructed softly.

Captain Grimes lifted his head slightly,

struggling to make his arm obey for a second to lift the dressing covering his wound. Admiral Sharpe could see where he was trying to lift and assisted him removing it. Elliot could see the wound, a six-inch stitched laceration with several smaller wounds around it, it was a deep purple in color with a web of pale yellowish streaks leading away toward the mottled gray skin surrounding. He could see pus coming from the stitches and the odor under the bandage was foul, it smelled of death.

"I hate to inform you boy." Elliot began, pausing when he could see Johnathan knew exactly what he was about to say.

"I know Sir. I won't survive this." Johnathan interrupted.

"I was going to say likely; you won't likely survive this. However, I believe your presumption is correct. I warned you about Crowsner, what a poor excuse for a surgeon. I warned you about that damn Scotsman, far too often in his cup and he consorts with a manner of pagan practices. I warned you Johnathan and I see like the stubborn mule you are you have ignored my heeding, likely to your death. My surgeon aboard the Endurance would've had every bit out and the wound cleaned proper, you'd be right to sail in a week." Sharpe scolded. "But no use for it now. Johnathan, you sent signal for tea. I assume your inquiry alluded to the order involving

East India Company ships."

"Yes Sir. Do you know anything Sir?" Grimes asked a sudden spark entering his composure.

"You there, you are the First Lieutenant am I right?" Sharpe asked to an onlooking William who seemed to snap out of some melancholy state hearing the Admiral address him.

"Yes Sir, I am, Lieutenant William Pike, Sir." Will replied.

"Very well. Johnathan, if you are to perish, do you have any qualms relinquishing command over to this lad?" Elliot asked flatly.

"None Sir, he will make a fine master and commander." Grimes said looking over at Will almost smirking at the dumbfounded expression on the young officer's face.

"Right then. Listen closely Will, your lot has joined the fleet at a precarious time. Now the order to remain a minimum of four cables distance from every company ship was given to my fleet four months ago. I received it from Governor Alton in Kingston, though I am unsure if it originated there. If you received the same orders from England, I doubt Alton is the only one involved." Sharpe said sitting onto a stool in the cabin.

"Involved in what Sir? What ends could these orders possibly serve?" William spoke up.

"I have reason to believe the East India Company is operating a slave smuggling operation in defiance of both parliament and crown. I myself lead a landing party inshore from the cove where the Endurance is currently at anchor. We came upon a prison camp and were thusly engaged by the men guarding it. I lost some of my marines in the exchange and one is still missing, taken prisoner I assume. It is purely suspicion at this point; however, I believe Africans are being taken by the company and shuttled here, then distributed from the camp I just mentioned." Elliot said looking intensely at Will.

"The governor is involved Sir? Are you sure?" Will asked. The situation seeming more and more formidable as the Admiral listed his suspicions.

"I am sure of nothing Lieutenant. I have my suspicions. What I am sure of is that there is slave trafficking through seas I am responsible for. If it is in fact the company, if the governor is involved, if anyone in London is aware, I cannot prove. What I can prove only makes me more suspicious. What I need right now is my fleet, upright and battle ready. How soon can you sail Lieutenant?" Elliot asked.

"It will be two more days Sir; the foremast needs to be replaced. We've repaired the rail and mended what we can of the gun ports. The lion's share of the larboard battery is good only for ballast at this point and any provisions we had that were not destroyed by the water taken on in the storm are now ruined. We are in desperate need of a proper refit in port Sir." Will replied reviewing their condition.

"I suspected as much and fortunately enough; my next destination will be Kingston. However, when we get there, I will require every able marine you have on ship. You will have twenty-four hours to take on what you need Will, not a minute more. I expect a very cold reception from Governor Alton and quite possibly a hostile farewell, our departure may be quite rushed." Sharpe extolled with a gravity that gripped both officers. "Use the carpenters I've brought over. Keep them for the sail to Kingston, likely you will need the hands with the casualties you've taken."

"My thanks Admiral." William replied gratefully.

"No son, it is I who should be thanking you gentlemen. If you hadn't engaged those pirates, it is likely they would have bottled us into that bay and harassed us with cannon fire to no end. Johnathan, you truly have embraced the name of your vessel." Sharpe said his voice going rasp as he looked over at the ailing Captain.

"Not her last by far Admiral. William shall see to it." Johnathan said in a trailing voice. His strength failing as he spoke, he lay his head back into his hammock surrendering to exhaustion. Elliot stepped over, checking him for breath. He looked over to William,

"He is still alive lad. But my guess is it won't

be long. Make your preparations for sail, two days son and then we sail with the tide."

"Aye Sir." William responded. He took his leave promptly, there was far too much to do and too little time. Two days had been a hopeful response to the Admiral's question, even with the additional hands.

Chapter 8

'Gazelle'
18 Sept 1808
17 Degrees 48' N, 76 Degrees 7' W

A hopelessness had engulfed everyone aboard the Gazelle. The sailors, who at first had taken a vigor to their work of sailing the ship as if their lives depended on it, had fallen into a surrendered temperament. The snappy shouts and crisp replies had faded to a tone of resign. The two ships off their stern had spent the day pursuing them at a pace the small band of sailors and inexperienced Africans just simply could not endure. As the sun drew lower into the west the sails grew larger behind them until detail of each vessel became more and more pronounced to the naked eye. When the winds began to shift from the east to southeast a sail adjustment became necessary. To the aggravation of the sailors aboard the line adjustment was too much for the four of them to accomplish without aid from some of the Africans. One of the African men who tried to assist them heaving a line lost his footing, causing the man next to him to trip and the team lost their line spilling wind from the sails at a critical moment. The lack of knowledge or coordination from the Africans enraged the sailors who were desperately trying to evade their pursuers and miserably failing to do so.

Dr. Lemeux stood on the aft castle looking out over the narrowing expanse of sea separating the Gazelle from the stalking predators behind her. The dark clouds overhead threatened another storm, which they could not weather and the ships approaching would have them in their grip before nightfall. The situation seemed utterly hopeless and Lemeux began thinking he may be responsible for signing death warrants for every soul aboard. Then, as if cued by his mental anguish, the stalking ships unfurled large black banners billowing out into the wind.

"Pirates, damn!" one of the sailors lamented.

"What of their banner? Is it one you know?" another asked.

"No. It's not one I've heard of before." the first sailor answered.

"Maybe it is good, an unknown pirate crew, maybe they aren't so terrible."

"Shut up you idiot," the first sailor balked, "It likely means they don't make a habit of leaving anyone alive to tell tales."

The horned skull floated over the decks of the imposing ships as the distance closed and Lemeux felt his heart sink farther with each passing moment. The menacing black eyes of the horned skull seemed to mock their waning attempts to flee and the trident canted behind drew a shiver from LeMeux as his eyes traced over it. He looked around the gathered Africans on deck. What business did he have starting a mutiny and sentencing all these people to their deaths? Would a pirate crew really murder a ship full of stolen men, women and children? His head swam in a furious circle of questions and fears as his eyes welled up until the banner behind them became a black blur floating over a formless ship. God damn them all. Damn these ragamuffin sailors, any crew worth its salt would have found a way to evade or be preparing to mount a defense. But now it was a forgone conclusion, they were far too close to have any hope of escape and fighting seemed an even more certain doom. Omibwe crutched his way over to LeMeux's side sharing the doctor's hopeless look.

"They will come and steal us away?" Omibwe asked.

"I don't know Omi, they may kill us all, they may take whatever goods we have and leave us to die of our own devices. Either way, it seems, I have doomed us all." LeMeux replied in a wave of sorrow.

"No. Not your fault doctor. The sailors on this ship, it's their fault. They are the reason we are here."

"I guess you are right my friend. But what does it matter whose fault it is, this is where we are," said the doctor.

"Talk to them doctor. Make them friends, you have a way. I know you can," said Omibwe with a spark of hope.

"I will certainly try my friend, I only hope they would listen but I fear that may not be high on their list of priorities." LeMeux's eyes fell to the sea as he spoke, "You should go be with Anaya and your mother, they will want your comfort now my friend."

The sailors aboard the Gazelle gave up all hope shortly after hearing a single cannon shot, raising a white banner into the stiffening wind. They loosed the sheet lines and spilled all the wind from their sails. It was a dreadful, somber feeling watching the pair of ships as they approached and enveloped the Gazelle. One of them drew near on the starboard rail and grapple lines were thrown over. With a few minutes the heaving sailors had drawn the ships close enough to drop a gangplank across. A filthy skinny man in ragged pants with no shoes or shirt scurried across, dropping onto the deck in front of the gathered occupants aboard the Gazelle. His wide grin revealed crooked and rotten teeth as he leveled a set of pistols into the crowd of sailors and Africans. Behind him a tall broad-shouldered older man strode across the gangplank with a swagger, he too held a pistol in each hand though this man maintained the muzzles skyward. LeMeux noted authority with this larger man, his beard and thick side chops were streaked with shades of gray and he nodded direction to several of the men following behind him, they reacted promptly.

"My name is Chibs and I am the first mate aboard the Drowned Maiden!" the man shouted out over the crowd on deck. "We are claiming this tub for our fleet and any crewman who wishes to defy this may meet me with steel in hand!" He looked around seeing the group of Africans huddled together on deck and a puzzled look crossed his face.

"Where be your Captain?" Chibs growled.

"The Captain of this vessel is dead." LeMeux called across in response.

"And who be you?" Chibs shot back.

"I am a Doctor, the reluctant doctor of the ship on which you stand. You should know you are boarding a vessel occupied only by captured slaves and men pressed against their will. There is little aboard for you to take," said LeMeux. Chibs seemed slightly taken aback, unsure of his next action. It was precarious, just a few of them had crossed onto the Gazelle and there was a crowd of Africans all around him. The possibility of an elaborate ruse by a ship of the East India Company still lingered in his mind. Behind him, Captain James and Lilith fanned out against the crowd, sword and pistols in hand. Lilith's hands became unsteady as she took in the sight of the Africans, her eyes choking back a welling of tears. Everywhere she looked, she could see her mother.

"Captain, we'll sweep below decks and sort this matter now. I've a feeling the good doctor here is telling his tale true, but let's be sure." said Chibs, his eyes unshifting from the Africans gathered around them.

"Aye Chib. Do that. Lilith, go with him." James replied.

"Aye Captain," said Lilith.

The pair made their way to the weather hatch through the crowd, the Africans parted to make way for the armed duo as they moved. Lilith looked over all the faces, her gaze stopping at a woman with a young girl by her side. Her eyes held a defiant glare, the look of a mother lion guarding her cubs. On the other side of the young girl under the woman's arm, Lilith caught the wide-eyed look of a young man leaning on a wooden board next to an empty pant leg. His eyes belied something else entirely, a look not unlike a few she had received from James in fact. Lilith felt her face flush slightly and they continued past, going below deck. The instant they entered the belly of the ship both Lilith and Chibs were assaulted by the same horrifying odor they experienced from the Shepherd. Remaining below deck became a severe challenge and the two searched through the compartments and cabins in a methodical sweep toward the bow as their stomachs churned from the stench. The cells were plain enough evidence, this ship was a slave hauler. The gun deck housed six cannons on each side, twelve pounders each appearing to be in worse condition than the one before it as they looked through.

"It's been a spell since they've seen any use of these Lilith, likely they've had escort ships along with them," said Chibs in his customary sailor's growl.

"This is wretched Chib, worse than the Shepherd was…" Lilith gasped, choking back gags as she spoke.

"My guess is she's been at sea quite some while lady. Africa is a month-long journey or better," he replied. "The conditions these poor souls endure…" his voice trailed off as his eyes led across the gun deck toward a cabin at the bow. "That's odd."

"What?" Lilith asked following.

"This compartment up here. Maybe it's an extra magazine or some such, it's just strange they would have it in the bow," answered Chibs as he trudged his way up the deck towards the compartment door, Lilith close behind. As they drew near a lock came into view barring the latch closed. Looking around Chibs grumbled something about shot and stepped over to the gun nearest the door. He hefted one of the twelve-pound balls that lay in a wooden crate next to the gun carriage and returned to the door. With a swift strike downwards, Chibs broke the lock under impact from the heavy cannon shot. Unceremoniously he tossed the shot to the deck with a heavy thud and removed the lock as the cannon ball rolled away. Inside the compartment as Chibs opened the door, Lilith peered into the dark compartment. There was no light except for that coming in from the lantern Lilith held. She could see gleaming chains hanging on the walls, shackles, whips. Suddenly Lilith was struck with a panicking urge, she could feel it like a lightning bolt through her legs and up her back, she wanted to run to flee these awful instruments and never lay her gaze on any like it. Chibs grumbled, something about killing the miserable sods who used these on people and Lilith felt her courage return. Her gaze fell to the floor of the compartment, where Chibs stood.

"I would bet that James will want to toss this shit overboard, but girly, I think we might keep it. It could be useful for chain shot. Have I ever told you of the time James heated chain in a fire and we defeated a Navy ship? We made him Captain after that." Lilith no longer heard what he was saying, her eyes remained fixed on the deck boards beneath his feet. Something was off about the spot where he immediately stood.

"Chibs, move." Lilith instructed.

"What?" he replied a little confused.

"Chibs, there's something under you," said Lilith pointing to the deck under him. He jumped slightly, fearing something sinister was under him and scrambled from the compartment. Looking closely Lilith could see the edge lines of the deck boards, running laterally across the deck. But there was an edge running perpendicular to the others, it seemed out of place to Lilith and as Chibs looked closer he noticed it also.

"Sweet mother's son! Lilith, good eye lady, good eye! Here, give me a hand," exclaimed Chibs. He withdrew a dagger from his belt and kneeled inside the compartment, he wedged the blade into the gap between deck boards and began to pry upward. As the board came loose Lilith reached over Chibs' shoulder to help pull the boards away. Underneath the boards lay a small compartment, but Lilith could not see very far into it from where she stood behind Chibs.

"What do you see Chibs? What's in there?" Lilith asked excitedly.

"Lilith go get James. He needs to see this straight away," he answered sitting up slightly. "Go girl, fetch the Captain!" Lilith startled a little by Chibs' short reply turned and raced above deck, grateful for a breath of fresh air. When she returned with James, Chibs was sitting on the cannon carriage hunched over facing away from them.

"Chibs!" James called, "Are you alright? What is it man?"

"Look here Captain!" Chibs gestured to a chest at his feet. The lid was opened and as

Lilith raised the lantern light up to it, she could see a brilliant sparkle of shining coin. "There's two more in there James, same size as this one."

"Chibs, are those Spanish coins?" James asked wide eyed.

"Some are. Some are French, some of them are American. There's no telling what that chest alone is worth, Captain."

"What would a slave hauler be doing carrying all this?" asked Lilith shifting her gaze between the two men.

"Well. It could be the Captain's purse." James started.

"Not a Captain of the East India Company James, this is more than any Captain could be holding for himself." Chibs answered with a grievous glare. "James, these riches were bound for someone. The crew likely had little knowledge they were even here. If they had known of an amount like this, they'd have mutinied on the bastard and this tub would be scuttled in some cove never to be found again. There's just no way."

"Who cares Chib? It's ours now! The profits of the slave trade, split amongst our crew!" exclaimed the Captain.

"James, you're not hearing me. Someone is expecting this bounty! When it doesn't arrive, there is going to be all manner of hell breaking loose. This is an East India Company ship, that means whoever is waiting on this gold holds position with the company and likely the damned Royal Navy. We need to scuttle her here and now and be gone. Out of the Caribbean and soon lad!" said Chibs, his voice betrayed a bit of panic James was not accustomed to from his steady first mate.

"No Chib, I don't think we'll be scuttling her." James began.

"Oh, damnit man! Will you hear me out? They are going to be watching for this particular ship! A brig of English make and mark lad! We can refit her and rename her, but that won't deter eyes for long! James, I'm begging you. We can take on all the souls, there's room aboard the Maiden and the Shepherd, between the two of us we can save them and be rid of this vessel. Use your reason lad!" Chibs was in a full fury now. Trying to dissuade his Captain from what he saw as an error of ego.

"No, Chibs. I understand what you are telling me. I get it clear as morning. But I have another idea," said James. His glance shifted between Chibs and Lilith and for a second, there was a devilish grin on his face and Lilith caught a gleam in his eye. Whatever thought he had cooked up; Lilith knew he would not let go easily.

"Clear every soul off this ship Chibs, just as you said. But get a prize crew aboard her, we make sail with the dawn. Northward."

22 Sept 1808
Kingston, Jamaica Colony

Dawn appeared behind the fleet as they sailed into the harbor in Kingston, sending long shadows from the tall ships stretching out ahead of them onto the gentle swells. With the Hunter in the lead they slowly eased into the broad bay towards their anchorage some distance off the long piers on the shore. An eerie calm lingered over the harbor which was usually fraught with activity no matter the time of day. Aboard the Endurance, Admiral Sharpe had come on deck for their entrance into the harbor. His keen eye missed little and he was soon on a razor edge with the change in activity. Typically, the fleet pulling into harbor would draw a frenzy of activity. Merchants and craftsmen would make their way to the piers to offer their goods and services, women would flock to greet the weary sailors and help relieve them of some of their pay. But this morning the harbor remained quiet, even for a day when they were not receiving the fleet. Something was amiss. The steady sounding of the linesmen calling out their measurements and the crisp orders from the quarterdecks of each ship was the only sound that met his ears. No music from town, no raucous brawling or shouting, no catcalls from women on shore. Elliot's face tightened and he could feel his skin prickle with goosebumps as he looked up to the fort overlooking the harbor. The battery guns were all run out.

"Lieutenant Harper." Sharpe called over his shoulder.

"Yes Sir?" the Lieutenant answered hurrying up to the Admiral's side.

"I want a detachment of marines armed and ready into longboats as soon as we drop anchor. From every ship. They are to man their watch and send me every other available marine and an officer from each vessel. Is that understood?" Elliot ordered.

"Yes Sir, straight away Sir," the young officer replied.

"And have the gun lines man their pieces. Don't run them out, they are to stand by. But I want them manned, something isn't right in Kingston."

"Aye Sir," the Lieutenant rendered a salute and hastily withdrew.

Over his shoulder Elliot looked back at the Valor following his flagship. His heart sank for Captain Grimes and he wondered if the stubborn rogue had parted from the world during their sail. No signal had yet been given from the Valor's acting commander, but Grimes' condition had seemed too severe for recovery. The Admiral could feel a burning tingling sensation in his nose, radiating up behind his eyes threatening to send tears forth. He cleared his throat and looked about the deck of his flagship quickly, he dared not show this emotion freely in front of his command. But the memories begrudgingly kept holding his mind. Shared drink and merriment with Johnathan as a young Lieutenant, hardships borne together and losses, a great many of them. Johnathan had been a Lieutenant under Elliot's command aboard the H.M.S Raven a frigate much like the Valor. He had mentored Johnathan where he could and even though the man was stubborn and prideful almost to a fault, he had developed into a masterful commander. Elliot gritted his teeth a bit thinking about his early struggles with Johnathan. He had a mind for tactics and he was devilishly clever but his sheer aggression often overshadowed his finer traits in his youth. True to form until the very end, he flatly refused to be beaten. The engagement long over and decisive as it was there was no contesting, the Valor had been defeated. Elliot chuckled a bit thinking, no, not for Captain Grimes. Not until the Valor was pulled to the cold depths would Grimes admit a defeat.

"Heave to boys! Prepare cables and anchor, haul up those halyards and make ready for longboats!" cried out a petty officer near the quarterdeck. Admiral Sharpe snapped his mind to the present, shaking off nostalgia. The present required his full attention and his command required nothing less than absolute focus. Johnathan would have scoffed at him just for the time he'd already dithered away reminiscing. Marines were already forming up on deck, preparing for the landing party the Admiral had ordered. As Elliot strode back to his cabin with the morning sun glorious in his eyes, he took note of the impressive appearance of the formation. Each marine was being picked over by a pair of sergeants ensuring they were ready for action, that bold look of determination flashing in each man's eye. Yes, Elliot thought, Grimes would have made a fine marine had he not been a sailor. The thought made him grin a bit as he passed the last of the formation and descended to his cabin. He donned his formal uniform coat and his hat, then strapped on his sword. It had been years since he had worn his sword for anything other than ceremony and tradition. Not even for the incursion of the cove had he armed himself, that's what he had marines for, but this interaction, this confrontation rather, was an entirely different matter.

"If that bloody American is there. God only knows how this will go." Elliot grumbled aloud.

"Pardon Sir?" Lieutenant Harper asked.

"Never mind lad." Elliot replied, silently chastising himself for breaking his reserve. "Actually. Lieutenant, get yourself squared away. You will be joining me, us, ashore." The young Lieutenant's face hinted a slighter shade of white.

"M-m-me Sir?" Harper bumbled.

"Yes. Strap on your sword and leave that damn sheepish look stowed away. You wouldn't want the marines to think you a coward son," said the Admiral. His disappointment was veiled behind his bearing, but nonetheless still there. Perhaps he would find another officer of Grimes' caliber, but Harper would not be it.

The line of longboats steadily made way under oar to the pier. In the lead Admiral Sharpe appeared to be doing his damn best impression of Washington crossing the Delaware, William thought. He did look formidable and that thought struck William suddenly. Was the comparison of Sharpe to Washington a sign? Was it some subconscious force at work warning him of their endeavor? William's mind was tangled, and his guts seemed to be following suit. They cramped and ached under his uniform coat as the longboats approached the pier. The sunshine was quickly warming the thick Jamaican morning to a stifling muggy, yet William's fingers ached with chill. His heart fluttered in his chest the way it had when the Valor first opened a broadside in the Atlantic all those weeks ago. The Admiral had business to deal with Governor Alton, but this was no routine calling. Their landing party was comprised from every ship at Sharpe's disposal, sixty marines and twelve officers and midshipmen.

The wooden thunk of the longboat bumping against the pier brought a flurry of action from each boat and William debarked in a scurry of activity. In short order the marines had formed into two columns to move out to the Admiral's objective, Governor Alton's mansion. They stepped off the wooden pier and onto dirt road marching their way past shops and taverns, every man well aware of the odd calm surrounding them. Windows were being shuddered along their path as the column crew up the road toward the Governor's residence and every so often a mother would be seen scurrying her children back inside. Along the left flank of the column a marketplace that typically teemed with activity was barren. This sight seemed to strike a chord with Admiral Sharpe, soon William began to hear the marines passing word to fix bayonets. Despite the sweltering sun a chill ran through him, attaching bayonets was as sure an omen of combat as the opening salvo of a bow chaser. But indeed, this would be a gritty affair, up close if it ignited and every bit as explosive.

The mansion stood tall in front of them, gated and with stone cobbled streets approaching the front. Admiral Sharp stepped to the side of the double column and let them pass until he saw William with the detachment from the Valor.

"Lieutenant Pike, I would like for you and

the marines of the Valor to accompany me inside to see the Governor when we get there. The rest of the party will secure the grounds and stand guard while we attend the Lord Governor," said Elliot briskly.

"Yes Sir. Is there anything else you need done Admiral?" Will asked, trying not to let his nerves show.

"Keep your saber handy and that imposing look, you'll do fine otherwise. If something should happen to me, get the men back to the fleet and respond accordingly," said Elliot. His impression did not change, nor his tone, but Will almost stopped in his tracks. What could he mean 'If something should happen to me', what did he expect would happen? They were going to confront a Governor suspected of crimes, yes, but not lining up against Napoleon's formations. The column finally entered the Governor's gated compound and orders began flying around. The marines fanned out and moved through the compound, cautiously checking corners, window and doors. Once the outside was secured, Admiral Sharpe, Lieutenant Pike and Lieutenant Harper made their way up the final steps to the grand front entrance. A pair of marines quickly moved in front of them and opened the double doors followed immediately by another pair who entered into the atrium.

Inside as Will and Elliot entered, they immediately noticed the mansion had been stripped bare, devoid of the excessive finery Governor Alton so famously indulged in. Paintings were gone, furniture overturned, and fixtures stripped everywhere they looked.

"What in hell?" said Sharpe, his voice betraying his confusion and an edge of anxiety.

"It looks as though someone may have beaten us here Sir," one of the marines said. Sergeant Wilson, one of the complement from the Valor was pointing out a blood stain at the foot of the curving staircase.

"So it would seem. Damn it! Lieutenant Harper get me a runner, we need to get word from the garrison and find out what the blazes has happened in Kingston." Sharpe snapped.

"Yes Sir." Harper replied slipping outside to fetch a marine for the task.

Will walked toward the rear of the house through a door where a desk stood amid a floor full of overturned bookshelves. On top of the desk lay several charts and a log. A small jar of ink had spilled over onto the desk and there was a deep gouge into the surface of the dark wood. William scanned over the charts, noting nothing of significance. He pushed one off of the next, sorting through the pile. They were all detailed charts of the coasts surrounding Jamaica. William raised a brow as an idea crossed his mind. Shuffling back through the charts he looked for the cove where Admiral Sharpe had discovered the slaver camp nearby. Twice over he sorted through the pile unable to find the chart for the location he was after. His search was interrupted by the sound of the front door of the mansion slamming open.

"Admiral! Admiral Sharpe Sir!" Lieutenant Harper called.

"What is it?" came the Admiral's reply as William ran out into the atrium.

"A column on horse approaches Sir."

"How many?" the Admiral asked quickly making his way to the door. The Lieutenant began to respond, but it was lost in Admiral Sharpe's next order.

"Form up marines. Make ready," he shouted, then turning to the marines inside the atrium, "To the roof lads, I want you to cover us from above. If a fight starts, aim smartly." Elliot stepped out into the burning sunlight to the sight of a column of men on horseback, entering the compound gates. Will fell in beside the Admiral and Lieutenant Harper as the column came to a halt. The lead rider approached to a few paces in front of the officers.

"I have brought a dispatch from Lord Governor Alton, Admiral," said the rider, pulling a sealed parchment from his coat.

"Tim, isn't it? As recollection serves, the Governor introduced us. Where is he? Governor Alton, I desire to speak to him," Elliot asked cutting straight to the matter.

"He has chosen to relocate for his own

safety. Due to your treacherous actions the colony of Jamaica is not safe," replied Tim, a grin forming with his words. "But by all means. Read for yourself Sir."

"Why would a Governor of a British Royal colony, Crown appointed, be sending his orders through an American?" Elliot said, making no move to retrieve the letter.

"To that I will not speak. Not that it is any concern of yours, you are a servant of the King, an order is an order is it not? Perhaps a more amenable commander could be found for your fleet should you continue your unruly behaviors." Tim's eyes moved upward toward the roof, "I heard I missed you in the cove. How unfortunate, meeting you there could have saved me some trouble. Now Admiral, be a good sailor and take your orders." He dropped the envelope to the ground. William could see Elliot's face flush red. He stood stone still, unmoving to the insults being laid on him by the arrogant American.

"And the fire sortie at the 'rebel camp', that was you as well?" said the Admiral, his voice lowered slightly and Will could see his anger beginning to boil.

"Yes. Your fleet performed remarkably in that respect, my thanks to you Sir. See? I can be a reasonable fellow, I just require some, cooperation. Your recent performance, however, leaves something to be desired." Tim drawled, as he spoke, the column of horsemen had fanned out making a semi-circle enveloping the front of the mansion. "I warned the Governor that you would become a problem. As usual, that fat oaf ignored good sense. I had planned to come see you in the cove, but again, we just missed each other. I thought for certain, and correctly, that you would be returning to Kingston. To confront Alton with what you found in the cove, yes?"

"You seem to have the measure of it." Elliot growled.

"Well, your interference can no longer be tolerated," said Tim, as he spoke, the bodies of four marines dropped from the roof. Tim rapidly drew a pistol from his waistband, leveled it at Admiral Sharpe and fired. Elliot recoiled and William reached out to stop his fall. Blood was already soaking into the Admiral's uniform coat as Will tried to help him get his feet back underneath himself. In a moment the grounds of the Governor's mansion became a battlefield as fire was exchanged between the royal marines and the mounted men. Tim had wheeled his horse and departed immediately after shooting Admiral Sharpe, leaving the rest of his men to deal with the aftermath. Gun smoke permeated the air and hung low over the ground; marines fell to shots as men were unhorsed from their accurate return fire. Will looked toward the road at the fleeing American, seeing a marine thrust his bayonet and impale a rider following the man. For an instant Will felt a clarity take hold of his mind in the middle of the chaos, the gunfire and screams seemed duller and he asked himself where the American could be going. Then it hit him, just as if he'd been struck by a musket ball.

"Get to the longboats, men, get to the ships! He's going to the fort! Get to the ships now!" he screamed. Will put the Admiral arm over his shoulder and began moving to the road as marines closed in to protect their movement. He noticed that Sharpe's arm had gone limp and he head hung down against his shoulder. "We're going to the ships Sir, just hang on Sir, I will get you there." No response came and Will's heart sank in his chest. He ran, heaving the Admiral with him toward the gate, through gun fire and swords and bayonets clattering. The marines had gathered around him, a far slighter number than had first marched up the road in the morning sun. Perhaps twenty remained, the rest lay scattered about the mansion grounds. Once they made their way from the cobbled street and onto the dirt road the mounted men ceased their fire. Will dared not slow his pace, unsure if they were regrouping to continue their assault.

"Get to the ships men and make sail at once! Cut anchor lines and just go, they are going to open fire from the fort batteries!" Will screamed, laboring for the breath for each word.

He could feel the pace of every man with him quicken and suddenly two marines had overtaken his hold of the Admiral.

"We'll get him the rest of the way Sir," one of the marines said.

Their race to the docks was unencumbered by any more fire from the horsemen, but just as Will's foot thudded onto the wooden pier the roar of a cannon shot pierced through the harbor. Will looked up in horror as the first shots impacted into the Hunter.

'Drowned Maiden'
22 Sept 1808
17 Degrees 13' N, 76 Degrees 12' W

The warm rays of the Caribbean sun held Lilith in their gentle grasp as she manned the helm of the Maiden. It had become her favored post on deck and as she quickly caught on needing less and less guidance and instruction from Chibs, she was often requested to the wheel. Her skill increased every day and as a convenient side effect, she was learning sail patterns more intimately and understanding them far better than when she had worked the deck or aloft in the rigging. An adjustment from the helm to the wind would work so far as the wind stayed consistent, any change of the wind relative to their course would require repositioning sails or resetting the pattern entirely. After several changes Lilith began to see a pattern to Chibs' orders. She began to predict, often correctly, Chibs' next order to the hands. It gave her a swell of pride and the feeling of belonging while at the same time the glorious sensation of freedom. When Lilith was not at the helm or engaged in another task she often lingered on the bow of the Maiden, looking out over the water, watching as the hull sliced through the blue green Caribbean. Gulls overhead and dolphins frolicking off the bow made an almost fantastical surrounding for a girl who had only known dirt floors, fear and suffering. Her heart soared higher than the mast tops. No thoughts of the future crossed her mind, the worries and sadness for her mother seemed to fade with each passing day. Lilith had found something she had relished after her entire life. She had a home on the Maiden, she had family with her crew and the protection of a fearsome band along with their captain.

Gently rolling waves and a constant wind out of the southwest made their sailing almost leisurely. The fleet of three ships was tacked onto a northerly course that James had described as 'waving the prize right under their smug noses'. He hadn't revealed his plans to Lilith, nor did she expect he would, but Chibs seemed to have his reservations as much as he tried to hide it. The wealth they had discovered aboard the Gazelle was beyond imagining, enough for every soul aboard the fleet to live comfortably for the rest of their days. It seemed madness to tempt fate any further, Chibs had insisted, but James would have none of it. He wanted to punish the slavers, lay their ships along the bottom of the sea and wet his sword in their blood. He had devised a plan to do just that and northward they sailed, destined for another engagement. The Maiden sailed in lead with the Shepherd abreast of her, the Gazelle followed along often it was everything their prize crew could do to keep up with the pair of frigates. The Africans who had been freed from the Gazelle were quartered now between all three ships. After being fed and well treated some began to lend into the work aboard ship. James offered passage to the nearest port for anyone who wished to depart, but that seemed to Lilith to ring hollow. Even if he delivered them ashore with provisions and perhaps even weapons, it would be only a matter of time until they found themselves in the custody of slavers. Lilith knew, from firsthand experience, as she readily told all of the freed captives, their greatest hope at freedom from bondage was the Drowned Maiden.

    A slight shift of sea current prompted Lilith to make a correction, it was minor and required no sail adjustment. Looking aloft as she moved the wheel expertly, she watched and shifting her glance between the compass in front of the helm and the lofty top gallant sails she made her correction while keeping her sails full and taut. The procedure had become second nature, repeated so many times a day it no longer required active thought. After her adjustment Lilith looked over toward the starboard rail and noticed one of the Africans they had taken on. He was leaning awkwardly on a makeshift board crutch, hobbling along next to the tall wiry white man that had come aboard with him. The young man was dripping beads of sweat and grimacing in pain, but stubbornly trudging onward under his companion's watchful encouragement. She watched as they made progress up one rail, across the stern and back along the other, walking several rounds of the deck before coming to a rest beside the helm.

"A few more days my friend and you won't need any help from me," the tall thin man exclaimed.

"I can walk with this. But I want to run, I want to climb and swim and run," replied the one legged African.

"No. Omi, I'm afraid running isn't in your future. You may learn how to swim or climb without your leg, but I don't see how you could ever run," the man replied, adjusting a set of wire rimmed glasses up his nose and wiping his brow with a dirty, stained kerchief.

"You did this. You took my leg from me. Now what do I do? Hobble on this for the rest of my life!" the African replied, shaking the board crutch in his companion's face.

"I've explained this to you Omi, it was your leg or your life. I am terribly sorry for the pain it's caused you, but that's far preferable to not breathing."

The young man slumped from his crutch onto the deck of the ship, looking exhausted and hopelessly depressed. Lilith looked on, silently admiring his tenacity while holding in a grimace for his obvious pain.

"I think you are brave," said Lilith. Her words floated across the deck like a strong favorable wind, filling the young man's sails. He looked over to Lilith and then back down at the deck.

"What is brave about not having my leg?" he replied.

"It's not missing a leg that makes you brave. It's the fact that you lost your leg and yet you refuse to give up. Some of the others told me you killed your captor's captain after he shot your father, that took courage." Lilith answered.

"I was not brave. Just scared and angry."

"Oh, but you were. In fact, all the braver because you were scared. There are grown men with both their legs who would not attack a ship's captain. You fought one who held you prisoner and defeated him. That is courage," said Lilith, looking over as he raised his eyes again. "My name is Lilith. What's yours?"

"Omibwe," he answered.

"I think you are brave Omibwe." Lilith encouraged. "There are scores of sailors missing limbs. Some captains even."

Omibwe stood, fueled by the attention of the beauty he had admired from the moment he first saw her. Now she was paying him compliments. The doctor stayed at his side as he made his way over next to the helm.

"How long have you been a pirate?" he asked.

"Ahh, two months, I think. I'm not completely sure. It feels like forever since I ran away." Lilith answered.

"Where did you run away from miss?" the tall man in glasses asked. Lilith looked over at him awkwardly, cocking her head and giving him a sideways look. His French accent skewed her countenance against him before she even really considered why.

"A cane plantation. In Haiti," her reply came in a curt tone.

"Oh lovely. I have wanted to see Port-Au-Prince and…" his rambling cut short as Lilith's right hand drifted from the wheel to the hilt of a sword at her side.

"I said nothing of Port-Au-Prince. Why would you? Where are you from Frenchman? Why do you have so many questions for me?" Lilith demanded. Her voice had become cold and cutting in an instant masking the flash of fear she felt that somehow this man had been sent after her.

"No, dear, I… I only meant to say Port-Au-Prince among other places I desire to see and explore. I've no interest in your past beyond conversation I swear it," the man answered, stammering out his words quickly as he backed away. He did not see Chibs approach behind him or notice until his back bumped blindly into the barrel-chested sailor.

"What's got you in a fit doctor? Lilith, did you frighten him?" Chibs poked, chuckling.

"He's asking too many questions." Lilith replied, replacing her hand back to the helm and her eyes to the compass.

"Not a wise thing to do aboard a pirate vessel Doc, best leave your inquiries alone until the crew gets a better feel for you. Myself included." Chibs intoned. He turned to Lilith, "Miss, I think we ought to expand our fencing lessons, if you're not opposed."

"What do you mean?" she asked, her eyes unmoving from the course ahead.

"We should have a few of these new folks. We are bound for a fight at some point and I think you've got a good enough handle, you can help me show a few of these fine folks what I've taught you." Chibs answered.

Lilith's eyes moved aloft, she adjusted the wheel slightly and a long pause went by. Then she pointed over to Omibwe, his eyes widening in alarm.

"Omibwe learns to wield a sword Chib. He

has the sand to fight with one leg and he hasn't even been taught yet. If you'll teach him, I'll help," she answered, a beautiful smile broadening across her face.

"That's a deal little lady," said Chibs with a wide grin as he fiddled with his pipe. "But you'll have to promise not to scare the life out of our new doctor just yet. We could be needing him."

"Needing me? I was under the impression I would be transported to my original destination Sir!" the Doctor interjected looking quite disheveled.

"Now what made you think that Sir?" Chibs asked flatly, his eye never shifting from the task of filling his pipe.

"You did. You told me I would be let off in Martinique at the earliest possible convenience."

"Ah. You seem to misunderstand doctor. I said as soon as we make port there. Well, I guess I did fib a bit, mostly in jest doctor. We have no intentions of sailing to Martinique, by all means, if we pass close and you desire to disembark then you are free to go. As a matter of fact, you're free to go now if you'd like. Au Revoir, I think it goes, enjoy your swim," said Chibs as he struggled to contain a belly laugh.

"I see. Well in that case, I could stay on until you pass near any French port."

"That you could doctor and we're only too glad to have you. It's handy to have a decent sawbones around when shot starts whizzing through the air and such.", Chibs continued, "The Captain has plans to skirt the cove again and wave the 'Gazelle' in those slave smuggler's faces. Likely they'll pile out right into our teeth. We'll keep you under good employ then Sir."

"I see," the Doctor's reply came feebly.

22 Sept 1808
Kingston Harbor, Jamaica Colony

"Pull! Heave men put your backs into it! Pull for your lives!" William cried out, urging the men rowing each of the longboats. They were in a race with death itself, rowing against their own fates. The longboats pulled away from the pier under plumes of seawater spraying from the near misses of the cannon fire from the fort battery. Men screamed, screams of fear floated above the calm waters of the harbor interspersed with the pleading cried of men encouraging one another. William struck a different tone than the others, he felt no fear that morning. With the cannon shot flying through the air, sizzling and whistling far too close for comfort, amongst the thick clouds of smoke from gunpowder and flame, William felt no fear. Through the chaos of the continuing barrage, through the losses of the initial engagement earlier that morning and the ensuing whirlwind, William felt a sharp and burning anger combined with a distinct sense of purpose and direction. When the Admiral had fallen, he became the senior officer present and immediately the sailors and marines and had looked to him for direction. William had not hesitated; his decisions came to him with clarity and resolution he had not experienced before. The men surrounding him were relying on him to make the right choices, his actions and chosen course would determine all of their fates.

The Hunter had taken the first hit from the battery. As they rowed towards the fleet in a fury several more direct hits had sent wood fragments and men flying from her deck. William looked on, helpless to stop the barrage as round after round impacted into the Hunter's deck and along her starboard rail. As the longboats neared, he could see the Hunter's gun ports opening and her cannon muzzles emerging to return fire. Every man looking on felt a spark of hope with each emerging cannon, knowing that return fire was the truest hope they held to slowing the onslaught. "Come on gents, run the elevation up and let fly! Come on, come on, what's taking so long?" William muttered to himself. His words were cut short by another thundering report over the harbor and a shower of shattered wood from the side of the Hunter. The impact crunched home sending a bone cringing wave through every man in the fleet, Will hunched down low in the longboat as the men rowing paused momentarily to see the deadly result. A waft of smoke began to billow from the Hunter, first from the hole of the impact and then in great plumes and clouds from gun ports and hatches. Anywhere smoke from below decks could escape became a thick cloud of churning acrid black smoke rushing forth. Every sailor looking on knew, these were her final moments. Several men aboard the Hunter leapt overboard, fleeing the flames that were now engulfing her in a desperate attempt to survive. An explosion followed, sending massive wooden chunks whizzing through the air, lifting the deck of the Hunter and seemingly splitting the vessel in half. Her masts toppled and stay lines snapped everywhere, the shock wave that permeated the sailors in the longboats could be felt down into their bones. In a matter of minutes, the only trace the Hunter had been afloat in its position moments ago was burning lamp oil on the surface and a scattered mess of flotsam in the water she had just occupied.

  The barrage from the fort continued without even the slightest pause. Their next target was the Bayonet, who had been anchored only a few hundred yards further out than the Hunter was. William bit his lip in apprehension, watching as the Bayonet elevated her guns as high as they would go to return fire. A round from the fort impacted the surface of the harbor sending a spray into the air short of the side of the Bayonet. "That's it lads, here's your chance, fire! They haven't got you dialed in just yet. Fire, boys, come on, come on FIRE!" Will found himself shouting across the water between them. A long moment of silence ensued and the men aboard the longboats, still furiously rowing toward the fleet began to wonder if the crew of the Bayonet had given up hope to abandon ship. Then, as it seemed they would never fire, the Hunter's battery erupted in a solid uniform roar as she let loose a broadside. Will turned to the fort as their longboats were approaching the bow of the Bayonet, desperately hoping their volley would impact somewhere that would effect the battery. Shouts and cheers erupted from the Bayonet and the longboats as a cloud of smoke and dust erupted from the wall of the fort at elevation with their gun line.

"That should slow their battery! Keep firing! Keep firing!" Will shouted up to the deck of the Bayonet as his longboat passed on the far side. Two of the boats with them had been sent from the Bayonet and those men climbed aboard with reckless abandonment to aid their crew in counter firing against the fort.

The remaining longboats rowed on, beating exhaustively toward the Endurance and the Valor. Only a few hundred yards of open water stood between them and the Endurance, which was now adding her gun line to the fray sending a succession of single shots at the fort. Her fire was precise and effective, erupting clouds of dust and debris from the fort. William, elated to see effects on the target from her gun fire, realized quickly that their efforts would be in vain if they did not make sail out of the harbor and soon. Another crashing impact sounded behind them as the longboats approached the Endurance announcing that the fort's guns were still operational despite the counter fire. William looked on to the Valor and saw she was under sail, grudgingly turning to exit the harbor before the firing of the fort turned on her as well.

"Look there boys! Lieutenant Shelton has the idea, let's get aboard the Endurance and get the ever-living hell out of here!" William called out for all the longboats to hear.

"Sir! The Bayonet! We can't just abandon them!" a sailor replied, looking up at Will with a forlorn expression.

"It's likely that they are lost already man. The best we can do for them is not to squander the time they are buying us," said Will. His voice fading into a tone as low as his spirit, he looked back to the Bayonet. Still standing their ground in the harbor, the Bayonet defiantly returned fire with another broadside against the fort battery. She was listing heavily, and smoke was rising from her decks, it would not be long before the fort battery no longer considered her a worthy target. They would shift their firing on the Endurance soon and Will did not intend to remain by idly like a sheep for slaughter.

The longboats clattered against the Endurance's hull as the men aboard scrambled to board her. William wasted no time, issuing a bevy of orders to get them underway.

"Cut away those anchor lines and let fly the main and foremasts. Main sails, top sails and tacks, hard larboard until we can tack her over." Will shouted on deck over the sound of firing being exchanged between the fort and the Bayonet. He leaned over the ladder well leading below deck and yelled down to the gun crews, "Starboard batteries, larboard batteries, make ready!" The answering echoes of his orders being repeated sounded back up from two decks of cannon crews. Will shifted his attention up to the bow, watching closely as the sails filled to his orders. The helmsman expertly came across the wind and just as Will had hoped, filled their sails. The ship lurched forward as she came under the force of her filled sail building speed slowly but surely. When the Endurance reached the midpoint of her turn, Will walked to the ladder well and waited. As soon as she completed her turn and the larboard battery aligned with the fort he screamed below to fire. The reply came back in an ear shattering roar as the full broadside fired. The Endurance rocked as two decks each fired fourteen guns sending twenty-four-pound cannon balls hurling toward the fort. A pattern of smoke and debris erupted from the fort wall eliciting a wave of victorious shouts and jeers from the deck of the Endurance.

"That'll fix the bastards!" Lieutenant Harper cried.

"It will be a disruption, little more. Get the hands ready, I want every stitch of canvas ready to fly when we reach the mouth of the harbor. The Valor is in no shape to be going alone and she has a lead on us." Will sharply replied, cutting the young officer's celebratory tone. "Get to it Lieutenant, we haven't a moment to waste and each moment we have was purchased in blood." Will almost did not recognize the words coming from his mouth as his own, it felt as if he spoke for the late Admiral and Captain Grimes as well as himself. His decisions were framed only in light of the survival of his crew and their effect on the enemy. He looked out over the fantail at the Bayonet in her final moments of defiance against the fort and its guns. Her listing had worsened, in her state she would be unrecoverable. Thick clouds of black smoke were the harbinger singing her death as desperate sailors resigned to abandoning ship. She did not explode as the Hunter had, Will thought it likely her magazine had been engulfed by seawater slowly invading her hull. As the Endurance, ran out of the harbor Will witnessed the agonizing end of the Bayonet, both burning and drowning while her hull resigned into the sea.

His heart felt low, as low as it had ever been. A knot in his throat formed as he turned and saw a group of the crew gathered around the body of Admiral Sharpe. Will wanted to approach, he wanted to console the men who had served with the Admiral far longer than he, but his legs refused to work. The thought of Captain Grimes laid up in his hammock, surely, he wouldn't last much longer. His condition had improved slightly before Will had departed on the sortie with Admiral Sharpe, but the outlook of his survival hung by a thread and would only be further jeopardized by their desperate flight from Kingston. Will's eyes glossed over, welling up with tears he could not hold back. He had taken orders to the Valor with high hopes of someday earning himself a command, this was not how he had envisioned it would come to pass. Deep in his guts he felt utterly hopeless and unprepared, any blunder he made moving forward would be measured against the command of men he thought he couldn't possibly hope to emulate. The breeze urged Endurance along and in less than an hour's time she came abreast of the Valor. Will forced himself to the rail and looked over the vessel. She was still in rough shape, sailing but not like she should. Her larboard gun line was still in tatters, only four of the fourteen pieces still workable. She needed refit in a proper port and resupply long before that could happen.

"Lieutenant Pike Sir! What course do you intend for us?" Shelton called out over the small expanse of sea between them. Will pondered for a moment, holding his breath as if it would churn along the gears of his mind faster. He could not chance another engagement until the Valor was in fighting condition again. Straying too close to any French colony was risky and there was still the matter of the two pirate vessels they had the engagement with by the cove. Will didn't know if the American had any naval power to go with his fort or his horsemen, but it was worth considering. Nassau was too far and required them to sail too close to too many French ports. St. Kitts lay over a week's sail away, that too was close to Martinique. There was Barbados, though as soon as it came to mind Will dismissed it as too far away. Standing at the rail of the Endurance, looking over to Shelton, he realized it had been long moments since the young man shouted his inquiry. Damn it all, Will thought, exactly as I feared they look to me for direction and I am japing over at him like a fool caught in a trap. Just call a heading, call a heading and make a plan below in the chart room, he told himself.

"Make your heading east by southeast. I will find a port for us to refit the Valor." Will called back.

"What happened in Kingston Sir?" Shelton asked.

"Nothing good lad. I will explain everything when we make port, until then you had best keep Valor on course ahead of us. Stay leeward if the wind shifts so we may assist you if necessary. Do you have any news of Captain Grimes?"

"He lives, but he is not well Sir. I fear he won't survive much longer." Shelton answered.

"Please signal if he passes." Will requested. The words almost caught in his throat. If. If he passes. Even a lay man could see by looking at the captain's wound that he was overdue to depart the living world. But in some small way Will was holding onto hope that somehow, by some miracle he would pull through.

Chapter 9

H.M.S Endurance
24 Sept 1808
17 Degrees 38' N, 76 Degrees 32' W

Dawn approached sending fingers of yellow light slicing high into the darkness, the glow of the sun just under the horizon heralded its return to the sky. Just past four bells William had awoke in the Admiral's cabin. It felt odd to him and he wrestled with pangs of guilt for occupying the deceased man's place. He rose from the hammock and washed his face in the basin. He reached into his linen shirt and was pulling on his boots when he heard a commotion above deck. Furious footsteps followed and Will heard a whistle, almost immediately he could feel the Endurance change course. "What in god's name?" he said aloud to himself. He rushed to the door and pulled it open to find Lieutenant Harper approaching.

"What is the commotion Lieutenant?" Will asked.

"Sir! Man overboard, spotted off the starboard side!" wheezed Harper, attempting to catch his breath.

William was off like a bolt of lightning up the ladder well, he raced on deck and up to the bow. A group of sailors were clustered around heaving on a line over the rail. Will skirted around them looking over shoulders and elbows to catch a glimpse of the soaked sailor. After a moment of jostling around Will looked and saw another form still floating in the water. A white linen shirt and pants, blood stained with a fan of long hair haloing the man's head. It took a second, but the identity registered with Will sending him into a panic.

"Captain!" Will cried, he grabbed a stay line and vaulted himself up onto the rail.

"Sir!" one of the sailors behind him yelled. But it was too late, Will launched himself into a dive, entering the water just feet from where Captain Grimes floated limply.

Will surfaced looking around, he pulled his hair away from his face and reached out for Grimes, pulling him near.

"Captain, Sir, are you alright?" Will asked spitting seawater as he spoke.

"I'm fit for tea with the King lad." Johnathan answered, laboring his words out. "We just fancied a swim."

"What happened Sir?" asked Will, he lifted Grimes' head up slightly to keep it out of the water.

"Cobb. Cobb's mutiny…" Grimes faded out of consciousness.

"Throw me a line!" Will cried up to the sailors on deck. With lifeline in hand and a dozen sailors heaving them up, Will had his commander aboard the Endurance. The sailors relieved him of Captain Grimes and lay him on deck next to the other man they had rescued. Will hunched over the two men, Lieutenant Shelton lay next to Grimes both men unconscious. Shelton still bleeding from a number of wounds. A boiling rage rose inside of Lieutenant Pike and he looked up over his shoulder into the rising dawn. The shimmering sunlight danced along the water, shining brilliantly into his eyes. Squinting and blocking some of the light with his hand Will could make out the silhouette of the Valor under full sail. She was listed slightly from the wind and making good speed.

"Many things I could say of Cobb, but he is an able sailor, damn." Will growled to himself. "All hands, full sail and beat to quarters, run out those chasers!" Will ordered as he stood to follow the sailors hauling the rescued officers below deck. "Fetch me when we're in range, if she turns, if the wind shifts, anything," he said to Harper and disappeared below.

  The rhythmic rocking of the ship did little to hinder the aging doctor in his examination and treatment of both men. Occasionally he would beckon Will to assist in some small way, holding a lantern, helping remove some article of sea-soaked clothing that was a hindrance. Will felt utterly helpless standing and watching. What little he knew about wounds was of no use in a room with a man who had quite literally been practicing medicine since before Will was born. After about twenty minutes of looking over both officers, the Doctor turned to Will with a stone expression.

"This one will live," he motioned to Lieutenant Shelton, "The Captain however, I'm not sure how he is still alive. He has recovered somewhat from his blood loss, but the infection is advanced. If it were in another part of the body amputation would be his only hope and still overdue. He may survive the day, not much longer."

"Thank you, Doctor. Please excuse me, if you would Sir. I'd like a few moments alone with them." Will replied, desperately trying to shrug off the doctor's prognosis of Captain Grimes.

The array of glass windows across the rear of the cabin began to shine with daylight as Will sat silently looking over his fellow officers. Captain Grimes lay mortally wounded, Admiral Sharpe dead by the American's hand, his contingent of marines was cut by two thirds in the engagement in Kingston. Half the fleet was lost in the harbor and now the Valor taken by mutiny. How quickly the Caribbean had chewed through them, Will thought. The first engagement nearly broke them, leaving the Valor in shambles. She still had not been fully refitted. The fact that she was making speed now was a testament to Cobb's seamanship. There was no denying, Cobb had a great deal of knowledge and skill for sailing. But his honor, that was another matter entirely. There were no doubts in Will's mind, Cobb had sown dissent amongst the crew since the exchange outside the cove. Having half the fleet gunned down by a British colonial fort before their very eyes only played further into his hand. Without question, he decided, there are men aboard following Cobb under false assumptions. But the frigate, even wounded, would still be capable of sailing circles around the cumbersome line flagship. Her larboard battery was in shambles, but the crew could, given enough time in fair seas, transfer some of the starboard guns over. Even at half power, with a proper commander, she was still dangerous. Will's mind ached with the possibility of engaging the Valor, men with whom he had served, many if not all would die in such a battle. How was any of this to be explained upon his return to England? A rogue Governor? An American conspirator leaving two ships sunk and mutiny aboard a third? Will felt as though he was drowning in despair. The words of the Admiralty board in London crept into his mind, *You are not yet ready for a command of your own*, they had felt like a hammer blow that afternoon in the roasting oven of the board room. Here, in the late Admiral's cabin, thousands of miles removed, the words stung more than ever.

Lieutenant Shelton came to first, a fit of coughing rousting him awake. Will grabbed the young man's hand and knelt at his side.

"You're alright lad, relax." He said, easing the Lieutenant back into the hammock.

"Will?"

"Yes, you're aboard the Endurance. My lookouts saw you in the dawn, thank god, any earlier and we'd likely have missed you both. What happened?" asked Will.

"Cobb happened. They organized a mutiny, I tried to fight them Will, but he's turned too many. They took the watch and locked the marines into the hold, when I awoke, they stormed the cabin. I didn't stand a chance Will." Shelton rasped.

"Ok. Ok lad take it easy now. Cobb's had his fun, now we'll see if he's got the stones to weather the storm he's just whipped up." replied Will.

"He's got enough to sail her Sir, but he can't fully man the gun lines at the same time." Shelton reported, is voice cracking to a whisper.

"Good. Fine job Lieutenant. You rest now, we'll see to the mutineers." Will eased the young officer to lay back into the hammock and turned for the hatch. He paused for a moment, looking over the pair. Shelton's wounds were not too serious, he should recover, but Captain Grimes should already be gone. The fact that he had survived as long as he did had given Will slight hope that the man would recover and plot their course out of this mess. "You would know what to do Sir, I am out of my class," he muttered. Captain Grimes stirred a little in his hammock and Will moved to his side.

"That's horse piss Will. I've no clue what you should do, nor what I would do. But, I have some advice for you." Grimes rasped out, his voice a mere whisper.

"What is it Sir?" Will pleaded, desperate for guidance.

"Do what you know to be right lad. Whatever this Governor is doing, he must be stopped," he answered.

"I've been wondering Sir. What if, well, what if this Governor isn't acting alone?" Will pressed.

"I've thought that too Will. How deep does it go? No matter, King and Country, all that, to hell with it. Piss on them. If the crown is somehow in league with this, I don't have an answer for that. Do what you know to be right, that's all the advice I can give you." Grimes said, grimacing as he finished.

"Rum Sir? For the pain?" Will asked looking around the cabin for the bottle he had seen earlier.

"No, don't waste it on me. I won't be much longer, and I know it." Grimes said with a slight wave of his hand. "Make sure you run that Cobb through when you get to him Will. A pistol shot is too dignified for a mutineer, run him right through his belly with your sword. You tell him I'll see him in hell for the rest of his penance."

"I'll do that Sir. Get some rest." Will replied. His bearing failed him as he turned to leave the cabin, fearing this would be his last talk with his commander. He departed the cabin to return on deck, hoping the wind would carry away the tears from his eyes before anyone could see them fall. The blurry outline of Valor's sails was pushing ahead of them on the horizon. The distance between them was slowly increasing, even under full sail the Valor would run out of their line of sight before evening fell.

'Georgia Spirit'
24 Sept 1808
17 Degrees 25' N, 75 Degrees 57' W

Tim Sladen scanned the eastern horizon through his telescope, scouring for any sign of a sail or mast. Since his first introduction with Admiral Sharpe at the Governor's residence, he had watched as his carefully constructed system came undone. The satisfaction he had felt in killing the Admiral had been an immense release of frustration, only to be replaced with yet another disappointment as he watched two ships slip his trap and exit the harbor. The ships at his command were privateers, originally hired to transport slaves from his holding camp in Jamaica to the American south and a few select destinations in Europe. He had chosen what he deemed as the finest as his impromptu flagship the 'Georgia Spirit'. At the head of a fleet of three ships he sailed in reckless, desperate pursuit to prevent his undoing.

The hunt for those remaining vessels consumed his every thought, making even the most basic of tasks seem heart wrenchingly urgent. If news of the true nature of his operations were revealed, he would be finished. It would be embarrassment at the highest levels, treason, heresy. The economy of the American agricultural machine in the south would grind to a crawl, costing him and countless others untold amounts of money. He had been tasked with assembling a covert network to continue the slave trade. France and Great Britain had both outlawed the acquisition and transportation of slaves from their native lands, it was only a matter of time until the slaves currently held would be ineffective for profitable operation in agriculture settings. So, his benefactors had retained him, at great expense, to ensure that their interests were safeguarded. A fortune had been spent soliciting cooperation from likely detractors, to little effect, Tim thought to himself while gritting his teeth.

Below deck in the hold of the Spirit, Governor Alton sat in a cell, naked and shackled. Tim had decided the pompous Governor could only be counted on to act in his own self-interest. Given the nature of his knowledge, that made him yet another liability. Yet he could still prove useful, unlike the Admiral, Governor Alton could be manipulated to do whatever Tim needed of him. That so far, had held as reason enough to keep him alive. If all else fails, he thought with a morbid grin, I could ransom the pig to the Crown and make an escape. As Tim lowered his glass from a weary eye, the Captain of the Spirit approached.

"Mr. Sladen, I fear they may have too far a start for us to catch them. Is there a destination you believe they could be headed for? Perhaps we could out navigate them," the Captain offered.

"British ports most likely. Nassau, Barbados, somewhere they could reinforce and refit. I'm afraid that my knowledge of these matters is limited, I'm not a sailor by trade." Tim answered in his gentle drawl.

"Barbados has the largest garrison, although St. Kitts is closer. We can hold this easting for a while, but if they lit out for Nassau, they're as good as lost to us Sir," said the Captain, hesitating slightly as he broke the last bit. Tim turned and looked the Captain dead in the eyes with an unbreaking stare.

"Failure here is not an option Captain. We will absolutely find those two ships and leave both of them at the bottom when we are done. That is the only outcome that is acceptable and that will be the only outcome where we survive. But I promise you, Sir. If we do fail, you will be going before I do. Do I make myself clear?"

"Yes, Yes Sir," the Captain replied with a stammer.

"I'm going below to pay our honored Governor a visit. Please inform me immediately if there is a sighting Captain. Keep your heading east, let's presume nothing about their destination yet." Tim snapped curtly.

"Yes Sir," the Captain's reply came. Drawing looks and raising a few eyebrows amongst his crew.

Below deck, Tim walked down a narrow corridor leading to the cell holding the Governor. As he approached, he could smell the rank odor of waste and sweat, the heat coupled with constant motion and the foul smell brought a wave of nausea. Tim stepped in front of Alton's cell, hanging a lantern on a hook outside the iron bars. The Governors figure sat slumped on the floor, pale and naked. His waste bucket had tipped with the motion of the ship and the foul contents covered the floor where he sat. Alton stirred for a moment when the lantern light spilled into his cell and he looked up through squinted eyes to identify his visitor. Tim saw his face was a mess, dried vomit streaked his face and clung to the stubble that had replaced his shaved and powdered look.

"You are a sight, Lord Governor." Tim mused.

"I feel it." Alton remarked. His tone was surrendered, missing the superiority and disdain Tim had grown accustomed to from him. "How long do you intend to keep me prisoner Tim. I don't know how much more of this I will survive."

"Oh, I can't say for sure. But you will survive Governor. You have my assurance of that, you are in fact no good to me dead." Tim drawled slowly. He took great pleasure in seeing the condition of the dignified Governor, it seemed to bring him solace from his current predicament.

"This whole ordeal, this entire thing has turned into an utter disaster Tim. What could I have done differently? Honestly, Tim? You blame me for this, but what could I have done differently?" Alton moaned before retching onto the floor.

"You should have brought that damned Admiral to heel or replaced him as I suggested. Your stubborn, pig headed ego has purchased you this fate Governor and I feel absolutely no pity for you. This all could have been avoided had you just replaced the Admiral. We would be sitting on your balcony right this moment enjoying a fine cigar and discussing whatever ridiculous topic you desire. But we are in fact in a very different situation and I have a question that has been smoldering for a couple days now." Tim drawled slowly, deliberately while measuring the effect of every word as it hit Alton.

"What is it?"

"The timing which Sharpe's fleet occupied my cove. It begs asking, Lord Governor. Did you betray us?" asked Tim.

"Betray you?" Alton cried, "Whose house has just been ransacked and robbed? Which one of us is currently covered in his own shit? No, Tim, if one of us is guilty of a betrayal, it is not me."

"Are you suggesting to me that I have done something which I did not warn you about? No, Governor, you were given every opportunity to correct this situation before it escalated out of control. I failed to see your true plan. You were one of three men who knew the destination and expected arrival of the 'Gazelle'. You were one of only three men that knew of the payments she holds. The chance arrival of your fleet into my cove the night before she was expected? I am many things Governor Alton, but I am not a fool." Tim hissed, his anger gathering as he leveled the accusation.

"No. No, Tim I swear it. It wasn't me. I had

no idea what he was doing. I was wrong, I should have replaced him, you're right. But I had no idea, you have to believe me." Alton pleaded, shaking his hands against the chains he was shackled by.

"Do I? And why is that? How do you think your pathetic pleas will hold up in front of The Order? Will they keep you from losing your head?" Tim snapped.

"You wouldn't. Tim, no…"

"What choice have you left me? Their payment has not arrived and is likely lost because of your reckless incompetence. We have now lost two shipments of slaves to Georgia and the Carolinas and as we speak there are two navy ships with a full day's sail ahead of us containing men who know entirely too much. You have left me with one course of action Governor, which I intend to execute with everything I have left in me. If it means I have to do it my god damned self, I will." Tim's voice elevated as he spoke until he was shouting.

"There is nothing left for me then Tim. Why don't you just kill me and be rid of the encumbrance." Alton said, tears welling up into his eyes as he looked through his cell bars at Tim.

"As much as I would enjoy it." He paused, sneering at Alton's plea, "If The Order does not accept the facts as I lay them out, I intend to ransom you for my safe escape. Don't get your hopes up, they will desire your silence far more than they value your life, Lord Governor," said Tim. "Perhaps if I can recover their payment and silence any outside parties, maybe things could be different…"

"I cannot help you Tim, I have no idea where they sail for. I have no clue where the Gazelle is, nor what has happened to her. As I said, you would be served just as well by killing me." Alton moaned in reply.

"Like I told you, Lord Alton. Not yet." Tim drawled as he stood up. He plucked the lantern from its perch and made his way back up the passageway, observing his usual custom of skipping any formal farewells.

Above deck, Tim had just taken his last step off the stairs leading up from below when he noticed the group of sailors huddled together near the bow. They stood near the starboard rail looking out over the seas to the south. Tim raised a brow and he curiously walked toward the group. "Over there! There's another one I know I saw it!" a sailor called out above the chatter of the group. Then from high aloft in the crow's nest a call came down, "SAIL HO! On the southern horizon!" Through the heat of the Caribbean sun Tim felt a chill flash through his veins, his pace broke into a run.

"Where is it? Show me," he snarled at the group of sailors, fumbling in a pocket for his telescope.

"There sir, right along four points off the bowsprit," a sailor replied, loosely gesturing out over the sea. The description did little to aid Tim and his inexperience with anything nautical revealed itself. He extended his glass out and was scanning the horizon almost due south, far off the direction of the sighting. Looks and grins were being exchanged at his expense, as though he hadn't noticed. Finally, he scanned far enough eastward he was looking at an azimuth about forty-five degrees from the bow. A white square floated above the water, faint even through the lens of his telescope. Four points, he thought to himself making a mental note, a forty-five-degree angle. He watched the small patch of white, desperately begging his eye to coax whatever information he could glean from the little white patch of sail far across the water. Through the distance he could not decipher even their direction of sail much less size or origin of the ship. It pained him horribly, but he decided to ask one of the sailors.

"Can you make what direction she is headed?" Tim asked in a low growl, warning them against taking further humor at his expense.

"Likely she will get closer before we lose sight of her sir." One of the younger sailors informed him, "She's either headed east or north with the winds from the southwest as they are. But we'll know her direction after watching her for a while. If she gets a bit closer, I can tell you for certain sir."

"Right. Good, please do that. The minute you have a good fix on her, I want to be the next man to know." Tim replied as he squinted back into his telescope. For the next several hours he was immovable from his post on the starboard rail, raising his telescope to his eye every few minutes to glimpse at the white square off in the distance.

The Black Fleet
24 Sept 1808
17 Degrees 8 minutes N, 76 Degrees 3' W

"Sails on the horizon!" the cry had come from lookouts aloft hours ago, setting the crew to preparations for engagement. Since then a steadily increasing tension had built. Lilith could feel it, hanging in the air and dancing between the masts, injecting every task with a sense of urgency. The wind had held steady out of the southwest and she kept her course steady while awaiting orders from Captain James. Nowhere amongst the crew was the excitement more palpable than with the Captain. The instant the call had floated down from the crow's nest, James armed himself and furiously assisted in battle preparations everywhere he could. Cannons were loaded and run out while arms were disbursed through the crew and staged on deck for quick access. Chibs appeared from below decks where he had been assisting the gun crews with their loading, a cloud of pipe smoke rolling behind him as he walked about the deck. Orders flew around the deck of the Maiden, sending hands new and old alike scurrying through preparations until finally no tasks remained.

The sails loomed larger and larger as the hours drug by and through the course of time it became apparent to Lilith that these ships were not the same ones they had engaged near the Jamaican cove. James gave the order to don the colors as they drew ever closer and Chibs raised their black banner above the stern. As it unfurled into the wind all eyes examined the ships for a reaction. Lilith took her eyes off course for a moment, stealing a glance up at the banner as she always did when it was run up. As she did, the lead vessel altered course northward.

"Captain!" Chibs cried out, "We've struck a chord in that lead crew, they are breaking to run!"

"Aye, So I see. Hold her steady now Lilith, are you with us girl?" James replied, noting her gaze upward.

"I am Captain," her sheepish answer came back. She felt a bit embarrassed to be caught off focus.

"Good, they have three vessels and we'll need every hand to have their wits about to come out on top. Watch those ships carefully and I want you to make a hard larboard turn the minute one of them comes about toward us. The wind favors neither of us at the moment, but one wrong move could give them the upper hand." James said to her. As he spoke the lead vessel had come back onto her original course.

"They're not sure what they want to do Captain." Lilith observed.

"I see. That will work in our favor. Hold her true Lilith." James said with an endearing smile. "I'll be close by my dear, worry not."

"I can take care of myself Captain." Lilith shot back with a smile and a glance from the side of her eyes.

"Oh, I don't doubt that miss. If we are forcibly boarded, you are on your own, it's every man and woman for themselves at that point as they say. I only meant that once the maneuvers begin, I will be close at hand to help you position the ship exactly as I want it. That is all." James said lifting his hands by his shoulders with his palms forward. "This won't be a sail by broadside. We will likely have to do some quick handling. But, if you insist on doing it all alone, I suppose."

James started to step away, but Lilith reached to stop him, grabbing his shirt.

"No, James, that's not what I meant," she chided back.

"So, then you want me close to you?" he

asked raising his brows with a widening gaze.

"Yes, yes, of course I do."

"How close Lilith? I wouldn't want to make you…" He began to reply, until his shirt collar was pulled, and Lilith planted a lingering kiss on his lips. She pulled away and set her gaze forward again to her task.

"Lilith, I, I…" He stammered.

"Shut up, don't ruin it." Lilith said cutting him off, again.

The two stood in silence for only a moment as they approached cannon range from the ships.

"Captain!" Chibs called back from the bow, "They're flying American colors."

"Just as well. Send a warning shot from the bow and one from larboard battery Chib. Perhaps their courage may waver again."

"Aye Captain." He replied and then turned to crewmen around him, "You heard him lads, one off the bow and one from the larboard battery, lead gun. Let's get to it!"

The first cannon shot from the Drowned Maiden echoed out over the expanse of sea in between the two squadrons of ships, followed shortly by another. Lilith was always struck by adrenaline from cannon fire at sea, it sent adrenaline shivers through her nerves and a chill up her spine even though she had heard it before. The bone rattling thunderous boom caused her to flinch slightly and the acrid smoke that followed seemed to penetrate her nose and eyes making them water. The lead ship of the enemy squadron held a steady course, unwavering through the cannon fire. Lilith adjusted the wheel ever so slightly to keep the sails taut and looked over as the Unholy Shepherd loosed several warning shots of their own. Though the ships were still several miles apart, Lilith began to wonder if both commanders were so stubborn as to let their ships collide before being the first to act one way or the other. Men are such stubborn creatures, she thought, they would let the whole world burn around them before allowing anyone think them weak. At first Lilith was amused by the thought, then the more she thought about it she became anxious and angry. The ships were drawing nearer and still James gave no orders. Lilith looked at the approaching enemies, then at Chibs and James, then over to the Shepherd and back to the enemy again.

"Are we just going to crash into them? James?!" Lilith rose her voice in despair. James walked to the starboard rail without giving Lilith so much as a glance and waved his hat at the Shepherd. She immediately made a hard-larboard turn, two men at her helm to execute, passing so close to the Maiden's fantail that Lilith worried for a moment if they would collide. As Shepherd crossed just behind Maiden's wake, James walked back over toward Lilith.

"Hard to starboard miss," He said gripping the wheel along with her, "Now!"

Together they hauled on the wheel turning the Maiden as sharply as she would go until she sailed almost due east.

"James, if they turn south, won't they have the weather gauge on us?" Lilith asked with a concerned tone as they reeled the wheel back to centerline.

"I'm setting a trap dear. Watch and learn." James answered with an unwavering confidence. "As soon as they see the Gazelle follow behind us, they won't be able to resist. Watch, you'll see."

Lilith cut her glances in between the enemy ships and the Gazelle, making her far wider turn to follow behind the Maiden. Just as sure as James had said, moments after the fantail of the Gazelle was visible to the American ships they turned to pursue. Lilith stole a glance back to the Shepherd to see that they had beaten their way to the west and would be able to turn in behind the following Americans.

"Once they close distance we will turn southward. They've taken the bait, full well knowing we are sailing under black banners they have altered course at the sight of the Gazelle. They are slaver ships; of that I have no doubts." James said with a devilish grin beaming across his bearded face.

"You are clever Captain James." Lilith

replied.

"Clever and handsome Lilith, you forgot handsome," he chided still beaming from the kiss she had stolen earlier.

"So I did, apparently humble isn't on your list though." She retorted playfully, rolling her eyes a little.

"Never has been!" he laughed "A humble Captain? On a pirate vessel? Confidence wins the day Lilith; a humble commander begs for a sword in the back and to be left afloat in his ship's wake."

"I see, but he's not too proud to be manhandled by a girl?" Lilith teased. She had embarrassed him a little earlier and she knew it.

"That was not fair miss, I wouldn't dare resist against you, and you know it," he replied smiling even broader.

"Well, if it wasn't fair then I suppose it would be wrong of me to repeat it," she stated flatly.

"I suppose it would. Best not do it again." James jested and made off toward the bow. He almost escaped her swinging slap against his shoulder, but not quite, and he continued on towards the bow with his mischievous laugh floating over the deck.

The sun was edging its way below the western horizon and the deadly dance between Captain James' fleet and the Americans had begun. Just as James had predicted, the ships eagerly turned in pursuit of the Gazelle, all but dismissing the two frigates flanking her at great distance. From her vantage at the helm Lilith was in the thick of the unfolding. She overheard nearly every command, every exchange between James and Chibs and listened intently when both men voiced their thoughts aloud. The moment the lead American ship had turned in pursuit of the Gazelle, she could feel shift aboard the ship like a change in the wind. Commands and answers became excited and hurried, James' demeanor turned cold as ice, his smile fading into stone faced resolution. Daylight was fading and darkness could be a great equalizer at sea, obliterating both weather and strategic advantage if an opponent could properly harness it. It would be less than an hour before the American ships overtook the Gazelle and tension was thick in the air. Gun crews all stood by at the ready, men aloft prepared for any order, the deck hands watched while the Gazelle slipped closer and closer to the grasp of the American fleet.

"Captain, they are going to take her. Shouldn't we do something?" Lilith asked.

"Let's hope they do Lilith and we are doing something. Don't worry about the lads aboard, they'll be slipping off soon. A little plan Chibs had when we first took her. You'll see." James answered, his eyes never leaving the lights of the Gazelle. The breeze gently whispered in across the deck of the Maiden, carrying the sounds of the choppy waves and the wash of the sea as her hull sliced onward. Then faintly, Lilith could hear another noise, an odd out of place creak and splash. Lilith strained her ears, thinking she must just be misplacing a sound from the Maiden, then it grew slightly, a creak, splash, creak, splash. She turned to say something to Captain James only to see Chibs standing next to him at the starboard rail, he was looking her way and held a finger over his lips in a hushing gesture. The noise ceased, followed by a dull clunk and within moments a group of exhausted men were climbing up over the rail.

"We've set it just as you ordered Captain, it should ignite when they open the hatch below," one of the men said through ragged pants as he was doubled over with his hands on his knees.

"Well done boys, my thanks to you. Extra rations and extra rum for each of these men Chibs." James said, his smile returning wildly.

"Aye Captain. A job well done indeed, let's hope it works." Chibs replied, ushering the sailors forward.

James turned back to Lilith, still smiling.

"Ready on the helm Lilith, they'll have her any moment now," James said in a steady, reassuring voice as they watched the dark silhouette eclipse their view of the Gazelle.

H.M.S Endurance
24 Sept 1808
17 Degrees 25' N, 75 Degrees 57' W

Darkness swept in around Will as he stood on the bow of the Endurance, far off in the distance the sails of the Valor crept further and further carrying his hopes of catching them away with every passing moment. His anger had subsided long ago, being drowned into a sea of sorrow and hopelessness. The tears he had been fighting no longer came and all that remained was a fatigue unlike he had ever felt before. Will glanced down at a coiled line at his feet, thinking back fondly to his early days as a midshipman when he and the other young officers would take turns stealing away naps atop a coiled bow line in the wee hours of the middle watch. The memory brought him a flash of joy and his reminiscing continued as he thought back to his introduction to the Valor. Captain Grimes, such a bold and skilled commander, he wished he had more time to learn from the man who was nearing his grave. Three French ships, he engaged three French ships, Will thought, some commanders, most in fact, would deem it reckless wanton glory hounding. But with Johnathan, even his brashness seemed measured, there was always a bigger plan.

Even the engagement which wounded him so grievously, at first look he had acted rashly to engage but on deeper examination he had acted to draw the pirate ship away from the Admiral's flagship, keeping them free to maneuver from the cove without being engaged.

William's thoughts kept him pinned to the forecastle well after losing sight of the Valor. He pondered over his situation, the Valor, the Governor and the American. His thoughts were interrupted by the unwelcome arrival of the ship's doctor.

"I am sorry to inform you Sir, but Captain Grimes has passed," he stated flatly.

"Right. Ok, thank you. I will see to preparations for burial at sea." Will replied, surprising himself with his manage on the emotions washing through his mind.

"If I could be so bold to suggest Sir, but wouldn't Captain Grimes have preferred the frivolities of a service at sea be forgone in the effort to retake the mutineers?" the Doctor said struggling his words out.

"You are right Sir. I can almost hear his admonishments now, we will bury the Captain just as he would have us, underway and in pursuit." Will replied finding his resolution.

"You'll find your way Sir, you have a streak of Johnathan about you, it is unmistakable," the doctor said as he patted Will on the shoulder before scuffling off to return below deck.

The yoke of command, he had wanted a command of his own since his youth. He had envisioned it as a shining moment on his career, bestowed upon him by a respected commander such as Johnathan or perhaps a Lord Governor in some embattled port. He had even considered it would come as the result of some battlefield action or attrition, but never like this. Every bit of circumstance leading up to his current role had been either grave misfortune or the dishonorable deeds of others. He felt lost and alone, torn between doing his duty and the compelling urge to turn his ship toward England and never return. He had no family awaiting him, his father died in the service while he was still a boy and his mother of cholera shortly after he had become a midshipman himself. There was no wife waiting his return, nothing to run home to but the familiar comfort of home. Home, Will thought, I don't even have a home. Some boarding house or another while I await orders to put to sea. No, the Navy is my home, the Valor was my home and that bastard Cobb has stolen it from me.

"We will not be returning home. Our place is here, I will stay until I spill that mutinous cretin's guts all over the deck of the Valor or he does so to me." Will said aloud.

"Well put Sir." A sailor replied, startling the Lieutenant.

Will turned to make his way toward the aft castle, he desperately needed something to eat and some rest. As he passed the foremast, he overheard a conversation among the deckhands, a salty old hand was spinning some yarn about seeing the mythical kraken right here in the Caribbean. Even in pursuit, even through adversity and combat and loss, sailors will be sailors, Will thought with a smirk. He remembered a similar tale he'd heard Cobb reciting to hands aboard the Valor, a ghost ship, he remembered. He'd had gullible young landsmen just taken on from the press watching for their lives and jumping at their own shadows all through the long middle watch that night. Will stopped in his tracks, that was the night they had come across the squadron of French ships. Until this point, Will had attributed them locating the French that morning to blind luck, or even divine intervention. It had been Cobb's clever tactics and an alert watchman that saved them from being caught at the mercy of a squadron, outgunned and outclassed. It felt as though he held a thought by a thread and pulling it could somehow unravel the gauntlet before him. Lieutenant Harper was overseeing the change of watch near the helm and Will made for the quarterdeck as fast as his legs would muster.

"Lieutenant, no bells." Will said just as a sailor was about to strike the hour. "Douse all the lanterns, no bells and no whistles."

"Aye Sir" the sailor replied.

"Sir?" Lieutenant Harper asked, looking confused.

"Cobb is a clever man Lieutenant. We outclass the Valor in gun count, weight and manpower. But an ambush in darkness could negate all that advantage and leave us exposed and at the mercy of a crew of mutineers. Double the watch and maintain course, I will be below in the chartroom, please inform me of any sightings." Will replied. His exhaustion hit as he had spoken, causing him to repeat several words.

"On in darkness then Sir, as you say." Harper answered hesitantly. Will knew the young officer's fears, they had once been fears he shared.

"Trust the watch lad, trust the watch and trust the charts. If I am not on deck at dawn, wake me." Will reassured.

"Aye Sir." Harper answered as Will descended below decks. He had intended to spend some time reviewing charts to decipher the course Cobb would likely take. But passing the door of the cabin he had made his proved impossible, his eyes were bleary and tired. The charts would have to wait, he thought, no use for them if I can't even think straight. He entered the cabin and shucked his jacket, then sat on a stool to remove his boots, the gentle rocking of the ship only increased his sleepiness. Finally, after removing his trousers and blouse he crawled into the hammock slung through the middle of the cabin. The gentle motion of the ship was tempered by his hammock, but still gave him a slight sway and stretched out in the hammock, Will finally closed his eyes to welcome sleep.

Even through his exhaustion, the wheels and gears of Will's mind ground away. It was a furious thing to him, so utterly exhausted and yet even as he lay in his comfy hammock, his brain would not allow sleep to grace him. He kept wondering on what course Cobb would sail, what his destination was. What had he told the crew? Those sailors threw their wounded Captain overboard, Will thought, it makes no difference what Cobb had told them, nor how he had persuaded them to do it. They would all die a mutineer's death, by sword, by cannon shot or hangman's noose. Their destination wouldn't be a British port, even if Cobb were so bold to attempt a masquerade in the effort of resupplying the ship, the rest of the crew would have none of it. No. They would steer well clear of any British port. Possibly he would take the Valor into a French or Spanish harbor, there was a chance with this though of being engaged on sight. Britain and France were locked in war in Europe, Spain being one of France's staunchest allies made the possibility quite real in their ports as well.

Will drifted off into sleep, the gears grinding out his plans lulling him into fitful dreams of sea engagements. The image of Admiral Sharpe's posture withering after the American fired his pistol replayed in his mind. Will knew it was coming, he had seen it before it played out in real life. Yet he was unable to alter the course of events, like a patron in a theater watching a play. The marines fell from the roof, impacting onto the ground with a dreadful thud sending a splatter of blood into the air. The American drawing his pistol, almost in slow motion. Will's entire body felt to be made of lead, impossibly slow no matter how much he tried. His voice made no sound as though it didn't even exist. Bits and pieces would replay, out of order but vividly clear. The smells were present, the same taste in his mouth, even the sounds he had heard. But every sequence of dream related to that day was followed abruptly by the American shooting Admiral Sharpe.

Chapter 10

'Georgia Spirit'
24 Sept 1808
17 Degrees 14 minutes N, 76 Degrees 8' W

The instant Tim had looked over the fantail of the Gazelle and seen her name painted in golden lettering, his heart soared. He looked again, making sure his eyes were not playing some trick on him and through the fading glow of the evening he confirmed to himself, it was indeed the missing ship, containing a massive payment for which he would be held responsible.

"Follow that vessel!" he screamed out to the helmsman, "Follow that ship, with all haste. She must not escape us!"

The Captain paced over next to Tim, a hesitant and pained expression plaguing his face.

"Sir, that ship is flanked by two hostile vessels, even if we can overtake her, we will be utterly exposed. It would be folly," he began, interrupted by Tim's dagger coming into his sight from its sheath. Tim's eyes locked onto the Captain and his lips curled up, baring his teeth like a wolf challenged over a fresh kill.

"I gave you a directive, Captain. You have been paid handsomely, should you fail your duties I will see fit to relieve you, permanently, and select a more effective captain from the ranks of your crew." Tim's reply hissed through clenched teeth, his anger and urgency boiling through.

"Yes, yes, we will pursue with all haste. Right to a watery grave," the Captain answered defiantly, "But, as you wish Mr. Sladen."

The course change came abruptly, shouted commands bounced around the deck for a few moments and the helmsman labored at the wheel. The crew made quick work of adjusting their sails to coax every bit of speed they could from the winds. Tim's morbid grin returned to his face as he watched the sails of the Gazelle, the Georgia Spirit gathered more speed and their approach quickened. It became obvious to Tim that they would overtake the ship in less than an hour. The last glow of daylight had faded, but lanterns aboard the Gazelle remained lit and with two more ships behind him, Tim was unconcerned about the two flanking vessels. He turned to one of the sailors who had paused working to take in the sight of their target as they approached.

"Go get my prisoner and haul his fat ass up on deck." Tim barked, "Dress the bastard and throw some water on him while you're at it. I'd rather not smell his shit."

"Yes sir," he replied, quickly scrambling to his new task.

Tim's eyes were immovable from the silhouette of the Gazelle, cast along the water by soft light from its lanterns. The dim light from the lanterns cast an odd glow up onto the Gazelle's main sails, outlines from a web of rigging splayed across. They looked like arms reaching up from a fiery hell, reaching toward some salvation that would not come. The smell of the salty sea air suddenly seemed like perfume to Tim's nose, the wooden deck at his feet no longer seemed as foreign. This setback would be just that, he thought, a setback. He had feared his undoing, but as long as he recovered the payment hidden within the hold of the Gazelle, he could secure his own future. Governor Alton would be another matter entirely, but Tim had never been beholden to Alton, much less loyal. When the time came, he would offer Alton up to the Order and rid himself of the ineffectual swine forever. Perhaps, he could even restart this endeavor.

    Governor Alton stumbled along as the sailor who was sent to retrieve him pulled at his bound hands. He had been given ill-fitting clothes that looked to Tim's eye to be something very near burlap in texture. Alton wore the look of a disgraced man, his station in life had deteriorated from statehouses and fine dining to wearing rags and sitting in a pile of his own feces.

"Un-hand me you son of a bitch, I am a Lord by rights!" Alton screeched furiously.

"There's no Lords in America, to me you're just a whiny fat man, stinking of shit," the sailor replied with a laugh.

"I'll take it from here sailor." Tim said elevating his voice slightly. The sailor gave a shrug and let go of Alton's shackles.

"Thank you Tim." Alton huffed, "Now could you get them to remove these? Please, Tim, I'm not escaping you with or without them."

"No, Lord Governor. I think shackles suit you for the time being and I would hate to have to kill you to prevent your escape. I'm afraid they are going to remain. Besides Governor, it's a good look for you, perhaps if you stay a prisoner you may even lose some of that excess weight." Tim jested, smiling broadly at Alton's misery.

The Governor groaned and grumbled something under his breath, unintelligible but still annoying to Tim.

"Alton, if you look just ahead of us, you will see, the Gazelle is within our grasp. I will have the Order's promised payment. Do you know what that means?" asked Tim with words dripping in condescension.

"No, Tim, I have no idea what that means. Why don't you stop clowning around with me and just bloody tell me what in the hell is going on?" Alton shouted angrily, shaking his shackles in a flare of rage.

"Calm down Governor. There is no need to

be that upset, I'll have you back down in your cell in no time. I just thought you would like to see the instant you become unnecessary." Tim quipped, smirking as he spoke.

"Un, unnecessary?"

"Yes, Governor. If I have the payment for the Order, I won't need to ransom you. In fact, they will probably greet me with open arms. I may even be able to rebuild this effort." Tim gloated.

"Whatever. Do what you will, do what you want. I don't give a damn anymore, just do it! Kill me, toss me to the sharks, drown me, whatever. But bloody well do it, I have had enough of sitting in that cell…" Alton raged, until Tim raised a finger as he looked out to the Gazelle. They were just yards from her now.

"In due time, Governor." Tim replied, "Why is there no crew on her deck?"

As they approached the Gazelle, Tim noticed the ship's wheel had been tied in place. No hands were about the deck, none aloft in the rigging. Nothing but the eerie glow of lanterns gave any clue that there was any life aboard the vessel. "Grapple lines!" the Georgia Spirit's captain called out and a half dozen sailors began tossing their grapple hooks over to bring the ship in closer. The metal hooks hit deck boards with a hollow thunk and Tim braced, waiting for the crew to storm on deck. Nothing. Sailors aboard the Georgia Spirit hauled on their lines and brought her in close. A crossing plank was secured. Tim had all but forgotten about the other ships until he heard the Captain give orders to the watch, "Be ready on the guns when we board boys, those hooligans out there aren't likely to give up their target so easily." It had never crossed Tim's mind, until that point, that perhaps the pirate vessels weren't trying to capture the Gazelle. Maybe, he thought briefly, they had already taken her.

"Captain, the Governor and I will let you handle this. The cargo I am after should be in a forward cabin on the gun deck. Let me know when you have it," said Tim closely guarding the concern that had dawned on him.

"Ok, Mr. Sladen, well, the boarding party will let you know whe…"

"You're not going over Captain?" Tim interrupted.

"Well, no Sir. A Captain stays with his ship Mr. Sladen, if something should happen, I need to be here, with the crew aboard the Georgia Spirit." The Captain explained apologetically. The Captain's answer visibly displeased Tim, but the Captain stood firm, offering no further explanation.

The boarding party moved methodically over the crossing plank, fanning out and searching over the Gazelle's deck. From the forecastle, Tim watched as the sailors slowly moved across the deck, carefully checking under her longboats and peering into her hold wells. His unrelenting stare remained as the boarding sailors opened the Gazelle's weather hatch and carefully, one by one descended below her deck. Moments drug by, Tim had to remind himself to breathe, the empty deck of the Gazelle stared back through the dancing light of the lanterns on board. The sails above flopped and snapped lazily in the wind, the wheel strained back and forth sporadically against the rope binding it.

    A shout from deep within the Gazelle sent Tim's heartbeat into a race, his mouth went dry and he stretched his spine, leaning over the rail in an attempt to hear what was going on. Running footfalls preceded a scream of "ABANDON SHIP!!" Tim wheeled from the rail, looking behind to where Governor Alton was slumped against the opposite side of the ship. Running as fast as his feet would carry him, he screamed at the Governor, "Jump, go, jump!" Alton, unaware of the unfolding events began to ease himself off the rail he had been leaning on when Tim collided with him, shoving him violently. Alton's rear hit the rail just as Tim savagely shoved him again screaming, "Get off the ship!" Both men sprawled over the edge limbs flailing into the night air, the pair hadn't broken the surface of the water when the darkness erupted into a massive explosion sending jagged shards of wood and hunks of metal flying. The force of the explosion from the Gazelle was so great it sent the Georgia Spirit reeling sideways with flames stretching high into the air licking at masts and sails. As Tim and Alton surfaced a deadly rain of debris fell, chunks of wood large and small, cannon shot, chain, ropes and planks fell all around them. Tim looked skyward to see flames spreading rapidly through the Georgia Spirit's sails and rigging, shadows of the chaos played through the smoke spilling over the rail as sailors fought against the spreading blaze. Screams could be heard from on deck and Tim attempted to call out for help, but his voice was choked out by seawater and smoke. A low whistle grew in pitch and volume until its source, cannon shot from the Gazelle ejected into the air by the force of the explosion, came crashing into the deck of the Spirit. Another, louder crash caused by a falling cannon hulk smashed through sails and yards before crashing into the deck, sending even more debris flying.

Through the pandemonium going on all around him, Tim looked around, to find Governor Alton clinging to a half-broken chunk of barrel. Light from the flames stretched out illuminating the side of the lurking pirate ship. One by one, he watched in compounding horror as its gun ports opened and the menacing snouts of its cannons protruded from each in turn.

"Governor, we need to get away from the

ship!" he cried, choking on smoke, "Swim man, go!" His plea was punctuated by the first incoming cannon shot. A plume of water shot skyward as the round impacted short of the Georgia Spirit, mere yards from where Tim and Alton floundered and scrambled in their attempt to swim away from the ship. Another shot thundered over the water, its shrieking whistle piercing into Tim's ears before impacting against the side of the Georgia Spirit. He and Alton paddled in desperation, clinging to debris for their lives. They moved along the side of the ship as it took several more impacts from cannon fire, pausing with each shot to shield themselves from the flying wooden shrapnel of obliterated timbers. Once they passed far enough behind the fantail of the Spirit to see the other side the scene was horrifying. Flotsam and flames dotted the plot of sea once occupied by the Gazelle but that was all that remained of the vessel that had just moments ago been sailing next to the Georgia Spirit. It sent a fury through Tim though he remained stone faced at their current predicament. He and his prisoner were overboard, one ship had been sunk and very soon, without intervention from the rest of his fleet, the Georgia Spirit would be following.

Tim scanned the sea northward for the vessels that were following the Spirit. He could see the hull of a ship slicing the water in approach and panic began to grip his soul.

Where were they others? Had they turned and fled? Cannon fire continued and the Spirit was taking a beating, each shot crashing its way through timbers and sending shards of wood flying in all directions. After some of the impacts screams of agony and fear could be heard rising from the bowels of the ship under barrage.

"Why are they not returning fire?" Tim raged aloud.

"It's likely they don't have enough men to by now." Alton wheezed in reply.

It burned Tim that he was bound in his circumstances to the pompous deposed official. Again, without possession of the payment for the Order, he was beholden to keeping Alton alive for his own sake. Once safely out of range from flying debris, the pair rested, bobbing along in the ocean current while the onslaught against the Spirit continued. Tim looked northward hoping to see the ship he had sighted swooping in to save them, but only found the empty darkness of the night and the sea. Helplessly they floated and waited, watching in horror as the vessel that had carried them into these waters was pummeled into a slow surrender and descent to the depths.

H.M.S Endurance
25 Sept 1808
17 Degrees 24 minutes N, 76 Degrees 2' W

William startled from his sleep to the sound of drums beating. Drenched in a cold sweat he took a second to gather his bearings, his heart was racing, and his fists were clenched so hard his forearms ached. On the deck above him he could hear the pounding of footfalls as men scrambled to battle quarters. Will pulled himself from his hammock, struggling in the dark to dress himself when an urgent knock came at the cabin door.

"Lieutenant Harper's compliments Sir, he has requested your presence at the quarter deck," a sailor outside informed.

"What is going on? Have we sighted the Valor?" Will asked, springing the door open and hurrying toward the ladder well. The sailor took off behind him, struggling to match his pace.

"An explosion, Sir. Miles to the south of us, flames were visible on the horizon and we've faintly heard some report from cannon fire. Not sure if it is the Valor, Sir," the sailor answered.

"Very well," Will turned and sprinted the rest of the way up the stairs, taking two steps at a time. He arrived on the quarterdeck to find Lieutenant Harper looking through a telescope toward the southern horizon.

"South by southwest of us Sir. It must have been a massive explosion to be heard this far away, followed by a ball of fire and now we're hearing cannon fire intermittently." Harper reported.

"Very well, time on deck and winds?" Will asked.

"Two bells in about a half turn Sir, winds still steady from the southwest."

"Damn if we're sailing in at a disadvantage. Lieutenant about face her, we'll beat our way west and turn south with the daylight. That should put us upwind from where the explosion was. If there is anything left, we can assess what happened," said William. His voice felt surer than his mind, his decision almost instinctive.

"Are we to break pursuit of the Valor then Sir?" Harper asked, lowering his voice slightly.

"No lad, for all we know that could be the Valor circling around to gain the wind on us to attack at dawn. That Cobb is a dangerous man, left to his devices. He is clever and malicious, most would be happy to take the ship and escape, not him, I believe he won't stop until he has put us on the bottom with every soul aboard." Will replied.

"Or we put him there." Harper said.

"Yes, well, that would be the idea. Let's get to it then, it's going to be a long day." Will said looking over the log to determine their position.

The bow of the Endurance swung around westward and Will took careful note of each cannon report his ears could detect. At first it seemed to be too slow and inconsistent for an exchange between two ships. Almost as if they were hearing the aftermath of a battle where one side was unrelentingly beating their enemy into shreds. Captains would often fire single guns and observe their effects carefully to conserve their valuable ammunition. One shot penetrating a ship's magazine would effectively end an engagement. Though, if the outset of their engagement was an explosion, then why all the following cannon fire? Will carefully considered the possibilities he could be sailing into, also, bracing himself for the possibility that he had just broken pursuit of the Valor for something that could be completely unrelated. A thought of the American who had shot the Admiral crossed his mind and sent a twisting feeling through his stomach. If I cross paths with that man again, Will thought while gritting his teeth, he will die at my hands. His thoughts were interrupted by more cannon fire, this time though the shots were more rapid. Then another round of successive shots echoed in over the waves, snapping Will to an alert posture, it had to be return fire. The reports of cannon fire continued as the Endurance raced her way westward. The direction of the sounds aided Will in judging his relative location to the battle taking place.

The early glow of dawn began creeping into the eastern sky when one of the lookouts cried down from the rigging.

"Sail behind us, she looks to be fleeing northward!"

Will looked out over the fantail, straining in the early light he could just barely distinguish the outline of a ship. They had no lanterns lit on deck and Will could not make out if they were flying national colors. He couldn't even distinguish the class of ship he was seeing, it was smaller, maybe a brig, perhaps a frigate.

"Helmsman come about southward, I don't think she's spotted us, but I don't want our stern exposed if she has." Will ordered, again he felt an unfamiliar confidence. His decisions felt more like finding a piece missing to a puzzle than they did carefully thought out and painstakingly weighed.

"Another sail, following the first," the lookout called down as the Endurance made her course change. Will looked again, scouring the space behind the first ship they had spotted. Sure enough, the silhouette of another ship followed along closely behind the first. The dawn grew in the east like a crescendo of light heralding the appearance of the sun and as the light increased every moment more details became visible from the deck of the Endurance. The ships fleeing toward the north were under full sail, even letting out auxiliary sails as Will examined them through his telescope. Neither ship made any indication of spotting the Endurance, their full attention seemed to be in a hasty retreat from the battle unfolding to the south.

Boom! The thundering report of a cannon from the second ship startled everyone aboard the Endurance, including Will, nearly out of their skin. The rallying dawn showed a cloud of smoke drifting skyward from the bow of the second ship. She was firing her bow guns at the vessel in front of her!

"Orders Sir?" Harper inquired with a look of dread.

"We don't know anything yet Lieutenant, hold fire and hold course. It's a matter of time until they spot us, and we'll be in the mix with the rest of them lad., Will replied.

"Aye Sir. Do you think that is the Valor?" Harper pressed. Will could hear an edge of fear in his voice.

"We can only hope lad. It would be a fitting end for Cobb to be taken unaware by a full broadside from this behemoth. Be sure the gun crews are all at the ready."

"Yes Sir!" Harper answered setting off at a near run.

Will watched the ships through the intensifying light, neither appeared to be the Valor. The second ship was being commanded by a bold and aggressive man, Will noted, her bow guns were firing as rapidly as they could be loaded, and scoring some hits from the sounds he heard floating across the water. He scanned the length of the second ship as more detail became visible, she was a frigate and under full sail. "You're damned determined to catch that bugger aren't you boys?" Will said aloud. He scanned back forward looking over the fleeing ship, she was a brigantine and there were crewmen scurrying about the deck dealing with damage from the accurate fire of their pursuers. Will looked aloft in the rigging of the fleeing ship and felt a cold streak run up his spine when his eyes fixed on the colors of the fleeing ship. Over the stern of the brigantine flapping in the dawn breeze floated old glory, the American stars and stripes. Harper returned from below to report back,

"All guns are run out and at the ready Sir."

"Very well Lieutenant." Will answered without removing the telescope from his eye. He scanned back to examine the pursuing ship again. With better light he could now see her crew clearer and they appeared ragged, without uniform, but well led and orderly. Will's heart fluttered as his eyes traced over the profile of the ship and then up the rigging at her stern. His vision caught their black banner as it fluttered in the wind, the hollow eyes of a fearsome horned skull seemed to burn right into his soul sending a stomach wrenching wave of anxiety and panic crashing over him. They fired their bow guns into the American again, prompting a creaking, groaning noise from the prey ship. The distinct crack of splitting wood could be heard slicing through the morning air and Will shifted his telescope back toward the American ship.

"God Damn." Will exclaimed as his sight lay on the American ship again.

"What is it Sir?" Harper pressed, eager to know more detail.

"They've taken out her aft mast with their bow chasers. Those gunners bloody well know what they are doing." Will answered. Then he snapped the telescope shut and stepped back from the rail, "Helmsman bring her about two points larboard. Lieutenant Harper prepare to relay fire commands." He ordered.

"You intend to engage them Sir?" Harper stuttered.

"I do, and hopefully overwhelm them with fire before they can answer now take your post Lieutenant, their stern will be exposed in minutes," said Will, his patience running out.

"Aye Sir," Harper said, his face going paler with the turn of each event.

Will had to wait only a moment for his course change to take effect and he was rewarded with the target profile of the pirate ship he had hoped for. It was something every commander strove for in combat, a shot encompassing her side and stern. With well-placed shots, her damage would be severe after even one full volley. Will's mind wandered to the American man, the image that had haunted him all night, his grotesque smirk and his smoking pistol.

"Lieutenant Harper, Fire!" Will called below.

"FIRE!" Harper screamed the command out to the gun crews on the larboard battery.

Both decks of guns opened fire, fourteen guns each, eighteen-pound guns on the top battery and twenty-four-pound guns on the bottom. The concussion was oppressive, hammering through the bones of every man aboard and rattling the ship. The smoke cloud took almost a full minute to clear and the damage inflicted on the pirate vessel was tremendous. Her fantail had taken several direct hits, as well as on her side. One large hole had been blown just above the waterline and with each wave she took on water. Screams floated up from her decks through the rigging. Will gritted his teeth and flared his nostrils as he recalled the exact feeling of what those souls were experiencing.

"Fire at will!" he screamed down toward Harper.

"Reloading Sir!" Harper replied back up, then turning to the gun crews, "Hurry lads, hurry, reload for your lives!"

Will could hear the crews sounding off below. Commands he was all too familiar with. Then in rapid succession,

"Gun one ready!"

"Gun two ready!"

"Gun three ready," commands and replies were screamed and all down the line on both gun decks gun crews came back to the ready. Then only the slightest heartbeat of pause and Harper screamed again, "FIRE!" The volley reverberated through the ship, causing it to rock slightly sideways, tilting the masts from the forceful collective recoil from twenty-eight guns fired nearly simultaneously. As the smoke cleared from his vision, Will could see the carnage he had unleashed on the pirate ship. Her aft and main masts were broken and had fallen, ripping sails and rigging, sending men from aloft hurdling toward the deck and into the water. Her battery facing the Endurance was all but blown away, massive holes had been penetrated through her side level with her gun ports and on her fantail, Will could see they had scored a hit to her rudder.

"She's dead in the water boys!" Will cried out to a mass of shouts and cheers from the crew. "That one's for Captain Grimes you bastards!" he yelled inciting another round of shouts and a roar of taunts and curses directed at the pirate ship. The shouts and jeers continued as the Endurance slipped past the rear of the pirate ship and Will examined her closely for any sign of continued defiance. As the ship's starboard side came into view it became obvious that the crew was abandoning her as they were lowering the intact longboat over the side.

"Shall we fire another volley Sir?" Lieutenant Harper asked, reappearing to Will's side from below deck.

"No. We've done her in, let the sea finish the deed," answered Will as he shifted his focus over to the American ship. From his vantage on the quarter deck of the Endurance, he watched as the American sailors labored to recover their ship. When they noticed the pirates putting to sea in a longboat several of the Americans took up muskets and began firing on them. The pirates made a futile attempt at returning fire in their desperate attempt to escape, but the accurate fire from the Americans was too much to overcome. After a few volleys of fire, the longboat bobbed along lifelessly in the current of the sea.

Will glanced over the longboat, limbs of the dead pirates protruded over the sides and its oars hung limp into the water. The sun rose higher into the morning sky revealing the scene of carnage in its bright and gory detail. The American ship slipped further north, having jettisoned their broken aft mast and resetting their sails.

"Shall we pursue them Sir?" Shelton's voice came over Will's shoulder. Will turned quickly, seeing the young officer had emerged from the Admiral's cabin.

"Lieutenant, what are you doing up here?

Are you well?" Will inquired with a concerned look.

"Well enough Sir. Please don't shove me back down into that cabin, I can't stand it." Shelton pleaded.

"No, lad. No, if you are well enough, I'm happy to have you." Will answered turning back toward the wreckage of their engagement, "As far as following the Americans, I don't know to what end. We are still bound by the articles of war and I cannot engage a vessel flying colors of a nation we are not at war with, unless provoked."

"The man who shot the Admiral…" Shelton began.

"We can't know if he is on board, nor even if he has anything to do with that vessel. We could certainly follow them, but I don't know if there would be any benefit to it. The Valor is still out there somewhere and there was another battle to our south and east. That would likely be a better course." Will interrupted.

"Something in that longboat Sir! Some cargo they didn't want going down with the ship!" called down the aft lookout.

Will stepped back toward the rail and extended his telescope. He could see nothing noteworthy in the longboat through tangled mass of perished. He handed his telescope over to Shelton, who looked through to the same result.

"Mr. Shelton, you have the ship. See the longboats are readied, I'm taking a compliment of marines to investigate." Will ordered, sending a wide smile across Lieutenant Shelton's face.

Drowned Maiden
25 Sept 1808
17 Degrees 14 minutes N, 76 Degrees 8' W

Smoke lingered over the water's surface in the morning sun, spreading an eerie thin veil over a scattering of flotsam and bodies from the sunken vessels. Flames still smoldered on several pieces of floating debris, occasionally carrying their fire to slicks of floating whale oil. The barrage had lasted long into the night and a subsequent engagement with another of the American ships had garnered similar results. The crew of the Maiden greeted the new day with high spirits and tired eyes. Though she would rather be on the helm, Lilith stood on the bow with Chibs as a lookout while they moved through the wreckage. The Unholy Shepherd had taken after one of the fleeing American ships in the darkness and James announced with the daylight that they would sail north to rendezvous with their sister ship. The fatigued crew was weary to chance another battle so soon, cannon fire had been heard to the north of them and Lilith feared they could be sailing into an engagement with the American ship instead of a rendezvous with a victorious Shepherd. Chatter she overheard throughout the crew indicated that she was not alone in her fears.

As the Maiden slid through the debris field Lilith looked over the wreckage. Burned and broken pieces of wood, shreds of sail, lengths of rope were all interspersed by the occasional floating body or body part. It was gut wrenching to the young woman to witness the carnage left in their aftermath. As they neared the edge of the debris, Lilith spotted a large man clinging to a broken barrel. She strained to see through the stinging smoke, but as her eyes found focus, she could see that he was clearly alive.

"Chibs!" Lilith said, tugging on his shirt sleeve and pointing to the man in the water.

"A survivor," he grumbled, rubbing his whiskers, "We'll haul the bugger aboard and see what he has to say for himself."

Crewmen on the Maiden tossed a lifeline to the survivor who released his desperate grip from the barrel that had kept him alive through the night. It took two tries until the hapless man could reach the line and at one point it appeared as if he would drown in the attempt, but he raised a victorious fist gripping the rope and the crew heaved to until he was close enough to climb a rope ladder they lowered. The man was in very poor shape and it took an inordinate amount of time for him to reach the deck of the Maiden. He finally climbed up the final rung, wheezing and heaving for breath on all fours at the feet of the crew who had saved him.

"Who be you?" Chibs barked at the panting man.

"M,M,my n,n,name is Geor Alton. I am the king's governor of the Jamaica colony." Alton stammered between gasps for air.

"Pleased to meet you Governor. My name is King George, and this is the H.M.S. Make Believe! What kind of a fool do you think I am? What is your name?" Chibs rasped. His face was flushing as his temper flared.

"I speak the truth to you good Sir. My name is Geor Alton…"

"Yeah, yeah and you are the kings own blah blah, whatever and what have you. I'm too tired for games." Chibs said as he turned away from the pleading man, "Take him below, lock him in the hold."

Several of the crew began to drag Alton away as he protested.

"I am the Governor of Jamaica! Treat me fairly and you will be rewarded! I can pay. I can grant pardon. Please I beg of you…"

Through the commotion, Captain James made his way forward from by the helm. He had been scanning the horizon keenly while the crew fished their new guest from among the wreckage. He strode over next to Chibs and pointed off to the northern horizon.

"There Chibs. What do you see?" he asked.

Chibs turned to see where James had pointed and squinted. A faint haze squatted over a small area of the edge where the sky met the sea and amid the bleary smudge of white and gray Chibs could make out a small white shape. He searched his pockets for a second and produced his telescope, he then fixed his gaze through it on the white shape.

"That's not the Shepherd, James. It's not that American brigantine either." Chibs replied, his look suddenly becoming even more fatigued.

"I assumed the cannon fire was from the Shepherd when I heard it earlier. They followed after one of the Americans that abandoned the fight last night. I didn't think anything of it then, but I suppose it is possible they were drawing her off to an ambush. Could it be?" James lowered his voice to not raise a panic.

"It's a possibility, sure. But likely any vessel they had wouldn't sit idle while we sunk one of their own." Chibs replied.

"The American brig couldn't have overcome the Shepherd."

"We will find out soon enough Captain. If Shepherd has been taken or sunk. Their next course will definitely bring them to us. The explosion from the Gazelle was big enough, I'm sure parliament in London probably felt it. I think we should push east, run with the wind at our backs and get as much distance between this mess and us as we can." Chibs encouraged. His face was long and weary, his voice missing the usual gusto Lilith had grown accustomed to hearing.

"We should run. But Trina and the Shepherd could be in trouble. She would sail to our aid Chib, we won't leave them to whatever fate they may have encountered." James was resolute.

"Aye Captain. I'll have the crew make ready, again." Chibs said, making his way to prepare.

Lilith, exhausted like everyone else aboard, lingered on the bow. She trusted and admired Chibs as well as Captain James, when they disagreed on matters, she found it most discomforting. There was little to be gained by inciting conflict between the Captain and his first mate, though on this particular issue she felt more aligned with James. Trina was a friend to Lilith; she was tough, and she had introduced Lilith to her new way of life. James had her heart, Chibs felt like the father she'd always longed for, but Trina was an older sister. Hard while still matronly, a friend when needed and a woman in the mix of a man's world aboard ship.

"You think we should be running? Like Chibs wants?" James asked, seemingly reading her mind.

"No. I mean, we are all tired James. I want to run as much as anyone else. But if they are in trouble, James, we have to do whatever we can to help." Lilith exclaimed.

"We will. I won't leave them to whatever fate throws their way. But I do hate to defy Chibs' advice, if it weren't for him, I would never have survived as long as I have." James looked troubled, conflicted about his decision.

"I treasure Chibs as much as any of you, James. But I think you are making the right choice. Whatever the horizon holds for us, we can't run forever."

"Just what does the horizon hold for us my dear?" James asked, locking his eyes onto hers. "Does the fair Lilith intend to spend her days sailing with a pirate crew?"

"I can't say James. Forever? No. But who knows what the future holds? For now, I am here. I will live my life as each day comes until I have a choice to make, I suppose." Lilith replied breaking her eyes away, back to the sea.

The two remained on the bow, watching the sail on the horizon without further exchange. Lilith felt a desperate anxiety to find out the fate of the Unholy Shepherd. Even under full sail, their progress felt like an agonizing slow crawl leaving nothing for Lilith to do but torture herself with the possibilities of what they would find of their sister ship.

Battle Wreckage
25 Sept 1808
17 Degrees 14 minutes N, 76 Degrees 8' W

Consciousness came and went, the gentle roll of the sea occasionally brushed debris into the set of planks Tim had latched himself to, awakening him for fleeting moments before he drifted back into another realm. The smoke streaked his face and stung his eyes when he had tried to open them. Exhaustion permeated his entire body to the point where simply staying atop the planks was all he could do. When the sun had lifted from the horizon in the early hours of the day it brought a welcome warmth from the chill of the constant breeze over his soaked clothes.

When the shadow of the pirate ship passed over him, he only noticed at first the missing warmth. Forcing his eyes open yielded only a glimpse of a moving wall of wood, he dared not move. If he was spotted, surely, they would fish him up only to end him, or worse, he would be taken captive. Sudden shouts from the deck above announced they had spotted a survivor of the carnage. Tim's heart exploded in a succession of beats that each felt harder and faster than the last. He remained still, silently hoping they had mistaken one of the floating dead for a survivor.

The Governor's driveling pleas for

mercy met Tim's ears and a flame of anger kindled within him. One of the men mocked the Governor's pleas and Tim almost smiled. He took a small comfort knowing that man would continue to suffer. Suffer you worthless incompetent swine, He thought, you've blundered everything and it was all handed to you so neatly. All the man had to do was follow instruction, do what he was told and collect his obscene payment. But he had been too timid to reassign the admiral, too greedy to keep from interfering in matters far above his understanding and too stupid and slow to execute anything with effect. Let him rot in a cell aboard the pirate ship, Tim resigned, I am as good as dead anyway. The floating corpses would soon bring sharks, if they didn't kill him the exposure certainly would.

    The shadow passed from Tim as the pirates made sail again. His planks bobbed gently with the gentle swells of the sea. He drifted, through the cluster of flotsam and dead just as helplessly as the thoughts clouding his head. The Order, his meeting in America with their delegation. The task he had been given and all the riches he had been entrusted with, reputations and livelihoods hung in the balance. Power, those who held it and those who sought after it. Was this his end? Was this to be the culmination of everything he had worked for? The comforting warmth of the sun had grown more intense and its rays soon became another torment against him.

Tim felt the edge of the timbers he lay on and shifted his weight back toward the center. His movement shifted him just too far and the small platform that had sustained him from drowning capsized. Jolted from his lethargy by the sudden drop into the water, he struggled to recapture his tiny wooden savior. Opening his eyes, Tim looked around. Above him, just out of arms reach the planks bobbed along in the slight chop on the water's surface. It looked like wrinkled glass, a ceiling reflecting the brilliant Caribbean blue sky with sun rays visibly protruding down into the water illuminating various shades of blue that darkened as he looked down further, until directly underneath him all that was visible was the abyss of the deep. It was near the edge of the darkness that Tim's eye caught a glimpse of movement. He adjusted his focus and saw the figure move again, his heart fluttered and out of the corner of his eye he caught another moving figure. With what remaining strength he had, Tim pulled hard in a desperate attempt to reach the surface. His lungs burned, pulsating, crying out for a breath of air. His second stroke yielded him the surface and he gasped in air, just as quickly as he had surfaced, he found himself back underwater beneath a small swell. He pulled again, refusing to forfeit to the deep and his head broke free again. He scrambled, paddling himself to the floating oasis of wood. When his fingertips had just brushed the edge, just as he felt his salvation was at hand, something brushed against his leg. In a wild panic, Tim fluttered his feet kicking at the water until he had a solid grasp of the lifesaving timbers. He clawed at the wood, pulling his torso up as far as he could, reaching up he took hold again and with what seemed the last of his fading strength pulled himself the rest of the way up.

    The small wooden platform barely longer than he was tall and only inches wider than his frame was enough to keep him from drowning, but just barely. With his weight on it, the chunk of deck stayed just below the surface. Every movement he made threatened to capsize him again. Propping up his head slightly, Tim searched around for any signs of other survivors. Broken barrels and other chunks of wood were scattered all around him, smoke still rose from several spots of still burning oil on the water's surface. Every direction he looked Tim found more corpses, none that he recognized, most were burned or disfigured beyond recognition anyway. As he shifted his head sideways to look out over his shoulder, the water's surface exploded in a rush of gray motion. A corpse that floated only yards from his improvised raft disappeared in a violent splash. Panic grabbed Tim like a giant hand, squeezing him at his armpits until he felt he couldn't breathe. He began to pull his limbs away from the edges of the wooden planks, only to feel his balance shift, then he froze. Every fiber in every muscle of his body tensed, his senses sharpened, and his heart raced. A shiver seemed to grip his spine in defiance of the heat from the sun and every perceptible movement flooded his body with another wave of panic.

    It seemed that he lay in a state of hyper alertness for hours, while the sun plotted its course toward the western horizon. His entire being was beyond exhaustion, staying balanced on the wooden boards had drained him to the point he was sure that if he slipped over again, it would be his end. Each time he began to relax his anxieties he would hear thrashing somewhere in the water surrounding him. He dared not move, even the slightest lean to gain perspective could tip his fragile balance and the platform keeping him afloat was his only barrier against whatever predator the seas had sent. He could only lay along the boards, tortured by the thought of what awaited him should he capsize again. All through the late afternoon he listened to the sporadic thrashings as the corpses disappeared from the surface down into the depths. Eventually he succumbed to his exhaustion, drifting out of conscious thought.

PART THREE
A Fitting Betrayal

Chapter 11

H.M.S Endurance
25 Sept 1808
17 Degrees 32 minutes N, 76 Degrees 12' W

Rowing into the floating carnage left behind by the pirate ship they had just sunk gave the men in Will's longboat a transparent uneasiness. At sea, all sailors are subject to many of the same risks and hardships. It fosters a kinship unlike other occupations, even between enemy nations and enemy vessels. The same crew that would blow your ship full of holes and set it ablaze was just as apt to risk their own lives to rescue imperiled men in a storm. It didn't help, William thought, that sailors are the worst kind of superstitious. He had long ago learned not to fight against it, it was often better to work around the lion's share of their ideas about luck and bad luck.

"The dead care nothing for your fears boys. Pay them no mind and they will do the same in return." Will said softly, trying to ease their gaunt expressions.

"There's women mixed up in them Sir. Have you ever heard of a woman pirate?" a sailor asked while pulling on an oar.

"Yes actually. There were several notable female pirates in the last century." Will replied as he looked over the body of one they passed. "But I'm not sure I've heard of an African lady pirate before. Hold stroke lads." Will looked over a woman, floating face up just feet from the longboat. She was young, perhaps in her early twenties, with a shot wound high in her abdomen and another near her shoulder. Her face had a strong beauty, even in death with her soaked braids floating around her head like Medusa's snakes, she had a defiant look even in unconsciousness.

"Fish her over to the boat," said Will, drawing a bewildered look from all aboard.

"That'd be frightful luck Sir..." said the sailor who had been asking about women pirates.

"You wanted to know about a female pirate, now you can have your look. Just pull her in next to us with an oar, I want to see something." Will said.

"I'd thought you would've probably already seen it by now Sir," another sailor jested, drawing a nervous chuckle from several others.

"Just bloody well pull the woman's corpse over to the damn boat." Will said resisting a laugh himself.

The sailors awkwardly reached out with two oars and as gently as they could, moved the body closer in toward their longboat, shuffling in their seats to the far side as she drew near. Will, reached down and took the woman's hand in his, pulling her arm slightly out of the water. He gingerly pulled back her loose shirt sleeve, exposing her wrist. Closely inspecting the wet skin of her wrist revealed scars, not fresh scars, old wounds from being bound that had healed long ago. Gingerly, he lowered her arm down and then pulled up the other repeating his inspection to reveal similar scars. As he was about to lower her arm back down, Will felt the hand in his grasp tighten with such slight force that it might have been a whisper. It was like he had been bolted by lightning he almost threw the arms away it gave him such a startle.

"She's alive!" he exclaimed. "She's alive, help me haul her in lads, come on."

The crew in the longboat tried as gently as they could, to lift her from the water. But as they lifted her from the tug of the sea the woman let out a painful groan.

"It's ok miss, we'll get you some help." A sailor said.

"Why would we nurse her to health? So we can hang her as a pirate?" another quipped, cutting him short.

"She is an escaped slave lad." Will said in a stern tone, "She's probably been through hell and back. We will nurse her to health if we are able. On my order, if you need a reason, but I would expect your humanity would suffice you."

"She's a pirate Sir. Slave or not, if we don't hang her, it's our necks," the sailor grumbled.

Will felt his face flush red, the line of conversation was gradually raising his blood in anger. He reached to his waistband and pulled his cutlass from its scabbard.

"She stays aboard, on my order. Now row for their longboat so we can finish this sortie lads." Will said in a low tone.

Looks were exchanged aboard the longboat, some of the men seemed unsure of their situation, others seemed unsure of the challenges their Lieutenant was receiving. Will reminded himself that these men, most of them, were not of his crew from the Valor. Even if they were, the Valor had mutinied, tossing Captain Grimes overboard to leave him for dead. As the longboat approached the boat of dead pirates, Will felt completely and utterly alone, clasping the grip of his cutlass as if the crew would rise against him at any moment. Among the dead bodies, most of them African Will noted, was a chest. The sailors painstakingly hauled it aboard, its weight requiring the full strength of two able bodied men. The exchange of begrudged looks halted when Will lifted the lid of the chest, his eyes growing wide in glorious surprise.

The afternoon sun cascaded into the chest as Will lifted the lid open, throwing the bright glow of gold against his face. Looking up at him from the inside of the chest was a stack of brilliant gold bars. Will reached in and hefted one, its weight cemented what he was experiencing as genuine and not some wild fever dream from the hot sun.

"Dear Christ in a manger," a sailor said over his shoulder. "That's more gold in one place than I've ever seen in my life!"

Will was dumbfounded, he had never seen that much gold, collectively, in his life. He reached in and examined another bar, each one felt to weigh about five pounds. The chest was full of them, Will's head started to spin as he mentally tried to tally how much value sat in front of him. He could buy a ship, an entire fleet with the contents of this chest. It was a fortune that would last a man his entire life and that of his children, likely even his grandchildren. This was the kind of fortune men would kill for, risk life and limb to steal away, or even mutiny against their commander over.

"Row for the Endurance men. We need to get out of here." Will ordered giving the handle of his cutlass a squeeze.

They rowed in silence toward the Endurance, through the debris and floating dead. There was no more grumbling of bad omens or cursed luck from the crew as flotsam and dead bodies bumped against the hull of the longboat. Will caught several looks between the rowing sailors that set his hair standing. The chest they had discovered was going to be a problem. At best, the position he was holding aboard the Endurance was fragile. In a matter of a few days all the senior leadership of the fleet had been lost. If Will could not maintain order aboard the Endurance, things would devolve into chaos beyond recovery. As they approached the shadows of the masts on the water's surface Will looked aloft to see a scurry of activity. Sailors in the rigging were pointing to the opposite side of the ship and shouts drifted down. The bell aboard the Endurance started a frantic succession of rings, followed shortly by drums signaling all hands to their battle quarters.

"Something is wrong," Will said aloud, his heart sinking.

"There must be a sail visible on her other side. Another damn ship to fight." grumbled one of the men pulling on the oars. "Another engagement and in less than a week since you clambered aboard in place of the old man, Lieutenant."

"Funny how a chest of gold makes mouths and hearts bolder. Tell me sailor, what exactly are you getting at?" Will snapped, fearing what the man would answer with.

"The Admiral is dead, as is your Captain, we were fired on by our own countrymen from the fort and now we're chasing a vessel that you say has mutinied, rescuing pirates out of the drink. Why would the fort open fire on us, unless you officers committed some treason? How far exactly do you think you will push before we deal with you Sir?" the sailor raised his voice, standing in the longboat, his long oar still firmly in his grasp.

There were three armed marines aboard the longboat as part of William's compliment, part of their duties charged them with maintaining order against mutiny. Will looked over his shoulder to one of the marines as the sailors ceased their rowing and stood around him. His eyes met the barrel of a musket.

"They have a point Lieutenant, why don't you put your sword down before this gets out of hand," the marine said.

"This only ends one way men." Will started, gently lowering his sword to the deck of the longboat.

"Your end is what you should be considering," another of the sailors quipped, "When we get back aboard, I say we clap this fool into irons and lock him below, head for the nearest British port and get this mess all sorted out. It'll be the gallows for him when the Crown catches up to him."

"Or perhaps, for you. Once you are discovered as a bloody mutineer." Will seethed, unable to check his tongue.

The longboat clunked clumsily against

the hull of the Endurance and the men aboard made quick work of attaching the lift ropes. In moments the craft was being heaved up while the crew aboard turned the capstan, it's lock clunking with every step. Will's furious outrage grew with every thud of the capstan as they ascended up toward the deck of the Endurance. Captain Grimes had implored him to do what was right and he now sat in the midst of the second crew to mutiny against his command. He felt completely and hopelessly alone. He looked down at the unconscious pirate laying at his feet, if he surrendered now, she was as good as dead.

The deck rail of the Endurance crested into view and Lieutenant Shelton stood with Lieutenant Harper watching as the longboat came level with the deck. Will stood helpless to warn his fellow officers with a musket still trained on him.

"Sail on the horizon Sir, we can't identify her colors... yet." Shelton started, losing his voice as he noted William's expression and saw the demeanor of the rest of the longboat party. "What is going on here?"

One of the sailors quickly disembarked, scrambling toward the ladder well and disappearing below deck. The marine who had his musket trained on William edged out from behind him as the remaining sailors unloaded the chest from the longboat.

"Lieutenants, I'll ask you to place your

officer's swords on the deck. Carefully. Or Lieutenant Pike here will be missing a large portion of his head," the marine said. His voice was calm and even, only a few of the nearest on deck noticed the situation that was developing. Shelton and Harper both unbuckled their swords from around their waistbands, easing them to the deck. Will turned his head slightly to look at the marine who held him at gunpoint from the corner of his eye.

"Are you quite sure the rest of the crew will be going along with this?" Will asked, shifting his eyes from the marine behind him to another that stood just out of reach at his side.

"I'm sure enough, but it won't matter once we've clapped you all into irons," his hissing reply came.

Will caught a look of hesitation from the marine by his side, the man was unsure, unconvinced of the events unfolding around him. That cemented Will's decision and he sprang into action. In a burst, Will threw his head aside of the musket barrel and grabbed it in his hand. He then delivered a donkey kick into the man's gut while heaving forward on the gun. The marine let out a guttural cry and stumbled backward, tripping over the longboat's edge and fell over the side. Will continued his momentum forward and swung the musket's butt hard into the jaw of the hesitating marine beside him, sending him sprawling. One of the sailors swung an oar toward Will in a savage arc. Will managed to retrieve his sword from the deck of the longboat and met the oar with his blade, inches from the side of his head. He countered with a thrust and ran the sailor through with his sword eliciting a shriek from the man that sent every eye on deck to the longboat.

Will withdrew the blade, kicking the sailor to the deck of the boat and adjusted his grip on the musket.

"Lieutenants retrieve your swords, this isn't over." Will shouted as another sailor in the longboat grabbed for an oar. Will caught him with his blade at the nape of the neck, splitting his collar open with a gush of arterial blood spewing forth. From below deck a bevy of armed sailors came rushing out, led by the disgruntled sailor who had first scrambled off the longboat. He raised a sword, pointing it at the officers.

"Whatever treasons you have committed to destroy this fleet, it ends here and now!" he cried out, "Seize them!"

His last word was annunciated by the musket in Will's hand, he leveled the gun and fired it like a pistol into the mutiny leader's chest. A moment of calm punctuated the deck of the ship as the puff of gun smoke cleared from the breeze. The man dropped his sword, clutched his chest with a look of pale dread and fell to the deck. Chaos followed as the crowd of sailors behind him rushed forward. Swords clattered and gunfire erupted. Will swung the barrel of his musket into one of the advancing men with a solid impact on top of his head and then ran the edge of his sword across the man's throat. Shelton had engaged two men with swords and was handily keeping both on their heels. Lieutenant Harper met another with his cutlass and delivered a swift kick to the man's knee, taking him to the deck while William caught a sword swing toward Harper's neck with his own blade. Marines came from below deck adding to the fray, instinctively circling around to defend the officers.

"Get the woman from the longboat and get her into the aft castle!" Will shouted to Lieutenant Harper, "I'll guard your flank, lad, come on!"

"Woman? What?" Harper looked frantic and then seeing her laying in the longboat snapped to his orders in a mad sprint.

A mad frenzy ensued as Will, with a handful of loyal marines and sailors guarded Lieutenant Shelton's movement into the great cabin of the aft castle, carrying the unconscious woman in his arms while sword and bayonet clashed all around. Will slammed shut the door behind them and turned to face the onslaught. More sailors had been rallied against them and the deck was littered with bodies of the wounded and dying, made slick from bloodshed. Scanning the situation Will's heart sank as he took stock of their dilemma. There was only a handful of men aiding him, a dozen at most and with each passing moment it seemed their odds at survival slipped away while more sailors would take up arms against them. A sailor scrambled forward and grabbed the rope handle on one side of the chest dragging at it with all his strength. Will stepped over to the sailor and with an odd calm swiftly kicked the man in his jaw, sending him sprawling over backwards. The sailor raised an arm up as will reversed grip on his cutlass and plunged the sword down through the man's chest. The sailor clawed at the blade with bare hands, slicing them to ribbons while Will leaned hard downward.

A sudden eerie calm settled over the deck of the Endurance as pistols and muskets had all been spent. The clash of sword and bayonet hushed and eyes across the ship shifted to the wails of the sailor Will pinned to the deck with his sword. Will looked up from the desperate sailor's eyes to see crew all around gaping at him. His fury only grew in intensity and in his rage, he kicked over the chest of gold bars, spilling them across the deck.

"All these lives lost, needlessly and over what? Some gold?" he screamed, glancing out to the sail on the horizon, "and even as we fight amongst ourselves, enemies draw nearer! If it's gold bars you want, take them! Take them and be gone! We will gladly shed your dishonor and count ourselves fortunate."

"You've gotten half the fleet sunk at harbor! Why in hell would we follow you any longer?" a sailor shouted in reply.

"Toss the gold, it's your head we want!" another cried out.

"Toss him! Keep the gold and the ship!" a sailor shouted.

Will looked back to the sail approaching, the sun was dropping low in the sky and the vessel would not draw near until after nightfall. By that time, he would either be dead or have such scarce crew left he would be unable to command a defense. If he surrendered now, he would be killed as would all who had stood with him and the woman he'd rescued. He did not hold enough of the crew to effectively sail the massive line ship, let alone man her guns as well. Surrender would not do. Fighting on would only prolong the inevitable, but his honor wouldn't allow him otherwise. A pistol shot pierced the moment of calm and Will felt a tearing, burning sensation high on his left arm followed by several sailors charging him. He parried and countered in a rolling retreat, falling in line with the marines who had stood with him.

Their stand on deck was short lived as they were pushed by the overwhelming number of revolting crew towards the aft castle. A marine opened the hatch and the men all scrambled in, Will rushed in just ahead of the last marine who took several pistol shots in the back, collapsing to the deck. The door slammed shut behind Will as he raced into the cabin. Around him the men braced the door as those from the outside attempted to force their way in. Three marines held the door while another two dropped a timber plank through braces on the inside. Shelton approached, exhausted from the struggle and wounded by a slash on his forearm.

"You're bleeding Sir," he said, opening Will's sleeve to examine the wound. It was a deep gash, but the shot had grazed his arm and missed the bone. "What happened Sir? How did we come to this so rapidly?"

"Gold, man. I've heard of mutinies over less, though I'd never expected it would happen to my first command, nor so rapidly. There's enough gold on deck to fund the entire Royal Navy." Will answered dropping his gaze onto the floor of the cabin where the woman lay, still unconscious. He took a deep breath and closed his eyes while the pounding against the door and shouting outside intensified. "It seems they take issue with my decision to rescue this one as well. We found her floating in the sea among the wreckage on our sortie." Shots sounded outside the door and one of the marines began to look panicked.

"Sir, if they lift a gun from below to blow down this door, we're finished. If they all rush us, we won't last but a few minutes," he implored.

"They can't keep up the siege forever and the approaching ship should be on us shortly after nightfall. They don't have the time to lift one of the heavy guns." Will said almost thinking aloud.

"But if they are another pirate crew or a French privateer, we'll be done in Sir. I won't be a captive, I'll die first." Shelton retorted.

"You may have the chance Lieutenant, but I won't surrender to mutineers. For now, we hold the line here, force those buggers on deck to make their move. Once that ship approaches closer, they'll have some decisions to make. Let's see how well they hash it out amongst themselves." Will said smirking. He walked to the fantail, pressing on one of the ornate glass panes above a wooden bench lining the rear of the cabin. The pane popped free and fell to the water below prompting wild looks between the rest of the occupants of the cabin. Will protruded his head out of the frame the glass had occupied, craning his neck to see the incoming vessel. She had full sails set and in skillful manner, she would intercept the Endurance in a matter of hours.

Drowned Maiden
25 Sept 1808
17 Degrees 32 minutes N, 76 Degrees 12' W

Night closed around the Maiden as she sliced through the calm seas northward. The last rays of evening dying out in purple and red hues gave way for the wonders of the galaxy to display themselves down onto the earth. But no eyes from the Drowned Maiden were sky larking amongst the heavens as she sailed for the last suspected location of the Unholy Shepherd. Instead, every hand on deck had their focus glued to the double decked line ship that lay ahead of them. As they drew nearer and the light of the sun faded from sight, it became apparent to Lilith that something was unfolding before them on the vessel across the water.

"Chibs, is that gunfire?" Lilith asked, furrowing her eyebrows.

"It sure sounds like it. They wouldn't be firing at us though, not yet, we're too far away…" his answer drifted away.

"They're fighting each other?" Lilith pressed dying to know more, even if it was Chibs' conjecture.

"It happens at sea, a crew will mutiny for any number of reasons, a skipper too harsh or even rations running low. Sometimes all it takes is too much time between port calls. But my guess is they saw the black banner and they're fighting amongst each other over what they will do. The captain will want to fight, the crew will want to flee. But that's only my guessing, we'll find the truth soon enough." Chibs drew on his pipe and smoke circled from his nostrils as he spoke. "James means to find out what happened with the Shepherd but judging by the flotsam in the water around her, I'm guessing she is what happened," he said pointing to the enormous line ship.

Lilith's heart sank in her chest. She felt a wave of dread and tears began stinging her eyes.

"Trina? Chibs, if something happened to her I swear…" Lilith started, a wave of anger rising in her voice.

"Don't write her off just yet miss, Trina is as hard as they come. By god, it's damn likely she's mixed up in the gunfire we keep hearing. Those poor navy men have no idea what they have gotten themselves into in that case." Chibs said cracking a smile while pointing the stem of his pipe across the water. "I'm afraid she may not leave any for us."

James paced into the midst of the bow where Lilith and Chibs stood, a wide-eyed excitement plastered his face.

"Do you hear it Chibs? They're fighting on the deck of the line ship. Can you believe our luck?" James exclaimed.

"Only that I'd seen it with my own eyes

Captain. If it were a story in a pub, I'd call the man a liar." Chibs replied.

"What would the crew size be on a vessel that big?" the Captain asked with a flash of an idea through his eyes.

"Oh, at least two hundred likely closer to three. But who knows, they could be half that now, especially if that's a mutiny we're hearing." Chibs said flatly, unexcited for what was to come.

"That's perfect. So long as the fighting keeps up, we'll run right up to her, perhaps we have a chance to take her!" James chimed. Chibs head twisted a bit, Lilith could see he was thinking and judging by the larger clouds of pipe smoke, he was thinking hard.

"I don't know James. She's a big brute of a ship, even if we took her, we would be hard pressed to sail her let alone man all those damn guns. We'd be far better off to take whatever we could and scuttle her, a ship like that draws a lot of attention too. There would be no changing names and banners and easing that thing into a port. The Royal Navy would be hunting her down to the ends of the earth!" Chibs argued. This time, Lilith agreed with him. He knew more about sailing than anyone aboard and he certainly knew more about the Royal Navy. The ship did seem gargantuan to her eyes, even from a distance, it looked big enough to get lost inside.

"I wouldn't want it for long. Just one

sortie and I'd scuttle her." James replied. Both Lilith and Chibs could see, yet again, he had his mind set.

"I suppose Captain, if it's doable, we'll do it. I'm with you." Chibs relented while rapping the contents of his pipe bowl onto the wooden rail. He let a deep sigh go as Captain James departed towards the helm.

"You ok Chib?" Lilith asked as he looked out over the water toward the large ship.

"Oh, I'll be fine my dear. We're in for a fight with this one and James won't have any other way I'm afraid. I'll follow him to hades gates, even if it's to talk him out of jumping in. Likely he won't listen there either, which is fine. But we've got some precious cargo aboard and the means to send them on to a prosperous life. Why take chances we don't have to?" Chibs replied. Lilith could hear a pain in his tone she hadn't heard before and noticed he was hiding his face from her. She leaned over the rail slightly and saw the starlight gleam from a streak down the sailor's face.

"Chibs, James wouldn't attack unless he thought the odds were for us. Would he?" Lilith implored, growing more concerned.

"No miss, he wouldn't. But why take the chance? Why rescue these people from their fate just to gamble it again? They didn't ask for any of this and why subject them to any further loss? The doctor was helping me speak to one of the women, she's lost her husband and her boy had his leg blown to ribbons. What business do we have risking their lives again?" he lamented.

"None of that was done by us Chib and if I recall correctly, you tried to keep me from the boarding party when I first came aboard. These folk will find their sea legs, or leg I guess in Omibwe's case." Lilith said placing her hand on his shoulder and hugging his arm. Chibs chuckled when she mentioned Omibwe.

"He fancies you, that boy." Chibs jested. "Every time the poor sod is on deck it's all he can do to keep his eyes in his head." Lilith slapped his shoulder, eliciting a full laugh.

"He does not, don't be cruel." She snapped through a broad smile.

"Would I lie to you miss? He is love struck by those gems you have for eyes." Chibs replied. "Can't say he's the only one. I would say the Captain would leave the ship for them, but we both know that is a lie. Just as well though, I'd have you find a gentleman somewhere, a better man than any of us." Chibs said, getting quiet as he spoke.

"How fatherly of you," Lilith said, hugging his arm again.

"Well, I haven't any children of my own. None that I'm aware of I suppose, Kingston perhaps, maybe one or two in India.

But I did fish your sorry skirt out of the drink in Port-Au-Prince and I've taught you as much as I know of what a father could teach his daughter, I guess." He drummed his thumbs on the rail in front of him, uncomfortable with the expression.

"How to wield a pistol and saber? Or how to trim the mainsail for broad reach?" Lilith poked.

"These are the things I know girl," he chuckled.

"You'll be the only father I'll ever claim Chibs. You're leaps better than the one I was cursed with at birth." She replied rising on her toes to plant a quick kiss on his cheek.

"Alright now." He said wiping his eye quickly and darting a look around to check for onlookers. "Better get ready miss Lilith. You're going to be making use of those sword lessons soon."

"Not going to demand I stay on the Maiden?"

"No, I won't spare those sailors your wrath miss, but I do have an ask for you dear. See to it the boy's mother doesn't get in a bad way." Chibs said, stone faced.

"Chibs? Really? You fancy her, don't you?" Lilith replied breaking a huge smile with a sparkle in her eyes.

"Just, Lilith, will you please?" Chibs asked again, rubbing his whiskers nervously.

"I will Chib." she said, grasping his

seriousness.

The spirited moment was broken by the whistle of a musket ball zipping through the foresail above them, followed by the thud of the report. Captain James cried out an order and the Maiden's decks shifted beneath their feet as she turned to a slightly angled course toward the line ship's forward beam. Hands aboard the Drowned Maiden gathered, James intended to take the line ship, so there would be no cannon fire. Lilith knew, the approach was the most dangerous for the ship as a whole, she could see James' plan taking shape. They would run at angle under full sail and turn into their enemy after passing out of the field of fire, with some luck they would escape the line ships' massive cannon batteries before they could mass accurate fire. Moving at speed would be their defense and once out of the field of fire they would board her.

Boom! Boom!

A double report thundered through the darkness and Lilith listened intently as the cannon shot whistled harmlessly behind the Maiden's stern, billowing into the water well beyond them. More musket fire sounded, along with voices carrying shouted curses. The musket reports sent no whistling near the Maiden and Lilith's heart soared. "They're still fighting on deck!" she cried out. Every hand that had taken cover for the cannon shots popped up to try and catch a glimpse onto the decks of the looming ship in front of them.

Another cannon shot fired over the Deck of the Maiden, this one sending a ball whistling just feet over her deck. Everyone aboard dove for cover again, scrambling to whatever refuge they could find against the next round which they were all sure would impact. Lilith looked across the deck in the gleaming light of the moon and she could see Chibs standing tall, unshakable. Lilith wondered for a split second if anyone else aboard the Maiden had witnessed Chibs in a vulnerable moment like she had. She suddenly felt even closer to the salty old pirate. The decks shifting again beneath her snapped Lilith's thoughts back to the situation at hand. They were turning in toward their target, just clear of the line ship's field of fire. With full sails set they rapidly closed on the line ship; Lilith could see how much taller her deck sat over the Maiden's. Almost as if he had read her mind, she heard James shout an order for grapple hooks and rope ladders. Above, on the deck of the line ship the fighting intensified and from the rear of the vessel something caught fire sending a forbidding orange glow muddled by thick smoke through the darkness.

Just before the hull of the Maiden collided with the large warship Chibs called for the sheets to be loosed, spilling the wind from their sails. The momentum they still carried slammed the wooden ships together in a bone jarring crash. Screams could be heard up on the line ship while the pirates tossed grapples aboard to begin their assault and Lilith felt her guts tighten into a knot. When the crew began climbing the rigging, Lilith followed the man in front of her, carefully placing hand after hand and foot after foot up the shaking rope web that served as their ladder. Glancing up, she could see the man directly above her was scrambling wildly and shaking the ropes, making a mess of the ascent for everyone.

"Steady now! Upward man, we can't get stuck here!" Lilith shouted up to him. He paused for a second and looked down at her through the hazy orange glow. "Go damnit!" she cried again. To her horror, as the man in front of her reached up for the next handhold a silhouette came into view above on the rail of the warship. The shadow popped into view and then disappeared for a moment followed by two more popping into view. Pistol shots roared down, first one and then another. The man above Lilith flailed from the impact of a ball round, letting out a wheezing groan before going slack and losing his grip. He fell as Lilith tried to shimmy herself to one side to avoid being torn from the web. His side slammed down onto her shoulder and their heads collided sending Lilith's face into the side of the warship. Her vision blurred and her right hand was wrenched from the rope, with her remaining grip she slid down a few feet, the rope gnawing into the flesh of her hand. Barely clinging to consciousness, Lilith summoned her strength to hold the rope. A moment passed and her vision cleared, she could feel blood on her face from the impact on the hull and her raw hand burned from the rough rope. She swung her free arm up and clasped back onto the web, scrambling her feet back onto the rope to gain support for her arms. As she regained her footing, she could hear Trina in her mind, *Always mind your feet* she had told her. The thought of Trina sent a bolt of lightning through Lilith's veins and she surged upward, bent on havoc and vengeance. Then the shadows popped back into view over the rail again.

H.M.S. Valor
25 Sept 1808
17 Degrees 14 minutes N, 76 Degrees 8' W

Under the night's brilliant blanket of stars, with just a sliver of waning moon aloft in the eastern sky, the Valor cut through the debris field scattered through a broad swath of sea. The previous night, after darkness had fallen, they had doubled back to ambush the Endurance. A massive explosion had risen from the horizon, followed by an onslaught of cannon fire, alerting the men aboard the Valor to an engagement they were hoping would be the death song of the Endurance. Cobb had skirted well around the battle ground through that night and they wound up sailing far to the south. At daybreak, they made their way northward in a search pattern through most of the day. The first sighting of debris from the battle came in the waning hours of dusk and they moved urgently to comb the wreckage. Daylight would be ideal for the search, but Cobb was impatient to discover the fate of the Endurance and confirm that he was forever rid of Lieutenant Pike.

Cobb stood on the quarterdeck, near the helmsman, watching closely as he navigated them through the scattered remnants. Sailors lined the rail watching for any sign that one of the sunken vessels had been the Endurance. The ominous glow of the lookouts' lanterns drew a pale-yellow circle around the Valor, illuminating debris and floating corpses alike. Grim observations overheard from the sailors set Cobb's teeth on edge and his temper flared short.

"It's bad luck, looking at the dead like this and at night too," a sailor grumbled.

"Just be watching for any sign of the Endurance. It's likely this was Pike, trying to do his best Captain Grimes impression and falling far short. Keep looking." Cobb snapped.

"That, or the Endurance will be sailing up our asses while we hold out lights in the dark for the whole world to see," the reply came in a low grumble.

Cobb gritted his teeth, trying to suppress a flare of rage and failing. His temples were throbbing, and his throat felt dry. A constant, nagging strain had plagued him from the moment he had turned the crew against Grimes and that idiot Shelton. Every moment he felt threatened that they would now turn on him and end his tenuously held leadership. Hearing grumblings as they moved through the wreckage had sent his blood into a fury. If they turned on him now, he would only be known as a failed mutineer, a cautionary tale for wide eyed midshipmen to hear aboard their first assignment. The thought of infamy was unbearable and the fear of it drove Cobb mad with determination to regain control of his destiny. If he could silence Lieutenant Pike, whatever he reported back to London would become fact in the eyes of the admiralty and crown. Maybe he could even gain a promotion. But everything hinged on him surviving and not Pike.

Convincing the senior members of the crew to his cause had been simple enough after the batteries in Kingston had fired on the fleet. With Captain Grimes too weak to stop him and Lieutenant Shelton too inexperienced to realize what was occurring until it was too late, Cobb turned the crew and took command of the ship with ease. He'd dealt with the only dissenters shortly after tossing Grimes and Shelton overboard, by noose and pistol shot, he'd whittled through any on board who would defy him. But a lingering feeling haunted his every step, a pressing paranoia that squeezed in on him relentlessly and caused him to look suspiciously on every man aboard, second guessing everything and everyone.

"This one's alive!" a lookout called back from the rail on the bow. Cobb ran to the rail, looking at where the man was pointing. In the dim lantern light, Cobb could see a man in ragged clothing floating atop a section of broken deck timbers. The pale-yellow light glittered off the rippling water where the floating survivor raised a hand, shielding his eyes from the lanterns as they approached closer.

"Get a lifeline out to that shark bait!" Cobb shouted, sending the crewmen scrambling. A line was thrown out, falling onto the surface of the water just out of the man's reach. He seemed aware of its impact, but unable or unwilling to depart the small floating platform to reach for salvation. Cobb gritted his teeth, "We should leave this sorry sack for the elements, he won't last another day bobbing about," then he turned to the crew preparing to throw the lifeline again. "One of you is going to have to go get him, he's likely too weak to hang on."

"Should we lower a longboat?" a sailor asked as Cobb brushed past them toward the helm.

"There's no time for that. But since you're so eager to find a better option, take two with you and you go. Drag him to the ship and you boys hoist him up, once we have him on deck, I want to make sail, far away from here." Cobb grunted, his temperament growing fouler and more urgent with every passing moment.

Three sailors climbed down the side of the Valor to retrieve the stranded survivor, easing themselves gingerly into the dark waters. One by one they slipped from the side of the ship and stroked their way through the circle of dim light put off by a few lanterns being held over the rail. Above on deck the crew watched in anticipation, both eager to see their shipmates return with the rescue and to vacate the eerie battle scene floating amongst the sea. Cobb gripped his weary fingers against the wood of the rail, tense to see results so they could escape the unsettling scene. Sailors were the worst kind of superstitious creatures and sending three men off the ship into a scattered field of debris and corpses from a recent battle was about as unlucky of a situation as any sailor could think of. The crewmen aboard were already grumbling about it.

Cobb watched while they made their

way out to the flotsam barely holding the marooned man out of the clasp of the deep. An utterance of conversation could be heard, no doubt they were trying to convince the man to swim back with them, to no avail it appeared. They were lingering off the ship far too long for Cobb's preference.

"Just drag him back, planks and all you dogs! We need to be making sail!" Cobb shouted at the rescue band. One of them turned and shouted back,

"He says he is an American and one of the ships that's departed the battle headed north!"

"Fine lads just get him up here. We'll have time a plenty to talk to the man once he's aboard!" Cobb seethed. Almost grudgingly, the men began to swim back, pushing along the planks with the American aboard. Their progress was slow and Cobb soon lost patience with watching, turning to head for the helm. He got no more than a few steps from the rail when an explosion of thrashing water echoed across the sea separating the swimmers and the safety of the ship.

"Ahhhggh! Help! Help me, dear go…" the sailor's screams shot across the water and ricocheted up into the Valor's rigging, drawing intense attention from everyone in earshot. Then his voice was suddenly and mercilessly snuffed down into the dark waters surrounding the platform they had been pushing along. Nothing remained but an upward cascade of bubbles among a thick froth of bloody water where the sailor had vanished into the depth.

"Sharks! Sharks! Swim for it lads, let's go! Come on!" Cobb screamed out in a panic. The two who were left dutifully pushed along the wooden planks carrying their marooned American, swimming in a frenzy to escape the killing field. One sailor swam at either side of the planks, paddling with one hand while holding onto their quarry with the other and Cobb could only watch in horror as things unfolded below. They were getting close, only a few strokes more and all three men would be climbing their way to safety aboard the Valor. Then the sailor swimming off the side nearest where Cobb stood on deck jerked in the water with a sudden and violent force. He let out a blood curdling scream, wrenching on the boards he had been propelling to lift himself up. He was drug under for a split second and then popped back up screaming and wailing, thrashing his arms to climb aboard the platform.

"Help me! Help! My legs! Help!" the sailor cried out while attempting to crawl onto the tiny wooden platform. The American sat up as the distressed sailor clawed his upper body onto the boards, he kicked his feet at the man pushing him off the fragile safety of the chunk of decking. The water became a thrashing froth of blood and screams again as the imperiled sailor clawed for the boards in vain. The platform drew close enough to the Valor that both remaining men began a mad scramble for the rope. The American gave no quarter in his struggle to be first aboard, drawing ire from the onlooking crew. The American kicked at his rescuer, forcing him under the water's surface momentarily while climbing onto the only salvation for either. Angry shouts drifted from the crew down to the murderous scene amid the fluttering lamp light and when the American had secured his grasp on the lifeline, he began to climb raggedly.

"Hoist him up." Cobb ordered to the men standing along the rail where the line led up.

"He can bloody climb his ungrateful ass up, Cobb," a response zinged back from the cluster of men near the rope.

Cobb felt the wave of rage returning, that throbbing in his temples coupled with the parched throat. He reached into his waistband and hauled up a pistol. "I told you men to haul him in. Now, haul the rope up and get that piss ant aboard, now." The crew stood motionless, staring back at Cobb in his fury as if he were impotent to enforce his order. He raised the pistol and cocked the hammer of the piece, aiming it indiscriminately among the gawking sailors. "Haul him up. Now."

The sailors brought in the line, hauling away slowly in deliberate short pulls. By the time the American reached the deck of the Valor, he stood for only a moment on unsteady legs before collapsing to the deck. The men only gave him a look before tossing the line back over to rescue their remaining comrade from a surely impending and violent death at the jaws of some barbaric sea creature. As the sailor sloshed and scurried to grab hold of the rope, the American drew looks over the shoulders of the watching crew. He was on his hands and knees, laboring breath and crawling for a handhold to help him to his feet. Cobb walked over, stepping into the American's view of the wooden deck and offering a hand to lift him up.

"You know how to make friends Yankee." Cobb grunted, hauling the man up. "We do you the courtesy of rescuing you, so that you can let our brothers squander and die in a feeding frenzy. Perhaps we should have left you to die."

"I am an American, but I didn't float all day balancing on those planks to be tipped into the drink by your men." The man dragged out through ragged breaths. "I'm sorry for your men, but you need to get this vessel moving. We have to go, now."

Cobb scratched his jaw and leered suspiciously at the staggering man. His clothes were tatters, but he spoke with certainty, like a man accustomed to position and influence. Over the side, thrashing water could be heard and a scream shot through the dense night air.

"That'd be the last man of your rescue party. I traded three able bodies for you and I certainly hope you are worth the cost. I have a mind to reintroduce you to your fate." Cobb growled, stepping up to the staggering man and grabbing a hold of his collar. The crew turned, gathering their focus on the confrontation with the image of their shipmates being torn to the depths of the sea fresh in each mind.

"I was aboard a vessel hunting traitors of the Crown!" the American blurted just as Cobb began to pull his collar toward the rail. Cobb stopped in an instant, realizing the man's narrative would reinforce his own claims, not only among the crew but also with anyone owing allegiance to the King.

"Go on." Cobb said, releasing his grip.

"My name is Tim Sladen. I am a tobacco merchant from the States, and I was in Kingston when Admiral Sharpe attempted his coup against the Governor. He failed and we set off under contract from Governor Geor Alton to hunt down the two remaining ships and return them to the King's justice." He rattled. "Since they departed Kingston, one of them has engaged a merchant ship named 'Gazelle' laden with payment to the Crown from the East India Company. I believe they have joined causes with a band of pirates to further their cause."

"Why would Lieutenant Pike join in with pirates?" a sailor in the crowd shouted over, red faced and visibly irate. "I manned helm on his watch, and I was there next to him when it was pirates that fired on us! It's hog spit, it makes no sense. But what I have seen, Cobb, is I have seen this bastard push three men who were trying to rescue him back into a feeding frenzy in the water! I say we toss his arse over and watch while they rip him to ribbons!" Several shouts of agreement rose from the crowd that was now encroaching on Tim's position on deck. Cobb shifted his gaze back to the pitiful looking American who had fallen to his knees.

"There is gold at stake here. The payment from the Company is a massive amount, all the profits from India and the Caribbean over the course of the last year. The Admiral's treasons were an attempt to seize that payment. They are pilfering riches from the East India Company," Tim pleaded, hoping the mention of gold would pique their interests. Cobb smiled broadly as a fortunate coincidence hit his mind.

"Who here remembers the flag signal we flew before the pirates fired on us?" Cobb shouted over the crew.

"Captain Grimes inquired the Admiral for tea," a sailor called back in reply. "Could he have been alluding to the East India ships?" Faces in the crowd of sailors suddenly shifted expression, trading knowing looks and shrugged shoulders. Cobb could see them drawing the conclusion he had aimed them toward.

"Snap to on deck," Cobb barked, "Ready on the main! I want full sail and taut sheets; we have a ship of traitors to hunt down!"

Chapter 12

H.M.S Endurance
26 Sept 1808
17 Degrees 32 minutes N, 76 Degrees 12' W

The incessant pounding and hacking at the barricaded doors of the aft castle cabin had gone on for hours. Near midnight, Lieutenant Shelton had come up with the idea for a sortie to buy time if not retake some of the ship. He and several of the marines who had taken refuge inside the cabin would climb out the fantail windows and up onto the stern, from there they would counter the assault and attempt to regain control of the helm. Will sat on a wooden bench rubbing his temples while Shelton spelled out his intent. He looked down where the unconscious woman lay on the deck and considered how much of their predicament could be accounted to his decision to aid her.

"It is our best chance, Sir. If we sit in here and cower among ourselves, eventually they will break down the door, barricade be damned. We cannot hold out forever." Shelton pleaded.

"Neither can they, with another ship approaching, their attention will have to avert to that and soon." Will countered.

"And if they are pirates? Or suppose she is a French privateer. Are we really considering another ship for our salvation? Sir?" Shelton pressed, his tone was plagued by the frustration of their predicament and becoming more challenging by the minute.

"It won't solve all of our problems. Only give them more to contend with. Damn it! This confounded crew of greedy bastards why am I so cursed?" Will shouted, kicking over a stool near his leg. "Grimes would know the answer, but better yet, Grimes wouldn't be in this situation to begin with. I've failed my commission, failed the Navy, the crew. I've failed. The board was right, I'm not ready for command of my own."

"You've only failed us Sir, if you surrender to it. So long as there is fight left in those of us with you Will, don't give up hope." Shelton replied with a hopeful look. Will's shoulders sagged for a moment, feeling the weight of every eye in the room falling on him at once. He shifted his gaze back to the woman on the deck and caught her stirring. She lifted an eyelid and pressed her arm outward against the deck, rolling herself to one side with a painful groan.

"She lives!" a marine uttered.

"Aye get water lad. Shelton, get these men ready. You're going to carry out your assault plan, but I want you to time it with the arrival of that approaching vessel." Will said, fighting the nagging doubt in back of his thoughts.

"Yes Sir. Let me have a look and see if I can spot her again," he replied with a renewed vigor as he paced back to the fantail windows.

Will knelt next to the stirring woman, seeing her confusion and shock to be in a large stateroom.

"Who are you? Where are we?" her question rasped in a near whisper.

"We are aboard the H.M.S Endurance miss, the Navy vessel that sank your own. I found you in the debris field and we fished you aboard." Will answered in a flat tone but not unkind.

"Why? Why rescue me just to hang me? You should have saved your efforts and let the sea take me," she hissed in her rasp.

"I'll not presume the King's justice, nor will I stay it. You may hang woman, but not now. I found you alive and I am honor bound to aid any soul at sea in need. Gallows bound or not." Will answered through a fresh battery of pounding at the door. "In any case, I may have pulled you from the frying pan and into the fire. Those are the sounds of a mutiny in progress and all the while we are being approached by another ship."

The woman sat up at the mention of another ship, wincing in pain as she did.

"What colors does it fly?" she asked opening her eyes further with a gleam of hope flashing through them. Will hesitated a second, if the approaching ship was in concert with this woman, they likely wouldn't take kindly to the man who had sunk their sister ship.

"I saw no colors, only full sails rigged on a three masted ship, a frigate class approaching from the south." Will answered.

"That'll be the Maiden and there will be hell to pay at her hands," she shot back with a smile breaking through her pained expression. "There may be some goodwill for rescuing me. But you killed two dozen others Captain James will want an answer for."

"If there is a price to pay for fulfilling my duties, then I will face that as well." Will said locking his eyes onto hers in a grim stare.

Lieutenant Shelton leaned against the framing of the empty fantail window, stretching to catch a glimpse of the approaching ship. His head snapped back into the cabin as Will spoke his last reply to the woman.

"She sails with a black banner Will and they're close, now is as good a time as any." Shelton was already sheathing his sword into its scabbard at his waist and slinging a musket around his shoulders.

"Alright lad, up you go. When you get to the helm, call out and we will join you on deck. Likely you'll catch them off guard and if that pirate crew boards it is going to be utter chaos out there." Will said in a low tone. "Keep your head about you Lieutenant."

Will followed him to the fantail windows and assisted each man trying to shimmy out the window and scale the stern up onto the aft castle deck. He handed out muskets and braced their legs while each climbed out into the dark night. Once the last man was away and they had scurried out of sight up onto the deck above, Will hurried back to the cabin hatch. He strained to listen through the steady drum beat of impacts against the wooden door separating him from the mutinous crewmen. Thump, thump, thump had been the dreadful steady death toll for hours since they had barricaded themselves inside the cabin.

The absence of a beat made Will's heart race. His thoughts flashed, too fast to grasp hold of individually. Had they spotted Shelton up on the decks? Was he alive? Were they engaged right now? Will strained to hear. Shouts muffled through the bulkheads sounded, he heard running footsteps and then a volley of shots. More shouts followed and again several shots thundered through the wooden bulkhead. Then Will could hear Lieutenant Shelton's voice distinctly, "We've got them on the run! For the Captain boys!" Will's smile spread uncontrollably across his face and he turned to the marines in the cabin. "Move this riff raff lads, we're going out to join the fray." He stepped over and knelt next to the woman on the cabin floor.

"Can you move on your own?" he asked.

"Aye. I hurt, but it will take more than this to keep me from a fight," she replied, wincing as he helped her to her feet. "Are you going to arm me then?"

"I'm not in the habit of slitting my own throat miss, nor handing a blade to one who would put it in my back." Will was taken aback at her request.

"You'll have to get over your damned self. You spared my life, at least let me defend it for what I can," she snapped back. Will reluctantly opened a trunk near the bench seat on the fantail and looking in found the sword belonging to Admiral Sharpe.

"Its last owner was an honorable man. It is yours for the fight, but I will want it to turn over to his next of kin," he sighed and handed the weapon over. She looked back at him with a puzzled frown, still wincing as she moved.

"Yeah. If we live, I'll be sure to return it soaked in sailor guts and blood. Next of kin is going to cherish that," she retorted rolling her eyes.

The marines pulled back the last reinforcement against the cabin door and Will moved to open it. Both marines stood shoulder to shoulder, muskets at ready with stained bayonets attached. Will grasped onto the latch and prepared to open the door into chaos when a jarring impact rocked the ship. Everyone in the cabin lost their footing and one of the marines discharged his musket into the ceiling of the cabin. Will slammed into the bulkhead where his arm had been grazed, firing a bolt of pain down his arm and into his fingertips. Struggling to his feet he didn't even give a glance over his shoulder as he threw open the cabin door and stepped out onto the deck.

Shelton and the marines above on the aft castle let another volley of shots fly into a gaggle of sailors as they struggled to their feet on deck. The helm stood between him and a retreating mass of sailors and Will could see masts from the vessel that had collided into the warship, throwing everyone violently to the deck boards. A lantern hanging from the main mast had been knocked to the deck, spewing oil and flame into a race across its wooden surface. The flames threw up a bright orange partition separating him from the mutineers and casting a ghostly glow against the fluttering slack sails of the assaulting vessel off the bow. Shots and screams carried back from the ensuing fight against the boarding pirates. It was as if hell opened its gates and sent a band of demons to torment the mutineers. A man who had been near the hanging lantern had caught fire from waist to shoulder and ran screaming for the rail as Will emerged from the cabin. Thrashing his arms in a wild attempt to escape the blaze, Will watched as his screams escalated from shock to fear, then panic and agony. The sailor ran headlong into the rail, tipping over the side in a flailing tumble to the water where he landed with an unceremonious splash.

Swords clashing together mixed with gunfire penetrated through the growing flames on deck singing a symphony of chaos to the onlooking officers and marines. They stood near the helm, shielding their eyes from the growing heat as fire engulfed the deck and began climbing the mast.

"The ship is lost." Will shouted over the roar of noise, "Make for the longboats, abandon ship."

"But Sir!" Lieutenant Shelton began to object.

"Now lad. I'll not waste another soul to this struggle; the ship is lost. We couldn't hope to sail her now even if we had the manpower. There's no time to quibble." Will said as the smoke rolled over the decks, they stood on engulfing them into the deathly orange glow that promised to soon devour the Endurance. They quickly made their way to the longboat Will had taken on sortie the previous afternoon, waiting for them in suspension over the water.

"Someone is going to have to stay aboard and lower it down, likely two with all our weight." Shelton said while he climbed into the small boat.

"I'll stay Sir," a marine offered through stone expression. Will felt his heart leap, after all he had been through, the utter selfishness and treachery he'd witnessed in the last few months, the man before him redeemed his faith in honor. Valor is not dead, Will thought as his eyes darted over the decks, looking for another solution.

"Unacceptable marine. That won't do." Will uttered.

"Sir?" his confused reply was lost on the Lieutenant.

"Shelton, get out." Will snapped. Lieutenant Shelton shot a bewildered look back and climbed from the longboat in haste. Will swung his cutlass into the aft rope, severing stands with each swing until the line snapped dropping the longboat to swing from the bow line. Wasting no time as the flames grew drawing nearer with each heartbeat, Will ran along the rail with reckless abandon swinging his saber into the bowline with every bit of force he could muster. With a single blow the line parted in a violent snap dropping the longboat into a free fall to the sea. "Follow Me!" Will screamed over his shoulder as he jumped from the rail, his limbs flailed wild as he slashed into the inky dark sea.

Drowned Maiden
26 Sept 1808
17 Degrees 32 minutes N, 76 Degrees 12' W

Lilith clung for her life to the rope webbing, watching in in sheer horror as a silhouette appeared along the rail above. For a moment that shadow was the reaper signaling her sure death as an arm extended with a pistol in its clasp. She grimaced against the hot bolt of pain she knew was coming and pressed herself as hard as she could to the wooden surface of the hull. A thunderclap reverberated through the thick night between ships and Lilith squeezed her hands harder onto the rope, drawing an ooze of blood from where her grip had been bitten by the course line. For a moment she shuddered, waiting for the searing pain to register. She could feel the shadow above wobble from the rail and felt the air flutter as her would be reaper dropped through swirling smoke and screams into the water's grasp. Lilith looked over her shoulder, half in panic and half in delight to see the stern face of Omibwe behind a smoking musket barrel. His precarious balance did nothing to slow him rapidly handing off the spent musket to the waiting hands of Doctor Lemeux at his side. The French Doctor reloaded as best he could to keep up with the fury of Omibwe who leveled accurate fire as quickly as he was handed a ready piece.

Hand over hand, Lilith resumed her climb toward the deck as the smoke and noise from above intensified. Finally reaching the rail with her forearms groaning in a dull ache of exertion, she peered through a scupper to witness fury and chaos aboard. Captain James had been among the first to set foot aboard and was engaging a group of several sailors by wielding a sword in each hand. Behind him a pair of pirates let fly with pistol shot and took up swords from the fallen on deck. When Lilith's bare foot made fall onto the deck of the big warship, it was already slick with blood. She looked about frantically for any sign of Trina, but with no success.

A sailor ran toward Lilith from her right side screaming as he swung a tomahawk in a sharp downward arc. She drew her sword and made a lunging dive onto the deck, causing the swing to slice harmlessly through the space she vacated. With her sword in hand Lilith rolled to her feet and turned just in time to parry a following swing from the screaming sailor. The forceful impact almost wrenched her backward but with a flash of speed the sailor could not anticipate she slid her blade out of contact with the tomahawk and plunged it hard into the man's throat. He dropped to his knees with a pleading look of fear spread across his face as blood surged from the wound in his neck. Lilith grabbed his tomahawk with her free hand and while driving her knee into his chest, freed her blade from its burrow of flesh. A moment later she buried the tomahawk firmly between the shoulder blades of another sailor who lunged at her. In a swift motion she parried his sword and side stepped while swinging the other blade deep into his back, dropping him to the deck in a twisting storm of agony. Lilith made no effort to finish the man and stepped further into the fray.

Flames clawed along the ship's middle, climbing her mainmast and dancing along each rail as it spread and cast a stark orange glow through the thickening smoke. Lilith caught a glance of James, a sword in each hand, dealing out pain and death to the ship's defenders. As bodies collected on deck, both navy men and pirates alike a crescent began to form around James as his deadly blows repeatedly finding their lethal mark began to give pause to the men around him. A flash of fire brightened the smoke hanging above deck as flames found the mainsail and Lilith saw a man lunge himself at James from his flank. The pirate captain caught the movement and parried with one sword while simultaneously driving the other right through the sailor's belly, then with a fluid grace his parry sword assaulted an onlooker within reach in a cross-hand slash finding his throat. James ripped his penetrating sword free just in time to parry another attack. He hammered blows for a moment against two attackers, parrying and swinging, the ringing clash of steel crying up through the dying ship's rigging.

Seeing the moment of peril her captain James faced, Lilith raced toward the scene, hacking and thrusting at sailors engaged by pirates every step of the way. She was almost near enough to aid James when he turned a block sideways and was caught by the blade of another on his forearm. He countered with a furious slash landing on his assailant's elbow and with his wounded arm drove his other blade right through an exposed chest. Lilith looked on as if time slowed while another round of attackers threw in against James. As he recovered from the first attack, he had to parry another advance with his good arm while trying to free his other sword from the clutches of ribcage. The sword was lodged and being unable to free it put a beat in James' timing. Another sword slash found him on top of his shoulder, he raised his blade to parry a following swing meeting steel but missing the lunge of another at his flank. The sailor who drove a blade into his side was immediately greeted with James' downward swing burrowing into his forehead from hairline to eyebrow.

Lilith felt as if she were wading through molasses, unable to stop the events unfolding just out of her reach as James drove his sword down onto a man's head and collapsed to one knee. She shoved her way through the last few steps separating them and caught a sword just before it completed a downward swing into the back of James' neck. Her counter slashed across the wielder's ribs and then plunged into his belly. She withdrew her cutlass and relieved the dying man of his sword with her free hand, raising both blades to ready in a standing vigil as James slumped onto the blood-stained deck.

Smoke clung to the deck of the warship swirling around the combatants aboard, its thick cloud captured the orange and red fire hues illuminating the night. Lilith's nose and eyes burned from the acrid pitch as she watched the remaining sailors begin to circle her position, just as they had with James. There was a moment of hesitation, shifting eyes darted between Lilith and the growing inferno consuming more of the ship with every passing second. Across the deck a man screamed at the top of his lungs, "Follow me!" The sailors around Lilith turned their gaze in the direction of the yelling for a moment and a fleeting glimpse of a man lunging overboard caught her eye. More shouts came from a group behind the man and through the haze of smoke and flame Lilith could see just a flash of a familiar female figure run to the rail. Lilith lingered her eyes for another moment to see as the woman turned to look over her shoulder and for a split second their gaze met. Trina's face locked into her mind sending a bolt of adrenaline racing through her.

    The first sailor to make a move toward Lilith was met with a furious torrent of sword blows that ended in a slash that split the man from collar to waist. Another plunged in, attempting to catch her off guard while she dealt with her first attacker. She made a sideways step and reversed her grip on one sword, driving it into the man's lower back up to the hilt. Lilith wrenched the dying sailor around to shield herself from another's sideways slash. Pushing her human shield to the side after the impact she lunged with her remaining blade into the sailor's chest, stopping him before he could recover for another strike. Her swords were both lodged, and Lilith panicked as her strength failed to free either, she panicked and wrenched on both and then one with no success. A sailor, seeing her plight from across deck, hoisted a spent musket by the barrel and ran with a bloodcurdling scream. Lilith looked up to see the man sprinting to bludgeon her to death, a final tug on the sword she was trying to free confirmed it would not move and she reached for a sword from the clasp of a dead man. Lilith heard the scream and felt each step as the man approached to deliver his deadly blow, as her hand gripped the sword, she raised it to deflect what she could of the impending swing and grimacing in anticipation. The scream cut off in a ragged gurgle and the impact Lilith braced against never landed on her sword. She widened her gaze to watch the man crumple into a bleeding contortion, dropping the musket to claw at a tomahawk that buried deep into his throat.

Snapping her attention to the source of the blade that saved her, Lilith looked onto Chibs, he stood among the scattered dead on deck almost obscured by a veil of thick smoke. Then she noticed the wound. He was holding his arm tight against his side and grimacing in pain with every breath.

"Lilith. Dear, we have to go," he struggled out.

"Chibs, James, we can't..." Lilith started to object.

"We have to leave him girl. I'm sorry, but the fire is spreading too fast. We have to leave him." He pleaded.

Lilith ran to Chibs and pushed her shoulder up under his good arm to help him over the rail. All around them sailors and pirates alike scrambled in retreat of the growing fury of fire on deck. Splashes broke the dark waters where those retreating could only find solace overboard. Chibs grunted and strained with each step down the rope webbing and Lilith could see in the glare of orange that his entire side from armpit to ankle was soaked in dark blood. Just a few steps above the Maiden's rail Lilith heard a sudden gasping groan and looked down to see Chibs struggling to hold the rope web with a single hand as his feet dangled free. His grip slipped and the big pirate fell, slamming on his back across the rail. Lilith screamed, "Chibs!" and pushed herself off the web jumping across to the deck of the Maiden. The landing impact shot up through her shins and into her knees and her hands took painful gouges from the deck timbers as she caught her upper half from hitting but the pain barely registered while she scrambled to Chibs' side.

"Chibs!" she cried feeling the world spin around her as he groaned with a labored breath, "Chibs what do I do? What can I do?"

"Get Lemeux and get us under sail dear. Let him tend to me, you get us out of here." He rasped as blood began to show at the corners of his mouth.

Her eyes became a fogged blur of tears while Chibs pushed at her shoulder, urging her to lead the Maiden away from peril. Lilith stood, pausing for a moment to take in the blurry figure of Chibs laying on the deck, blood pooling around his wounded side. "Doctor!" she screamed whirling around to see what few crew they had beginning to huddle around. "Get that damned French doctor! And get sheets set on the main, we're making sail!" Her shouts were met by a moment of hesitation, surprised looks and unbelieving eyes and then as if their realization came all at once the deck went into a flurry of activity. Sail sheets were tightened, and the mainsail filled with a crisp pop, Lilith went to the helm and pulled at the wheel for a starboard turn. Slowly, grudgingly, the Drowned Maiden pulled free of contact from the dying warship. Like a crescendo of destruction, building toward her ultimate fiery fate, the blaze spread while the Maiden crept by her bow stem. The fire had danced its way across her deck, consuming them until chunks and pieces had fallen through. Her foremast was by now a pillar of flame, creeping its way out the yards to feast on its sails in bright flashes of fury.

Lilith feared, as Chibs did, that the magazine would catch before the Maiden would be out of range from the catastrophic explosion that would result. Their progress away from the floating firestorm gained momentum when the crew set topsail and began to work on the foresails. After a moment, the line ship was astern of them and Lilith grabbed Omibwe as he hobbled by on his way to the stern.

"Take the helm Omi, hold us on this course," her order sounded as if it came from somewhere else, even surprising herself a little.

"I don't know how..." Omibwe was hesitant and a little intimidated.

"I'll show you how Omi, it's easy enough. But for now, just hold the wheel steady," she said while placing his hands on the helm holds. "Hold steady pressure, you'll feel it resist a little but keep it right around here. I'll come help if we need to make a turn." He seemed willing but ill at comfort. "I need you to do this now Omi."

"Ok. I'll try," he managed.

Lilith went to where LeMeux was looking after Chibs on deck. The big pirate was grimacing with every breath and pale as a ghost, wheezing curses while the French worked on his wounds. The pool of oozing blood at his side had grown and Lilith felt a chill as their eyes connected briefly when Chibs opened his eyes from the squinting grimace.

"I'll mend miss, the Doctor has it well in hand." Chibs rasped. Looking up at Lilith, LeMeux didn't seem so sure.

"He has lost a lot of blood and this wound on his side is deep. I don't know," he began to lament, but stopped when he saw the girl pirate's expression take an icy change.

"Your fate is tied to his Doctor. If he bleeds out and dies on this deck, so will you. Understand?" her eyes narrowed and locked with his.

"Y, Yes. Yes, I will do everything I can," the doctor replied and snapped back to working on the wound.

"Lilith, let him be, get me a totter of rum miss, I'll be good as new by sunrise," he said with a chuckle and then stopping with a pained expression. Lilith fought off tears, looking at the dark red circle on the wooden deck as it soaked into wood grains.

"Longboat off larboard rail!" the cry came down from a hand working the top gallant.

Lilith snapped out of her dread and looked over the rail, remembering the familiar face she'd spotted through the flames. The outline of a longboat stood off the Maiden's larboard side no further than a cable length. She couldn't make out faces, but one figure stood up and waved arms in a frenzy to be seen and even through the darkness Lilith knew who it was.

"Get a line out!" Lilith yelled, "It's Trina! She's out there and it looks like she's not alone."

H.M.S Valor
26 Sept 1808
17 Degrees 28 minutes N, 76 Degrees 11' W

The looming feeling he was about to meet a grisly end still hung over Tim's every thought. Being pulled from the debris field and the reach of the sharks improved his situation, though as Tim observed the demeanor of the sailors on deck, only slightly. He sat on a bench near the weather hatch under the vigilant glare of a duo of sentries. His treatment had been a degree better than if he were a prisoner, but Tim felt as if the men lingering on deck were imagining terrible ways to rid the ship of him. His panicked reactions during the rescue won him no friends aboard this vessel, everywhere he looked was a grim face or a menacing stare. Their leader, Mr. Cobb, seemed to appreciate Tim's value to a certain degree. But only so far as it concerned the recovery of gold. This was an unfortunate problem as Cobb likely intended to take whatever riches they came across while Tim desperately needed to deliver that payment to the Order. The night air held a cool edge to it, the first notes of a retreating summer and a reminder of the timeline to which he was encumbered. A meeting of delegates would be held within a month in Charleston and if he failed to deliver, the consequences would be severe.

"If you're being false with us, I won't be able to stop this crew from tearing you to pieces. Nor would I try. Gold, Mr. Sladen, gold will be your salvation, or your doom should it not be there." Cobb said climbing from the weather hatch.

"The payment was aboard the company ship Gazelle, Sir. If it is to be had at all, it will be aboard the Endurance and in the hands of traitors. Though I'm not sure why you are so interested, it is profits to the honorable lords in ownership of the East India

Company and belongs to them as such." Tim sighed in resignation, already knowing exactly what this Cobb was thinking.

"A prize sum will surely be awarded to the crew for the recovery. Unless you haven't told me some detail, but you wouldn't lie to a crew of men who rescued you from certain death, would you Tim?" Cobb cut sarcastically. "None of this makes any sense to me. The Admiral and Captain Grimes aside, why would a payment for the lords in ownership be ferried through the Caribbean? What aren't you telling me?"

"Mr. Cobb, I can only tell you that you are getting yourself and your crew involved in matters far beyond your understanding. You would be well served to kill me here and now and forget everything I've told you. Make for some foreign shore and never speak of what I have told you, but you won't." Tim replied indignantly. "But you won't, and that's fine. However, this plays out, from here on, you've been warned." Cobb's eyebrows raised in a look of cautious apprehension.

"Right. I've been warned. You're a nutty one. I mean to see the Endurance sunk, but for my own reasons. If there is gold aboard her to be had, all the better." Cobb said with a dismissive wave to Tim's warning.

"What reason have you to sink her?" Tim asked.

"The man assuming command of her is

on some treasonous errand of the Admiral. We made port in Kingston and as you well know, something occurred there between the Admiral and the Governor. Half the fleet was sunk by our own fort battery. I suspect a coup of some sort, not that I can prove anything beyond what I've already told you. Something was afoot and if the men involved knew about the payment you are so eager to recover; I would consider that was likely their motive."

Tim could not believe his ears; this man honestly had no grasp of the reality of his situation. He was clever, and Tim suspected there were motivations for sinking another navy ship that he was not sharing. Whoever Captain Grimes was he likely knew some of the details the Admiral had deduced. Mr. Cobb seemed ignorant so far as to the true nature behind the unfolding events. Tim fought a smirk while he thought it over, Cobb hadn't even questioned how an American privateer would know the details of payments being shipped through the Caribbean. So long as there is something he is hiding, Tim thought, he will be reluctant to keep pressing me.

"Where do you intend to sail, once you have sunk the Endurance, Sir?" Tim asked.

"How did you know there was a payment aboard a specific vessel bound for Kingston?" Cobb shot back. Tim's heart sank in his chest, he could feel the last strands holding his web slipping. Cobb looked down on him with an air of disdain as Tim sat huddled on the bench, still soaked through and beginning a shiver in the chill night breeze. "It's obvious to me there is some deception you are attempting here, Tim. If that is even your true name. You can have it. But keep your questions to yourself. If at the end of this ordeal, we can both serve our own ends perhaps an arrangement can be made. Until then, I think it best you just go along with things as they were, lest I turn you over to my crew."

"That seems reasonable, Mr. Cobb." Tim said with a grudging sigh.

The night wore on with a stiffening breeze bringing another wave of chill over Tim's body. The sliver of moonlight traced silvery edges along the crest of gentle swells contrasting the darkness of the seas. The winds slipping through rigging aloft and the gentle lapping of water against the wooden hull lulled Tim into a tranquil, dreamless doze as he sat on the bench. His guards seemed to relax as their watch drug into the early hours of the morning, nodding with heavy eyes where they stood. In between little jaunts of drifting sleep, Tim pondered his situation and how he could change events into his favor. Cobb believed his commanding officers were attempting a coup, if he held to his current course, there was no need for any deceptions. He could sail to the nearest British Colonial authority and report his suspicions, to a hero's welcome. But, upon questioning, he had become defensive. Tim concluded it was likely that Mr. Cobb desired to cover some past transgression, or that his intentions upon recovering the gold and sinking the Endurance were more self-serving than he would admit. Tim opened an eye, peering around the deck lit only by lanterns and the waning moonlight. One of the sentries standing guard jerked his head suddenly, snapping out of a doze while he leaned against the bulkhead behind him.

"Is Mr. Cobb the commanding officer?" Tim asked in a low tone.

"What's that?" the sentry growled in reply, looking confused and fatigued.

"Mr. Cobb. Is he your commanding officer? I only ask because he was not wearing an officer's coat. In fact, he appears to be no more than a petty officer." Tim pressed, drawing a scorn from the guard.

"He's in command now, that's all I'm concerning myself with. It's a shame the officers dishonored themselves the way they did. I don't blame Cobb for putting them overboard, likely I'd do the same if they hadn't." He answered, looking uncomfortable with the exchange.

"And what exactly did they do?" Tim asked hoping to glean a perspective from someone besides Cobb.

"They landed a party of marines from

the fleet to overthrow the governor of Jamaica. You said so yourself, what are you getting at?" the sentry leaned away slightly, off put by the line of questioning.

"What if I told you that the officers and marines of the fleet were ambushed by a band of pirates in Kingston? It was pirates who took the fort and opened fire on your fleet. Your friend Cobb has committed a mutiny and made you all his accomplices. That's why he put the other officers off the ship." Tim said in a low hushed voice. He watched as his suggestions kindled in the sentry's mind, just as he had hoped they would.

"Why would Cobb be so desperate to get after Lieutenant Pike and the Endurance then?" the man hunched lower to speak with Tim.

"He has to silence anyone who can report his mutiny, of course." Tim said with a flat condescending tone.

"By god. What have they done? And now we're all mutineers!" the sentry hushed his exclamation, gritting his jaw afterward.

"By my reckoning, the only chance you gentlemen have at not feeling a noose bite your neck as your last living moment would be to take the ship and restore order aboard." Tim suggested, looking away into the night to let his words work on the sailor's mind. It could not have taken more perfectly if Tim had planned it. The guard hadn't questioned the motives of the American feeding him lies and leading him where he wanted, he just drew the conclusions Tim led him to. Aboard a crowded vessel at sea, it would take only hours, but the seeds he had now planted would grow into a violent problem for Mr. Cobb, one Tim hoped he could get in front of and use to his own advantage.

"Fire on the horizon! There's a ship out there aflame!" the cry echoed down from the forward lookout. His shout was followed by a flurry of footfalls against the wooden deck as everyone moved to get a look. Tim stood and leaned over the rail to take in the sight. An orange dot on the horizon was all he could make out, but as he peered longer it seemed to grow in intensity. Chaos was what he needed. If Cobb and his crew were distracted by an outside event, Tim had a chance to effect some change in his situation. That growing orange blot on the horizon promised some distraction and offered the chance for some chaos to take hold. Maybe, Tim pondered, the doubts I've planted with this nitwit will take fruit amid some action, perfect.

Cobb appeared from below deck and shot a suspicious glance toward Tim on his way to the bow. It had been mere hours since their departure from the debris field and Cobb looked as if he hadn't slept at all in that time. The orange glare flashed, growing in intensity as flames likely caught hold of sailcloth. Cobb stood near the bowsprit, with an extended sight glass raised to his eye. He leaned over and said something to a nearby sailor and soon a couple men scooped Tim off his seat on the bench and drug him up to the forecastle. Cobb had a wide grin that gripped Tim's innards like a vice.

"Would you care to have a look and see the source of flame?" Cobb sneered.

"My eyes aren't what they once were. Just tell me." Tim was apprehensive at the sailor's joy.

"The Endurance. She's the only vessel that large in these waters and she is lost to the flame. I imagine we will hear her magazine go at some point soon. Pike must have run across someone far better suited to naval combat." Cobb jeered. "And it looks like my problem has been solved for me."

"And mine? Where does this development leave our arrangement?" Tim asked somberly.

"Oh, Mr. Sladen. Your problems have only started." Cobb said with a broad grin.

Tim bit his lip, trying to contain the furious torrent of cursed insults that sat at the front of his mind for this sailor. He was clever, though not quite as clever as Tim. With any luck, the seeds of doubt and deceit he had sown with the crew earlier would be coming into play.

Chapter 13

Drowned Maiden
27 Sept 1808
17 Degrees 34 minutes N, 76 Degrees 14' W

The plume of smoke from the burning warship trailed along the surface of the sea, hanging heavy in the air. Its acrid odor clung inside of Lilith's nose fouling her smell and stinging her eyes. Everyone aboard the Maiden was exhausted and precious few had escaped without some form of injury. Chibs lay on deck, resting after having been wrapped in bandages by the doctor. With dawn's first fingers stretching high into the starry skies the crew aboard the Maiden hoisted a longboat filled with battle weary faces, including one very familiar to them.

"You look a beautiful sight Lilith!" Trina called up as Lilith stood at the rail above to greet her.

"You look a mess Captain!" Lilith called back down. The men occupying the longboat with Trina seemed taken aback. Several of them exchanged glances among each other and the man in the prow with an officer's coat slunk his head down, rubbing his eyes.

"Who have you brought along

Captain? Prisoners?" Lilith called down. She held a cutlass in one hand, its point dug into the wooden rail as she leaned against it.

"These men saved me Lil, they plucked me from the wreckage after the Shepherd went down. The one in front was their commander. They mutinied when he refused to throw me overboard for the fishes." Trina called back up, Lilith saw her exchange a glance with the officer in the prow and the man looked up at her afterward.

"Hold the capstan," Lilith ordered over her shoulder and then called back down, "And who would you be navy man? A pirate hunter?"

"My name is Lieutenant William Pike; I am the commissioned first Lieutenant aboard the H.M.S Valor. No, our tasking was not to hunt pirates, although any navy ship is duty bound to do so on sighting them." Will answered.

"And so why would I hoist a crew of men, duty bound to kill pirates, aboard my vessel? I thank you for rescuing my friend, but I won't be meeting a sword point to my back once you're up here, will I?" Lilith demanded. She held up a hand as several of the African crew gathered at the rail with muskets in hand.

"No miss. I have no reason to commit treacheries aboard your ship. Enough has been done to me in the last few weeks." Will replied, his glances swapping back and forth between

Lilith above and Trina in the back of the longboat.

"No. That's not good enough. You're not setting foot aboard unless I have your word, on your honor, that you will be loyal to the Maiden and her Captain. Anything less buys you a volley of shot and a grave in the deep." Lilith called down.

"Lilith, they saved my life! Hoist us up and we'll discuss terms." Trina shouted up, growing irritated with her stubborn protege.

"He saved you from what? He saved you after they blew the Shepherd to pieces? And I'm supposed to thank him for it? You said it yourself, this crew won't have freeloaders aboard. If they mean to come aboard, they'll do so as part of the crew or not at all." Lilith yelled back down, her voice beginning to betray the anger she tried to keep veiled.

"What? Where is James? Or Chibs? Have them come to the rail and speak Lilith, I want aboard." Trina replied.

"James is dead. He fell at the hands of the crew of that warship and Chibs is wounded Trina." Lilith called back with a cracked voice, her eyes welling up uncontrollably as she spoke.

"Oh, love. Dear, hoist us up. These men will do you no harm, you have my word. If they put a finger out of line, I will gut every one of them." Trina called back up; her voice softened with her temperament when she saw the tears streaming down the girl's face. Lilith turned to the crew at the capstan, "Hoist away, bring them up. But all the rest of you, arm yourselves."

    The growing dawn brought into stark reality just how much damage the crew had sustained in the battle. Though the ship had faired remarkably well from its impact, Lilith could only count fourteen aboard that had returned from the fight. Most of those were wounded as well. Chibs had ordered a group of the Africans, mostly the women and children, to stay aboard the Maiden and that made the total number still less than thirty souls. As the longboat edged its way up to level with the deck an uneasy crew gathered around, weapons in hand.

    Trina was first to step onto the Maiden's rail, leaving the men aboard the longboat to exchange hesitant glances and wonder for their collective fate. Lilith met her and the two friends embraced.

    "I am so sorry Lil, about James." Trina whispered.

    "He died the way he would have it. Too soon and with a sword in each hand." Lilith whispered back through tears.

    "Where is Chibs? I'll want to see him." Trina said as they released each other, still holding onto each other's hands.

    "We've made him as comfortable as we

can by the helm, he insisted." Lilith replied as Trina dried her face with a rough hand.

"Sounds like the old sea dog hasn't changed." Trina said, drawing a laugh from them both.

"Not in the slightest." Lilith replied with a smile returning.

"These men, Lil. They saved my life, that has to count for something. What do you intend to do with them?" Trina's tone lowered.

"I'd like to hang them all, for the Shepherd, Trina. But I have something else in mind." Lilith answered, looking over to the men still anxiously waiting in the longboat. "Go, see Chibs. He's not well. I'll have a word with them." Trina left with a reluctant parting glance to each of them, lastly lingering on the strapping Lieutenant Pike. She shot a smile his way and then walked off to see Chibs.

Lilith looked over the Maiden's crew and then to the men in the longboat. They were all a sore and sorry sight, no one would win from another fight today. In a step she was up to the rail, leaning her weight back onto the hilt of her sword while the tip scratched into the grain of the wood.

"I meant what I've told you. If you mean to board this vessel it will be as members of the crew or not at all. I'll have no turncoats stabbing my crew in the back and taking this ship for their own." Lilith laid it out flat for the men to consider.

"I can assure you miss; we are in no position to incite a mutiny aboard your ship. These men are free to do as they would. But, for myself, I will not swear any oath to a pirate banner. I am honor bound to King and Country. If that means my life, so be it." Will cut back with an unflinching determination.

"Oh, what a fool you are man! Do you think us a bunch of savages? That I would rather cut you down than add you to the fold?" Lilith looked across the faces of the men in the longboat, squeezing her grip on the sword. "I don't want to kill you, William. But I won't have any of you roam the decks freely," she said clinching her jaw and turning to the crew behind her. "Bind their hands and stow them all below with the other prisoners. If any resist, kill them." The Lieutenant sitting just behind Will had a pleading look in his eyes that met with Lilith's for a passing moment, she dismissed it as her crew boarded the longboat to restrain them.

Lilith paced toward the helm, putting the forlorn looks of her new prisoners out of her mind. They aren't slavers, she thought, but they land on their side if they won't join us. Ahead of her, Trina was sitting on the deck next to Chibs. The two were both facing her as she approached, Chibs looked ghastly pale but he was awake and overjoyed it seemed to be with Trina.

"And what of this one?" Trina said

loud enough that Lilith could hear, "She's come a spell since you fished her out of the drink Chib. Perhaps she'll make for a Captain."

"She has my vote Trin." Chibs chimed beaming a proud glare at Lilith.

"That's not funny. Trina, you will Captain." Lilith replied feeling a pang of shock and confusion.

"No love. I am a Captain, of the Unholy Shepherd. She lay at the bottom, very much full of holes. James is gone dear and a good many of the crew with him, as Chibs just explained. You, though, sweet Lilith. You don't even realize it. The crew was rallying behind you when Chibs called you back to the Maiden. When James fell, it was you they followed." Trina said while digging a dagger into the wooden deck. "Be it because you are one of us? Or because you didn't shy away when the battle was grim. Whatever the cause, unless there is dissent, you command the Maiden dear."

Lilith felt a flush come to her face, her mouth dried and in an instant the wind dancing against her skin seemed to bring a chill. Trying to formulate a response only yielded her to looking at Chibs. She swallowed hard, her tongue feeling as if it were double its size.

"Chibs? Why not you?" Lilith said, fearing the answer more than any sword swing or cannon shot.

"I'm in no condition to command anything girl. Besides, that's not my way. I'd dither about and second guess my every move. No. You will Captain, Lil, and you'll have me and Trin here at your side. You'll be sick of us soon enough." Chibs announced, grimacing at his final words and grabbing at a wineskin in Trina's grasp for a big long drink. "But you don't fret over me, it's going to take more than a sword stick and a few scratches to kill me. I'm rigged to fight."

"Sail Ho! Southern horizon!" a voice shouted down from aloft.

Lilith ran to the stern, Trina springing up to follow. The sun had crested into the eastern sky, bringing with it a brilliantly painted morning of pinks and oranges beating back the starry darkness of the night. Along the southern edge of light Lilith could make out a rig of sails. Broad mains and top sails below with smaller gallants and royals above trimmed out on their edges by auxiliary sails. Her commander was plowing ahead toward them and flying every stitch he could to get there. Lilith scrambled back to Chibs.

"Chibs, I need your sight glass," she said while scrambling by to the weather hatch.

"Check your cabin dear, there's one in a chest right by the door," he gruffed, sitting up a bit with a wince. Lilith froze in her tracks for a second.

"My cabin?" she asked with a confused squint.

"The Captain's cabin girl! James kept a sight glass in the chest right by the door. In YOUR cabin," he answered with a booze fueled smile.

"Right!" her answer floated back as she disappeared below.

Lilith raced below and into the cabin, throwing open the chest right where Chibs had promised it would be. It was filled with James' few personal effects and for a moment, Lilith had to pause, she grabbed the sight glass and exited quickly to ward off a wave of emotions that threatened to crash down on her if she lingered too long. On her way back up the ladder well, she found herself face to face with William, being led to their new home in the hold and an idea struck her.

"This one is coming with me," she said to the escorting crew as she grabbed Will's coat. "You are going to be of some use to us, Lieutenant, or you will learn to swim with your hands bound."

Lilith drug the officer along, though he wasn't resisting he just could not quite match her hurry, above deck and up onto the aft castle. With sight glass in hand she extended it and looked through to the incoming vessel. It was a frigate, comparable in class to the Maiden herself, but still too far off to count gun ports. Lilith handed the glass over to Trina and turned to William.

"Do you know that vessel?" she asked, giving him a side eyed glance.

"I could. It is hard to tell with a naked view at such a distance." Will replied with stone expression. Trina handed him the glass.

"Have a look for yourself, I can see no colors. But she sails with a purpose towards the smoke plume. Could that be the last of your fleet Lieutenant?" Trina posed while giving the officer a stern look.

Will focused on the vessel, giving nothing but a long silence back to his captors. He studied her bow through the foggy distortion of the glass until his eye began to ache with strain. Then he handed the instrument over to Lilith and looked down at the wood grain in the rail to his front.

"I believe it to be the H.M.S Valor, manned by a crew of mutineers. They surely saw the fire in the night and are no doubt investigating." Will's eyes lifted back to the sails on the horizon as he spoke.

"And how do you know this?" Lilith pressed, squeezing her hand on the wood of the rail at her hip.

"The damage she, we, sustained in our engagement with you. Her forward larboard rail, it's barely visible in the sight glass, but the damage matches what I know the Valor to have sustained. Also, I believe she would be making such a maneuver to come about on the

Endurance at some point, with the wind at her back." Will answered. His tone was flat, monotonous while conveying information with no ill feeling toward the pirates or to the crew that had mutinied against their commander.

"How many guns?" Trina pressed in closer to Will.

"She's rigged for twenty-eight, fourteen guns per side. When you landed your broadsides eight guns were destroyed on the larboard battery, leaving six on that side. My guess is they will have moved guns over from the starboard battery by now to even trim and firepower. That will mean she has ten-gun batteries on both sides, eighteen pounders with two long nines on her bow. She's a force to be reckoned with, even short crew." Will rambled, staring out over the seas with a glossed overlook.

"How short is her crew?" Lilith asked.

"You killed near twenty immediately with your broadsides. Wounded another dozen, of those four survived. We were short crew when we put to sea though." Will began.

"How many?" Lilith raised her voice, gripping her cutlass and causing Will to take a step back.

"Fifty-five able bodies, at the most. I don't know if any were lost to the mutiny, it could be less," he stammered out, flustered by the young woman's sudden anger.

Lilith took a step back, feeling the blood drain from her face. She looked at Trina while a helpless feeling washed over her soul, sucking her into depths of a sudden despair she could not express.

"Trin, we don't have that many. And what we do have, we can't sail and man the guns, we can't outrun her…" Lilith's voice trailed off as her eyes locked on to Trina's.

"We will find a way girl. Now is when you need to be brave. Not for you, "She paused, pointing out to the crew on deck, "For them."

All three of them looked out to the horizon, those little white sails were already growing larger.

"Trina." Lilith said, again squeezing the grip of her sword.

"Yes girl." Trina replied, breaking her stare to look at Lilith.

"Fly the colors." Lilith said, her eyes still locked onto their approaching enemy.

"Aye Captain!"

Drowned Maiden
27 Sept 1808
18 Degrees 20 minutes N, 76 Degrees 12' W

Will looked aloft, standing next to the beautiful young pirate captain while her banner unfurled into the wind felt surreal, a dream which he did not remember falling asleep for. The rising sunlight danced across the white of that devilish horned skull and trident, the image up close seemed even more imposing than the day he had watched a pair of them sail away from his crippled ship. He could still hear the screams of the wounded sailors in the recesses of his memory, for a moment he felt his throat tighten, his face flushed. At one point, he thought, not long ago I vowed to lay this ship along the bottom, now they are my salvation. His stomach knotted and his temples throbbed, the slight motion of the deck he was so accustomed to suddenly seemed exaggerated, intolerable. He was not sick, so much as he was thoroughly unsettled. The black fabric mocked him, snapping in the breeze as it reached its perch above the stern. Will's eyes began to gloss, the wind in his face felt hollow, lacking the sense of freedom and adventure he longed over when he was ashore.

"Take him below, with the others." Lilith told Trina when she returned from raising the harbinger of death and chaos over his head.

    Will gave no resistance to being led below, he felt as if he were a ship with slack lines and no rudder, dangerously adrift. The warmth below deck closed in around him as they proceeded up the passageway, invading his nostrils with the smell of cramped quarters, wood and tobacco smoke, the brine of the sea meeting the musk of timbers. It was a familiar smell, usually comforting, but today he took no solace in it. As the iron hinges squealed on the first of two heavy doors, Will peered in. A rotund man dressed in rags and smelling like death sat alone in a corner. Will looked at Trina for a fleeting moment, finding no mercy in the eyes of a woman he had saved from death. Letting out a sigh of resignation he entered the cell, hearing the squeaking cry of the hinges and then a clunk as Trina closed the door firmly behind him. The patter of sea against hull and voices in the cell next to him brought his situation into stark reality.

The man in the corner hardly moved, except for the quick rise and fall in his chest and belly, Will would have thought him dead. He opened an eye, staring up at Will for a moment and then closed it dismissively.

"Have they taken a Royal Navy ship now?" the man asked, through his labored breath.

"Taken. Never. They've sunk the Endurance." Will answered, trying to quell his stomach from the awful smell of the man.

"Admiral Sharpe. That is a shame, I held hope he would get me out of this mess." The reply came as he relieved himself without moving.

"There is a bucket." Will cut, no longer hiding his disgust. The fresh smell of urine mixed into the already foul odors permeating the small cell. The man hadn't bathed and was sweating profusely, to add to the concoction his bowel movements were handled in the same matter as his urine.

"What's the use? We'll be dead soon enough, you as well, so you can dispense with your comments. I won't be taking inquiry today, nor ever again," his hand waved in a grand dismissive gesture.

"Who are you? How did you come to be on this ship?" Will asked through a squint, trying to see the man's face in the dimness.

"What does it matter? I can be King George and You Admiral Cornwallis; it makes no difference lad. We will die at the hands of these savages. Did you see? They have Negroes commanding, they will skin us or slit our throats if they don't run us aground first," the man dithered in sobbing tones.

"She seemed seaworthy to me, maybe short of crew, but…" Will began to interject but was interrupted.

"They are all savages! Fit for cane and cotton field, nothing more! I wouldn't even let them work in the bloody kitchens!" his drivel turned to screams, the voices in the next cell quieted.

"Lieutenant Pike? Everything alright over there?" a voice from Shelton echoed in from a barred porthole in the door.

"Yes. Yes, we're fine in here." Will answered, then turned to the filthy man, "What is your name Sir? We likely aren't going anywhere soon; I'd just as soon know whose piss I'm standing in."

"I am Lord Geor Alton, the King's appointed governor of the Jamaica colony if you must know. But you will find that rank and title are lost on these buffoons. Privilege and position mean nothing to animals, so I wouldn't waste your breath," his answer inflated and Will took it as another sarcastic tirade.

"Right. Well, I'll certainly remember the time I was imprisoned with a mad man who claimed to be a lord while pissing himself." Will snorted, leaning against a wall and looking for a clean spot where he could sit.

"No, I meant it. I am a Lord, I am the Lord Governor of the Jamaica colony." Alton huffed.

"Yes Sir. Let me fetch the Endurance off the bottom, Lord Governor, and we will get to rendering honors." Will quipped, tired of the conversation by now.

"You served aboard the Endurance?" the filthy lord demanded.

"Not originally, I was assigned as first Lieutenant aboard the Valor." Will said, finally finding a spot to plant his seat.

"I gave special orders for the H.M.S Valor to search for a missing merchant ship upon their arrival to Nassau. The Carolina Shepherd, I believe it was," he spat, leveling his stare at William.

Will's mind went into a race, who else

could know this but the man who signed the order?

"How did you get here?" Will asked, still guarding against some evil jest he suspected was coming.

"Oh, I've been working my way to this for a good while I suppose. A year since I was approached by that Mr. Sladen, months and weeks now whilst things have gone all awry." Geor Alton babbled, gesturing his hands while he spoke.

"Sladen. Tim Sladen? An American?" Will asked with a quickening pulse as his temper began to rise.

"Oh yes, that's the devil. You've met?

"Met him? I saw him kill Admiral Sharpe. He and his men ambushed our shore party, we lost half our compliment of marines. Wait? You were working WITH this man?" Will's anger grew, rising up into his voice.

"Why yes lad. I hadn't much choice in the matter. These are powers you cannot even comprehend, let's not complicate our last hours, why fret about it now?" the governor waved at him, a gesture he knew dismissing him to silence.

"Or, Lord Governor, you can answer my questions. Perhaps enlightening me to what in the King's bloody name created such a blunder of things." Will seethed through clenched jaw.

"Oh, the King bloody well knows

what's occurring. Who do you think cleared the way for this sailor?"

"What? The King cleared the way for what? What are you talking about?" Will snapped, drawing a confused look from the ranting Lord.

"You really don't know what this is all about? The slave trade boy, Parliament in all their wisdom passed the abolition of the slave trade last year. Against the wishes of our monarch." Geor babbled through his labored breathing, "After the rebels in America won their independence, he cannot afford more unrest, nor look weak in the face of Bonaparte. So, he instructed a more, well, discreet method."

Will sat with his back pressed into a corner of the cell, staring into the face of the deposed Governor. The knots he expected in his stomach did not come, only a tingle into the palms of his hands, a heightened awareness of the sounds surrounding him. The shock of this revelation fell flat, and Will knew it was because somewhere inside, he had suspected something of this nature all along. Ever since the day he met with Captain Grimes on the bow of the Valor, a lurking unrest had haunted him. Then a thought struck Will and his hands began to clench.

"You knew of this. All of it. And you let this Sladen murder the Admiral? You let him fire on the fleet? Do you have any idea how many souls were lost in the harbor that day?" Will's tone rose into shouts, evoking a tremble from the Governor.

"No, lad, no, Sladen took me captive. When the Admiral sent a shore party into the prison camp, Sladen thought I had betrayed him to steal a large payment. I had no part in any of that. When the fleet was under fire, I was in a cell in the fort."

"So, you say. Lord Alton, this is treason."

"Against what? The Crown? Use your head boy! Who do you think arranged for this?" Geor shouted in reply, leaning forward in a struggle against his gut. "You have no idea what you are stepping in son. You would be best served to forget this mess, die with a clear head."

"I don't intend to go quietly Governor. You may have surrendered your honor, but I refuse. Whether this was your doing Lord Alton or the King's, it is treason and I will not go along with this." Will glowered, rising to his feet.

"What exactly do you think you are going to do lad? You are a prisoner, same as me. They will kill us both, it's only a matter of when." Geor snorted, prodding his finger in Will's direction.

Under his feet Will could feel the Maiden shift course in a hard turn, prompting him to brace himself on the bulkhead at his side. In the cell next to his, Will could hear several of his men topple over.

"Governor, you're going to explain this to me. How does this operate? How have these arrangements been made?" Will said as he straightened from the ship's lurching turn.

"I don't see why I would. I told you, I intend to spend my last moments at ease," his driveling speech cut short when Will's boot set firmly against his throat.

"You're going to tell me everything Geor, or you will die here, at my hand, traitor." Will seethed, pressing his boot into the Lord's neck until his face began to change color, then removing it suddenly to a fury of coughing and spit.

"What? What is it you want to know?" Geor hacked through wheezing coughs.

"How is the American involved?" Will pressed, raising his voice higher.

"He works for an apparatus called 'the order', he is their chosen representative."

"The Order?"

"A combination of both American southerners and British Lords of the King's choosing. They have met twice now and their next council approaches soon." Alton wheezed, still clutching at his throat in dramatic fashion.

"Give me names." Will demanded.

"I have none to give, son. I've never met a single one of them, like I said, Mr. Sladen is their sole representative. I don't even know the date or location of their next meeting," came the sniveling answer.

Will stepped away, weighing his position, his options. They were few. Any way he went about things now, if he were to stand by his honor, he would be branded a traitor. If he could somehow get off this ship and return to England unscathed, he wouldn't be able to live with himself. *Do what you know to be right.* Captain Grimes' words rang through Will's ears almost as if he were in the room with him. He took a deep breath of the fouled air in the cell, letting it out slowly while stepping towards the cell door.

"Guard!" he called out, "Get Trina down here, or your Captain. There's something they need to hear."

H.M.S Valor
27 Sept 1808
17 Degrees 34 minutes N, 76 Degrees 14' W

Salt water sprayed in the wind as the hull of the Valor slid through the waves, her sails stood taut, harnessing the wind in their haste northward toward the smoke plume on the horizon. On the quarterdeck, Cobb paced between rails checking course and wind, eyeballing sail and line and helm. The gradual approach toward the ominous column of smoke slanting upward into the sky maddened him further with every passing heartbeat. His mind was wholly consumed by verifying the doom of the Endurance. Each glance and look from sailors on deck brought amplified his mistrust of the men around him, making him manic to a point of intolerance.

The morning sun had brought no comfort, even though the night had an edge of chill, it laid bare the frayed looks and distraught temperament of a crew he no longer trusted. And he was beginning to see the feeling was mutual. He turned on his heel, making another swift plot across deck to face the sun.

"Sail! North of the wreckage, heading north by west!" The forward lookout called down.

Before the call was repeated Cobb was off in a run to the bow. His looking glass in hand, he weaved between crewmen as they gathered around to catch a glimpse for themselves. He extended his glass and raised it to his eye, scanning from left to right over the debris field where the smoke continued rising from scattered flotsam and a hulk of ship still protruding from the water's surface. At first pass he saw nothing, empty horizon and smoke. Then, edging out from the pillar of thick black and gray wafting from the water in a slanting cone from the wind, he caught a glimpse of her. She was angling away from their approach and using the smoke screen to cover her movement. Cobb turned skyward to the lookout.

"What can you see of her?" he shouted.

"Just the mainsail Sir. She's blocked by the smoke!" the lookout called back with a shrug.

Cobb gritted his teeth in frustration, wanting to rap the sailor across the mouth. His frustrations becoming more and more apparent to the crew standing around him. His gaze fell to the deck and then lifted to the men around him.

"Well! If we can't see them yet what are you lurking about for! Back to work!" he screamed, flailing his arms before making a threatening grasp on the hilt of his sword. He turned back up toward the lookout, "Call out as soon as you can see her colors!"

"Aye Sir." the reply fell flat onto the deck while Cobb looked aft and stomped his way toward the helm.

Cobb trudged his way past sailors tending lines and the petty officers minding them. Each giving him glances with a varying degree of both fear and contempt. By the time he reached the helm, Cobb could feel the eyes of every hand on his back. He quickly wheeled about, facing back to the bow only to find the men at their tasks. Am I going mad, he thought to himself while watching the activity aloft. Sailors in the rigging seemed occupied with their minor adjustments, coaxing every bit of speed they could from the Valor. On deck it was more of the same, hands were either absorbed in their tasks or looking out over the bow. "Keep it together lad, you're cracking up." Cobb grumbled under his breath.

    The wafting pillar of smoke drew nearer and nearer as the Valor cut their way north, the smell of soot and burning wood thickening as they passed the debris field off the larboard rail. Cobb examined the protruding hulk of ship as it bobbed at the surface, its surface spotted with flames and smoke. Even through the hazy field of smoke he could make out the distinct figure carved beneath the protruding bowsprit. Her lovely figure was being consumed by flames gnawing away at the wooden bodice, the face already lost to a blackened char, she was all that remained of the Admiral's ship the H.M.S Endurance. Cobb felt a presence step beside him along the rail and looked to see the hollow face of Mr. Sladen.

    "That'll be the end of it. A failed rebellion." Cobb announced, loud enough for crew around him to hear.

    "I wouldn't be so sure, Mr. Cobb." Tim replied with his signature drawl. Cobb turned to face him, irritated by his reproach.

    "Cobb! She's flying a black banner!" the aft lookout called down, just as Cobb was about to berate the American. His mouth froze, still beginning to form words when the cry came down from above. He exchanged a look with Tim and grew more irritated when he found that his alarm was met by a glance of indifference from the American.

"Do you intend to engage them?" Tim asked with a wily grin. Cobb squinted at the question, rubbing his chin and poking in his mind at what the American could be getting at.

"Yes. She is flying a black banner. Of course we are." Cobb snorted.

"Keeping up appearances?" Tim quipped.

"What are you saying? Just bloody be plain about it! I've had enough of your sniveling weasel speak." Cobb's grumble grew into a shout.

"I'm only observing. It is curious that a man in the service of the Royal Navy would take so much joy in seeing the Admiral's ship destroyed," his tone was elevated and Cobb could sense he was being baited, though he couldn't see to what end.

"The Admiral was in open rebellion; I've told you this." Cobb rebuked, noting that sailors on deck were beginning to take notice of the exchange.

"And I've told you, privately, that pirates were the true cause behind the unrest in Kingston. But you have obviously not informed your crew! What exactly are you trying to accomplish out here? Have you led all these men into a mutiny against their appointed commander for some personal mission of revenge?" Tim's voice was now raised so every hand aboard could hear. "My only intention is to recover property belonging to the East India Trading Company, as I was hired to. It appears to me that you have some motive of secret agenda Mr. Cobb. These fine men aboard deserve an explanation!"

"What? What are you saying? No, the Admiral was attempting…" Cobb began.

"A what? The Admiral was attempting a rebellion? To what end Mr. Cobb? Stealing gold? Does that seem plausible to any of you?" Tim shouted aloud, gesturing to the sailors looking on.

"You snake bastard!" Cobb hissed under his breath. "Clap him in irons and lead him below!"

A moment of hesitation passed, while the crew of the Valor looked on to the quarreling men, unmoving. Tension mounted through the silence as Cobb looked around to the crew hesitating against his order. His face flushed, growing hot against the wind and his temples began to throb with his racing pulse. Looking around him, Cobb saw confusion in the men instead of resolve.

"I said clap him in irons and lead him below! What in the bloody name of Mary are you waiting for? An invitation?" his voice cracked as sailors gathered around him, seemingly unconcerned with his tirade.

"You've forgotten an important detail of maintaining order on a ship Mr. Cobb." Tim said with a widening smile as the sailors began to circle behind him.

"And what is that?" Cobb stammered.

"Once you mutiny against a commander without good cause, eventually, it will be you next." Tim said. Cobb didn't have time to react. From both side sailors approached and seized his arms, preventing him from drawing his weapon. In an instant his head was covered in a burlap hood and only fleeting small glimpses of the outside world were available to his eyes through the gaps between its course threads. An impact along the back of his neck and head shot blinding pain wrapping around his skull, dropping him to his knees. He began to protest, but a second impact struck between his shoulders on his back, sending him sprawling across the hard-wooden deck. Before he could get his hands under his torso to lift himself up his arms were grabbed again, and he was bound wrist to wrist behind his back.

"This man has made mutineers of all of you! Unknowingly, you men trusted his word. But I am here to tell you now that you have been deceived! I've told you the truth as I know it and too late it seems to save the Admiral or Lieutenant Pike, but follow me and I will do everything I can to deliver you all from the gallows!" Tim shouted over the gathered crew. His speech was met with a quick cheer of assenting shouts. "Those pirates have sunk the Endurance and robbed them of payments to be made to the Lords in ownership of the East India Company. Follow me and we will exact revenge on them for the loss of your countrymen and recover that payment, for which you will be handsomely rewarded!" More cheers and shouts followed. Cobb tried to shout his dissent, but it was lost under the burlap and as the voice quieted a single kick landed in his ribs, stealing away his breath.

In the clamor of shouts and cheers Cobb was lifted onto unsteady feet. He struggled to breathe through the pain in his ribs, which shot through his torso with each attempt to inhale. He could feel hands all around him, shoving and prodding at him and then there was a driving sharp point pressed hard against his back.

"And what do we do with this one?" a voice shouted out above the others.

"Throw him over for the cold depths!" another answered.

"No! Hang him! He committed mutiny and brought us all along for the ride, let him taste the noose!" yet another cried out.

Cobb's heart pounded harder and harder with each response while the crew's appetite to see him dead was voiced. A slight jab from the point in his back prodded him forward to some grizzly fate he could not yet see. Footfalls on the wooden deck around him urged him on through driving mystery hits on the bag covering his head. He stumbled, but before he could fall hands were grabbing at him, forcing him to his feet and the point in his back continued urging him on. The process repeated several times as they marched him blindly up the deck, Cobb knew they were moving toward the bow, but he couldn't see enough detail through the tiny holes in the bag to collect where he was exactly. The voices around him hushed slightly and the point pulled away from his back. Hands that had been tugging his blouse pulled away and Cobb was left standing alone with the deck shifting beneath his feet. A sudden hit to his belly doubled him over, driving the wind he had just recovered right back out again followed by another to the back of his legs collapsing him to the deck, driving his knees onto the hard wooden planks.

When the burlap hood was ripped away a world of blinding light rushed into Cobb's eyes. His vision was blurred, and his head pounded from being struck, blood trickled down from his brow and ear where he had been hit several times on the march up the ship. The bleary forms of sailors crowded around him and as his vision began to clear, he could see they were all looking down on him with dreadful expressions of murderous intent.

"Let me see him." Tim's voice came from behind the crowd, parting the sailors until Cobb could see him, looking down from the forecastle. "Mr. Cobb, as you can see, your crew holds no great love for you. I suspect they never have. We will make your departure from us as dignified as you deserve." Sladen said with a sickening grin.

Shouted threats and insults pelted Cobb from the crowd while an abrasive course rope was lowered from the rigging. A sailor standing by Mr. Sladen fashioned a noose from the bitter end of the line while they all continued to hurl insults and jeers down on him. Tim's stare focused in on Cobb and when their eyes locked all faded from existence to Cobb but that grotesque smile. He was lording victory over the ousted commander and using Cobb's own crew to do the deed. The heavy loop of a noose dropping over his head broke their death stare and even before it was cinched tight, he could feel it gnawing at the flesh of his neck. Cobb was dragged to his feet in a rough manner by a sailor at each side.

"Heave away and farewell Mr. Cobb," Tim said with a sloppy mocking salute repeated by many of the sailors surrounding him. A crew of men out of sight from Cobb began to heave the heavy line taking slack out in long jaunts until the rope was taut. The next heave took Cobb's feet from the deck, biting the fibers of the rope into his flesh. He sucked for air getting only a gulp before his airway closed, the next heave rose him in a violent leap well over the heads of the sailors on deck. Cobb struggled against his wrist binding while the rope at his throat burned while it tore at the skin under the strain of his weight. His heartbeat screamed in his chest, sending a throbbing up through his neck radiating around his head. Cobb's eyeballs felt as if they would explode with pressure while his lungs burned for air, pulsating against the airway closed off by the combination of rope and gravity. Another heave on the line sent a gush of blood from Cobb's throat down amongst the crowd of sailors on deck, he could feel the warm fluid running from his ripped flesh down his chest and belly. Through bulging eyes, he could see the pirate ship, not so far off in the distance. A black banner rippling through the wind behind her stared back at him with hollow eyes from a menacing horned skull. Cobb kicked his feet and bucked himself, straining his bound hands desperately. His vision blurred and doubled, pain seared the fibers of his mind, white hot and relentless. His body tensed and seized erratically beyond his control. All sound faded from the world and he could feel another warmth drip from his pants as he lost control of his bladder. His final fading thoughts seemed to echo over and over in his mind. *Good. Piss on them.*

Chapter 14

Drowned Maiden
27 Sept 1808
19 Degrees 12 minutes N, 74 Degrees 03' W

The sharp smell of smoke still lingered in Lilith's nostrils, drowning out the brine of the sea and even Chibs' pipe which he puffed at with the same fervor, sitting at the aft castle bulkhead behind the helm. Her attention lay absorbed in the Maiden's sails and her course. After consulting Chibs from his position on deck with a chart in hand, she had devised a plan which would rob their adversary of the advantage of both guns and numbers, but only if everything worked in her favor. She judged wind speed and direction and agonized constantly over the wheel and sail positioning, making minute corrections every few minutes. By Chibs' reckoning, they would make round the southern point of west Haiti before the pursuing ship was within firing range. But only if the wind held.

Every sail change required close guidance and it quickly became obvious that maneuvering while running the gun batteries would be out of the question until her crew was far more experienced. "We'll use a different strategy is all Lil. It makes no difference how you beat their commander, so long as you beat them." Chibs had told her. While the sun rose high above into the sky, they had made the best use they could of the smoke screen rising up from the wreckage of the Endurance, shielding their own movement from the ship far to the south. Shortly after noon though, it became apparent that they had been spotted by the ship Will had identified as the Valor, which skirted the wreckage and made sail on course toward the Maiden.

On deck it felt like an ongoing funeral procession. The hands with experience either grieved for their lost captain or could see the impending danger approaching from behind while the Africans who had recently become part of the crew quickly realized how few an ineffective they were while executing basic sailing tasks. The only chance they had to best a seasoned crew, as Chibs had told Lilith, was to outthink them. The Valor was a Royal Navy warship, even without her commander she would have a seasoned crew, weary to almost any trickery a sixteen-year-old girl could produce. "So. You'll have to do something that will catch an old sailor off guard. And it just so happens, you've got an old sailor on deck girl. We might just fare alright." It did little to ease Lilith's mind as the sails behind grew larger while the Valor continued making headway against them, gaining on them with every passing hour.

Trina was a comforting presence, ever patient and instructive with the green crew of African rescues as she was with Lilith those first few weeks after she had joined the ranks of the Maiden. When the guard she had posted below to watch over their prisoners appeared on deck requesting Trina come below, Lilith thought nothing of it until Trina had been absent for some time. When Trina materialized on deck with Lieutenant Pike at her side, she didn't know what to think, other than Trina must have held a soft spot for the man who had spared her life.

"He says he is ready to do as the Maiden requires Captain, as well as the charges he came aboard with." Trina said.

"Just hours ago, he was ready to die before committing service to the Maiden. What changes? Should I expect a sword at my throat the minute I look away?" Lilith cut back, giving Will a suspicious glare.

"I met your other prisoner. He has enlightened me to the circumstances behind what has occurred since my arrival in the Caribbean." Will uttered with a somber stare.

"The governor?" Chibs chimed, "Piss on that fat old dirtball. He's so full of lies I'm surprised a sailor would give any credit to his hot air. Just a bunch of flotsam and dredge yield if you ask me."

"No, Sir. He is genuine, and he is the governor of Jamaica. He has proved as much to me based purely off information only the governor would be apprised of. The conclusions I have come to are disturbing. But based on them, I cannot in good conscience stay my present course. I will aid you in your effort, miss. So long as the ships you engage are not law-abiding merchantmen." Will replied in a curt, matter of fact affect.

"Fine. Relieve them of their restraints and put them to work Trin. But don't arm them yet. I'm not quite convinced this won't result in my throat being cut from behind." She gave Will a side glance while she spoke, "Or at least, I'm not convinced they would try it."

"Try and fail girl. I saw what she can do with a sword aboard the Endurance, Lieutenant. Don't let those princess eyes fool you. She'd drop your corpse to the deck and step into her next sword swing, that's a fact." Chibs added, pointing his weathered finger at the officer with a squinting glare. Lilith wore his protective threats like a shield, raising her eyebrows at Will, inviting his response.

"I have no intentions of the sort. The Valor is my charge, whether the crew has mutinied or not, I am responsible for her actions and if she is aiding the slave trade, I will see her to the bottom while I live and breathe," his words drug out as if he could barely annunciate them. "I'll serve to that end, in any way that I can."

Lilith furrowed her eyebrows in a

moment of thought, Trina gave her an encouraging nod, yet it was not quite enough but with so few able bodies aboard she needed every strong back and willing heart. Chibs shifted in his seat, looking over everyone that had congregated in front of him. His tightly wrapped wounds showed no sign of infection yet, but the French doctor still held a concern over his long-term outlook especially after Lilith's vows to hold him directly accountable. The salty quartermaster grimaced, pulling himself up by a ledge from the stairs he sat next to onto shaky legs. Lilith darted to aid him, only to be gently rebuffed.

"I'll get it, girl. I can't have you powdering my arse the rest of my damned life. Let me be." Chibs insisted, groaning with each movement up to his feet. When he finally stood erect, he leaned forward into a movement of the ship and nearly lost balance, recovering it after a little shuffling of his feet. He grabbed onto Lilith's shoulder and looked over to an onlooking Will.

"You can use the help Lil. I say release them from their cell, let them aid us, hell, I'd arm them if that ship gets close enough for it to matter.", he shifted his eyes over to the beleaguered officer, "He knows if any harm befalls you miss, it'll be me he answers to. Even wounded, it's a stretch too far for most men, this one won't be a problem."

"Aye, Chib." Lilith replied, then

turning, "Trina, release the Lieutenant's men and see them to work. No weapons for them until we absolutely must."

"Yes Captain." Trina's response came sharp and clear.

The addition of Will's sailors and marines brought an immediate renewed vigor into the lifeblood of the Maiden. For hours the mournful glances between pirates old and new had told a tale of certain defeat to come, after only a few minutes on deck the disciplined and spirited men had every soul aboard tacked onto a new course. Urgency and resolve became the new theme, replacing exhaustion and despair. Sails were trimmed tighter and changes made with precision, quickening their pace. In less than an hour the Maiden had gone from losing ground and hope to steadily increase their lead. It was a lifted weight from Lilith's shoulders, a stay of execution. The palpable relief felt through the crew lifted her spirit momentarily, until Will approached her on the quarterdeck as she looked back toward the Valor falling further behind.

"We can delay them a while like this. But if she jettisons some ballast and makes a few sail changes, they will catch us. What do you plan to do miss Lilith?" he asked with a sober expression.

"Captain Lilith." She cut back, correcting him.

"My apologies, Captain." Will said with a sheepish grin.

"Do you have a suggestion Lieutenant Pike? Or are you just going to glower at my ineptness?" Lilith said, annoyed by his smile.

"I do, Captain Lilith. If you'll take it." Will replied. "We can't outrun her indefinitely, but there are things we can do to keep her at bay until the opportune moment to strike. I recommend you lift a gun onto the quarterdeck, they will be hesitant to run within range if you fire an occasional shot off her bow."

Lilith was intrigued by his suggested tactic, but still unsure of trusting him.

"Is it so important to fire at her bow that I should weaken the strength of my broadside?" Lilith asked in scouring tone.

"I don't intend that you should weaken anything that is not already emaciated Captain. The simple truth is that even with the few men I have that can contribute to your fighting power, we don't have enough to sail and execute gunnery. We need to delay and stall them until we can gain a tactical advantage either by sea condition or using the chart to our advantage." Will answered with a steady even cadence, his eyes locked onto hers. "I meant what I have told you Captain. My only aim is to see their end."

"Aye, so it would seem. Alright Lieutenant Pike, we will move the gun. See to it yourself and use whatever you need to get it done. As for using the charts to defeat our adversaries, you can rest assured Will, I have a plan," she shot him a confident smile while he stepped off the quarter deck to effect his contributions.

Lilith looked back out over the seas separating them from the Valor and noted the sun hanging low in the sky. Chibs huffed his way up next to her, the evening light playing on his face and seeming to give him back some of his color.

"You really should be below Chib, resting." Lilith said, knowing full well the response she would get.

"Aye, I should be a rich old fat man, eating and drinking my fill and surrounded by beautiful women, but here I be." Chibs grumbled with a smile, "I heard you gnawing at the Lieutenant. Now I'm curious girl. What is this plan of yours?"

"How long of a run is it to the cove Chib?" she asked with a daring flash across her eyes.

"What? The slaver cove?" he looked stumped.

"No, Chib, the cove we refitted the Shepherd in. The Haitian cove." Lilith said lowering her voice as Will came back on deck with a couple sailors in to aid moving the gun.

"Well, not more than a day. But what do you plan there Captain? It's folly to try and outrun them. We'll surely still be in sight range, so we can't hide. Once we're in the cove Lil, we'll be trapped." Chibs replied growing exasperated as he spoke.

"I don't intend to hide Chibs and yes, I will make sail into the cove in full plain sight of them. But if all works according to my plan, it will be the Valor sailing into my trap. I just need to keep them at bay through the daylight hours." Lilith's eyes narrowed as she spoke, looking at Chibs she tried to gauge his response to her ambiguous outline. He scratched his foot along the deck, looking hesitant.

"The Lieutenant should be able to keep them at length Captain, for a day at least. And yes, any commander worth his salt will sail right after you and bottle us into that cove. What could you possibly hope… to…" Lilith watched the realization hit as he spoke. A broad smile spread across his face and a shimmer of understanding came to his eye. "Girl, that's going to bait them right in perfect. She'll be a sitting duck."

"Yes. And I don't intend to take prisoners afterward quartermaster. See to it the crew is understanding. If the new members have a change of heart when the time comes, I want them dealt with swiftly as well."

"Aye Captain. No Quarter." Chibs replied with a satisfied grin.

H.M.S Valor
27 Sept 1808
19 Degrees 22 minutes N, 74 Degrees 13' W

Cobb's body swayed with the pitch of the ship, still dangling from the noose against the backdrop of red and purple evening glory in the Caribbean sky. His face remained twisted in a grotesque expression of pain and panic while his body remained rigid. The soft creaking of the thick line suspending his corpse sounded with every pitch and sway of the ship, death's mocking serenade. The promise of gold payment for timely capture of the pirate ship ahead fomented the crew to action after the grizzly end of their mutinous leader, they had drawn together for renewed purpose before the dripping blood from his neck had ceased.

Tim largely ignored any sideways looks he'd had to endure before Cobb swung, afterward it seemed as if the crew around him had galvanized at the promise of opulent payments. How quickly they forget, he thought, of their brethren I fed to the creatures of the deep, how beautiful a thing greed can be. Sails snapped and popped in the wind as the crew made adjustments to regain on their prey who in the waning hours of daylight, had made a remarkable increase in speed. Tim cared little for sailing and knew even less; his only concern remained the recovery of what remained of the money owed to the Order and silencing every voice who could give accurate details to anyone of consequence.

Evening burned its way beneath the waves of the western horizon and the skies were soon littered with a million brilliant jewels of light, glittering and shimmering off the rippling seas. With the sunlight gone the night brought a chill which Tim cursed along with the never-ending sawing sway of the deck. His stare remained locked onto the sails on the horizon, even when they had gained back the distance lost earlier and drew even nearer, he could not bring himself to remove his eyes. His trapped focus was more than a tunnel vision of blind hatred. He was afraid. He feared losing the ship to the night or being left at too far a range to regain their position. He dreaded the possibility that she was manned by a seasoned crew of pirates that would ambush them from some position along the coast. But more than that, with the ever present creaking of Cobb dangling above on his noose, Tim feared losing the promise of payment for the crew and the inevitable retribution that would occur when some of their uttered oaths were no longer lost to the glitter of promised gold.

A slender moon did little to illuminate the night, but what light she did cast play along the pirate's sails marking their position long into the darkness. Tim's vigil on the bow outlasted the darkness of night as he stubbornly refused to allow the fleeing pirates a moment unwatched. Fiery columns of morning stretched their way into the sky, invading the heavens and slowly drowning the light of their brilliance. His eyes and legs ached, and his back felt as sour as his mood when he finally relented to sitting down at a bench near the helm. Tim had spent his life around soldiers and considered himself one still. Sailors were a different breed entirely, hard men for certain, but peculiar in Tim's eyes. Some soldiers he had worked with were superstitious, which Tim considered a sign of lower intelligence, but it seemed almost every man aboard the Valor was concerned at some point or another about the bad luck of this or that. Just hearing it exhausted him as his mind reeled through constant reasonings to disprove their archaic beliefs.

Morning wore on and the sun edged it's way free of the embrace of the horizon, basking the seas in it's warm glorious light. Tim remained seated on his bench, closely observing the helmsman while regularly peering out over the bow to make sure the sails they pursued hadn't somehow eluded them without his constant watch. A grizzled petty officer approached him, unshaven and barefoot with horridly crooked and stained teeth, the man pulled a pipe from the clutches of his bite and pointed it toward the weather hatch leading below deck. His rambling brogue came across to Tim as utter gibberish, incoherent and undecipherable. Tim furrowed his brow at the rattle of the petty officer, trying to make sense of what he was saying. "What?" The response came even faster and less understandable. A younger seaman heard the exchange and approached behind the petty officer.

"He's saying, we need to shove off some of the ballast below decks to make better speed, Yankee. Except he's a damned Scot, so he talks like his arse is on fire and his tongue is swollen. Do you want us to?" the sailor spat.

"Do we need the ballast? Is this something we will all be regretting later?" Tim inquired with a thoughtful glare.

"No, she'll handle differently, sure, but we can make do. Even if the weather kicks up, we'd be doing well to have a touch more freeboard, Sir," the reply came back in the sailor's gravelly rasp of voice. Tim thought for a second how wretched these sailors all seemed and yet were so competent at their craft.

"Yes. Let's be rid of what we can. Make all haste to catch that ship. I'd like to be walking over the corpses of her crew by nightfall." Tim drawled out.

"We'll have it done then. Sir."

The wrecked cannon hulks that had been secured in the hold as ballast crashed into the water as they were dropped overboard. One by one they were sent hurtling towards the bottom with a loud clap against the waters' surface and an explosion of bubbles trailing upward as heavy barrels disappeared from view. Almost instantly, as the last of the damaged cannons left the ship, Tim could feel their added speed. The petty officer he hadn't been able to understand barked some garbled order aloft and sails were quickly adjusted adding even more speed to their pursuit. Soon the black banner waving behind the fleeing ship ahead was close enough that Tim could stand on the bow and make out it's details clearly through a sight glass. The satanic looking skull seemed a typical fare for pirate crews along with a canted trident, yet another staple symbol of nautical marauders. But the object on the banner that vexed him played across the bottom of the black field. A chain, broken in the middle directly beneath the leering hollow eyed skull. Tim pulled his eye away from the glass and pondered a moment over the symbolism on the black flag. A broken chain, it could be anything, he supposed silently, but a pirate crew that displayed it on their flag while at the same time that he had lost two shipments of slaves bound for America? Could it be that this entire time he had mistaken the effort of these pirates for a betrayal by the Governor and his Admiral? He picked over events in his mind, deciding if that were the case it was far too late now to reverse course. He couldn't take back the ball he had shot into the Admiral's chest nor raise the ships he and his men had sunk in harbor. But a lingering feeling began to overcome him. The feeling someone gets when they discover they have made an egregious error and it's about to be unveiled to the light of day.

Tim's face flushed and his heartbeat quickened as he looked again through the glass, studying the ship they were drawing rapidly closer toward. The Valor was almost near enough that he could make out the form of individuals on the pirate's deck. He scanned their rigging through the flapping of the massive black flag, he could make out forms aloft, climbing ratlines and scurrying along the spars. Their shirts were what stood out, dirty and stained white cloth, the rest of their form was still too vague to glean any detail from at their distance. He angled the glass back down to the stern and as the pirates altered their course slightly the billowing black cloth revealed a split-second glimpse of the quarter deck. Tim's hands seemed frozen and his heart skipped, the breath he had been about to expel stuck in his throat almost choking him. In the void behind that infernal black flag he had spotted two blue navy coats and three spots of red that could only be royal marines. He recoiled the glass from his eye almost involuntarily and slammed a closed fist onto the wooden rail of the bulwark. His jaw clenched and he felt his teeth gritting from tension and strain. Above, the rope that still suspended Cobb over the bow decks creaked like a mocking raven offering its morbid note. Tim shot a seething glance to the dangling dead man as if Cobb had created this web of failure.

Tim stormed back toward the sailors on the quarterdeck in furious purpose.

"When can we begin firing on them?" he demanded with impatient fervor. The sailors exchanged glances and carried on while a petty officer took a step over to the irate American.

"We're still out of range. It'd be wasted shot and powder to fire on them now. On toward afternoon we might be close enough. But firing the chasers won't likely do us much good, we'd have to get an angle and aim for her rudder or the aft mast. I've seen it done, but that's master gunnery, not likely," came the sobering reply.

"As soon as we can levy effective fire on them, do it. I won't relent until we have what is ours." Tim said dryly.

"We'll be approaching the coastline soon, judging by their course. Haiti. We'd best stay well clear of French waters," cautioned the man.

"I care not for your concerns, continue the pursuit, whatever we encounter. I trust you men are capable to deal with any manner of complications." Tim retorted, unflinching. The sailor hesitated a moment, then gave a nod and continued to his work. Tim's jaw clenched again, grinding his teeth as he tried to formulate a plan should sailors aboard the Valor be confront with the sight of their countrymen aboard the pirate vessel. His schemes would unravel in his face, again. He doubted, if the truth behind his haphazard web of schemes and lies were revealed, that even the promise of gold would placate the crew. If the true nature of Admiral Sharpe's demise was revealed, Tim knew, he would suffer a fate much worse than Mr. Cobb. Somehow, if he managed to survive his current predicament, he still had to face his failures with the Order. Suddenly, swinging from a rope off the foremast seemed a tolerable end.

A single shot pierced the midday calm, with a puff of smoke rising up from the Pirate ship's stern. Tim heard a whining shriek and saw a geyser of seawater spray high into the air where the ball impacted. The Valor still lay outside of their range, Tim understood that much at least, but the pirates were sending him a message. Things were going to get precarious and soon, the coast of Haiti was now in view along the eastern horizon and shortly after passing the south western tip of the island, the pirate ship edged their bow over to a northeasterly heading. By evening they would be well into the gulf created by the southern and northern fingers of Haiti's west coast, and the sailors aboard the Valor assured him, the pirates would have no escape. They kept the Valor's course just west of the pirates and continued their distant pursuit, just out of cannon range.

Drowned Maiden
28 Sept 1808
19 Degrees 34 minutes N, 73 Degrees 4' W

Late afternoon whipped the warm southern wind across the Maiden's deck, filling her sails and the hearts of her crew. If these winds held, Lilith would be able to execute her plan just as she had imagined it and her heightened spirit was felt by all on deck. Chibs' gait seemed to liven as the coast came into sight, a mix of rocky outcroppings and low-lying sandy beaches. The bottom rose up to greet them like a long-forgotten friend as they made their way into the broad gulf off the western end of Haiti, fading the darker shades in the water to a brilliant blue just deeper than the sky. Lieutenant Pike and a couple of his marines had set up one of the twelve-pound cannons on the Maiden's stern and were periodically letting fly one of the deadly projectiles to warn off the pursuing Valor. The acrid powder smoke floated over the stern after each round before catching in the wind and dancing all along the deck before dissipating into nothingness.

The low beaches and rocky shores of Haiti rose up as the afternoon sun wore low, peaking in high rock faced cliffs that lorded over the sea edge, painted in subdued hues of the sunset shining on them. Lilith checked the rigging and the helm, making certain everything was in order. She rigged a red sash around her waist, which was now holding a cutlass, a smaller rapier and two loaded flintlock pistols. Lilith could feel the rising tension throughout the crew as they drew nearer to the mouth of the hidden cove. Her plan demanded a perfectly executed turn and masterful timing, but if they could pull it off their pursuers would have no chance to counter before their situation spiraled out of control.

Lieutenant William descended from the steps of the aft castle to where she stood near the helm, an expression of concern riddling his features.

"It won't be much longer Captain Lilith, once the light of day fades, they will make their move despite our gunnery work. If you have a plan, the sooner the better, as they say," he relayed his warning cautiously.

"Aye. I have a plan Lieutenant, but the more I think it through, the more I've realized I'm going to need your help," she said removing the air of distrust her heart had harbored.

"How can we be of service?" Will replied.

"That ship was in your command, correct?" she asked, giving him a glance from the side of her eyes.

"It was. She is crewed by mutineers now, men I wouldn't dare to count on." Will said with an edge of disappointment in his voice, "I would not rely on using me to parlay any truce with them, miss."

"I am not interested in any truce; I intend to give no quarter to the souls aboard. My interest is solely in your desire to see their end. Are you capable of killing the men you served with Lieutenant? Would that stain be more than your precious honor could bear?" her voice rose slightly as she laid out her concern, demanding an answer.

"I see it not as a treachery, Captain. Her crew mutinied against their lawful commander, that was treachery. Her King has bypassed the will of his people to continue inflicting harmful practice against humanity, that is treachery. Sending her to the bottom with every hand on board would not be a treachery in my eyes, for what that is worth, it will be a triumph of good over evil." Will replied in his even tone and then repeated his offer, "How can we be of service, to further your plan Captain?"

"I need your gunnery skills Lieutenant.

When the time comes, I need accurate fire, one gun at a time if need be. But we must absolutely score hits with every shot." Lilith implored.

"Gunnery I can do for you Captain. But if she draws near enough to board us Lilith, I fear we are too few to hold our own. If we're boarded, we will lose the ship along with our lives." Will said, his face a model of concern.

"Leave the finer points to me Lieutenant. Just have those guns ready to fire and make certain they strike true." Lilith said over her shoulder while she shuffled down the stairs onto the weather deck.

The mouth of the cove was coming into range and her timing couldn't have been better. The setting sun lit the back of Maiden's sails with a vibrant array of orange and pink. Untrained eyes would focus on her deck and on her sails for telltale signs of what she intended to do next and when she executed her intended maneuver, even old sea hands were likely to miss what Lilith truly had in store for them.

"Full canvas on the jibs, brace the fore yard and ready cables!" Lilith called out to the hands on deck. She leaned over the larboard rail keeping a keen eye to the water's surface. The detail she awaited would only offer her a split second to react and any hesitation would spell certain disaster for the ship, only to be compounded by the rapidly approaching enemy. Trina repeated her command and through the rigging the song of different accents reverberating the echoed orders lasted near a minute. Lilith loved it, she loved the business of running the ship and she was about to flex her newfound power as hard as she could.

The moment approached and Lilith saw exactly what she was looking for, a blurry white blotch under the surface of the seas adjacent to the cove opening. She paused for a heartbeat, waiting for the exact moment. Trina was aloft sitting along the far larboard end of the topsail spar up the foremast.

"Lilith!" Trina cried in a pleading shout.

"All hands hard to larboard! Take in gallants and tops and stand by to man the guns!" Lilith screamed.

The Maiden lurched hard, pitching over with the force of her turn, the steep angle of her decks made walking difficult. Then as the bow swung over to face the mouth of the cove her deck leveled again, bobbing up and down slightly from the force on her sails but trim and steady. In a tense moment every hand aboard glanced back at their pursuers, under full sail and lurching toward them in a rage. Lilith examined their stern and could barely make out through the brilliant light of the setting sun in the background, the dangling body of a man hung by the neck off her foremast. The Maiden nosed into the shadows cast by the rock face guarding their cove entrance. To our pursuers, Lilith bemused to herself, it must look like we've disappeared into the sheer cliffs themselves.

When the last edge of dusk had slipped from the Drowned Maiden's stern and she made her way into the deeper body of the cove Lilith was struck by a memory, just weeks ago she had looked along the towering cliffs as a fresh face on Maiden's decks. The way the bluffs faded from the guarding towers toward the sea down to a gentle slope, covered in grasses and overhung with a lush canopy of rain forest. She thought of James and the night he had spent teaching her the names of pictures in the stars, how his gentle manner had contrasted to violence he displayed just earlier that day.

"Captain!" Chibs' cry slapped her back to the present, "Now or never girl!"

They had sailed into the deeper part of the cove, aligning with the small opening behind them. The time had come for Lilith to finish setting her trap, the most audacious part of her plan.

"Helm, hard starboard," she shouted to Omibwe, snapping him back into action. "Ready the fore anchor and stand by at the cable!"

Crew scrambled as the Maiden made another hard, lurching turn, wheeling to face their battery at the mouth of the cove. "Anchor away! Loose all tacks and sheets, brace for impact!" Lilith screamed. The anchor slapped into the water, barreling through twenty fathoms of water in seconds. The Maiden reeled hard, pitching to her side again while crewmen held on for dear life to the rail. "Cut it away now!" Lilith cried, fearing her tactic was going to tip the vessel on its side with the violent force. A hand had stood ready for the order and with a ferocious swing of an ax, he cut away the anchor cable which recoiled into the water like a whip from tension. The Maiden settled back to trim relieving Lilith's acute fear of tipping, but there was no time to celebrate. As she looked out over the starboard rail, the Valor's bowsprit was edging its way into view at the mouth of the cove.

"A little farther lads, then you can turn right in." She uttered aloud, then turning to the open hatch leading below, "Lieutenant! Run them out!"

"Aye Captain!" Will shouted back before scrambling out of sight on the gun deck. In seconds, Lilith could hear the gun ports clanking open, one by one and then starting back at the rear cannon, creaking ropes and wheels as the men below ran them out. Her attention shifted back to the mouth of the cove, where the bow was now visible as the Valor made her turn inward. A tense moment passed, Lilith could feel her pulse echoing through her entire body, soaking her muscles with adrenaline and sharpening her state of alertness. Then, just as Lilith's mind began to think it would not come, a sickening growl reverberated through the cove. The sound of wooden planks being ripped asunder into the belly of the Valor by that threatening coral formation James had warned her of all those weeks ago.

The Valor shuddered under the impact, sending hands aloft hurtling from their perch down onto the hard-wooden deck, their sickening screams ending with an unceremonious hollow wooden thump. Crashing timbers and snapping lines sounded into the cove while the Valor heaved from the force of her sails against the hull crushing itself into the coral formation. Panicked screams floated over the gentle ripple of the cove to the waiting ears of Lilith's crew. A broad smile drew across her face, her eyes lighting up like burning embers from the inferno of tension and anxiety that had plagued the last days. Her heart soared as the crew let out loud cheers, almost drowning her shouts down into the gun deck.

"Now Lieutenant! Fire at will!" her cry pierced down into the gun deck, ushering a moment of silence. A heartbeat elapsed and the first cannon fired, roaring it's thunderclap through the cove and eliciting another round of raucous cheers and shouting from the

Maiden's crew. The impact slapped into the hull of the Valor sending jagged shards of wood careening across her bow, devouring flesh and sail alike. Another roaring report sent a cloud of smoke up from the Maiden's gun line, obscuring Lilith's view of the carnage they were inflicting for a brief moment. The second hit scoured part of the Valor's bow rail and penetrated into her foremast, sending another volley of wooden shrapnel flying about on deck to deadly effect. When Will fired the third and fourth cannons, Lilith began to see men abandoning the Valor in desperate attempts at self-preservation as their ship was being ripped apart from coral below and pummeled by iron shot above. When the first full volley of ten guns was complete, flames could be seen on the Valor's decks, creeping along freshly cracked and severed deck timbers deploying a wispy blanket of smoke of the horror scene.

"One volley will do for now Lieutenant. Load them and stand by. Well done." Lilith said, looking down onto the smoke-stained face of Lieutenant Pike who appeared to be taking no joy in the victory. "You have served the Maiden exactly as you pledged to. Once I've made certain their crew has all perished, you will be released from my service." The officer's expression remained unchanged and Lilith felt an annoying tug in her spirit telling her she was not done with the

Lieutenant for his part. Her unease faded as she turned to an ecstatic Trina and Chibs greeting her in celebration. Trina grabbed her into a hug, kissing her forehead while heaping praise onto her. Another round of cheers sounded high up into Maiden's rigging while flames from the Valor brightly flared against the fading dusk as one of her sails began to be consumed.

Chapter 15

Pirate Cove
29 Sept 1808
19 Degrees 36 minutes N, 72 Degrees 59' W

A cool dawn stretched over the skies, pouring its light into the low hanging smoke still lingering over the water of the cove. Will rose from the bed he had made of coiled line on the Maiden's bow, stretching his muscles that were still tight from the activities of the evening before. His face still covered in smudges and stains from gun smoke and with a stubbly growth of beard that nagged and itched. Celebrations on board had gone long into the wee hours of the morning until finally a watch was set and everyone retired. His back ached from hauling on the gun lines, his ears still holding a soft hum from the reverberating reports of each shot. Will's mind spun from the whirlwind of what had occurred in the last few weeks. Looking out over glass calm water, with a dense mixture of fog and smoke clinging to its surface, he began to feel a ripple of calm overtake him.

William's life had been wholly committed to crown and country. Service had given him purpose and family where he had none. Until now, he had considered the cascade of tribulations had ripped away these values which he held so dearly. Last night as he fired each cannon, watching their devastating impacts onto the ship he had been commissioned to serve, he considered himself stripped of his traditional honor. This morning, under the new light of day, his mind was considering the totality of his circumstances. He had not surrendered his honor, quite the contrary. Will knew in his heart, while he looked out over the wreckage that remained of the Valor, he had done what is right. The pungent aroma of smoke mixing with the salty sea air clung to his nostrils and he breathed in deeply, savoring the smell while pondering his future. He closed his eyes and craned his neck, lifting his face to the skies in the slight chill of the cove, still shaded from the rising dawn. Lilith's approaching footsteps interrupted his reflective vigil and he gave her a warm smile, which she returned.

"I meant what I told you Lieutenant. I will not hold you in service against your will," she said, "But if you choose, you may stay on with the crew."

"I don't suppose sailing master is a billet offered aboard a pirate vessel?" Will replied, only partly in jest.

"Accommodations could be made, Chibs will remain Quartermaster as long as he wishes to, and Trina will always hold my trust as well. But I believe, if it is what you want, we have a place for you with us," her voice found his ears softly, inflecting a question she would not ask, only imply.

"I can only speak for myself; the marines and Lieutenant Shelton will have to decide for themselves. But I suppose much of it depends on your intentions after this. Where does the Maiden sail after this? And what does her Captain intend?" Will asked, rubbing the irritating scruff under his chin.

"There is a chest of gold below deck, enough to outfit an entire fleet and there is a cane plantation I intend to pay a visit to in Haiti. Captain James made it his purpose to reap benefit from destroying the slave trade. I intend to continue toward that end," fire lingered under her voice as she answered.

"And the legitimate merchantmen plying their trade across the seas?" Will pressed with a note of apprehension.

"I've no interest in wanton murder or thieving. If I kill a slave master or the one delivering the people kidnapped from their homes, that's another matter," her response came without hesitation or thoughtful pause.

"That is purpose I can commit myself to captain," his smile stretched wide and was met by hers.

"Then we'll be glad to have you Lieutenant," she said, walking off to greet Chibs as the sun finally broke over the canopy on the east shore of the cove.

The sunlight washing over the rock faces and sandy shores of the cove revealed brilliant colors to William. Blue and green hues reflected up from the water and its calm glossy surface soon held a mirror quality Will noted his image in, looking down from the bulwark. The scene of the cove was a surreal contrast of paradise marred by the aftermath of mayhem. The water's serene surface reached from a pristine white sandy strip of beach out in deepening shades of blue to emerald and finally dropping into a shade of deep blue where it blanketed underneath the hulk of the Valor, still lodged onto the blur of white reef. Her form was still smoking from smoldering timbers where her deck protruded from the surface. Most of her larboard side had keeled into the water, taking sea into where William's gunnery had breached the hull. Her foremast lay tipped backward over the deck in a mess of rigging and spars that failed to arrest it's fall. The stern had risen as the highest point of the remaining hulk, with daylight visible through its scuppers along the fantail and her rudder laid bare to the world.

In the water around the Valor's corpse floated all manner of debris, wooden and flesh as evidence of their violent end. Will noted that a sortie should be mounted to check the wreckage for survivors and salvage any useful goods from her decks. The governor remained below deck as well, with all his knowledge of the King's apparatus, "The Order". This first clash complete, Will gathered himself to speak with Shelton and the marines that had come aboard with him.

"If I am to remain as part of the Maiden's crew, I had best explain my reasons to them, their poor souls never asked for this mess," he said aloud.

"No need Will." Lieutenant Shelton said, walking up to clap him on the shoulder. "We go where you lead Sir," his smile was slight but genuine.

"What constitutes treason when the monarch betrays his people?" a marine added.

"Likely that line won't be drawn for us, should we face the crown or it's representatives again." Will replied with a grim tone.

"We'll face it together Sir. We're here to stay the course with you." Shelton said, reaffirming his earlier commitment.

"Better be ready to hold fast then Lieutenant Shelton, I have a feeling the girl captain has no intention of gathering barnacles on her keel in port."

Thank you for reading the first installment of
Treachery and Triumph
Be on the lookout for the next titles in the series.

Find my other book series, sign up for newsletter announcements including special releases and giveaways.
Just scan the QR code below.

Follow along on Facebook and Instagram for cover reveals and special announcements.

If you enjoyed this title, please be sure to leave a review on Amazon or Goodreads.

Printed in Great Britain
by Amazon